Melokai

IN THE HEART OF THE MOUNTAINS
BOOK ONE

Rosalyn Kelly

Melokai
by Rosalyn Kelly

This paperback edition (1) published by NValters Publishing
UK October 2017
Cover design © Damonza

Publisher's Note
This novel is entirely a work of fiction.
The names, characters and incidents portrayed in it are the work
of the author's imagination. Any resemblance to actual persons,
living or dead, events or localities is entirely coincidental.

For more information about this and other titles by this author,
please visit www.rosalynkelly.co.uk

For my mum, Ann

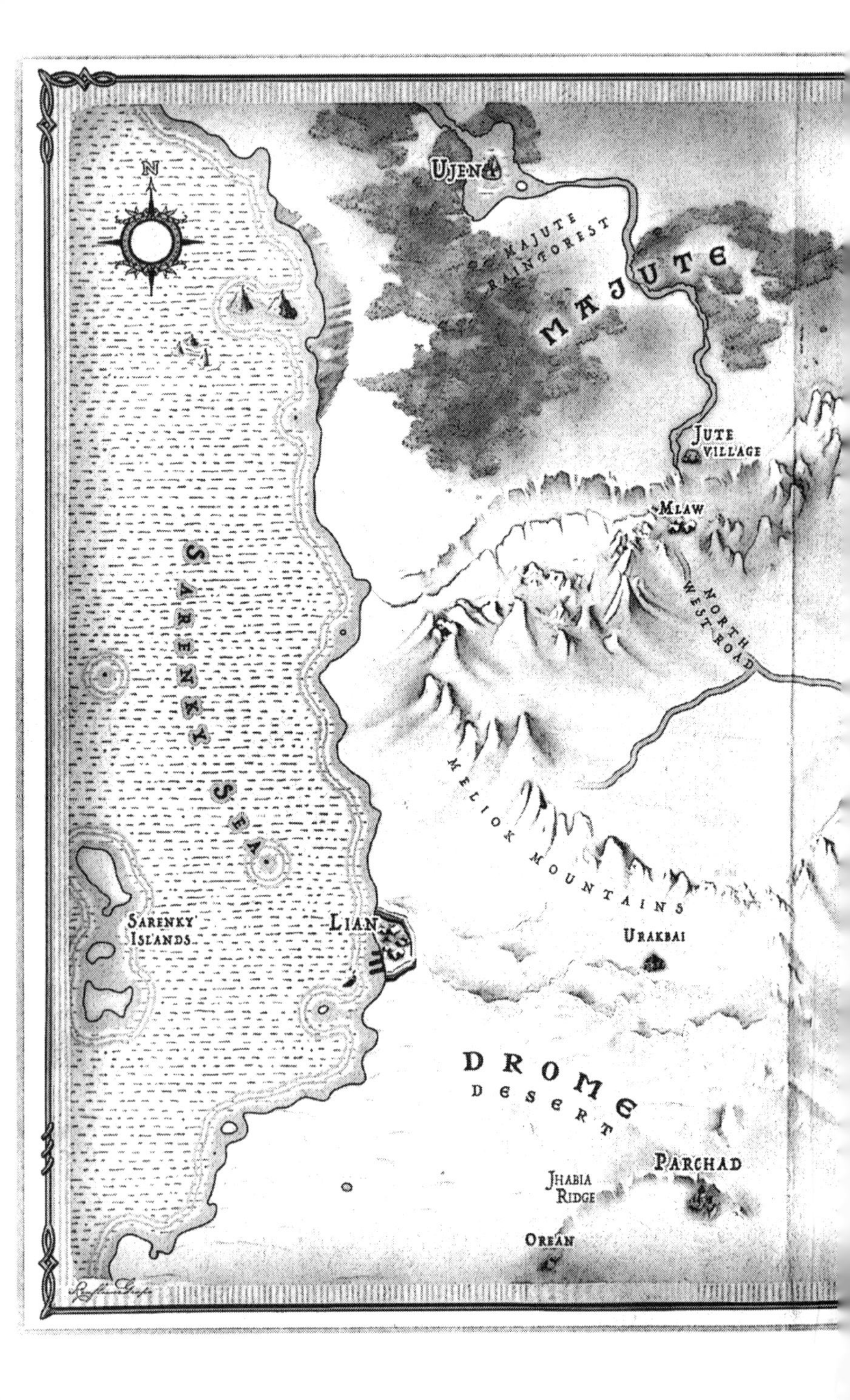
N
UJEN
MAJUTE RAINFOREST
MAJUTE
JUTE VILLAGE
MLAW
NORTH WEST ROAD
SARENKY SEA
MELIOX MOUNTAINS
SARENKY ISLANDS
LIAN
URAKBAI
DROME DESERT
PARCHAD
JHABIA RIDGE
OREAN

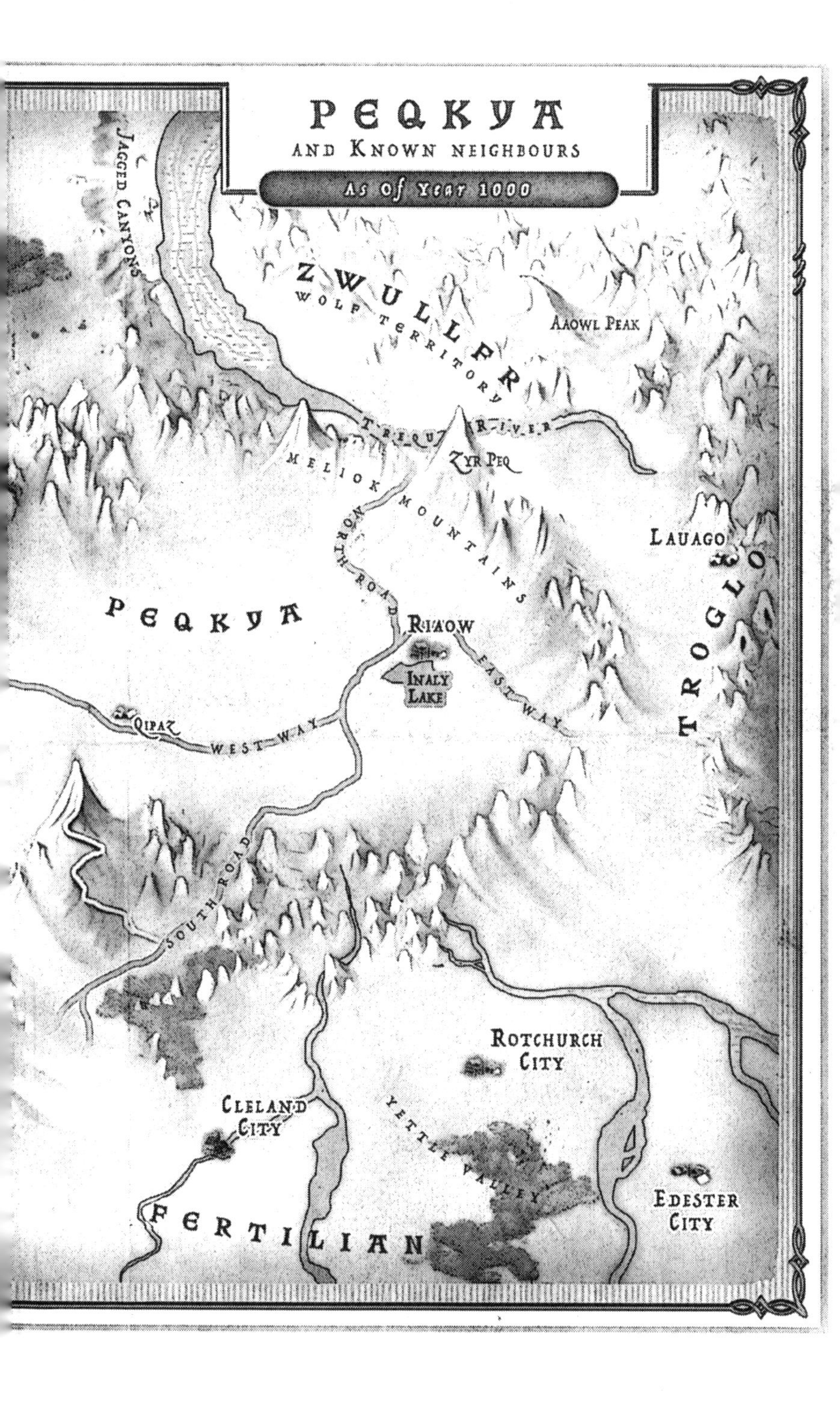
PEQKYA
AND KNOWN NEIGHBOURS
As of Year 1000
JAGGED CANYONS
ZWULLFR
WOLF TERRITORY
AAOWL PEAK
TREQU R-IVER
ZYR PEQ
MELIOK MOUNTAINS
NORTH ROAD
LAUAGO
TROGLO
PEQKYA
RIAOW
INALY LAKE
EAST WAY
QIPAZ
WEST WAY
SOUTH ROAD
ROTCHURCH CITY
CLELAND CITY
YETTEE VALLEY
EDESTER CITY
FERTILIAN

1

RAMYA

Ramya liked her tongue. She wasn't ready to give it up, not yet. The Melokai rolled it around her teeth, touched it to the roof of her mouth and brought it down with a satisfying *cluck*.

She glanced at Chaz. The scholar's mottled black and white hands cupped his face, his body rocking with the movement of his horse, eyes glazed. They continued through the circular streets of the city in silence, both soon to lose the ability of speech, but neither with anything to say.

Most Melokais ruled for a decade, Ramya had ruled now for two years longer than most. *Your time is up!* She was certain this was the cats' message. They had been frantic all morning. Their mewing, trilling, yowling sounded different. Urgent, worried. They had scuttled about under her feet as she limbered through her daylight dances, slapped paws at the goat's milk in her washtub rather than lapping at it, and as she had dressed, they clawed at her fur cloak, looking up at her with knowing marble eyes. When she had left her chambers to head to the busy dining hall, a swarm of squalling, hissing fur had trailed behind.

Ramya had made the oath, she knew what happened to

old Melokais. Her tongue would be taken and she would be banished by the Stone Prophetess Sybilya, cast out to wander the mountains alone. Sybilya cautioned that those who had tasted power were reluctant to relinquish it, and forever strived to wrench it back, causing unrest, violence and war. Without speech, old rulers cannot poison the minds of others and bend them to their will, and out in the wilderness there was no one to corrupt. *The Stone Prophetess knows best, she lived through the Xayy atrocities after all.*

Ramya had made this trip to see the Stone Prophetess every week for the past twelve years, since she was sworn in as Melokai of Peqkya. She couldn't shake the feeling that this would be the last.

The end of her rule was upon her, and she was dreading it. *Melokai no more.*

She found her tongue, formed words. "It will happen today."

Her counsellor and Head Scholar jolted out of his reverie. "I expect so, my Melokai. The cats…" He didn't need to finish, it seemed Riaow's entire feline population had emerged from every cranny to chitter at them as they passed.

"The Stone Prophetess will proclaim, 'It is time', and name four women to participate in the Melokai Choosing Ceremony and I will relinquish the title, be muted and banished."

"Yes," he replied, shoulders hunched.

Chaz, and each of Ramya's counsellors, would also be muted, as was custom, but they were permitted to stay in the city. Ramya's jaw clenched. Losing a body part was one thing, but gnawing at her insides, pummelling at every organ with vicious blows, was the banishment part. Ramya feared loneliness. She had no desire to go back to the solitary days of her childhood, where her volatile anger had scared off any would-be friends. She had learned to control it by throwing herself into warrior training, or leadership, or anything that kept her busy. As Melokai, the love of her people was a close friend. One she did not want to part with.

"You have achieved a great deal, you should feel proud." Chaz swept his hand to indicate the thriving city.

They passed rows of colourful dome-shaped huts fashioned on the first people's nomadic tents. Ramya had constructed homes for every Peqkian and ensured every Riat had a job, built the House of Knowledge, a centre of learning and documenting with a library open to every Peqkian, including the peons. She had set up the fresh waterflows with channels for drinking and to fill new public baths, as well as improved the underground sewers. She'd created wider, tree-lined streets as part of a city-wide roadway update, and opened more parks and healing centres. And had even introduced a swapping system, where produce and goods could be exchanged for items of an equal value, so there was no need for money.

"I've been busy," she said.

"You have earned your title and earned your people's love, my Melokai."

Ramya nodded at Chaz's reminder of her first visit to the Stone Prophetess after she had triumphed in the Choosing Ceremony twelve years earlier. Sybilya had looked into Ramya's eyes and deeper into her soul, and purred. The thrumming reverberated through Ramya's body. Sybilya had moved her hand, indicating for Ramya to sit on her lap. Ramya had wrapped her arms around the prophetess's neck and rested her cheek on the great lady's chest. Sybilya held Ramya tight and stroked her cropped black hair. She had felt wholly at peace. The prophetess had declared in a sonorous voice, "Welcome, my Melokai. Earn your title and you will earn their love."

Since then, no words had left Sybilya's mouth. Ramya longed to hear the purring again, to be stroked so tenderly, but silence greeted her. No response, no movement, just blinking eyes staring out into a different place, a different world. *I will hear Sybilya today, but she will tell me what I don't want to hear. Melokai no more.*

"I've been trying to distract myself from the upcoming," the eunuch pointed at his mouth, "by considering what I might write for my entry into The History of Peqkya. Every Head Scholar is duty bound to summarise their Melokai's tenure. Care to hear?"

Ramya welcomed the distraction and gestured for him to continue.

He cleared his throat. "Melokai Ramya's progressive governing principles combined with *relevant* traditions and *applicable* ancient laws ensured the city of Riaow remained a well-ordered settlement. She did not shy away from reforming old rulings or customs. As we know, the Meliok mountains surround the high plateau of Peqkya, making it a safe enclave with no bother from erratic neighbours or threat of invasion. However, under Melokai Ramya, Peqkians, both in built up areas and roaming the mountainous plains, have flourished. Our nation is prosperous, peaceful, happy."

"Maybe a bit much…" she mumbled, but internally swelled with pride.

"It's not all good."

"Really?"

Chaz cleared his throat again. "It is to be noted that Melokai Ramya has done much to improve the conditions faced by peons. This has received considerable criticism. Early on in her reign, seemingly on a whim, she suggested softening the severity of peon punishments at a public assembly, but this was met with uproar and rejected outright. She has not brought it up again."

She nodded with the briefest of smiles. Chaz had been the only one to support her that day and she had learnt a very valuable lesson. To pick – and communicate – her battles meticulously from then on.

Someone shouted her name. The group was passing through the cloth quarter, past the silk and brocade workshops. The heavy snows of the last few weeks had eased and the bright day had melted much of it, bringing the workers outside of the large goat hair works that made fine thread, ropes, rough-hewn bags as well as rugs and carpets. The women, bundled up in furs, and the peons, in goat hair overcoats, sat on small stalls weaving and spinning yarn in the sunshine. The call had come from the owner, who now waved.

Ramya halted her horse. "How is business, Glendya?"

"Better than ever, my Melokai. Our carpets are the finest in the city. I thank you every day for granting me the land and resources to build this workshop."

"And I admire you for bravely presenting your new weaving method at the public assembly all those years ago. I'm pleased to hear of your success."

Glendya bowed, beaming, and Ramya continued, "We must be off. Goodbye weavers."

The women waved back, the peons kept their eyes on their work, apart from a skinny one with swollen, raw hands, who stared a little too hard.

"Ready yourself for the fumes!" Chaz declared as they entered the bustling medicinal quarter where ointments and potions were conjured up and two of Ramya's healing centres were housed. Vast vats of bubbling concoctions, huge jars containing countless herbs and cages of creatures lined the street. The pungent fumes whooshed up her nostrils and whirled about her skull. Her vision blurred and a rising heaviness crawled up her throat and clutched at her tongue. She babbled a few greetings to the healers and chemists who ambled about their business, half intoxicated. As they passed out the other side she gulped down the fresh air and, when she was certain no one was looking, her warrior's restraint wavered and she slumped, rubbing circles on her temples before jolting back to her disciplined stance.

The smell stirred up her dread.

Steadying herself, the Melokai quashed the rising panic, which would only open the door to anger and recited one of the principles from the revered woman she was on her way to see, ingrained in the lives of all Peqkians, 'Embrace change, for when it comes you cannot stop it'.

An icy nip in the wind cut at her round face. Ramya was not beautiful. The height of Peqkian attractiveness was feline features – oval face, almond eyes, small nose and delicate, pointed ears, of which the Melokai had none, all her features were wide. Wide face, nose, lips, teeth. Even her bright green eyes were set a little too far apart. But her wide smile was warm and endearing. She was short and squat, not long and lithe like so many fellow warriors, but at thirty-two her body was still strong and her black skin glistened from her milk baths.

She turned to the fierce, young warriors who rode behind, Violya, Lizya and Emmya. There was no danger, their presence was custom, like the daggers strapped to Ramya's biceps. Her blades hadn't tasted blood in many years, not since that pygmie fray on her first warrior campaign, five years before she became the Melokai. She touched her mutilated left hand to her mutilated left ear. An ugly memento.

"We gallop from here," she said. If the warriors were surprised by the command they didn't show it. The group never hastened through the city, the journey to see Sybilya was leisurely, Ramya enjoyed greeting and speaking with her people. Not today. She ran the tip of her tongue over her lips. *Let's get this over with,* she thought as she kicked on her horse.

The group lurched to a stop at the foot of the sacred Mount of Pines. Ramya paused to rest the horses. The place was deserted, as always. The Melokai and her small delegation were the only ones who set foot here, not because of any law, but out of awe for who lived there.

Ramya bowed her head in greeting and then urged her horse on at a brisk walk, followed by the others. During the time of Melokai Tatya, three hundred years past,

Sybilya had returned from the gruesome Wolf Expulsion, sat on a tree stump atop this hill, and hadn't moved again. She was slowly turning to stone.

Ancient Sybilya had spent many lifetimes criss-crossing the land. The endless walking had given her gigantic feet attached to her tall, slender body, cat-like face and extraordinary red hair. The legends claimed her exquisite beauty used to stun Xayy men into silence when they looked upon her. That was before the momentous day a thousand years earlier, when she had conjured magic powerful enough to turn two immense male armies into stone in the midst of the Battle of Ashen. Putting an end to that pointless war ravaged her body, and scorched a circle in the earth she stood on.

Sunlight flashed on and off Ramya's face as she passed under the majestic row of pine arches that lined the path, like a snake curving its way up the hill. Each arch was carved with ancient symbols and painted the blue of mountain poppies. The paint was peeling and blue flecks fluttered on the breeze. A chill settled like a veil over her and with every step closer, the beloved prophetess's presence intensified. It was all encompassing, weighty but benevolent.

The horse slowed to a lumbering plod as they climbed and its clopping echoed off the decaying arches. The fading grandeur saddened Ramya. She hoped, as all of Peqkya hoped, that another would be found soon. Her messengers brought news of babies who might have a spark of magic in them from Mothers across the nation, but the spark always flickered out. Before the Battle of Ashen, when Peqkya was still Xayy, there had been many with The Sight and journeys to mythical Zyr Peq, the highest and most inhospitable mountain peak in the realm, were customary. Now, Sybilya was one of a kind and no one visited Zyr Peq.

Soon after the prophetess had arrived on the hill, so too had the cats, both normal and the larger clevercats that were trained to speak. Then the tigers. They had never before come close to the hut when Ramya was there, but – as if she needed any more indication that today would be momentous – she caught glimpses of striped skin lounging under the pines. The normal cats, usually as languid as the tigers, came rushing down the path to squirm around the legs of Ramya's horse, hissing when their tails were trodden on. As her group neared the hut, their purring became thunderous and the musty, intrusive smell of the creatures choked the earthy pine scent.

Ramya jumped down from her horse and patted its neck. She wanted today's visit and after, the public assembly, to be over quickly so she could get drunk. *Tonight I shall drink my body weight in sweet wine. To toast the end of my reign. And then I will call for company, enjoy myself whilst I still can. Before I am ban– No!* she cut into her thoughts. *Pointless to dwell on the inevitable.*

The warriors stationed themselves outside the simple hut as Ramya and Chaz entered. He took his position standing by the door and she sat crossed legged on the ground, rested her hands, palm up, on her knees and humbly looked up at Sybilya.

The prophetess's colossal feet were now stone, two unmovable slabs, and Ramya could see the stone creeping up her legs and into her hands that rested in her lap. The tips of her long flaming red locks had faded to white, her once black skin had turned grey and the threadbare rags that still clung to her body were weighed down by a layer of grime. As usual, Sybilya's eyes were fixed ahead and her shallow breath wheezed through her teeth.

A cat came and sat on Ramya, hot and bony. She twitched her arms and tensed her thighs, trying to subtly shoo it off without moving her hands. It licked its lips and made a foul choking noise, hunching up its body and then spewed out a slimy fur ball on Ramya's ankle before scampering away. She itched to flick it off, but moving her hands at this point would be disrespectful. She closed her eyes, focused on her breathing, calming her thoughts and willing Sybilya to speak to her.

After about an hour, the Head Scholar coughed to bring the Melokai out of her meditation and signal it was time to go. She wriggled her fingers and stretched her stiff legs, finally wiping away the revolting congealed cat sick. Her eyes darted to his and he gave a tiny shrug, a look of relief on his face. *There had been no words. I am still Melokai and he is still Head Scholar.*

Confused, Ramya stood, bowed to the prophetess and turned to leave. But then… a feeble grinding, like stone on stone.

The Melokai froze.

The Stone Prophetess dipped her head and was looking straight at Ramya. Chaz gasped. All was silent. A faint purr from the great lady grew louder in the hut, shaking the wooden walls. Every one of Ramya's bones vibrated.

She met Sybilya's gaze, two luminous beams that suffused her in light. Without breaking eye contact, Ramya approached and slowly sat on Sybilya's lap. There was no hair stroking this time, the prophetess's stone hands were still, but the mouth creaked open. *Issee! I will hear her voice again… she honours me with her words after so long! I was right… it is time for a new Melokai.*

With extreme exertion, Sybilya spoke. Her voice trembled, but the words were clear. "Welcome, my Melokai. Trouble will come from the east. A wolf will claim the throne."

2

FERRAZ

Ferraz stood in a bucket of cold water in the centre of his gloomy cell, scrubbing his body. Although the window shutter was closed, a bitter breeze circulated. His room was five paces by five paces, with a bed against one wall and a wash area against the other. His loin cloth, robe and cloak were folded neatly onto one shelf under the tiny window. He had few belongings. He patted himself dry with some rags and then rubbed scented oil into his skin, ignoring his shivers. He dressed and welcomed the warmth of his fur cloak.

Ferraz lit his candle, took his razor blade from the shelf, carefully shaved his scalp and massaged the oil there too. He trimmed his beard with sharp lines and smiled at himself in the mirror. His dazzling blue eyes sparkled back and his thick lips parted to show his straight teeth, perfectly aligned with his small nose and square jaw. Dimples in his cheeks set off his fine face and he winked at himself in appreciation before blowing out the candle.

Tonight she will call me, it has been three days since her last release, and I need to be in peak condition.

He had spent the morning honing his physique in the training yard, focusing on endurance, strength and quick recovery. Ferraz had mastered the art of performing at an exceptional standard every time, in quick succession if required, and this was why he was Melokai Ramya's favoured pleasure giver.

The PG lay on his bed, hands clasped behind his head, a faint smirk playing at the corners of his lips. He had worked hard to get here, and was proud of his status. He remembered his pen childhood, his earliest memory was being lectured by the Mothers.

"There is no use for useless peens," his pen-Mother used to say. "There are two reasons that peens still exist, to pleasure women and to produce babies. If we could continue our race by ourselves, we would. We only allow a small number of peens to pass into peonhood so you need to excel in a profession or you *will* be ended."

A string of peons gave talks about what they did, but until the day a pleasure giver arrived, Ferraz wasn't sure what was for him.

The PG had told them, "You need to be skilled at one thing. Sex. You need to pleasure every woman every time and each woman is different. If you fail, the customary death sentence awaits. Your cock is cut off, stuffed in your mouth and you are rammed on a pole in the marketplace and left there to bleed, die and rot in shame. If you have an unwavering commitment to learn about women and remember what they desire, then you should consider this profession."

From that day on, years of tuition from PGs had ensured Ferraz wasn't ended on his fifteenth birthday, unlike so many of his pen-mates who failed their peen usefulness tests. He had been given the PG assessment of entertaining a courtesan and he pleasured her so intensely that she called for her friends to sample him too. Four women had vouched for his skills and he had been welcomed into the PG set. *Nearly twenty years ago now.*

He started by servicing the lower rank courtesans and notable women from various professions. He built a solid reputation and was soon in demand among the high-level women. But he wasn't satisfied. He asked other PGs what the highest of them all, Melokai Ramya, enjoyed and gleaned information whilst pleasuring her courtesans. He memorised every word so that when the time came to please the Melokai, he would be ready.

Nine years into his career as a pleasure giver, he came to Ramya's attention. She called for him along with four of the best PGs and six of the most accomplished courtesans. But there had been a glitch.

Ferraz laughed out loud in his cell at the memory.

He was paired with Hanya, one of the Melokai's favoured courtesans, and was not required to go anywhere near the Melokai. Ferraz administered his most trusted moves, but Hanya was bored by it all. And the Melokai's attention was drawn by the couples enjoying themselves. Not once did Ramya look their way. So Ferraz stopped and asked, "Tell me, what can I do to please you, Hanya?"

"Finally, you ask me," she had chided and then told him specifically what to do.

He obeyed and, before long, Hanya's noisome ecstasy drew Ramya to them. The Melokai clapped her hands, thrilled. Then, as quickly as Ramya had appeared, she moved off to watch another couple.

Half a year passed before Ferraz was called to Melokai Ramya's chamber again, and he had started to lose hope. But this time, it was just him. And he had brought her pleasure, multiple times. She continued to call him and he never disappointed her, reading her mood and providing what she required.

Fifteen years into his career, and five years earlier, he had become her exclusive PG. He had to be available at all times for the Melokai and no other woman was permitted to have him, including the courtesan Irrya, who had been in love with him.

Over the years, he had fallen for Ramya and done everything he could think of to make her fall in love with him. He believed they were a good match, although he knew deep down that it wasn't a profound love, and probably not love at all, but he had to call it something. Ramya barely spoke to him, but he serviced her so proficiently that she hadn't called for another peon in five years. He was attracted by her power rather than her personality and certainly not by her face. Ramya was not the prettiest kitten in the litter. *I make up for her ugliness with my beauty.*

She still dismissed him with a brusque "Go", a flick of the hand and no eye contact. He always promptly left so as not to disturb her. However, two nights ago, before he retired from her chamber, he had dared to approach her and kiss her head gently. His courage had paid off, she had looked up at him, confused, but for an instant there was a hint of warmth, before she turned back to her papers. He deemed her reaction to that kiss, however small, as a good sign. *She is softening towards me. I've become more than just a cock to her.*

Ferraz leapt from his bed at a bang on his door. Light trickled in as it opened wide and there stood the washer-peon, come to collect his bucket. Ferraz picked it up and took it to him

"Any news?" Ferraz whispered. Court PGs were shut off from the outside world, always on call for the important women they served and not allowed out of the PG quarters. Gossip reached them late.

The washer-peon glanced down the corridor for the set administrator. She was occupied, talking to one of the warriors who guarded the PGs. He leaned in to Ferraz's cell and whispered, "Women be declarin' more peons as their soulmatches. Tis very fashionable of late. A lot of peons ain't happy with their lot, there's plenty of disgruntled talk n' us washers be plannin' a protest…"

"Peon," yelled the set administrator, "hurry up and get out of here. I'm fed up of your stench."

With a wink at Ferraz, the washer-peon grabbed the bucket and darted off. Ferraz shut the door and glimpsed the outline of his face in the dark mirror. *Soulmatch.*

Women had been pairing since Year Zero, but it had become acceptable in Melokai Ramya's rule for women to partner with one peon if he was to their liking. That woman would declare the peon as her soulmatch and move him into her home, marking him as off limits to other women for the rest of his life. Pleasure givers were designated for the Melokai and her court, but otherwise women could select any peon for sex and he could not refuse. If the peon proved unsatisfactory, he faced the same death sentence as the PGs. But now peons could say, "I am sorry, mistress, I cannot pleasure you for I am soulmatched to…" and this tiny seed of power had caused ripples of excitement through the peon population.

Ferraz narrowed his blue eyes. *I have work to do… It is not enough to be Melokai Ramya's favoured PG, or for her to love me, she has to declare me her soulmatch. Then I will be safe for life and can live out my days comfortably and without fear of a horrific death.*

And my son… Being Ramya's soulmatch will help me to protect my son.

His child with Ramya was three years old now, blue-eyed like his father, strong and handsome. Ferraz had been illegally watching him since birth and if discovered, the PG would be executed. *I've doubtless made children with other women but this one has the blood of the most powerful woman in Peqkya coursing through him. He is worth the risk.*

By chance, Ferraz had watched his son's birth, Ramya going into labour whilst he serviced her. Medics were called and in the commotion, he had shrunk into the shadows, forgotten. The first cry of his little boy almost broke his heart with love.

Ferraz never had any opinion about the Peqkian custom that dictates 'No baby will ever know it's parents and no parents will ever know their baby,' until Ramya had borne this peen. The baby was taken, moments after birth, like every other, and put anonymously into a pen to be cared for by the Mothers until fifteen when they entered a profession. Ferraz's baby would have the same start in life, the same chance to prove himself on his own merit. He could not rely on bloodlines or prestigious parents.

But my son does have a prestigious parent. In the time of Xayy he would've grown up to become the Melokaz, as the Xayy male rulers had once been called. He would be the most powerful male in the nation and not a lowly peon. Ferraz thumped the wall and his mirror rattled. He steadied it quickly, not wanting to draw the set administrator's attention.

Be grateful, peons are treated a little better now than before. In the thousand years since the Xayy armies were turned to stone by Sybilya, the attitudes to peens had softened in Peqkya, although the penalties for disobedience remained severe. Female and male babies were now nurtured together by the Mothers and given the same early education, but the peens still had to prove their worth to the nation. The girls, of course, were exempt from these trials.

A jolt of fear made Ferraz's legs tremble. *Even now, my body still remembers.* He had been petrified about being ended and lived each day in fear of failing the tests. In the early years of her rule, Melokai Ramya had reduced the peen cancellation quota, allowing more peens to pass into peonhood. *But my son will still have to face the same terror... When I am Ramya's soulmatch, I will find a way to save him from the usefulness test.*

A gong sounded. Ferraz left his cell and stood, silently, in the corridor with all the other PGs emerging from their cells, facing in the direction of the set administrator. She looked down the line, satisfied all were accounted for, and led them to the PG communal area.

After lunch, the PGs lounged in their designated room. Here they stayed all afternoon and into the evening, ready to be called.

Ferraz sat alone. *Ramya will be exhausted after her public assembly as usual, and in need of tenderness. I will sate her and then*

I will whisper, "I love you, soulmatch," in her ear. Will she be brave enough to declare me her soulmatch officially? Yes. She will be the first Melokai to do so, and she likes to be the first to do things. And I will be the first PG to be claimed.

A fluffy white cat jumped onto his lap and dropped a ball with a bell in. He picked it up and threw it. The cat bounded off, grabbed it between sharp teeth and sauntered back to him, presenting it to him like a gift.

He threw it again and listened to the other PGs chatter on. They boasted about which courtesans they had been with, who had been selected for deflowering ceremonies, the gossip they had gleaned from warriors and the women they might service later.

Ferraz watched them openly with arms crossed and a smug, amused look on his face. He had no need to contribute, he was the Melokai's PG. The cat returned and he threw the ball. But the fluffy thing ignored it and curled next to him. *I wonder what it might be like to attend a court dinner.* No peons were allowed apart from the eunuch Chaz, who had been in Ferraz's childhood pen. The PG grinned. *When I'm Ramya's soulmatch I'll get to go! I'll be the first* whole *peon.*

Late into the night the first messenger clevercat came to request two pleasure givers.

"Mistressss issss wanting two. Wild. Who issss ssssuitable?" the sheep-sized clevercat hissed and the set administrator beckoned to two burly PGs and signed them out. They left with the messenger who mewed her approval.

After that the messengers came thick and fast, as the women started to return home and the PGs filtered out to answer their needs. *I will be one of the last to be called, the Melokai has much to do and many people to talk to.* But every time a messenger came and Ferraz realised it wasn't Bevya, the Melokai's black and white, long-limbed clevercat, a creeping doubt clogged his mind. *Perhaps she wants her courtesans tonight...*

Before long, he was on his own in the communal area. The set administrator put her head in her arms and fell asleep on her desk. The cats deserted him to find a nook to settle in, but Ferraz refused to leave and go back to his cell. *I will be called soon. She will send her messenger for me soon.*

That night the call from Melokai Ramya never came. It would never come again.

3

RAMYA

ᢀ

The Melokai was rattled by the shock words from Sybilya and for the first time in her twelve-year rule she cancelled a public assembly in order to hold an urgent council meeting. She was sure her people would understand, considering the circumstances. She couldn't concentrate on anything other than the prophecy anyway.

Ramya sat with her body in its neutral position after years of warrior training, alert but unmoving, conserving strength. Her right hand rested on the hilt of her sword, the other on the grand table that was carved in the likeness of Peqkya, depicting settlements and natural landmarks. Sun streamed through the window and reflected off the polished wood, setting the council chamber aglow.

The noise of warriors grunting and steel clanging drifted in from the barracks training ground. Usually a soothing sound, now it irritated her. *I was expecting to be told my time is up... But not only am I still in power, I have a prophecy to deal with – the first Sybilya has spoken in hundreds of years.*

Ramya watched her Head Scholar, he hadn't left her side since they had returned from the Mount of Pines. He paced back and forth, tapping a white finger to his muttering lips. Chaz had been born with mottled black and white skin and, through a handful of pale spots on his head, white hair grew stark against the black. He had been identified as having The Sight with one white patch over his right eye in the exact shape of their country, but he had no magic in him.

He was destined for other things. From childhood, he had been determined to be a scholar, excelling at his studies, but one thing stopped him. It was an honoured job for women, peens weren't taken into the scholar profession. So Chaz gelded himself in his tenth year, believing this would demonstrate his unwavering passion for the job to the Mothers, and if not, then he'd die of blood loss anyway. He cut off everything between his legs, hobbled into his pen-Mother's office and threw the flesh in her fire before collapsing in a puddle of blood. He survived. An exception was made to the ancient rules and at fifteen he took the scholar profession assessment. Not only did he pass, he achieved higher marks than his fellow female students, and he was trained as a Scholar, eventually to become head of the profession and Ramya's counsellor.

The Melokai's other six counsellors sat around the great table. Relieved that they weren't about to become mutes, they were now all talking at once, the usual decorum forgotten.

Only Head Teller Omya stayed quiet, listening. She sat perfectly straight, thin lips pursed, fingers interlocked on the table. Her tightly plaited hair coiled up to a neat bun and pulled at the skin on her hairline.

Ramya held up her hand and the room fell quiet. "I appreciate this is a shock, but we need to approach it systematically. I want to go over everything. Chaz, please refresh our memories as to what lies to the east of Peqkya."

"Yes, my Melokai." The eunuch swept over to where the Eastern Melioks were carved on the table, placing his hands over the peaks. "To the east is the cave nation of Troglo. The Trogrs descended from humans, adapting to live in the colossal network of caves under the eastern length of the Meliok mountains. No Peqkian has ever passed through these caves. In the time of Melokai Annya, five hundred years ago, attempts were made to facilitate a trade route that ran east from Riaow into the lands beyond. Going over the avalanche-prone peaks proved impossible so the decision was made to go *through* the mountains. Four small openings were found, and exploratory groups ventured in to map the natural tunnels aiming to find an exit on the other side and, if not, to excavate one.

"However, this plan also failed. The Peqkians who entered those dark caves invariably never returned. The few who did told of the brutal destruction of their groups by strange creatures that looked like us but could see in the dark.

"Melokai Annya sent in the army. We had the numbers and the fighting skills but the creatures had the advantage. They knew the caves, every tiny crevice, and excelled in the dark – rendering our warriors useless when the lights went out and leading them down maze like passageways to be ambushed, or leaving them to aimlessly wander, lost, until they died.

"The Eastern war went on for four years and after terrible losses, Melokai Annya changed tactic. She called a truce and set up business with the cave creatures themselves. Trade terms were negotiated and borders agreed. And since that day, we have had a mutual understanding with the Trogrs, both nations stay inside their borders and Peqkian merchants can buy and sell at one designated trade point, in the twilight zone of the largest cave opening." Chaz pointed to the location on the table.

Hanny cleared her throat. She was Ramya's Head Courtesan, the one counsellor a Melokai was permitted to choose, the others having been elected by their honoured professions. Ramya's only close friend, Hanya was the epitome of Peqkian beauty, with her perfect feline features and voluptuous curves. She asked, sweetly, "What do we trade with them?"

Ramya's plump Head Trader Rivya twisted an extravagant, garish ring around a fat finger and said, "We give them vegetables, spices and grains, stuff they can't grow in the dark, as well as cloth and Fertilian salt and they give us the delicacy that is known as swiftlet nests, which they harvest from their caves."

"Ah yes! Bird saliva from the east, I've eaten that before," Hanny proclaimed, looking around at the others, glossy ponytail swishing. Her long hair was not coarse and curly like most Peqkians, but smooth and straight, and she styled it with a heavy fringe that fell just past her eyebrows.

"Indeed. It makes us a lot of money when sold to the Ferts, who prize it for its rarity, its unique taste and perceived benefits to the body," Riv said.

"But what lies to the *east*, Chaz? *Past* Troglo?" Omya's first words at the meeting were sharp and she turned her face to the scholar, scrutinising him through eyeglasses propped on her severe nose.

Chaz's expression changed from animated to downcast. "I… I do not know what is farther east, no Peqkian has ever got that far, and no being has ever come to us from the lands east of the Melioks. Regrettably, there is a gap in my knowledge."

There was a brief pause as the council considered this.

"Thank you, my Head Scholar, for that excellent summary," Ramya said. "I think the next question is, what *trouble* do they pose us? Please, speak freely counsellors."

Ramya regretted the instruction as soon as it was out of her mouth. Her counsellors all spoke over each other again, even Omya voiced her opinion. The Melokai listened for a few moments and then raised her hand.

"At this stage, we watch Troglo closely, for any hint of what trouble is brewing and try to pre-empt any issues."

Ramya turned to her Head Warrior. "Gogo, please increase warriors along the border with Troglo, send out discreet scouts to watch all four cave openings, and send a spy with Riv's traders to monitor the Trogrs. Also, set out a strategy for a possible invasion."

Gogo grunted. A prominent vein throbbed from the woman's forehead to earlobe on her lumpy, bald head. Hating the inconvenience of hair, Gogo had used potent pills from the chemists to destroy it when she first started her warrior training at ten years old. Her body was now completely hairless.

Ramya continued, "Zecky, map out a plan for managing an infectious illness in case the Trogrs are suffering from some kind of virulent disease that might spread to Peqkya."

Heavily pregnant with her sixth child, Head Speaker Zekya huffed and tutted as the bump got in her way. Zecky hated being with child, and she hated peons, but loved to be pleasured by them. Sybilya had forbidden the chemists from inventing any kind of potion to prevent conception as babies safeguarded Peqkya's future. The Head Speaker furiously fanned her hot face with a wedge of parchment sheets. She placed them on the table, jotted a quick note on her action and then continued to fan.

"Riv, look at your trade routes and merchants to redirect our products elsewhere if they intend to cease trading with us."

The Head Trader acknowledged the order by reorganising her heavy frame on the stool.

Omya tutted. "That would stop a steady income, impacting our finances."

Ramya said, "And that is why, Omya, I'd like you to consider how we could replace any lost income."

The Head Teller frowned.

Ramya looked to her Head Scholar. "Chaz, you mentioned that each year the soil here in Peqkya is warmer than the year before and there is less winter ice cover on Inaly Lake. Can you investigate if this change has triggered a shift to the Troglo cave environment that is forcing them out into the open. Also examine a possible evolution of the species, if Trogrs can now tolerate sunlight."

Her Head Scholar mumbled his agreement.

"Kafya, please can you ensure we are teaching Peqkya's children the latest information on Troglo, so our future warriors, thinkers and administrators are fully equipped with this knowledge."

"Certainly, my Melokai," Kafya, the Mother of Mothers, said in her gentle voice. Her kindly smile, stooped back and soft bosom always promised a warm embrace and Ramya instinctively smiled at her.

"Now, let's move on to the second part of the prophecy…" Ramya began but a knock at the door interrupted her. "Enter."

Bevya, her clevercat messenger, jumped up on the table and then placed her two front paws on Ramya's shoulder hissing in her ear.

"My Melokai, I can confirm, assss requesssted, that dinner issss ready."

Ramya sighed. "Yes of course. I will be there shortly. Thank you, Bevya."

Bevya meowed and darted out of the room. Ramya addressed her council. "We will retire for the day and pick up early tomorrow. Thank you all for your counsel, it is well appreciated."

***

"More wine, my Melokai?" a serving peon asked. Ramya held her cup for him to pour. She had gulped down too much already but couldn't stop, still unnerved by Sybilya's words. Even the dancers, musicians and delicious food couldn't distract her. She made brief conversation with her court, and was relieved when they sensed she was not in the mood to chat and politely excused themselves from her presence. She sat drinking and half listening to Peqkya's best pipe player.

She turned to Chaz, who was sat silently brooding to her left. "Chaz, *can* the Trogrs see in the dark?"

"An interesting question, my Melokai," he gushed,

clearly pleased to be given an opportunity to talk about a topic he was well versed in. "Trogrs are a fascinating species. They spend most of their time in utter blackness so evolution got rid of their eyes and heightened their other senses to 'see' their surroundings. They emit a noise into a space and analyse the echoes that bounce back. Their large feet and hands feel reverberations in the caves and they tell each other apart by smell and by 'tasting' the air. Extraordinary really..."

"Freaks," Gogo seethed as she passed behind them on her way to her seat after leading an evening training session. The Head Warrior's torso and defined arms were crisscrossed with scars from years of instructing warriors. She was sweating and on her collarbone, fresh scratches dribbled blood where a lucky warrior had managed to land a strike, moments earlier. "You should not admire them, Chaz."

Chaz's white Peqkya patch flushed red around his right eye. "Well, I don't admire them exactly – I admire evolution. As well as not having eyes, the species also…"

But Gogo stalked off and didn't listen to his reply. Ramya watched her sit, tear off a chicken leg and start gnawing at it. Gogo's clevercat messenger arrived, spoke a message in the Head Warrior's ear, and with a grunt, Gogo stood and stomped from the hall. Chicken leg in hand.

Across the table, a peal of laughter from Ramya's Head Courtesan Hanny caught the Melokai's attention. The job of the courtesans was to entertain high-ranking women. Courtesans lived in their own apartments, free to do as they wished and could refuse a call if they so pleased. Hanny was entertaining Captain Denya tonight, a respected warrior. "Denya is such a hard one to please," Hanny always quipped to Ramya when they were alone, "But once she's warmed up there is plenty of fun to be had!" The courtesan noticed Ramya's gaze and winked mischievously.

A flash of black and white fur startled the Melokai.

Bevya jumped onto her shoulder. "My Melokai, I have an urgent messssage from Gossssya."

Ramya nodded for her clevercat messenger to continue.

"There issss a prissssoner that you mussst sssee immediately. Come at once," Bevya recited the Head Warrior's message.

"Odd. Why would I want to see a prisoner?" Ramya asked, knowing that Bevya could not answer.

The cat tilted her head. "Gossssya told me it issss urgent, my Melokai."

"Tell her I am coming now." Ramya watched Bevya leap off the chair and run with her message. The Melokai stood, waited for everyone in the dining hall to stand and bow to her. She bowed in return and then left the table. The warriors guarding her followed behind.

She found Gogo waiting outside the small, mostly empty, prison wing.

The Head Warrior swallowed her mouthful of chicken and threw the bone on the floor for the cats. "My Melokai, my warriors guarding the eastern border have brought a prisoner here. They rode as fast as they could. The detainee came willingly and is, so far, well behaved."

"Who is this prisoner, Gogo? Why have you called me away from dinner?" Ramya snapped, and then immediately regretted it. She was horribly impatient when drunk.

"It's a Trogr, my Melokai. A cave creature. We will need a scholar who can translate."

Ramya stared at the warrior in disbelief. *Trouble from the east. So soon.* "Bevya!" she screeched, "get Chaz here now!"

The messenger's whiskers twitched and she darted off on her errand. Ramya tottered up and down the corridor, trying to walk off the wine, flinging a hand out to the wall every few steps to steady her. The Head Scholar arrived.

"My Melokai," he panted.

"Chaz, there is a cave creature in our prison! Gogo, tell us everything."

Gogo cracked her knuckles. "Five days ago, at first

light, my border guards captured a male cave creature. He was deep in our territory, a long way from the caves, in direct breach of our truce with Troglo. It appeared he had been beaten and was laying naked. The warriors started to move him to a holding cell but as the sun touched his skin, it burnt and started to smoke, and he screamed. So they kept him in the shade. The freak did not struggle as they bound him and came willingly to the capital. This is the first time that a Trogr has come so far west. It is suspicious. He is a spy. I will torture him for information."

"Before you torture him," Chaz said, curiosity etched across his face, "have your warriors tried to communicate with him?"

"Of course," Gogo scowled. The lack of brows and lashes making her eyes bulge. "But he speaks his language and we speak ours. That is why you are here, scholar, to translate."

Chaz's chin hit his chest. He glanced at Ramya.

"Please take us to him, Gogo," she ordered. "Let us glean as much from him as possible before we use torture."

Chaz clapped his hands. "What a learning opportunity! I cannot wait to write today's entry in The History of Peqkya."

"And I cannot wait to kill the thing," Gogo rumbled.

4

RAMYA

The cave creature was chained in a barred cell with no windows. Four warriors stood in the cell, with swords drawn and pointed at the oddity, poised to eliminate any danger. Vigilant for the slightest hint of aggression, their eyes didn't waver from their target as the Melokai entered.

But the prisoner was not hostile. He sat, back against the wall with his knees up to his chest and arms wrapped around his lower legs. As Ramya neared, his head came up and he took a deep breath through his nose. The four warriors bristled at the movement.

Ramya gawped at him through the bars. She had never seen a Trogr. His skin was dry and cracked. It was so white to be almost translucent and she could see veins and sinewy muscle. Blue bruises and cuts dotted his torso, and an angry burn with pus-oozing sores covered his left hand and lower arm. Fine, almost transparent hairs all over his body glinted in the candlelight and in place of eyes, he had pale pink lumps.

Gogo drew her sword and stood slightly in front of Ramya, primed to protect the Melokai should the need arise.

Chaz crouched near to the bars ogling the creature and jotting notes on scratchy parchment.

"Why is he that colour?" Ramya asked the scholar. She could not take her gaze off the Trogr.

"Trogrs have no colour pigment in their skin as they live in the darkness so it is not necessary, my Melokai. That fine fur heightens his sense of touch."

The creature turned an ear towards the voices.

"Ask him what he was doing in our borders."

Chaz spoke in the Troglo language. A guttural, ugly noise that came deep from the creature's chest, replied.

"He was banished from Troglo," Chaz said.

"Banished? Why?"

Chaz communicated with the creature and it responded with rapid grunts.

"My Melokai, he says that it is shameful, that he would rather die than repeat it to anyone. But give me some more time with him and I'm sure I can prise out the tale... He made a request."

"He is a prisoner! He does not make requests," Gogo thundered. She started to open the barred gate ready to thrash the captive.

"Wait, Gogo." Ramya held up a hand and the Head Warrior stepped back. "Tell me what he requests, Chaz."

"Water, my Melokai. He asked for water."

Ramya gestured to a prison guard to fetch some. She felt drawn to this creature, perhaps it was the wine, but her instinct said to help him.

The four warriors parted and a cup of water was put in the creature's hand by the prison guard, who stood to one side in the cell. The creature's hand was shaking as he sniffed it. He lifted the cup but rather than drinking, he splashed the liquid on his face.

"You insolent cockface! You ask for water and then throw it away," the guard shouted and punched him viciously, sending him sideways onto the ground. The warriors sprung forward, four sharp blades pressed the prisoner's neck, not yet breaking skin but with the clear intention to do so.

"Enough," Ramya bellowed. She had noticed his face had changed, from pain to that of relief. He slowly pushed himself up off the floor, tracked by swords. "Why did he do that, Chaz?"

"Caves are humid, my Melokai. They do not drink water like we do, but instead absorb it through their skin. It has revived him. Look, the skin on his face is already dry. Remarkable."

Ramya was as mesmerised as her Head Scholar. "Does he know where he is? Who he is speaking to?"

Chaz spoke to the creature and slowly the Trogr stood up to his full height, the warriors, unperturbed that he towered over them, moved back a step into a better position to attack. Gogo raised her sword and Ramya touched her fingertips to the hilt of her own. He put his right hand to his chest and bent forward, uttering a few words in his language.

"He says he is honoured to be in the presence of the ruler of Peqkya and that he is at your mercy. He declares he should be dead, that his own people wanted him dead," said Chaz.

Standing, the cave creature was magnificent. Taller than the average Peqkian male, broad shouldered with a sculpted body, long limbs and huge hands and feet.

"Ask his name."

The creature answered Chaz's demand but continued to face Ramya.

"His name is Gwrlain," Chaz repeated and added, "My Melokai, he asked if he could see you."

"He is blind. How can he see me?"

"He will use his exceptional other senses," Chaz enthused.

"This could be a trick by the freak, my Melokai," Gogo warned.

Ramya knew she should be suspicious. A cave creature inexplicably out of his cave and stood here unwelcome in her realm, but instead she was overwhelmingly curious.

Gwrlain, his name is Gwrlain.

"Yes, he may." She nodded at Chaz, who then spoke to Gwrlain.

Gwrlain's nostrils flared and he took a long breath that expanded his ribcage. He stretched his arms out to the sides with palms up and let out the deepest, throaty hum that thumped around the space and bounced off Ramya, shaking her with its power. The hum stopped and Gwrlain listened. He then made the noise again but this time in quick pulses, moving the angle of his head on each pulsing hum. He stuck his tongue out of his mouth for a few moments, took another deep breath and spoke.

Chaz listened, eyes widening with each word. He translated, "My Melokai, he says there are six nearby, five females and one half-male. He says that the Melokai stands in front of him behind bars, about five paces away and that she smells of milk. He says that the Melokai is missing two fingers on her left hand and most of her left ear."

Gogo glowered at Gwrlain, the skin on her bald head taut.

Ramya felt unstable on her legs again, stunned by the creature. *Is he the trouble from the east?* "Chaz, please come back here tomorrow and learn everything there is to know about his banishment and report back to me in the evening."

"He is a threat, not an object to study! Give him to me, my Melokai, and I'll give you all the answers you'll ever need in a few hours," Gogo said.

Ramya's mouth went dry, she could feel her anger rising at the challenge to her order. A crackle of smoke from the fire that raged deep within. She stared at her Head Warrior who stared back, mouth clenched. Chaz took a step backwards. Even the warriors guarding the prisoner flicked quick glances over to this explosion about to ignite.

After a few heartbeats Gogo deferred to the Melokai, and cast her eyes down.

"It's time to leave." Ramya turned and the others moved to follow. But a sound stopped her.

Gwrlain was singing and the entire room swayed around her. Chaz dropped to his knees and she even saw Gogo falter as the sweet melody flowed over them and, as it seemed to Ramya, into them. He had the loveliest voice she had ever heard. She didn't know how long he sang for, but when he stopped the world was a brighter, more wonderful place. All in the room were silent, dazed, and Gwrlain smiled for the first time. An honest smile.

"Give him as much water as he wants and then bring him unchained to my chamber immediately," Ramya blurted out and strode into the corridor. *The wine has made me reckless!*

Gogo grabbed Ramya's shoulders, shaking her whilst she shouted, "Ramya, no! This is madness. We have no idea who he is or why he is here, he is likely a spy. He could murder you, he could do anything. Think of the prophecy!"

The Melokai drew her dagger and held it to Gogo's throat, pricking her neck and drawing blood. "You dare to question your Melokai," she spat in Gogo's face.

Ramya's speed and sudden fury surprised her as much as her Head Warrior and as quickly as Ramya had angered, she softened. She withdrew her dagger. "I understand your apprehension, Gogo, and I am indebted to your unwavering protection, but he will not harm me. I am sure of that. If he attempts anything I will squash him quicker than a nipping fly."

Ramya forced a laugh, attempting to lighten the sour atmosphere. "Let's hope he's entertaining and doesn't bore me!" She reached out a hand to her Head Warrior and said quietly, "I'm sorry for the cut…"

Gogo stepped out of Ramya's reach. The warrior's skewering glare told Ramya that she was furious, but there were no more words.

***

Later that night, there was a knock on Ramya's door. It opened and Gwrlain was pushed in. He crouched to go under the doorframe. He stood there, and she noticed that they had dressed him as a pleasure giver in a leather loin cloth with an ankle-length robe wrapped around his shoulders and tied with a cord rope. She made no sound and watched the incredible being. Everything inside of her whispered, *he poses no threat.* But still, she had hidden her daggers nearby.

He took a deep breath, hummed and listened, sniffed and stuck out his tongue. His head turned towards Ramya. Using pulsing hums he navigated his way across her chamber, effortlessly avoiding chairs and obstacles. He stopped in front of her and then dropped to his knees, head down.

She noticed that his skin no longer looked so dry and cracked, the water had soothed it and he smelled musky. She brought a hand to his head and stroked the delicate hair. He shivered. *Heightened senses,* she remembered. She lifted his chin up so she could see his face and drew him off his knees so he was standing at full height. She undid the cord and pushed away the robe.

She took Gwrlain's giant hand and led him to her bed. He picked her up and lay her down gently, starting to sing. Her skin prickled. Still singing, Gwrlain started to massage her methodically from toes up. When he came to the bottom of her linen nightdress his hands stopped and he waited. She pulled the dress over her head and threw it by the side of the bed. He continued his attentions to her neck.

He turned her over so she was face down and started again to knead her feet and upwards, singing all the while. She brought herself up on her elbows but he pushed her back to the sheets with one large hand between her shoulder blades, pinning her down. No PG had ever dared to stop her and she submitted, thrilled. He traced his way down her torso with his mouth, until she felt his hot breath between her legs. Gwrlain started humming, low and long at first and then rhythmically pulsing, holding his mouth against her, so she had the full force of his throaty vibrations.

Ramya shuddered at the most intense, satisfying feeling she had ever experienced. She looked down at Gwrlain who was grinning.

"I want you now." Ramya sat up, ravenous, and ripped off his loin cloth.

5

DARRIO

It was a gloriously sunny day, although very cold. Crisp. Darrio trotted behind the pack over a light snowfall, through the glades. Every now and then moving from cooler shade into the bright sunshine and enjoying the sudden warmth on his fur.

The two alpha wolves were in front, Arro the fierce, male breeder and Lurra his mated female, just as ferocious but with a kind heart. Darrio made a point of thanking her every day, for without Lurra's generosity, he and his three pups would be long dead. He had been adopted into the Wulhor-Aaen pack around four seasons ago and his pups were strong because of Lurra's milk.

He knew that adoption of an adult wolf into an established pack was extremely rare and that he and his pups risked being ripped apart by their own kind, but he'd had no other choice. In utter desperation Darrio had skulked into the Wulhor-Aaen pack's den, a narrow fissure in weathered rock that opened into a large, high ceilinged cave. It was hidden by heavy undergrowth but the scavenger magpies and ravens squawking at the entrance, drawn by the smell of rotting carcasses within, signposted the way. He carried his body low to the ground on all fours, with his fur flattened, ears lowered and tail between his legs. His pups, barely a few days old and still blind and deaf were bundled in the skin of a deer, that he carried by his teeth.

He remembered how the dominant breeding pair lay in their cozy, dark den's resting area, next to the tattered remains of their last kill. To either side were their children. Pups from that year's litter as well as young wolves one to three year's old. Their older children had left to form packs of their own. As Darrio crept towards the couple, the intimidating grumbles and snapping jaws of the beta wolves convinced him this would be his last day under the sun. As he approached, Arro unfurled to his full height on his two back paws, his black hackles raised and eyes aglow whilst Lurra sat on her hind legs, staring at Darrio with mouth open, ears forward and nose wrinkled.

Darrio had dropped the bundle and whispered, "Please. Am packless. Have three pups in need of suckling. Please adopt me and pups. If no need of me, I beg you take my pups as your own."

Arro dropped down to all fours and had taken Darrio's muzzle in his jaws. Darrio hunkered down further, dropping his ears as low as they would go and turning his eyes to the ground. To show any aggression would be certain death.

"Why, stupid wolf, would we do that?" Lurra had asked, she was missing a chunk of her top lip which exposed her right fang and the gum above, adding to her formidable presence. She took her time to get to her feet, raising tail high and preparing to spill blood.

"One pup is female… she stands." Darrio struggled to speak as Arro still had his snout between his teeth. Darrio knew that this was his one chance, to intrigue them and at the very least they would keep his female child, Sarrya.

"A standing female? No such thing exists. You lie." Lurra leapt forward and snatched open the deer skin. The pups spilled on the floor and whined pathetically, all three were starving and in desperate need of a mother's milk.

She shoved Darrio out of the way and sniffed at the pups. She identified Sarrya and licked her chest to make the pup wriggle her legs.

Lurra barked and leaned back, startled that Sarrya had stretched her forelegs as the males did and had their wider back paws. She shook her head and then came near again, nudging Sarrya onto her back for a closer inspection.

"It is true. A standing female. Never heard of such a thing. Never seen such a thing." Lurra glanced up at Arro in amazement, who let go of Darrio's snout to look for himself.

The alpha Arro had approached the pups and Darrio's eldest, Harro, started to wail and whimper, helplessly rocking his tiny, pink head. Darrio moved to go to comfort him but Arro stood between them. The distress of their brother set off Warrio and then Sarrya herself started up, all three crying with hunger, begging for some nourishment.

"Shut up!" Arro exploded over the din.

Darrio had silently said goodbye to his pups at that moment, willing them to understand that he had tried to do right by them, to try to be the best father after their mother had left. Saying sorry under his breath that he had brought them here to be ripped apart by other wolves and thinking that dying from starvation would have been a better way to go. He hoped that the alpha pair would kill him first so that he wouldn't have to watch the death of his beloved pups. He had closed his eyes and waited for the mauling.

When it didn't come, he dared to peek. Lurra had flopped down on her side exposing her belly to the pups. She used her paw to bring them closer, guiding their tiny little mouths to her swollen teats. By instinct, Harro latched on first and the other two followed him. Guzzling contentedly, white froth around their little lips.

Arro stared at Lurra and said, "You are sure, mate?"

Lurra gazed down at the babes suckling and nodded.

"If father submits, we keep him too. Want to know everything about the special female."

Darrio had gladly taken the lowest position in the pack as omega, below the beta wolves who were still pups, to secure his life and that of his offspring. Arro and Lurra knew, as did their children, that he was more than a subordinate and should have a pack of his own, but he never attempted to elevate his status or compete with Arro for breeding rights. His pups were safe, that was all that mattered.

Now, a year later, they were fit and healthy. All had his colouring, a rich brown, although Sarrya had creamy fur around her head and between her shoulders and rare orange eyes. Beautiful. Apart from Arro who was black, the rest of the pack was grey or mottled grey and black. It still surprised him to see Sarrya stand tall on her two back paws with the males and not stay on all fours like every other female wolf. Lurra was proud of her, and did not deny the rumours that circulated around the neighbouring wolf packs across the Zwullfr mountains that Sarrya was her child.

Darrio was determined that the truth of his pups' parentage would never come to light. He repeated the same story to his pups and the alphas, which had been accepted. He had lost his pack to the madness disease, watching them all catch a fever and then convulse, be fearful of water and refuse to drink, slipping into unconsciousness before dying. He was the only wolf not to catch the devastating illness, surviving to wander on his own. This much was true. Darrio then told a lie, repeated so often that he almost believed it himself. That he had stumbled upon a lone female wolf who had lost her pack to the same ailment. They had mated with the ambition to form a new pack but then she had died in whelping. Knowing he could not provide milk for his pups, Darrio had determined to find another pack to adopt them and the Wulhor-Aaen pack had been the first he had scented.

And now here they were.

As he jogged under the snow blanketed canopy he stole a glance back at the yearlings behind him. His three loped along with two sons of Arro and Lurra. They were not old enough to join in the hunt but able to keep up with the pack and to watch it from afar, learning techniques that they would one day put into practice themselves. Sarrya ran close to Arro and Lurra's son Ricarro. Born in the same season as her, the pair were inseparable. It was assumed that once these two had matured in the next year or two, they would be mated and form their own pack as the alpha breeding pair. The thought pleased him. Perhaps they would produce more standing females, Sarrya being the first, and establish a new age for wolves.

Warrio and Harro were jumping on each other and play fighting as they kept up with the rest of the pack. Full of energy and with well-defined human features. This detail Darrio kept to himself and hoped that no other wolf noticed. Warrio spotted his father looking and sprinted to catch up to him.

"Pappy! You run like an old wolf." Warrio nudged Darrio's nose with his own.

"You still have pup fluff on your chest," Darrio said and in a swift movement he stuck out his back leg tripping Warrio headfirst into the undergrowth. "You run like a suckling newborn unsteady on his paws." Darrio laughed as his youngest son righted himself and leapt onto his father. They rolled around clamping each other's jaws. Soon Harro had joined the fray and all three tussled, licked at faces and tried to nip each other's muzzles.

"Ugh, Pa, don't encourage. Stop being so embarrassing," Sarrya groaned, rolling her eyes with snout to one side.

"C'mon, sis! Help us pin down Pa!" Harro shouted and grabbed at her front paw to try to bring her into the game, but she pulled it away with a huff and a shake of her head.

Determined female, thought Darrio and a fleeting memory

of her mother came to his mind.

Arro's howl brought them to attention. The hunting pack assembled in a ceremonial circle, nose to nose and wagging their tails. Each was on all four legs and Lurra gave orders about the prey that had been scented, a lame deer that was lagging behind its herd, and her plan for attack.

"Children, stay low, silent and out the way," she told the young wolves. "Watch. Listen. Arro test you on return to the den."

The younger wolves, including Darrio's three, dropped their heads to show they understood.

Arro, Lurra, the three beta wolves Marro, Zirrio and Herra, plus Darrio, spaced out and edged forward, noses to the forest floor to pick up the scent. Zirrio found it, standing alert and pointing his nose and ears towards the target. The hunters stalked along after Zirrio, picking up their pace as they drew closer and the scent intensified.

The lame deer stood apart from the herd, and the wolves positioned themselves around it, twitching their tails as they crept forward. Lurra gave the signal and rushed at the animal, whose innate response was to flee towards the other deer who, sensing the danger, also started to run. The six wolves gave chase. Darrio, Arro and Herra forced their way between the lame deer and the safety of its herd, isolating it. It bolted away from its kind, and straight into Lurra, Zirrio and Marro. It saw them and lurched again, running down a slope and towards the river.

This was not what the wolves wanted. The deer picked up pace on the downhill, dragging the bad foot. The pack's territorial boundary ended at the bank and across the river was the Lost Lands. Darrio picked up speed and overtook the deer, aiming to get to the river bank first and force it to turn left or right, rather than enter the water and attempt to cross. Herra followed behind him whilst the others trailed the deer's path. His plan didn't work as the deer bounced left and then bounded straight into a shallow part of the river, breaking the thin ice and plopping through into the flowing water. It swam across and heaved itself out on the other bank. The pack pursued at full speed, the thrill of the chase and desire to catch their prey overshadowing any thoughts of venturing into the Lost Lands. The pack hadn't eaten properly in days, their last two kill attempts failing and then no prey scented on their patch.

"Turned into a long chase," Arro shouted. "Pace yourselves, save energy for kill. Don't let dinner get away!"

Darrio winced as he dropped into the icy water. *Deer not as lame as hoped.*

As the wolves heaved themselves out of the river and sprinted after the deer, Darrio felt uneasy in the unfamiliar forest. It smelled different, there was a faint scent on the wind, long forgotten but distinct. The deer ran deeper into the forest of the Lost Lands but it faltered, it was tiring at last. The pack readied itself for a kill. It hobbled into a small grassy clearing but Darrio was stunned by glare from the sun. He scrunched up his eyes and they adjusted in time to see Zirrio stand upright and launch himself at the hindquarters, as Marro and Lurra closed in ready to lunge at the animal's neck to sever the artery.

But Zirrio didn't reach the deer. A spear came whizzing from the shadows of the trees around the edges of the clearing and lodged itself in his throat. He barked in surprise as it hit and then whimpered pitifully as he slumped to the ground, blood flowing from his wound.

The wolves skidded to a stop and squatted low behind Zirrio's body, snarling. The deer shambled away. Arro started to howl savagely. Darrio and the others joined him howling.

A flurry of spears was launched from the menacing shadows and the wolves turned tail, running back into the safety of the forest, hearing the whooshing and thudding noises as spears landed in the grass around them.

"My son! Zirrriiioooo," Lurra wailed.

They retreated a safe distance away and sat, heads lowered, behind the ripped up, gnarly roots of a fallen tree, keeping their noses alert for changes in the scents on the wind, but they were alone. The young wolves had fallen behind but soon caught up to them, and all were full of excitement at crossing the river. They fell silent sensing that something was very wrong as Lurra swayed and lamented her loss. Darrio found his three pups and hugged them to him, licking their faces with relief that they were safe.

He recalled the faint scent and what it meant. "Peqkians," he growled.

***

Arro sent the yearlings back to the den and told them to send Moirra, who had been on guard watching the new litter whilst the rest of the pack was out hunting. Once she had arrived, the wolves scouted the area, locating the humans and assessing their numbers and position. They regrouped a distance away.

"Established camp, fifteen humans. Majority female, carry weapons. Spears. Peqkians consider land as theirs, defend it," Arro said.

"Once our land," Lurra thundered. "They stole it from us. They have no claim over water or earth or sky or air. We are stronger now, males stand, we have standing female. Time to test our strength. They must die as my son died. Wulhor-Aaen is most powerful in Zwullfr, we avenge Zirrio's death. We attack tonight."

Darrio was reluctant and as the subordinate wolf in the pack he knew he should stay quiet, but he decided to voice his opinion. "Do I have permission to speak, alphas?"

"Speak," Arro replied and Lurra snorted her approval.

He said, "No good will come of human attack, more come in their place and make trouble for us."

"You are weak on humans, Darrio. You either with us or with them," Lurra snarled at him, her tail high and quivering in warning.

"With you, Lurra," Darrio replied and kneeled on his forelegs in submission.

The juvenile wolves were troubled and huddled together muttering and barking. Scared and confused at the loss of their brother as well as their odd surroundings.

"Moirra, Marro, Herra. Speak," Lurra said.

"Ma, Zirrio has died, do not want same. Lost Lands smell of death. Never fought humans, frightened," Moirra replied, the eldest of the three. Lurra crouched and jerked her snout, beckoning her children, who crouched around her. Arro joined them but Darrio, as an outsider of no blood relation and the omega wolf, sat off to a distance. He listened in.

"Lost Lands smell of death as death is what happened here. Zirrio's bones will rest with the bones of our ancestors. Hundreds of years past, many wolves lived here. Then Peqkians came down from the Small Mountains, greedy for the land. For thirty suns and thirty moons the human savages cleared the forest of wolves. Burning dens with newborns still wailing inside. Any survivors crossed Great River to north and we lost south Wul-Onr valley to the humans. It offended Great Mother Wolf and male pups were born across Zwullfr mountains with ability to run both on four paws and on two hindlegs, to take revenge when time right, on equal footing." Lurra paused to look at each of her children and then continued, "We are the first wolves in the Lost Lands for many generations, but we must not be afraid for we belong here. You will all be mated soon and your territories can be here, should be here. We take revenge for Zirrio and for our ancestors tonight."

"But why us?" Marro blurted.

"Why not us, Marro?" Lurra soothed. "We are here, we were brought here and the time for revenge has come, for Zirrio, for wolves. This is beginning. For reasons I do not know, the Wulhor-Aaen has been chosen to lead the charge for our kind. Be proud, be brave."

The pack was quiet after that, contemplative. Darrio paced, every sound in the new forest catching his attention. He willed the sun to stay in the sky. He did not want to fight, but had no choice. He had to obey his alphas or he and his pups would be packless again.

Darkness fell upon them and Lurra spoke the words Darrio had been dreading.

"It is time," she said.

For the second time that day the wolves stood nose to nose in the hunt ceremony, wagging their tails. Arro led the pack. They picked their way carefully uphill and upwind of the Peqkian camp and then turned back to it. With bellies low to the ground, they edged closer and closer.

The stars were out and the night was still. The humans slept in tents next to the dwindling fire, apart from one female on guard. She patrolled around the camp, a well-trodden and obvious path. With little effort, Arro and Moirra stalked behind her and took her down without a sound. The absolute shock on her face etched itself into Darrio's mind. Arro jutted his human blood-spotted chin and pointed his nose, directing his pack silently. The six wolves surrounded the camp with ease and on Lurra's piercing howl they attacked.

The female human fighters were targeted first. The pack howled as they bounded through tent openings and lunged at the sleeping bodies, crushing necks with their devastating jaws and moving on to the next. The warriors who were still alive, when they understood what was happening, grabbed their weapons and stumbled out of tents, bravely fighting back but the assault was relentless. Bloodlust and hunger spurring the pack on. In less than an hour all the humans succumbed, apart from one warrior left fighting stubbornly and, thought Darrio, heroically. The pack encircled her, biting at her limbs, clawing at her flesh and snapping at bloody fingers that clutched her spear. This taunting went on for a long time and Darrio felt ashamed, willing it to end.

She tripped and fell at Darrio's feet, her spear rolling out of reach. He stared down at her.

"Finish her!" Lurra screamed, but Darrio froze. Not with fear but with a painful longing for a time in his past. His delay almost cost him his life as the warrior turned and grabbed a sharp rock bringing it up to smash his head. Lurra jumped forward and tore out the human's throat with a gurgling sound that chilled Darrio to his bones. Lurra growled at him in disgust, narrowing her eyes, questioning his hesitation.

"Where's sister Herra?" Moirra shouted and Lurra moved away from Darrio, searching for her daughter.

Herra lay dead a few paces away, stab wounds covered her body. She was slumped on top of a dead warrior, the blood-soaked dagger still clasped in the human's hand. Herra's mouth was clamped around the warrior's ruined skull. They lay in a gory red puddle. Lurra yowled, devastated by the loss of her second child that day.

"Eat your fill, savour human flesh. We leave at daybreak," Arro told the pack.

But, like Darrio, Arro didn't eat. He crouched next to the cold body of his daughter Herra and nuzzled his nose into her matted fur, breathing her scent for the last time.

6

RAMYA

Ramya woke eager to interpret the prophecy.

"Go." She pushed at Gwrlain's hefty body so he would get the hint that he was dismissed.

But he didn't get out of bed, instead he nudged her back.

"No. You need to leave!"

Gwrlain's cheeky grin made her pause. His hand closed around her wrist and brought it to his face, kissing the tips of her fingers and leaning his face into her palm. The tender moment was shattered when he pushed her and she rolled backwards off the bed, tangled in the sheets.

The Melokai sprawled on the floor. *I'll destroy him.* She scanned the room and pinpointed where her nearest dagger was, kicking off the sheets to get it. As she was rising, the Trogr leaned his head over the edge of the bed and grinned again.

A surge of playfulness doused her warrior reflexes and she threw back her head and laughed until her sides ached. *He thinks this is some kind of game. There is no menace.* For the first time in many years she felt like a carefree child, and forgot the stresses of ruling a country. She pulled at the white giant and he didn't resist, tumbling on top of her.

A few hours later, Ramya was woken by Bevya pawing at her ankle and mewing. For a fleeting moment Ramya was confused. It dawned on her that she was wrapped up in Gwrlain's arms and still on the bedsheets on the floor. She felt ridiculously content.

"Your council issss waiting, my Melokai," the clevercat hissed.

"Zhaq," the Melokai swore and scrambled up. Gwrlain sat and hummed as she pulled on her clothes and strapped on her daggers and sword.

"Tell them I am coming, Bevya. And then send some food up for Gwrlain and find him some more suitable clothes, not those of the PGs."

The cat dashed from her chambers and Ramya followed close behind, but as she reached the doorway she turned back, ran to Gwrlain and kissed his forehead. He made a move to stand. She placed a hand on his shoulder and pushed him down.

"Stay here. I will be back soon."

Grabbing her cloak, she ran through the corridors and burst into the council chamber. Her counsellors ended their conversations abruptly and all turned to look at her as she fumbled with her stool and hurried to seat herself. She was flustered. She had never been late for anything.

"Let's begin, shall we," she managed and then flung her cloak around shoulders and swallowed down the excited frisson that bubbled between her ribs. Her counsellors continued to stare, Gogo struggling to mask an expression of utter contempt. Hanny winked at her. "Tell me of the wolves," Ramya exclaimed, desperate to turn their attention from her. She felt undone. "Chaz, say something!"

The Head Scholar frowned at her and then cleared his throat. "Yes, of course, my Melokai. We are here to discuss the second part of Sybilya's prophecy, 'A wolf will claim the throne.' I believe a good place to start would be to discuss which throne, then to discuss which wolf and then to decide what is meant by the word 'claim'. I believe that the throne Sybilya refers to is ours, as she is most concerned with Peqkya, but it could also be the thrones of any of our neighbouring countries, or perhaps even the wolf throne itself."

As the counsellors started to debate this, Hanny stood and glided over to Ramya. Without speaking the Head Courtesan raked her fingers through Ramya's short hair, teasing it into place. Ramya watched the mouths of her counsellors move, but could not focus on the conversation unfolding around her, snippets found their way into her ears but her head felt as if it were full of thick honey. Images of Gwrlain clouded her mind. Hanny adjusted Ramya's cloak and then sat back on her stool, a twinkle in her almond-shaped eyes.

Concentrate. Ramya curbed her thoughts. She rearranged her body in her warrior's stance and said, "Wolves… We have not had any sightings of wolves for many years, correct?"

Her Head Scholar replied. "You are correct, my Melokai. The last recorded sighting was in the time of Melokai Tatya, three hundred years ago, during the Wolf Expulsion, when we cleansed their kind from south Trequ valley in order to push our north-eastern border to the far side of the Melioks."

Ramya nodded. Chaz started to ramble, and Head Speaker Zecky chattered over him. Ramya's skin tickled with a memory imprinted there. *Gwrlain's arms around me, like a warm cocoon.* The frisson started to bubble again. She fidgeted on her stool, as if she was sat on hot coals. *I want to get back to him.* She placed her hands on the carved table and, interrupting her counsellors, said, "Well, I believe the best course of action is to take precautions to stop *any* wolf from getting anywhere near *our* throne. If they are nowhere near Peqkya, then they cannot *claim* it. Agreed?"

"Well, yes, my Melokai," Chaz said.

"Excellent. We keep a close eye on the northern border

with the wolves, track everything and be alert for anything. We put the same preventative measures in place in the north as we have in east. Agreed?"

Ramya's counsellors mumbled their assent.

Ramya stood. "Please continue to discuss the finer details, if you must, my orders are clear. I thank you for your counsel." She hurried out of the council room as fast as she had entered and did not look back.

A fizz of excitement swelled in her as she opened the door to her chambers. Gwrlain ran to her, picked her up around the waist and swung her in a circle, smiling and laughing at her return. *No one has ever been that happy to see me.*

That afternoon they wandered the city streets with one of Chaz's translator scholars and three warriors. Ramya pointing out various landmarks and quarters, explaining carefully through the translator the history and meaning. Gwrlain listened intently and Ramya enjoyed teaching him. She introduced him to curious Riats who crowded around the strange foreigner.

The Melokai took him out on Inaly Lake and from the boat, she had indicated Sybilya's hill with the snake of blue arches. Gwrlain could not feel Sybilya's positive, kind presence, like every Peqkian, and Ramya had vowed to organise tutors to educate him in her Sayings, on the Peqkian way of life based on her philosophies.

After, they visited various Riat businesses and workshops, where – much to Ramya's delight – Gwrlain had cheerfully tried his hand at weaving goats' hair, wood carving, playing the Peqkian pipe, as well as painting ancient symbols.

That evening they ate dinner in her chambers and lounged happily by a crackling fire.

The Trogr spent another night in her bed and the following morning Ramya taught him the daylight dances. She organised for two baths to be placed side by side. He bathed in hot steaming water that sunk into his skin and left him soft to the touch, she lounged in milk, whilst reading him poems from the latest collection by her courtesan Irrya. Although she knew he did not understand the meaning, the flowing rhythms of the language read aloud was like a song and he listened, rapt.

As they dressed, he sat on the edge of the bed and pulled her to him. He positioned her so that she stood in front of him, his hands holding her hips. He put his mouth to her belly and sung the sweetest melody. It made Ramya's entire body tingle. He rested his forehead on her belly, murmuring in his language.

"What are you doing?"

He smiled up at her, knowingly.

As Chaz's history tutor taught Gwrlain, a few paces away Ramya sat with her Head Scholar and Head Speaker, Zecky. Both her counsellors stared at the Trogr.

"My Melokai, have you not considered *he* is the trouble from the east?" said Zecky. Her chunky horse rider's legs were crossed, as were her thin arms, and she swept her waist-length, rope-like braids over one side of her head and then back to the other side as if her hair infuriated her.

"Of course I have," Ramya snapped. "But he shows no signs of aggression or deceit. He is a guest of Peqkya."

"Guest! The *peon* was a prisoner two days ago, my Melokai." Zecky snarled at the word peon. She was a staunch supporter of 'keeping peons in their place'. In the early days of Ramya's rule, Zecky would pluck a peon who took her fancy off the street to rut and then declare him unsatisfactory to watch him face the customary death penalty. Ramya had forbidden her to continue this unnecessary, callous habit and Zecky had never quite forgiven the Melokai, insisting it was her right. "The *peon* should be in the PG set, not in your chambers."

Ramya's breath stalled in her lungs, her anger was knocking. She kept the door firmly closed and her voice softened. "I am keeping a close eye on him." She noticed Chaz and Zecky exchange a fleeting glance. *I don't care what they think, he is charming and entertaining and, for now, I'm enjoying his company.* She changed the subject. "Zecky, I won't be attending the public assembly later today. Chaz, I'd like you to go in my place."

Chaz huffed and pursed his lips. Public assemblies were held in the grand assembly hall and could be attended by any Peqkian woman. It was where they discussed issues collectively, such as community facilities, new housing required, appropriate punishment for any disobedience, profession succession and various other things. They were long events, usually tedious but occasionally entertaining and, on the rare occasion, such as when Glendya the weaver had presented her new technique, inspiring.

Zecky tossed her rope braids to the other side of her head. "Are you leaving me to deal with the washer-peons' issue, my Melokai?"

"Yes, Zecky, but confer with Chaz first on the best course of action."

"What issue?" Chaz said.

"The stupid washer-peons refused to work in protest at their conditions. They believe that they should be allowed to wash every once in a while," Zecky sneered.

Chaz's eyes widened. "I see, that is troublesome…"

Gwrlain laughed at something in his lesson and Ramya glanced at him. "It was peaceful, Chaz, nothing to worry about. Perhaps grant them a wash once a year in the public baths."

Zecky shook her head. "But that will only make every peon demand a wash once a year, and the public baths are women-only. They need to be punished, my Melokai, and brutally, to deter any peon protest again."

"Well, I'm not sure I agree…" Chaz said.

Ramya sighed. "Counsellors, enough. This is something you can discuss at the public assembly *without* me."

"My Melokai, you have never missed a public assembly.

Are you sure this is wise?" Chaz said.

"Exactly, Chaz, I have never missed one! I have dedicated twelve years of my life to running the country, caring for the Peqkian people and the world around me. Peqkya is a prosperous and safe nation that runs smoothly because of *my* rule. You two, and my other counsellors for that matter, can manage without me for a little while, you are all meant to be at the top of your respective professions after all. The prophecy is in hand and if I'm needed urgently, then send for me. I'm not going anywhere, I'm just taking a little time off."

Chaz opened his mouth to argue, but Ramya cut him off. "You and Zecky will attend the public assemblies without me until further notice. You are both dismissed."

Later, Ramya and Gwrlain rode horses in the forest. Gwrlain had never ridden before, and seemed to have an enigmatic influence over the beasts who whinnied and yielded when he touched them. He also basked in the adoration of the cats, with two or three fighting to doze in his lap the moment he sat or lacing between his ankles if he stood still for long enough. *When he hums it sounds and feels like their purring. The cats' love for him is a good sign.*

Whilst they were in the forest, Ramya decided she would introduce Gwrlain to archery. Peqkians enjoyed shooting birds with arrows. The smaller the better for a challenge, and Ramya was a skilled archer.

"You pull the string back like so, aim like so and…" Ramya let go of the string and the arrow hit the target, a sparrow in a low branch of a nearby tree. It squawked and dropped to the undergrowth.

Gwrlain balked. "No!" He pulled the bow from her hands, flinging it on the ground. A torrent of words spilled from his mouth in his guttural, ugly language and he pointed at her and then at the tree. Ramya glared at the translator for an explanation. *I have never seen him so angry.* Her hand twitched towards her sword.

Gwrlain finished and the translator gabbled in a hurry, "Birds are sacred in his culture, my Melokai, like cats are sacred for us. He is upset that you took a bird's life."

"I understand. I'm sorry." Ramya let go of her sword and stroked his cheek. He nodded.

He held out his palm and made a high-pitched squeaky sound. A swift swooped in and landed on his palm, chirping as if telling him an important message. He beamed at Ramya and tried to get her to hold the thing, grabbing for her wrist. She refused, taking a step back from him and shaking her head. *I don't want that dirty thing in my hand!*

He then whispered back to the bird in his guttural language, too muffled for the translator to hear. The bird's little head jerked as if listening. He stroked its feathers and it took flight. Towards the east, noticed Ramya and stared hard at him, her brows furrowed.

Gwrlain's face was full of wonder and his arms were outstretched to the sky, exalting in the bird's flight. Ramya's forehead slackened. *The direction the swift flew off in was by chance, it is not anything sinister.*

A blissful week passed and Ramya set off with Chaz and her warriors to visit Sybilya. Every step the horse took away from Gwrlain her heart seemed to constrict.

"My Melokai, you are enjoying the company of the Trogr?" Chaz asked.

"I am." Ramya had never felt so attached to a male, or to any woman for that matter. *He holds some kind of influence over me. He is not like the PGs, he has a strong will and is not afraid to show his emotions.* Gwrlain was not dull like Ferraz, who was good at sex but nothing else, and the Trogr constantly surprised her. He was more like an equal. *This must be what women feel when they declare a peon as their soulmatch.*

"You favour him as I favour the PG Martaz, my Melokai."

"I do."

"I am pleased for you, my Melokai. Truly. It is wonderful to find such a connection." Chaz shifted on the horse.

"There is something you are not saying, Chaz. Out with it."

He cleared his throat. "It is this, my Melokai. Will Sybilya be happy for you? Will your counsellors be happy for you? Will your people be happy for you? You should take care, not all will approve of this match with a cave creature, or appreciate that you are distracted from rule."

"I am not distracted!"

"As you say, my Melokai."

She kicked on her horse and moved in front of her Head Scholar. *I can do both, rule and love. He'll see… everyone will see.*

A second week passed, then a third, and Ramya fell deeply in love with Gwrlain. The Trogr learnt enough words for longer conversations, and they discovered each other's past, the complex experiences that had made them who they were now.

"Farming my work," he told her one evening as they curled up on her sofa, in front of the fire. "I managed team to grow and find food. Not responsibility like you, you are very important. My responsibility to team, we fed my people."

"Then you had a great responsibility, Gwrlain, for without your leadership, your people would have starved," Ramya replied.

"Maybe," he agreed with a shrug.

"I'm sure they miss you. Why did you leave?"

She felt his muscles clench.

"Who your mother?" he asked, avoiding her question.

"In the pen my Mother was Kafya," she said. "She was warm and encouraging, always insisting that I could do anything I wanted. Some Mothers are cruel or cold but Kafya was fair and nurtured her charges to get the best from them rather than use force or fear. She taught me how to control my temper. She treated the peens and the girls the same, as long as we all behaved. She believes that peens are essentially good. Yes, they can become selfish and power crazed if allowed to, but as children they could be taught humility. Kafya rose in her profession from managing that pen to become the Mother of Mothers, the one who oversees all the Mothers in the land, and became my counsellor. And although I now rule over her, she will always be my mentor, an inspiration. Who is your mother, Gwrlain?"

"Her name Gruack. Beautiful. Laughing always. There for me, taught me bravery, belief in myself. Died horrible death. Miss her." Gwrlain's body tensed again and a purple colour blazed under his skin. He clamped his mouth shut.

She hugged him into her. "Why did you leave? Did something happen to your mother?"

He wriggled out of her embrace and stood a few paces away with his back to her, arms crossed.

Ramya wanted to know the truth of how he came to be in Peqkya, to be able to tell her counsellors that he was not 'trouble', not some kind of sinister infiltrator. "Trust me, like I trust you. Tell me what happened, why were you banished?"

"No."

Angered by his cold shoulder, Ramya stood and positioned herself in front of him. "Tell me what happened."

He turned so his back faced her again.

She grabbed his arm. "Zhaq, Gwrlain! Tell me, what are you hiding?"

"No!" He shoved her away. She stumbled, the force surprising her.

He stomped back to the sofa and took up one of his exercise books, writing out the letters of the Shella language.

***

In the deep of night, he crawled into bed and curled himself around her, his chest pressed against her back.

He whispered into her neck, "I'm sorry. I will tell you in time. You are my soulmatch, Ramya. Am I yours?"

Ramya hesitated. *It is true, I* do *want to spend the rest of my life with this male. But my time is running out… soon I will no longer be Melokai and will be banished from him. For as long as I have left, my everything is Gwrlain and will always be Gwrlain.*

"Yes, my love. You are my soulmatch."

He gathered her up, holding her tight and planted little, rapid kisses all over her.

7

RAMYA

"Table… chair… window… door…" Gwrlain repeated the words he had learnt that morning to his three tutors as they pointed at different objects. He was fanatical about learning Ramya's language, pushing himself and focusing all his energies on perfecting his pronunciation. She admired his rapid progress.

"Sssawwlung." Gwrlain struggled with the word and one of his tutors snickered at his articulation.

"No, no, no you see-through fool! It's ceiling. Try again." She laughed, getting too comfortable in her role and taking advantage of Gwrlain's good humour when he made a mistake. Gwrlain shrugged and attempted to form the word, but for the Melokai she had gone too far.

Ramya sprang up, crossed the room and slapped the girl, yanking her out of her chair by her hair. "How dare you insult the Melokai's companion so brazenly. You are here to teach him, if he makes a mistake it is your fault and not his. Violya," she shouted at the warrior she knew was stationed outside the door.

Violya entered, tall and lithe. She was loyal, unquestioning, deadly, and she was now Gwrlain's personal body guard.

"This cockface insulted me. Cut out her scornful

tongue, chop off her limbs and then feed her to the hungry pigs so she can hear them chomping on her body as Gwrlain had to hear her dreadful voice ridiculing him." Ramya shoved the snivelling tutor towards the warrior.

"It will be done, my Melokai." The warrior grabbed the condemned woman's arm to lead her out the room.

The tutor fell to her knees, trying to twist out of Violya's grip and begging the Melokai to have mercy on her, to give her one more chance. The warrior picked her up with one hand under the chin, rendering her speechless and pulled her out of the room.

"Wait," Ramya yelled. Violya paused at the doorway and turned towards Ramya.

The Melokai took a deep breath and shuttered the raging emotions inside her. *That was my anger speaking. Control it. I am not cruel.* "Take the tutor to the prison instead Violya, a week in the solitary cell should be enough time for her to reflect and repent on her actions."

"It will be done, my Melokai." Violya strode away dragging the tutor who babbled in relief.

Ramya turned to the other two terrified tutors. "You are both dismissed for the day. Tell Chaz that I expect the best of the best and any sub-standard scholars will suffer the same fate as that one."

"Yes, my Melokai," the tutors uttered in unison and fled as if an army was at their heels.

She turned to Gwrlain, and found she could not look at him, embarrassed that her temper had flared so spectacularly in his presence. She worried what he might think. "I'm sorry," she muttered.

Gwrlain stood and took her in his arms, chuckling into her hair. "You fight for me, I like. I do same for you."

"I do not doubt it," Ramya mumbled into his chest, her cheeks still burning. *He doesn't judge me, he accepts me. He has witnessed my anger, my greatest fault, yet continues to love me.*

"Let's eat." Gwrlain asked an attendant to bring his favourite lunch, vegetable dumplings with a spicy dressing and roasted trout. He didn't eat much, hardly anything compared to Ramya, but he liked tasting new foods having survived on bats, salamanders and insects in the caves.

They sat down at the table, Gwrlain patted his knees at the feast laid out in front of him and got stuck in with his right hand clasping a half-moon shaped dumpling, but before he could put it to his mouth there was a knock at the door.

"Enter," Ramya beckoned.

Hanny came into the chamber and Ramya felt a pang of remorse. She hadn't seen her friend in weeks. Before, they would meet every few days. Ramya had been too busy luxuriating in Gwrlain's affection. *A love I don't have to earn, like my people's. A love I hadn't been seeking, but now I could not live without.*

"My Melokai, there is a matter of great urgency and the council humbly requests your attendance at a meeting," the courtesan stated. Her manner was frosty.

"Hanny, darling." Ramya jumped up and hugged her friend, but Hanny stood still with arms tight to her sides. Ramya held Hanny's shoulders and kissed her cheek, but her friend didn't respond.

"Thank you, I'm coming now," Ramya replied, watching her friend leave the room without another word.

The Melokai swept into the council meeting, determined. Gwrlain followed her, their fingers interlocked.

The counsellors exploded, shouting over each other, standing up from their stools, banging the table in uproar.

"How dare you bring this outsider to our council meeting!"

"A *male*! You bring a *male*. You disgrace our hallowed Stone Prophetess."

"Do you have no shame? Keep him for your bed if you must, not to discuss the future of our great nation!"

"This freak cave creature cannot be here. He's a spy!"

"Have you gone absolutely insane, Ramya? Have you

forgotten the prophecy already?"

Ramya refused to be provoked into justifying her decision and, for once, she didn't want her counsellors' opinions. She took her seat, unhurried, and then gestured to her Head Trader. "Riv, please move so that Gwrlain can sit to my left."

Riv looked horrified but heaved up her flabby frame, picked up her ornate glass flask filled with a creamy soup, and moved away from her stool. Ramya noted her elaborate outfit with disgust, an oversized cloak made of various furs stitched together with gold thread, draped over a brocade smock dress with a fine silk scarf tied in a bow around her neck. It was in complete contrast to the simple attire of Ramya and her other counsellors. The Head Trader had always dressed with a flourish insisting that her trading travels opened her tastes to new garments and materials, but recently she had been overtly displaying signs of wealth. *The amount of jewellery she wears is obscene. I must find time to speak with Riv about this privately.*

Ramya addressed her counsellors, "Keep your thoughts to yourself or remove yourself from this council chamber. You all know if you leave before the end of your term then custom dictates that you are beheaded so you can never repeat what you have heard in this room. Gwrlain is my soulmatch and he stays, make your choice."

The counsellors shot glances at each other.

"My Melokai," Chaz braved. "You know Gwrlain shouldn't be here."

"*You* shouldn't be here, Chaz. Rules change, as you well know. Gwrlain is my chosen companion and he will be attending these meetings from herein. I have spent much time with this Trogr and I do not believe he is the trouble the prophecy warns us of. And besides, we shouldn't immediately fear those who aren't like us, we should embrace them and learn from them. Now, let's begin."

A thick, cloying silence filled in the room.

The Mother of Mothers, Kafya, stood up and looked

sadly at the Melokai. "You have desecrated one of our most time-honoured traditions, Ramya. I am appalled. I did not bring you up to turn your back on your people and on our customs or to be so easily led astray by this outsider, this stranger. I would rather die than be part of it." She shook her head and shuffled out of the chamber.

Hanny leaned her elbows on the table and dropped her head into her hands, Zecky muttered and Riv's mouth was so wide it looked as if her face might split in two. Ramya stared after Kafya in disbelief. Ramya's cherished Mother of Mothers, her beloved pen-Mother, who had given advice and devotion for the past thirty-two years had chosen to die rather than support her. Ramya's tear ducts threatened a deluge and she blinked quickly to halt the flow. With extreme effort, Ramya repressed her grief. *Kafya made her choice. There will be time later to mourn.*

"Speak. Do not keep me waiting," Ramya addressed the remaining council members with a quaking voice, as firm as she could muster. Gwrlain sat alert and listening, sensing the heated atmosphere.

Chaz cleared his throat and stammered, "There are a few urgent matters to discuss my Melokai..." But talking was too much and he choked with emotion, tears streaming down his cheeks.

Gogo picked up. She was clearly livid at Ramya, but as all good warriors she kept her emotion in check. "Ten days ago, an entire camp of border patrol guards was slaughtered as they slept on the north-east border. Ten warriors and five serving peons."

Ramya, still reeling with the shock of Kafya leaving, gulped for air, winded by this second blow. "Fifteen of our people have died? How? Why?"

"Two dead wolves were found, one at the scene and one nearby. The wounds are consistent with a wolf attack and some of the bodies had been eaten. The reason is not clear. When the camp did not check in to central border patrol as usual using fire signals, a warrior was sent and found the devastation. A messenger was dispatched to the capital, but the terrain is treacherous and arrived this morning."

Ramya noted the deliberate slight as her Head Warrior didn't address her with the customary *My Melokai*, but let it go. She said, "Why would wolves attack us now? This must be linked to the prophecy somehow."

"It seems Chaz's admired evolution has meddled with the zhaq wolves over the years," Gogo continued. "The female was what we expected, as noted in our records, but the male was… deformed. It's back limbs and paws were shaped in a way to allow it to run on two legs as well as four. It had less fur on the face and chest and a shorter snout than the female. The bodies of our warriors are on their way here now to be given a warriors' burial, the peons were buried on the site. The camp has been cleared and re-established with a temporary group of border guards, until a decision is made about what course of action to take. The two wolf bodies will also be brought back, packed in ice, for Chaz and his bookish little underlings to dissect and waste time pondering."

Gogo slammed her fist on the table and raised her voice, "This is an invasion, the first time in Peqkian history that a warrior has been killed on our soil by an outside force. We retaliate with ruthless violence immediately. The wolves cannot cross our borders and murder our people with no comeback!"

Chaz stood and paced, pausing as far away from Gogo as the room allowed. "Before we make war with the wolves, I think we should find out more about them, my Melokai. I am intrigued that they are no longer the wolves we once knew. They have changed, and we don't know how many there are. This could be a one off, freak incident."

Ramya looked down at her finger stumps. "The blood of ten warriors and five peons has been shed. We cannot let the wolves get away with this. We don't trade with them; we owe them nothing. I do not want to make war or spill any more Peqkian blood, but we need to teach them a lesson. Make them fear us and stay away from our kind, from our borders. And then watch them to ensure they are not planning anything that might threaten Peqkya or our people again. If they are, then we will have no choice but to annihilate them. Gogo, up the guard along that border and prepare a plan to take thirteen wolf lives in reprisal. Then they have lost the same number as us." *A wolf will not claim the throne in* my *lifetime.*

"We need to tell the people something, my Melokai, otherwise the burial ceremony might trigger panic," Zecky said. "We have not had one for some time so there is sure to be a big crowd for ten warriors."

"Agreed, Zecky. Make an announcement at the next public assembly."

Zecky pushed a thick rope braid out of her face and flung it over her shoulder. "May I suggest *you* tell the people at the next public assembly, my Melokai, your absence is sparking some *nasty* gossip."

"Gossip? Are my people unhappy with me?"

"Oh, just silly drivel, my Melokai," Zecky said, backtracking. "Will you attend the next public assembly and make the announcement?"

"I will, and I will explain that I took some time out and now I'm back." Ramya tapped her fingers on the mountains carved into the table, suddenly eager to get the session over with so she could retreat back into her worry-free world with Gwrlain. "Right, let us move on to the next issue."

"We have an update from the er… east, my Melokai," Chaz announced. His white spot glowed crimson as he looked at Gwrlain. Ramya motioned at her counsellors to continue.

"We upped the border guards and so far, nothing unusual has been spotted on the watch," Gogo reported.

Riv added, "Trade continues as usual, the same Trogrs

bringing the same stuff. However, my traders mention that the atmosphere has changed. It is now tense, the Trogrs are watchful and edgy. Perhaps they know that our warrior numbers have increased or perhaps it is nothing and will pass."

"Keep watching and stay alert to any slight changes, however insignificant they seem." Ramya glimpsed at Gwrlain, his demeanour was neutral. It seemed as if he didn't know they were talking about his homeland. "Move on to the next point."

"My Melokai, Fertilian has sent a messenger. The Fert insists on delivering you the message personally. Most unusual for the southerners to try to communicate with us other than through trade channels and Riv's traders," Zecky said.

"Bevya! Fetch the Fert messenger." Ramya was intrigued but also wary at a message from the southern lowland country, so called for its fertile lands.

The messenger was brought in by two warriors, who held daggers to his throat. He was sweating profusely. He stood upright and although his life tottered on the edge of a precipice, he had an air of arrogance about him, of entitlement and contempt for the company he found himself in. All male traits that the Peqkians, including Ramya, despised.

"Speak," Ramya demanded.

"My gracious, most worthy, Melokai Ramya. I am Duke Ranulf Hawkins, son of Martin, grandson of Michael, great grandson of Peter, duke of Burlay and once squire to the Prince Hugo Salmon, now King Hugo Cleland of Fertilian. The King Hugo and his Queen Jessima send their humblest salutations to..."

"Get on with it!" Ramya snapped.

"Um, yes of course... There has been a war raging in Fertilian these past twenty-four years. King Hugo wishes to open negotiations with the honoured Melokai of Peqkya to find a mutually beneficial agreement that sees the mighty and feared Peqkian army supporting his cause, and to end this pointlessly destructive war once and for all. King Hugo would offer ample recompense…"

"Truly I am insulted," Ramya seethed, disgusted that this pompous male would be sent to deliver such a crude request. The Peqkian army was not for rent. "Send the messenger back where he came from. But first, cut out his tongue, cut off his penis and carve into his chest this message in return – Send The Queen."

The messenger was dragged out of the room before he could reply and before Ramya could change her mind. Zecky smirked at the harsh sentence and Ramya's rage collapsed. For the second time that day Ramya almost shouted "Wait!" to correct an impulsive decision. She no longer had a thirst for blood as she had as a young warrior, and she strived to rule with compassion not brutality, but she could not be seen to be soft. The meeting had already been traumatic and she had no desire to quarrel about lessening the Fert's punishment with her counsellors. *This sentence stands.* Abruptly, Ramya stood and touched Gwrlain's shoulder to indicate it was time to leave. "If there is no more to discuss let us be gone from here. Thank you for your council."

Head Teller Omya pushed her glasses up her severe nose with a carefully shaped fingernail. "There is one last thing, my Melokai. How do we propose to *pay* for this wolf skirmish plus this increase in warrior numbers along the eastern border? It will drain our depleted treasury."

"Pay?" Hanny blurted out, her mouth working quicker than her brain.

"Yes, dear. Pay, dear. With money," Omya mocked, full of derision for the courtesan who had never had to pay for anything in her life.

"Explain yourself, Omya," said Ramya, sitting back down. This issue of lacking finances had never come up before. Peqkya was prosperous and no one wanted for anything. *As far as I know.*

"My Melokai, your exchange system works effectively on the street for smaller items and quantities, however we often need to pay with coin. We have enough monies to keep Peqkya ticking over at our current population, but we are growing in numbers every year. May I suggest that our *new* Mother of Mothers culls a higher number of useless peens at fifteen? I know you relaxed this number six years ago, however I believe we cannot be so lenient anymore."

"The number of peens who pass into peonhood is something we can discuss at a later date with the new Mother of Mothers," Ramya said. She had fought hard to allow more useful peens to survive, believing it was the right time to update the one-thousand-year-old quotas, and wasn't prepared to go back on this ruling so easily. "Go on."

"We have spent our excess funds on infrastructure, and public buildings and services, as you know, and we have sufficient monies to keep these running. But we now need to find *additional* coin to transport warriors to the north-eastern border, and transporting food and necessary items up and over the Melioks and around Zyr Peq pass will be tricky and therefore *expensive*, my Melokai. Also with more warriors deployed outside of the capital to the eastern border, we will need to identify and train more girls to take their place to keep up our numbers here. An increase in our army will mean an increase in food, shelter, weapons, pleasure givers for entertainment and so on. It all adds up."

"Understood, Omya. We up our trade to up our funds. Riv, what are your thoughts?" Ramya directed the question to her Head Trader who gazed out the window stroking the white fur lined hood of her ostentatious cloak. Hearing her name, she jerked to attention.

"My Melokai, I will need time to consider ways to *up* our trade. It is not so easy. For example, we would need to make our farmers produce more, or our artisans and tradespeople manufacture more goods for us to sell more.

As dictated by the majority of our trade agreements, we trade our products for products we want from our neighbouring nations, rather than sell for money. As this council will remember, I have made many petitions to update these agreements for us to fill our coffers, all of which have been denied as our blessed Stone Prophetess advocates against useless material possessions..."

"Avarice is a despicable quality, Riv." Ramya tutted and then repeated one of Sybilya's Sayings. "'Power does not come from material things. Power comes from action and from love.'"

"As you say, my Melokai… Well, we make a lot from selling the Troglo birds' nests to the southerners as this foodstuff is highly valuable and cannot be simply traded for any other product. However, trade with the Trogrs is currently… *problematic* should I say. And you have just sent a messenger back south to Fertilian without his tongue or penis, so I would suggest that relationship might be a little… *strained* from herein too. However, there must be something. Please give me two days to discuss with my merchant network and come back to you with a plan."

Ramya winced at the reminder of her harsh treatment of the messenger. "Granted. How much money do we need to make, Omya?"

Omya peered over her eyeglasses. "Give me two days and I will come back to you with a budget, my Melokai. I don't think Riv will be thrilled, unless her plan involves getting her hands on the nests of all the swiftlets in the sky."

Gwrlain had remained silent the entire meeting but taking care to pronounce each word correctly, he spoke, "Harvest nests here. I will show you how. I help you make money."

8

AMMAD

Crown Prince Ammad chased after the ball, urging his camel on relentlessly and kicking up a cloud of dust. He swung his long bat and thwacked the ball into the goal, the opposing team having left it wide open. The crowd roared in approval and Ammad pumped his bat in the air. That was his eighth goal of the polo game, and soon after, the gong sounded for full time. His team mates rode over on their camels celebrating the victory by circling him, their champion.

He looked up at his father Mastiq, the Ruler of Drome, who stood applauding energetically and then adjusted his headdress which had slipped to one side. Ammad's mother Jakira sat a little way back, she clapped less enthusiastically, she knew what the outcome of this game would be well in advance. The scoreboard said nine to three to his team the Parchad Prowlers. The losers, from nearby town Orean, conceded defeat graciously, no doubt thinking about the gold that Jakira would furnish them with later.

Ammad knew his mother fixed the games, but his father had no idea so Ammad kept silent and basked in the glory. Jakira told him, "the people need a hero," and she did all in her power to orchestrate his popular public persona. It was also his dear mother, one of many women in Mastiq's harem but celebrated as the most beautiful due to her tiny nose, who had ensured that Ammad was picked by Mastiq as Crown Prince rather than his eldest son Hallid. Born to Mastiq's official wife, Hallid was, by custom, the first choice to be named the Ruler's successor, but Hallid was so shamefully drunk and obese that he was hidden from public view. Mastiq had ordered Hallid 'cleaned up' on several occasions ready to stand in front of the people of Drome as Crown Prince, and all wine and food was forbidden and exercise enforced. This always seemed to work at first, until Jakira found a way to sneak in Hallid's vices. Mastiq had given up in despair and after a brief period of depression, announced his second eldest son and fifth child, Ammad, as the Crown Prince of Drome on Ammad's sixteenth birthday, to the delight of the Dromedars and relief of his mother. Hallid was swiftly forgotten.

After the celebrations, Ammad and his team selected several pretty street girls from the crowd and his guards pulled them from the throngs of people over the fence and led them to the stables amongst the exquisite, expensive polo camels. He and his team mates took turns fucking them in the hay or leaned up against a camel. Once they were done, he called in his guards and stable hands to have the girls too as he retired to his private room.

Five slaves poured bucket after bucket of water over him and as he was washing the grimy sweat off his brown skin and the dust out of his shoulder length black hair, his mother walked in. She said something to him but he pointed to his ear and shrugged, indicating that he couldn't hear her through the rushing water. She clicked her fingers and the slaves scurried out of the room.

"Mama!"

"I said, hurry up, son. The High Priest is at the palace demanding your presence."

Ammad huffed and looked around for a cloth to dry

himself whilst his mother stood in the slight breeze from the window and smoothed down her glossy brown hair that fell to her hump. She twisted it into loose curls and positioned the strands so they seductively framed the glimpse of her breasts through a strategic slit in her gown. The vibrant hue of turmeric spice, the silky fabric hung seductively from her curvaceous figure. She had no need to show too much of her honey coloured skin. Men didn't need to look at her body, they fell in love with her smouldering golden brown eyes. Jakira was Drome's most beautiful woman. Ammad felt awkward when his guards stared at her, his mother, but he was also proud and every time he looked in the mirror he saw he had inherited her fine features and stunning eyes. It was rare for his mother to be the one fetching him, and he knew the reason that she was here would be revealed soon enough.

"Yes, Mama, I'm hurrying. Since you are here, could you rub oil on my hump, I can never quite reach it… What does the High Priest want do you think?"

She took his oil and stood behind him massaging it into his back, like she used to do when he was a small boy.

"High Priest Ganni is talking about the coming wrath of God again and pushing for a cleansing of Our Ruler. We need to convince him that a sacrifice is what is needed. A cleansing is a big strain on the body, especially of an *older* body." She patted his hump and swept out of the room.

Ammad rubbed oil over his lean limbs and then called for his slaves to dress him in the fine, soft cloth imported from Peqkya. *She does not want Father to have to go through with a cleansing as it will kill him. But then I would become the Ruler of Drome! Clearly it is not yet time. Mama knows best.*

He left the polo grounds carried by his slaves on a litter, surrounded by guards, and headed towards the palace. *I'm ravenous.* He was tempted to stop off at the palace kitchens and have them make him a feast but knew better than to keep his mother waiting. He distracted his thoughts from his growling belly to take in the passing streets of the capital of Drome.

Parchad was an incredible city. Constructed in the centre of a massive crater, in the middle of a desert, formed a millennium ago by a falling piece of star. Inside the crater was paradise compared to the endless sand outside. There was a plentiful water source, grass and trees, and the wall formed a natural shelter from the severe winds that whipped up the dunes beyond and blew whole towns to smithereens. The Wakrime clan first found the crater and settled near to the water. There had been devastating battles as other clans tried – and failed – to take the crater for themselves, and the nation of Drome had been established with the other clans deferring to the Wakrime's rule, in order to stay on the inside.

Ammad was honoured to be a descendant of this clan, Ammad el Wakrime. The Wakrime royal clan had a back hump smaller and rounder than other clans, and his perfectly formed hump was a sign of his heritage. Royalty had plenty of water, so had no need of a large hump. The poorer clans, like the majority Affarah, had ugly, misshapen lumps on their backs and could go for days without a drink.

More and more people had arrived from the inhospitable desert looking for water and work and the crater became one big sprawling city. When there was no more space on the crater floor, buildings started to spring up on the steep walls, clinging to the sides and looming over those below. The wealthiest either lived up the sides of the crater which afforded a staggering view, or near the palace which was located on the lake and next to the water spring. Now, there were dwellings circling the outside of the crater, where the most impoverished survived. There were three main ways over the high crater wall and down into the city, the safest and quickest route was for the royal family and military, another route was for the Qacirr holy and Tamadeen noble clans and the third route was the busy road used by everyone else. But once you arrived in the haphazard city, the narrow roads and alleys were used by everyone.

There was little open space apart from the palace and its spectacular grounds, the stadium where Ammad played polo, the holiest of holy temple ceremonial square, and the teeming marketplace. In the eastern corner of the city were the glass works, where the Drome sand was melted and then formed, coloured and shaped into glorious glass of all kinds.

A large area near the lake was given over for rearing livestock and growing vegetables and fruit in vast glasshouses and sheds. The crater floor was lower than the desert outside and the earth was adequate. Ammad knew the Dromedar merchants brought in fertile soil from Drome's longtime enemy, the country of Fertilian, via the Peqkian hisspits, who claimed it was from their mountain lands to appease his father. The irony made him smirk. Drome once had access to the sea, at a place they called Vaasar, but two thousand years ago, the Ferts had captured it, slaughtered all the Dromedars and renamed the place Lian. Drome had been trying, and failing, to retrieve Vaasar from the thieving Fert occupiers ever since.

The streets and alleyways of Parchad were chaotic, it was crowded, noisy and smelly but Ammad loved it. His mother kept a grand villa high up on the craterside near to the royal road and he often escaped there when he needed a little respite and fresher air, but he spent most of his time in the palace, in the choicest part of the city.

"Crown Prince, sit back," Qabull shouted as they passed through the heaving snake alley where charmers practised their trade before entertaining in the market or in elite craterside villas. Qabull was Ammad's longest serving guard, the brute had protected him since he was a boy, and although Ammad hated to admit it, was perhaps more of a father than Mastiq.

There was a persistent danger from the Khumarah Assassins, the underground minority clan that had formed its own offshoot religion and made a name for itself by murdering members of the royal and holy families. Mastiq was always ordering crackdowns on the Khumarah and persecuting any who he deemed close to the Assassins, but Ammad had never been hassled. He was sure that there weren't that many left. However, to appease his mother, he kept a heavy security detail around him at all times.

As he neared the palace he saw Riv's donkey train being unloaded with a number of achingly beautiful Peqkian women surrounding it. The glossy black skin and lean bodies of the warriors made him hard every time he thought about them. He would have any mountain hisspit if he could, but after many scorch seasons of trying, he had yet to succeed. They didn't sell sex and had no interest in it.

There had been one incident a few scorch seasons back when two palace guards had attempted to force a warrior who had happened to be on her own. She had cut the bollocks off one before slitting his throat, and then shoved her sword up the anus of the second, pulling it out and leaving him to spill his innards on the ground. Even so, Ammad still lusted after them, but there was one in particular. Jozya, Riv's assistant trader, had pronounced feline features with huge almond shaped eyes. She had a small frame and was always laughing and talking. Every time he saw her he started sweating and couldn't form any words. He hoped Riv had brought her along on this trip. *If she is here, I will woo her this time.*

He was still imagining all the things he would do to Jozya when he walked into the great hall and saw the High Priest reclining on the floor cushions with Mastiq and various advisors, drinking mint tea and nibbling on dates and dried apricots. Jakira was stood at the end of the room with others from Mastiq's court. *I need to get through a meeting with this Qacirr holy fool before I can see if Jozya is here.*

Mastiq's elite guard The Cuttarrs, or cutthroats as they were known behind their backs, stood close by.

Resplendent in elaborate uniform and fingers twitchy on their swords, the cutthroats were made up of the first-born sons of the high status Tamadeen families. Taken on their tenth birthdays and indoctrinated to love and protect their ruler, the boys were punished with death if they disobeyed strict rules. In reality, they were hostages and a way for the Drome ruler to keep the Tamadeen clan in its place. If a family did not have sons, then the most beautiful daughter was taken as an exclusive Cuttarrs concubine. Ammad felt uneasy in the cutthroats' presence, his body reacted as if he'd sinned when he hadn't, and he was about to be discovered. His palms sweated, his stomach churned and an aching, hollow feeling crept into his chest.

Ammad eased himself down onto a cushion and popped an apricot in his mouth, trying to convince his body that he was, in fact, guiltless.

"Ahhh, here is my son, the Crown Prince," Mastiq exclaimed.

The Ruler of Drome still wore his elaborate headdress which looked like a hand stuck on top of his head at the wrist, palm facing forwards with fingers spread. It had been made with a wire frame which was wrapped in luxurious materials including Peqkian brocade, and adorned with bells, jewels, gold, and other trinkets hanging from the fingers. Small bones, thought to have belonged to his father, were tied on with colourful thread and knocked together with a revolting sound. Two long strips of cloth fell down Mastiq's back, pinned either side of his hump, which was on show through a slit in his gown and painted in a silver and gold pattern. Each Drome ruler had a headdress commissioned at the start of his tenure, and the bigger the better. Ammad felt relieved that he would not have to wear Mastiq's monstrosity when he was crowned. He often daydreamed about his headdress and how it would be the most elegant of any Drome ruler.

"He's just been playing polo, High Priest Ganni, an excellent game, of course his team won, and he scored…

was it seven goals, Ammad?" Mastiq leaned across the holy man, his large belly squashing on Ganni's knees, to pat his son's ankle.

"Eight, Father. It was a tough game, but the Parchad Prowlers smashed it as usual." Ammad grinned at Mastiq who nodded fondly back. The ruler cleared his throat, coughing up phlegm into a tissue that a slave held out for him.

"We are not here to talk polo," the High Priest sputtered.

Ganni was a straggly, thin man with a huge nose and a lazy eye. His hair was long, twisted in elaborate plaits, apart from a shaved line from ear to ear over the top of his head, believed to bring him nearer to God. Ammad noticed a nick of clumped blood over his right ear and tutted inwardly. *How can he have any respect for himself, going into public with such an obvious, pitiful scratch.* If Ganni hadn't been born into a holy family, he would be a nobody. Instead he was a pious, powerful man picked by the seven Qacirr families as the holiest of holies, the man supposedly closest to God in all of Drome. When he was old enough, Ammad's mother had taught him discreetly about how their religion truly worked, how it was all about making money, and what he had been taught by the wisemen as a child was a myth. He played the game though, pleased that he was no longer ignorant. His father, however, was obediently devoted, being a simple man.

"The wrath of God is coming and we need to cleanse Drome of its impurities to temper His anger. The people are impure, the royal family is impure. It is time for the Ruler and his Crown Prince to be immersed in blood! To bleed and drain themselves of the dirt and ask God to exonerate their evil deeds," the High Priest exclaimed with booming voice and arms raised.

Mastiq leaned back in his cushions, a hand over his heart, believing that God spoke through this man.

"If God requires blood, we shall sacrifice a hundred

more goats, pigs, sheep every day. That should quench his thirst. Don't you agree, Father?" said Ammad, attempting to coax his father and manipulate his response as Jakira had directed.

Mastiq looked confused. "Why yes, son, that is a good idea…"

"No," bellowed the thin holy man, surprising Ammad with the intensity. "Sacrifice will not appease Him this time. You are the leader of this people and they must see you cleanse, they follow your example!"

This is not going to plan, thought Ammad as he stole a glance at his mother who raised an eyebrow. A gesture so subtle that only Ammad could understand. He could hear her voice in his head telling him, *'Do not allow Mastiq to cleanse, he did it once and it almost killed him. You need to take his place.'*

"I will cleanse, High Priest. It is I who has sinned, partaking in sexual activity before I have wedded. Partaking of mind altering liquid and powder as well as neglecting to say my daily prayers. Our Ruler is a devoted man, God is angry at me and my indiscretions. It is time, I must cleanse," Ammad pleaded, touching the High Priest's hand, bending his chest towards the floor and touching his forehead to the man's stinking feet.

The High Priest's lazy eye twitched and he agreed hurriedly. "You shall be cleansed and renewed, Ammad, son of Our Ruler Mastiq, son of God. I will announce to the people tonight that you will cleanse in the temple square."

The High Priest stood to leave and all on the floor cushions scrambled up, touching their right hands to their hearts and then up to the sky in the religious sign. In response, the High Priest put his hand up to the sky, touched it to his heart and then swept it outwards across his body with palm upward to demonstrate how he was the channel of God's love and he was distributing it to all God's children who stood there. Ganni turned and left the hall.

"Very agreeable, son," Ruler Mastiq mumbled, "very agreeable."

Jakira touched Ammad's shoulder. To his relief, she was smiling in approval. "Come, let us eat dinner with Riv."

***

A decade before, the Peqkian Head Trader Riv first visited Parchad to negotiate trade deals with the Dromedars. Riv had wanted to see the opulent bazaars and Ruler Mastiq had instructed Jakira to show her the sights. Riv and Jakira had become firm friends. Although Riv had capable assistant traders, she still came to Parchad regularly, rarely to negotiate trade deals as these were solid, but to gossip with Jakira and go shopping, their favourite pastime.

The two of them had set up a commerce enterprise in Parchad and with Riv's business acumen and Jakira's vast network of contacts it had turned into an empire. Riv took great pains to hide this from her fellow Peqkians, and especially from her Melokai. Most of the spoils of her hard work were stored at Jakira's craterside villa, "waiting for a rainy day in Drome," Riv would laugh and Ammad would explain that it *never* rained in Drome, until he was old enough to get the joke. And although Jakira never mentioned it, she had become the most powerful woman in the city.

As Mastiq's court lolled on floor cushions around a low table savouring the feast in front of them, Ammad lost track of the rapid conversation between the two women, changing topics quicker than he chewed a mouthful of food. Riv had learnt Dromedari long ago and was fluent but every now and then Jakira would say a few words in the Peqkian language of Shella. Mastiq sat at the other end of the table, with his official wife and various nobles, merchants and powerful people. His twenty favourites from his vast harem sat at the other end with the eldest of his twenty-three children. Fat Hallid was absent as usual.

Every time Riv's emphatic laugh exploded, Mastiq gazed over wishing he was having that much fun.

During the eighth course, as the slaves put the sweet dishes on the table and the sensuous belly dancers commenced the evening entertainment, the conversation between Riv and his mother turned from jovial to serious and Ammad noticed that they were whispering.

His mother fell quiet, and he saw his chance to speak with the Peqkian, who had known him since he was a child and who he considered family. "Aunty Riv, tell me is Jozya with you this time?"

"Yes, Crown Prince, the lovely Jozya is indeed in Drome," Riv chuckled. She knew he had a soft spot for her assistant and had warned him off many times. "If you so much as touch her, or any of my women, I will bring all kinds of destruction on your head, boy."

"He won't go near them, Riv, he has plenty of well-paid whores to satisfy his urges." Jakira glared at her son.

"Ladies, really! I only want to say hello and ask her how trade is going. Besides, all my whoring has led to a cleansing, so I need to ease off on that for a while I think," he joked. In truth, he was scared witless about the cleansing but hadn't yet talked to his mother about it. Jakira would know what to do.

Jakira leaned in to him. "Come to the villa tomorrow, my son, we have something important to discuss."

***

When Ammad arrived the next morning, Jakira and Riv were sat on floor cushions on the terrace, sweating in the heat but enjoying the slight breeze that came with being higher up the crater wall. Riv was dressed in her lavish 'Drome clothes' as she called them, kept in a closet in the room that his mother saved for the Peqkian's exclusive use. His lanky brother Selmi, now with fourteen scorch seasons behind him and four less than Ammad, was in the paddock trotting in circles, exercising his racing camel.

The women were talking business, so Ammad slumped

down on the carpet and helped himself to mashed aubergine and flatbread. A house slave monotonously waved a large palm frond trying to create more breeze. Another slave handed him a cup of lime juice, honey and water. Earlier that morning he had hung about the women's guest quarters at the palace waiting for Jozya to make an appearance. He'd worn his finest clothes and had his slaves oil his body, shape his beard and trim his eyebrows.

She was nowhere to be found, and now his skin was crawling, clammy as oil mixed with perspiration. Beads of sweat formed up and gathered in the crease of his belly. Suddenly he couldn't bare it and stripped off his shirt. He flexed his arms, admiring the defined muscles.

"Son. We have much to discuss. I know you are worried about the cleansing, but we will not talk about that today so put it out of your mind, we have another matter to attend to," Jakira told him.

It irritated him that she still spoke to him like a child, even now that he was Crown Prince. He couldn't stop thinking about the cleansing, no matter what she demanded. He shrugged his shoulders and slouched on the cushions.

"Riv has told me what is happening in Peqkya. Melokai Ramya is failing her people and there is a current of discontent that gets stronger each day. The nation is at threat from the north and possibly from the east. It is penniless. The Melokai is consorting with a freak from the caves in the east and is allowing her realm to go to rot. Riv sees an opportunity."

"What kind of opportunity?" Ammad asked.

"To make my beloved Peqkya rich and powerful," Riv replied, passion burning in her eyes.

Jakira touched her friend's hand before continuing, "Remove the Melokai, usher in a new rule for Peqkya. One that makes the nation rich. One that allows people of merit to keep the coin they make, rather than distribute wealth amongst the ungrateful people."

"What's in it for me… I mean… for us?" Ammad sat up straight, his hump prickled in anticipation.

Jakira smiled. "A new Melokai will be chosen once Ramya is no more, and that Melokai will have a husband. He will rule and be called the Melokaz of Peqkya, like in Xayy times."

"You want me to rule Peqkya? Yes! I'm in. I'll have a harem of the finest women Peqkya has to offer."

"No, flesh of my flesh, you will be Ruler of Drome." Jakira nodded towards the paddock. "Selmi will be Melokaz of Peqkya. You will each rule a nation and be close allies. Together you will take back ancient Vaasar from the vile, thieving occupier Ferts, to indescribable glory. The two most powerful nations our history has ever known. Riv will have more money than she knows what to do with, no longer having to hide her wealth. And I will be the mother of two rulers."

9

FERRAZ

Ferraz sat in a dark corner of the pleasure giver communal area, brooding. The Melokai hadn't called him in nearly two months and it was clear to him, and to the other smug PGs, that he had been demoted. *I am no longer Ramya's favourite. A nobody. A PG with no status. What did I do wrong? I thought she was falling in love with me, that she would declare me her soulmatch.*

There were rumours she had found another peon, but it was not another court PG, which was baffling. There were no other suitable peons, unless she had found one from outside the capital, who was in another profession but even so, he would be taken into the PG set and given a cell with the rest of them. Ferraz could no longer get the latest gossip from the washer-peon, his tongue had been lopped off. The washer-peons' punishment for speaking out about their work conditions.

Ferraz was open for business, the best looking and most skilled PG in Riaow, but no one wanted him. He was tainted, the Melokai's reject. *I expect every woman thinks that Ramya is too kind to state that I failed her, and instead of sending me to my death, she is no longer calling me.* He would end up as one of the wandering old PGs, cast out of the PG set when women stopped calling for them and left to grow scrawny and sad.

I could request an early elimination, no one would miss me, no one would care. He only needed to ask a Speaker to terminate his life, as others did when they felt their usefulness had passed or if they were suffering from an incurable illness. No Peqkian wanted to be a burden on others and there was no reason to suffer when you didn't need to, and he was suffering.

Ferraz watched the PGs, waiting for the first calls to come in for the evening. A group in the middle were laughing and pointing his way.

"Did you forget where to put your cock, Ferraz?" Lomaz shouted. Known as Licky Licky Lo due to his skills at oral sex, and one of the courtesan Hanny's favoured PGs. His friends cheered and whooped, urging him on.

"Do you even know what to do with your pathetic slug, Licky Licky Lo? When was the last time you got it out?" Ferraz shouted back, he was in no mood to be taunted.

"Well at least I get some action! Your cock must be shrivelled up collecting dust it hasn't been used in so long."

Ferraz stood and in two strides fronted up to Lomaz, who got to his feet to meet him. Fighting was forbidden, anyone found breaking the rule was eliminated. *I'll beat him senseless and then they can reward me with death. I want to die.*

"Your tongue gets so much action it is swollen in your mouth and you no longer have control over it. It says things that get you into trouble." Ferraz shoved his chest against Lomaz, sending him stumbling back a couple of steps.

Lomaz looked cautiously over at the set administrator who was preoccupied with some paperwork.

"Come on, fat tongue!" Ferraz goaded.

Lomaz lurched but two of his buddies held him back.

Ferraz brought his fists up but a PG called Slim Stavaz blocked his way and another, Mikaz, grabbed Ferraz's arm.

"Lads, lads. You don't want to do this. Let's all get

back to playing nicely shall we," Mikaz said.

"You're not worth it." Lomaz stomped to the other side of the room and glared at Ferraz.

"Zhaq you," Ferraz mouthed.

Mikaz led Ferraz away. "Come on now, mate. Life ain't that bad."

Mikaz was the eldest of the PGs in the capital. He was still going strong, seeming to get more handsome as he aged, and had taught many of the younger guys, including Ferraz.

"I fell in love with a woman once. It came crashing down. The misery will pass," Mikaz told him gently.

Slim Stavaz added, "There are other things in life to be happy about."

Ferraz nodded. He had no words and hunched next to them. He appreciated their kindness. Ferraz was a loner, before he had no need for allies. *But now she has made me nothing.*

An image of his laughing son came to his mind. *I do not want to die, I want to see my son grow. Everything I do now, I must do for him. I have nothing else.*

The sky darkened and the calls started. Slim Stavaz was requested by a courtesan along with another PG, Stav's speciality was anal pleasure due to his slim penis. Mikaz went to service an older warrior, who often wanted a cuddle and a chat.

Licky Licky Lo was called and sneered at Ferraz when he passed. "Another night of wanking for you then, dusty cock."

Once again, Ferraz was on his own. He paced in circles and then crumpled to the floor leaning against the wall. He rested his head on his knees and hugged his legs to him.

"Ferraz, a messenger is here for you. Let's go," the set administrator said and she checked him out in her register.

With his heart in his mouth, Ferraz left to meet the messenger. *I'm coming to you my Melokai!*

***

Ferraz waited in a bed chamber he had never been in before. When the messenger was not Bevya, he thought that perhaps the Melokai had a new clevercat. But when they had turned in the opposite direction to the Melokai's quarters, his heart started to ache. There was no hope the Melokai would call him again now – he was free for anyone.

In stark contrast to the Melokai's apartment, this one was decorated lavishly with fine fabrics, sumptuous carpet, wood carvings and beautiful paintings. It was cluttered with colourful glass vases, ornaments and whittled chests piled high with coins. A crystal bowl full of exotic fruit he had never seen before, glistened on the bench in front of the bed and a dressing table was overrun with baubles and sparkling jewellery. But his curiosity was drawn by a massive gold bar the size of his foot, displayed on a small plinth by the side of the bed. He moved towards it and stared, reaching out a tentative hand.

"Don't touch that."

A woman entered dressed in expensive cloth. She wore jewels around her wrist and on her fingers, unusual for a Peqkian. A large silvery pink orb hung on a chain around her neck, shimmering in the candlelight. She was flabby around the waist and a double chin thickened her neck. Ferraz guessed she was nearing forty years of age. He yanked his hand away, dashed over to her and knelt low at her feet.

"What is your pleasure? Let me pleasure you," he said in the customary way.

"Sit down, Ferraz."

He did as he was told and found a chair at a table by doors that opened onto a courtyard and gardens, edging it out so as not to catch the drapes trailing to the floor. She took the chair opposite him and started to gorge on the bread, yak's cheese and grapes laid out there, as if she was scared the food was about to run away.

"Do you know who I am?" she asked and pushed a cup over to him.

"I do not, but I look forward to making your acquaintance and pleasuring you in any way you desire."

"I'm Rivya, the Head Trader of Peqkya. I don't want you to touch me, I want to talk. Drink some wine and fill my cup. I'm exhausted, I got back from Drome a few hours ago."

Ferraz rushed to fill her cup and then half-filled his own, not wanting to insult her by appearing greedy. She took a sip and gestured to him to do the same. He drank deeply, too much. He hadn't tasted alcohol for many years, PGs were given it by their callers but most wanted PGs on top performance and that meant sober.

"You *were* the Melokai's favourite. Tell me, PG, what happened?" Rivya looked squarely at him, expecting an answer.

I have to obey her, I have to answer but why does she want to discuss this? One wrong word and she would order his penis chopped off.

"Yes, I had the pleasure of pleasing Melokai Ramya. Every woman has unique and varied desires."

"You love her."

"As does every Peqkian." Ferraz put the wine glass down, it was starting to wobble in his hand.

"I want you to be honest with me. How does it make you feel to know that Melokai Ramya has a cave creature in her bed, pleasuring her?"

"A… a cave creature? Er… well every woman has unique and varied desires. If that is my Melokai's desire, then she should fulfil it." *I need to stick with the customary responses, this must be a trick.*

"I think it is an abomination, Ferraz. I think this freak creature is warping her mind."

"I… don't know… I have no opinion…" Ferraz stuttered, trying very hard to keep his face neutral and his tone calm. *Rivya has slandered the Melokai! The penalty is death if anyone finds out. Why is she talking like this to me?*

"There are many who think the same. Melokai Ramya is bringing shame on herself, and shame on her realm. She is neglecting her duties as the ruler of Peqkya and our great nation is faltering."

Ferraz panicked. He couldn't agree with Rivya as he would be slandering the Melokai, he couldn't disagree with her as it was his job to obey women. So he stayed silent and still, staring at a chip in the table in front of him and holding his breath. Any small movement could indicate his assent.

"Drink some more wine." Rivya pushed the jug towards him and he obeyed. The liquid warmed his insides. "Come, let me show you my pets."

She walked out the doors and Ferraz followed. They rounded a corner and there was a line of cages with various sized animals. All looked miserable and a distinct fug of unhappiness clogged up the area: urine, vomit and rotting food that piled up in the cages. A serving peon swept up the mess. Rivya waved him away.

"I have monkeys, snakes, birds and this here is a dog from Fertilian. But my favourite is this one." She pointed at the biggest cage and moved close to the bars, picking up a bucket of water.

Ferraz studied the odd creature. It was a straw colour with two huge humps along its back, a curved neck with big droopy lips. Its eyes were soulless. He felt sorry for it and looked back down at his feet.

"Here camel, camel, camel," Rivya beckoned, sloshing the bucket of water and holding it to the bars. The thing lumbered over and moved to take a drink, it's lips parting a finger's width away from the wet surface. Rivya pulled the bucket back, chuckling. The animal looked up at them, blinking.

"This is a camel from the Drome desert," Rivya told him. Ferraz had been taught geography at the pen and he knew where Drome was, south west of Peqkya.

"It can go thirty days without water apparently, I am testing out that theory. Currently we are on day twenty-four. Isn't he majestic! The only one in Peqkya. I offered him to the Melokai but she declined, an *unnecessary possession.*" Rivya snorted and turned back to the camel, reaching in a hand to stroke its furry neck. The camel suffered her touch, drool sploshing on the floor as it looked longingly at the water.

"He hates me right now, I can tell. As I can tell that *you* are unhappy with the Melokai. She toyed with you for many years, and then suddenly she no longer wanted you. You weren't enough, you were nothing to her." Rivya waited for Ferraz to reply. He stared harder at his foot and hunched further in to himself, trying to escape her intent gaze. After a few moments, she spoke again.

"She has no more need of you, which is why I could call you tonight. And how do you feel? I think you feel angry. Do you feel angry?"

The wine made him feel bold and he glanced up at her for a fleeting moment.

"You are not the only one angry with her. She is failing her people. Ramya has ruled for twelve years and it is high time we elect another Melokai. Dear Sybilya is simply too old now to declare another Choosing Ceremony and it's up to Ramya do it, but she is clinging on to power." Rivya slammed her fist into her palm. "She must go."

Ferraz eased his taut shoulders, which felt as if they were up by his ears, and unclenched his jaw. He was not alone, this eccentric woman shared his loathing.

"Will you help me, Ferraz? Will you help me to cut her down?"

He looked around the courtyard, trying to see – or sense – if there were people listening as well as the pitiful animals. *Is this really happening?*

"We are alone, for now. However, this will be a dangerous undertaking. I need to know if you are in. And if you are, then you must be discreet. If you are not, then I will tell the PG set administrator than you were unsatisfactory and you know what will happen then."

His predicament was plain. Refuse and tomorrow be flayed and left to decompose in the marketplace with a pole up his backside. Accept and likely die anyway when the Melokai discovered the plot. He thought of his son and braved, "Do you grant me permission to ask a question, Head Trader Rivya?"

"You have my permission."

Ferraz settled his gaze on Rivya's chin. He was trusting this woman with his biggest secret, it had to pay off. Slowly, quietly he confided, "I have a child with Melokai Ramya. He is three years old and is in the pen cared for by Mother Samya."

"Go on," she said.

"I know which peen he is as I have watched him since birth. If I am to help you, I beg of you to help him."

Rivya thought for a moment and then gestured for him to continue.

"I wish for him to be safe and to be loved, to not have to go through the fear of being ended. He has the Melokai's blood in his veins, I wish for him to be in a position of power one day..." Ferraz trailed off. He had said too much.

"The Melokai's blood is rotten, I would not try to flaunt parentage as protection for your peen."

Ferraz noted the vicious edge to her tone. *I'm a fool.*

"However," she continued, softer. "I will do what I can for your son, if *you* do what *you* can for me."

Ferraz acknowledged her deal with a brief nod, it was all he could hope for. "What would you have me do, Head Trader Rivya?"

"There is much to do, and it's too dangerous to write anything down so it is all up here." Rivya tapped her temple. "So, first things first. We need loyal supporters here in Riaow who will remain underground and silent until the time comes, when we will rise up together against rotten Ramya. We need a courtesan, we have a job in Parchad for an exceptional, determined, *dependable* woman."

"Parchad in Drome? The cammers?"

"Yes, Parchad in Drome. Don't look so horrified, the Dromedars are reliable trading partners and will support us. However, there are a few *un-supporters*, shall we say, that we need to take care of and there is a great deal of work to do there before we can have the unyielding support of the people and full force of the Drome army behind us."

Ferraz knew better than to question respected women in high power positions. *The Drome army! This is bigger than I imagined. Rivya must know what she is doing, I need to trust her.*

"Irrya," he blurted.

"What?"

"The courtesan you need. I think Irrya might help."

"Irrya. The one with long hair braided with orange cloth. She is stunning to look at and her poetry recitals are delightful, but I have never spoken with her at length. Why do you think she is our woman?"

"I have not seen Irrya for many years, but there was a time before I was *busy* with the Melokai that she always called for me to entertain her. I believe she was in love with me."

"In love with you? That is a big claim, PG."

He had kept this secret buried deep for many years. He exhaled, dragging it up from the depths. "After the Melokai took me as her favoured pleasure giver, Irrya wrote me many secret letters and poems declaring her devotion to me, how she was wretched that she could not see me anymore and her loathing for Ramya, who she considered her love rival. I destroyed the letters and did not reply. Eventually she stopped. This was a long time ago."

The memories of Irrya came flooding back to Ferraz. He had rebuffed her love for years, servicing her as required of a PG, and even enjoying her company, but he had remained emotionally aloof. *I denied my affection for Irrya in my ambition to reach Melokai Ramya. Pointless. Ramya never cared for me, Irrya did.* He desperately wanted to see Irrya again. *Would she want to see me? Does she still love me?* "I need to see her, to talk with her."

"And how do you propose you see her?"

"Send a message to her now saying that I am available to give pleasure again, that you had me and I was exceptional. I do not know for certain, but I think she will call for me – and soon. She blames Ramya for taking me away from her, it was not my decision to leave her."

Riv looked at him, surprised. "That's a *good* idea, Ferraz. I will send the same message to a few others in my close network so it does not seem odd for her to solely hear from me. I will do it tonight. You might be busy, and not just talking," Rivya sniggered to herself. "Go now and wait for Irrya's call, I hope it comes. I will summon you tomorrow for an update."

"Ferraz! Your third call tonight, a late one," the set administrator shouted.

Rivya's message had been well received and he had just come back from pleasuring a high-ranking warrior. He used all the techniques he had honed with Ramya and the warrior lapped them up like a thirsty kitten. He led her to orgasm quickly, so she would have no further use for him and send him back to the pen. He did not want to miss Irrya's invitation, he felt certain she would call.

The messenger was not known to him, but he remembered the way to Irrya's apartment and they started following that path. Ferraz was elated.

The clevercat showed him into Irrya's bed chamber and then closed the door. He breathed in the courtesan's lavender scent. Irrya was stood at the window, bathed in moonlight. She turned and tears fell down her smooth cheeks. Ferraz rushed to her and fell at her feet, his forehead touching the ground in front of her.

"Issee! Is it really you? After all these years…"

"It is I," he mumbled into her dainty toes and dared to bring his fingertips to lightly caress her ankles.

"Look at me, Ferraz, let me see your endless blue eyes and Peqkya's finest peon face."

He obeyed, slowly lifting his head and bringing his gaze up her body. He hesitated, staring at her navel. He could not look in her eyes, for fear of what he might see there. *Will she look upon me with love like before? Is that time gone forever?*

He whispered into her belly, "Forgive me, Irrya."

With the softest of touches, she lifted his chin. But he still could not meet her eyes. "Speak your mind, I give you permission. I always gave you permission to be yourself and I always will."

"I was a fool, Irrya, I denied you, I denied your love. I was so blinded by my ambition, to become the Melokai's PG, that I rejected my feelings for you. And you, you risked so much to love me, I see that now."

"It is true, it was not appropriate for me to fall so deeply in love with a PG, with a peon. I was derided by my fellow courtesans. Then the wider court noticed that my poetry bloomed with romantic themes and that started the gossip. I suffered it awhile but I couldn't bare it. To put an end to the whispers I admitted it publicly, that I was in love with you."

"You are so brave."

"No, not brave. There is much I regret. I should have asked permission of the Melokai and declared you my soulmatch when I had the chance, but I thought I had done enough. Everyone knew I favoured you, Ramya knew. Yes, you were called to pleasure other women occasionally, but most in the court respected my feelings and didn't call you out of consideration for me." Irrya's silky voice hoarsened with disgust. "But *she* took you from me anyway. She didn't spare a second thought for me, Ramya only cares about feeding her voracious sexual appetite. She takes what she wants to satisfy whatever animal lurks between her legs, just like with the cave creature, she wanted him so she took him with no thought about the consequences."

Silent tears rolled down Ferraz's face. *Irrya wanted to declare me her soulmatch!*

She snarled, "Ramya is as repugnant as a Xayy *man*, I hate her!"

A sharp intake of breath betrayed Ferraz's shock at Irrya's offensive smear of the Melokai. *I should not be surprised. The Head Trader insulted Ramya earlier today too, it seems many people hate the Melokai.*

Irrya's voice softened as she continued, "I was inconsolable, I retreated into my poetry, producing more than ever. And she… she championed my work, as if nothing had happened, as if we were friends. She insisted the scholars make copies of my collections and distributed the books around her court and encouraged my public readings. She clapped and cheered when I first recited my now famous poem about my hatred of snakes, completely oblivious to the fact that it was about her. Stupid woman."

Irrya has suffered so much for me. He flicked his gaze up to meet hers and a heavy weight lifted from his shoulders as he saw love. She sank to the floor so they were kneeling and facing each other. She took his square jaw in her hands.

Ferraz looked into her soul and then into his own. All his repressed emotions burst forth from the cage he had locked them in. "I love you. Could you find it in your heart to love me again?"

"I never stopped. Being apart for so long has made me love you more. I felt upset at first that you did not reply to my letters, but I knew it was dangerous and I was expecting too much of you. I realised that I would rather you stay alive, than be caught and killed for writing a silly note to me. I have waited patiently, hoping that you would come back to me. And here you are."

"Irrya, my stunning Irrya. I have missed you so much." He stroked her neck, taking her in. "How is it possible that you have grown in beauty, that you are even more wonderful now than all those years ago."

She traced the sharp lines of his beard with a fingertip. "And you, my love, you are like a vision. I have dreamt of this moment every night since you were taken from me. I think I am still dreaming."

Fiery lust shot through him and he grabbed Irrya's waist, lifting her up and carrying her to the bed. "Let me show you this is not a dream."

She enjoyed his caresses, but as he moved her legs apart she held his head up to hers and whispered, "No, Ferraz. Not yet. I have not had another peon since you left me, let us wait, let us find each other again first."

Ferraz's breath caught in his throat. *I am more to her than just sex.* He lay by her side. "As you wish, whenever you are ready. I am happy just to be near to you. Let us never be apart again, call for me every night."

"Always, my love, for this is the only place I ever want to be," Irrya sighed into his chest.

The PG leaned his head on hers. *I have two things to live for, my son and Irrya.*

10

FERRAZ

Ferraz watched the sleeping courtesan. He twirled an orange braid around his fingers and slowly her eyes opened. She smiled at him. Soon he would need to return to the PG set.

"I need to ask you something," he dared. He felt bold after his meeting with Rivya, like he was important somehow, part of something momentous.

"Anything."

He took a deep breath. "There are a few who want to remove Ramya from rule, saying she is neglecting her duties as Melokai, that her mind has been warped by a creature from the east."

"I have heard this also. I have seen the creature, an aberration of nature. She brings him to court. It is repulsive. I cannot comprehend how she could choose that over you."

Ferraz's body tensed involuntarily at the mention of Ramya's new love. He was ecstatic to be reunited with Irrya, but the Melokai's rejection was still raw.

She hugged him tight. "Her loss is my gain. I will never discard you like she did."

He brought a braid up to his lips. "She is welcome to the freak. I have all I need in my arms, my Irrya with the orange hair."

She sat up abruptly and placed a hand on his chest. "Many people detest her. Many people want her gone. There is a lot of chatter at court, none of it good. The woman is oblivious. What is it you want to ask me?"

"A group is no longer talking, it has decided to take action. It has allied with Drome." Ferraz waited, expecting this news to shock Irrya, but she nodded for him to go on. "I support this group. I was hoping… I was hoping you would support it too."

She paused, studying him. "Yes. I am with you."

"There is an issue with the cammers in Drome. A courtesan is needed in Parchad. I do not know what will be required."

"Parchad?" Her eyes widened with apprehension but then she ran a hand over his defined stomach and pressed a fingertip into his belly button. "I will do it for you. To make you happy. I will do anything for you, my soulmatch."

***

Two nights later Rivya, Ferraz and Irrya met in the trader's lavish bed chamber. To outside eyes it looked like a rampant sex session.

"Welcome on board, Irrya," said Rivya and patted the courtesan's knee. "I'm delighted that you have chosen to join our cause, to rid Peqkya of rotten Ramya. I have a task for you. Are you willing?"

"I am, Rivya. Please, tell me," Irrya replied. Ferraz beamed at her, admiring her courage.

"Oh, do call me Riv, dear. We have friends in Drome, and we need to assist them to trigger widespread public support for our cause. You will travel to Parchad with my assistant trader Toya. You can trust her. I vetted my two personal assistants to see who might be of the same *mindset* as us and Toya passed. The other is Jozya, brilliant at her job but sympathetic to the Melokai. I will find something *outside* of the city to keep Jozya occupied so she does not ask too many questions. Toya is well known in Parchad and she will guide you."

Irrya wrung her hands. "I cannot simply travel to Parchad, it will raise too many questions."

"I have already taken care of that. I heard from Ferraz that you were on board yesterday so I went ahead and told the Melokai that you will be travelling as the night time companion of Toya, in your capacity as a courtesan. I hinted that the two of you were in love, and have been for a while, and couldn't bear to be apart. Ramya made some silly comment about finally knowing who 'The One' is from your love poems. I flattered her, saying how clever she was for unravelling that mystery!" Rivya's chins wobbled as she cackled.

The courtesan glanced at Ferraz and his cheeks burned. *I am The One.*

Irrya waited for Rivya to compose herself and then asked, "What is my task?"

"When you arrive in Parchad, you will be met by my close contact who will instruct you on your task. Her name is Jakira. She is a courtesan of sorts, like you." Rivya's eyes narrowed and her voice hardened. "You must obey Jakira."

Irrya nodded and Ferraz noticed her hands shaking in her lap, although she clutched them tight. He whispered to her, "You will do well, consider this as an adventure that you can use in your next poetry collection."

She nodded at him and then turned back to Rivya. "I understand. When do I leave?"

"Tomorrow."

Both Ferraz and Irrya exclaimed "Tomorrow!" Ferraz grabbed the courtesan's hand and she stared at him. *We have been reunited for mere days, and now she is going. I must be strong, for her.* He remembered they were in the presence of Rivya, and took his hand away.

"No point in delaying things. The sooner this happens the sooner we can pull Ramya off her perch," Rivya said.

Irrya rallied herself, "I will be ready to leave in the morning."

"Excellent. You and the trading party will be guarded by the warrior Ashya and several of her warriors. Do you know who Ashya is?"

Ferraz shook his head but Irrya replied, "I believe I have heard her name, but I know little about her. Can we trust her?"

"Oh yes, dear. Ashya despises Ramya! Probably more so than any of us. She's old but is still a formidable warrior, and she has a legion of loyal warriors under her command. When Ramya became Melokai there were two names put forward by the warrior profession for the Head Warrior and counsellor position. Two exceptional warriors had received the same number of votes, Gosya and Ashya. Ramya chose Gosya, saying Ashya was 'past her prime'. She actually used those words!" The Head Trader cackled again. "Do you have any further questions, Irrya?"

"No, Riv. I will do as the cammer Jakira bids."

"I will see you on your return then. You'd best go and pack." Rivya stood and ushered Irrya from her chair and towards the door. Ferraz stood but Rivya placed a firm hand on his shoulder and pushed him back down. "Stay. You can go to Irrya once we are done, to bid her farewell before her trip."

Ferraz watched as the courtesan gracefully wrapped her fur cloak around her shoulders and walked to the door, turning her face to him briefly as a goodbye, before she left. He stared for a long time after her, in awe of her resolve. Rivya paced the room and came to stand behind him.

"You have done well. Irrya is perfect. I now need you to further support our cause, and to ensure Irrya's efforts are not in vain."

"Anything, Rivya. Anything." Ferraz wanted Irrya to be as proud of him as he was of her.

"We need to enlist more people to join our cause. I am

trusting you to recruit PGs and peons from other professions. I will manage the women."

***

In a secluded corner of the PG communal area, Ferraz waited for Mikaz and Slim Stavaz to return from their calls. Following the altercation with Licky Licky Lo, Ferraz had gravitated towards the pair. He had received a few calls since Rivya's announcement and serviced the women adequately. Nowhere near the volume of his heyday before Ramya had sunk her claws in, but he had no desire to be at the top of the PG profession anymore, he just wanted to get in, pleasure the women quickly so they could not complain, and then get out. All he could think of was Irrya. The courtesan had set off on her journey a few days ago, and to stop his pining, he turned his attention to his own task of recruiting peons, but so far hadn't made any progress.

Mikaz came back into the pen after his fourth call that night, with a rag in his hand. He'd washed ready for the next call and his wet hair fell in tight ringlets to his shoulders. He plonked himself next to Ferraz, bent forward and vigorously dried his hair with the rag, sitting back up with a huge black cloud of fluffy curls framing his face. Grey hair peppered his temples and was creeping into his beard. Mikaz poured a few drops of oil into his hands and started to rub it over his face. The crinkles around his eyes looked deeper tonight, tired. Then, still seated, Mikaz slowly smoothed some into his torso and legs, struggling to lift his arms. Ferraz gestured for Mikaz to sit on the floor in front of him. The old PG slumped down and Ferraz massaged his back.

Mikaz sighed deeply. "I'm getting too old for this. I'm so tired of pleasuring woman after woman, of living in fear of the day that I'm not good enough."

Ferraz kneaded his knuckles into Mikaz's tense shoulders and said, "But what would you do if you weren't doing this?"

"I like you, Ferraz, and I'm going to be honest with you. Stav and I are more than friends. We have been liaising secretly in our cells for years. We are in love. I'd be with him, in the open."

Relationships between PGs were banned, a PG's attention needed to be on pleasuring women and relationships were deemed a distraction. Ferraz squeezed Mikaz's neck. "You have my blessing." He was happy for the pair, but was worried for them. He patted Mikaz's arm. "You're done."

"Thank you." Mikaz took a moment to gather his strength and then hauled himself back onto the sofa next to Ferraz. He whispered, "I want to live in peace with Stav. I want to choose another profession and I want to grow old without the fear of a horrible death if I fail a woman."

"There could be a way for that to happen," Ferraz replied quietly.

Mikaz leaned closer. "What *way*?"

"You were honest with me, so I will be honest with you." Ferraz looked around the room, but no one was near them. This was the one place pleasure givers could socialise. It was forbidden to gather in the cells. "There is a group who is planning to remove Melokai Ramya from rule."

Mikaz's eyes widened but he didn't move or utter a sound, not wanting to draw any attention to them. He blinked quickly and Ferraz took this as a sign to continue.

"A rebellion. Things will change. If we are part of it, then we can ensure that *our* situation changes, improves. Have you heard the rumours from the city?"

Mikaz nodded. "Peons are unhappy, frustrated. But it is just talk."

"Now is the chance to do more than talk, my friend, now is the time for action."

Mikaz winked, a grin lighting up his crinkled eyes. Ferraz felt bolstered by the old PG's excitement. *I have found my first supporter!* "Will you help me to find more willing peons, *outside* the PG set?"

"Issee! An adventure. I love an adventure," Mikaz exclaimed, drawing glances across the room and making Ferraz laugh before shushing his friend.

***

His foot tapped as he waited in his dark cell for Mikaz.

They had agreed to leave the PG set that night, deciding the best time was between four in the morning and midday, after their calls for the evening had ended and before they had to check in again the next day. It would coincide with the morning market, where many worker peons congregated. Mikaz was confident he could find a way to sneak past the set night manager and into Ferraz's cell, and Ferraz had entrusted the old PG with a closely held secret – that in his cell there was a way out into the city.

Ferraz had found the secret exit by chance. When he had first been given his cell, nearly twenty years ago, he had been keen to start pleasuring women, but instead had fallen ill with a fever in the hot, summer months and found respite by laying naked face down on the cool stone floor. He heard what sounded like rushing water. The fluffy ginger cat who always came to his cell in those days was sprawled next to him and Ferraz noticed his fur moving in a breeze. He didn't think anything of it, until he had rolled over to lift himself up for a sip of cold ginger and a stone had dipped down in one corner with a thunk, pulling up in the opposite corner. Curious, he had dug his fingers under the stone and found it came up. He lifted it and the whoosh of the torrent beneath roared in his ears.

It was a year or so before Ferraz lifted the stone again. In the dead of night, he had used a candle to see what was there. A long dark hole down to black water. To gauge the distance, he lowered the candle using the rope from his robe until it hit the water. The hole was about as long as he was tall and must've been excavated by the cell's previous occupier, or perhaps the one before that. Who knew how old the hole was, but it was there and Ferraz had found it.

Ferraz had fashioned a longer rope from his robes, claiming to the PG set administrator that he was always leaving his ropes behind, saying that women enjoyed pulling it off and flinging it away, unable to be found again. He secured this extended rope to his bed and dropped it down the hole. Before he had first been called by Ramya, in a moment of recklessness, he had plunged down the hole, keeping his hands on the rope. That first time he thought he would suffocate. He had drifted underwater through a tunnel and popped up outside the Melokai's enclosure walls, floating along a slow stream. He scrambled onto the bank, vomited, looked around to gauge where he was and then used the rope to heave himself back against the current and pull himself up into his cell.

He hadn't used the exit again until Ramya had born him a son. He longed to see the baby and when he thought his head might finally burst, he had jumped, wearing the rags they used to dry themselves, that were given to old PGs when they are cast out from the set. Ferraz roamed the city, going from pen to pen with the desperate hope he would come across his baby. On the third trip, he had found his son. The blue-eyed peen was in the courtyard outside a pen with other peens of a similar age, rolling around in a shady, fenced enclosure and minded by a mother. Ferraz hid and watched for as long as he could. He had tried to visit the pen every week since, watching his healthy, handsome, laughing little peen grow up. They were not always outside, and for months he could go without glimpsing his son. But then a lucky day would come and the peen would be outside for Ferraz to watch from the shadows.

Mikaz tapped softly at the door and snuck in. "Ready," he whispered.

Ferraz eased up the slab of stone, pushing it to one side and dropped the rope. He lowered himself down, took a deep breath and dropped into the rushing water in the tunnel below, holding the air in his chest until he thought his lungs might burst. Then, as usual, he surfaced in the stream, and pulled himself onto the bank under a mass of trees. This was where the Melokai rode her horses, but he never saw anyone.

Mikaz burst up, gagging and with arms flapping. Ferraz heaved him onto the bank and watched as the old PG bent double and retched.

"I was the same, the first time. It will pass, my friend." He rubbed Mikaz's back as he vomited.

Mikaz wiped his mouth, inhaled through his nose and spoke with a twinkle in his eye. "Right let's go, I want to make mischief."

They passed through the bazaars, not yet awake, and into the marketplace which was buzzing with activity. Merchants set up stalls, farm hands arrived with buffalo drawn carts full of vegetables and grains. Goats bleated, the bells around their necks ringing, as milkers drove them into small cages, ready to be sold for milk, meat, skin or all three. There were worker peons everywhere, the women ordering them around from seats on their carts or from the top of a donkey.

The PGs hid behind hoods. They stooped to give the impression of old peons. No one paid them any attention so they were able to linger, watching and listening.

Ferraz didn't know what he was expecting to hear. "Any hint of dissent," Rivya had said. Mikaz was silent next to him. They shuffled to different spots in the market, and when business was finished, they went down nearby passages eavesdropping on various peon conversations, venturing deeper into the maze of alleys that led off the square.

Mikaz was a few steps in front and beckoned Ferraz to his side. The old PG pointed to a makeshift hovel propped against a wall, down a dead-end passage between two dome huts. There was a handful of dishevelled, dirty peons sat on stools, pallets or the ground. Ferraz had no idea what profession they belonged to.

One peon, with ginormous biceps, slammed his fist into the palm of his hand and declared, "Why should *men* be second class citizens? Why should peons 'ave no say? We should be equal to women! We once *ruled* over women!"

The rest of the group grumbled in agreement and there were a few "hear, hears!"

Dissent. Ferraz winked at Mikaz. *These are our peons.*

11

DARRIO

Marro saw the first one. Hanging from a tree near the river. With paws hacked off and throat slit. It was not a wolf he knew, not one of the Wulhor-Aaen, but it had frightened him and he had come dashing back into the den to tell the alpha pair. The next morning, five adults went to see, instructing the yearlings to stay behind at the den to mind the newborn pups in case there was danger.

The adults came across the rotting carcass and Marro coughed up bile. No one spoke for a long time, dumbstruck by what could have happened to this wolf. *Where are his paws?* The question kept repeating in Darrio's mind.

"Split in two." The alpha male, Arro, broke the silence. "One go left along river, other go right. Keep low and out of sight, stay together and go for as long as you feel safe. Then return to den, by sundown. Look and smell for signs of who did this and why."

Lurra, Marro and Moirra headed left, Arro and Darrio headed right. They trailed the river, sniffing the ground and the air, the two trotting on all fours, side by side. The reeking odour of another pack hit Darrio's nostrils and he huffed to get Arro's attention.

The black wolf padded over to him and inhaled deeply. "Norra's pack. Xulr-Aaen," he snorted. Norra was Arro's daughter from a few year's past. She had left the pack before Darrio had joined.

The black wolf and the brown wolf continued onwards, into territory heavily marked by this other pack. Both trod carefully, they were scouting and did not want to bump into another wolf and risk a potentially fatal scrap.

"Smell humans," Arro growled.

"See traces of humans," Darrio answered, pointing his nose and ears at an area of ground that had been trampled down by many feet.

They tiptoed on and within a few paces of the flattened forest floor, there was another dead wolf, a female, hanging from a tree. Mutilated in the same way as the first. The two wolves stood on hindlegs to their full height to sniff at the corpse. They did not know her.

Arro raised his eyes at Darrio and they continued creeping forward. Human voices carried on the wind and the pair froze, crouching low to the ground to listen. Without saying a word, Arro set off downwind of where the noise was coming from, Darrio followed.

A large pack of humans was gathered on the other side of the river, in the Lost Lands. Too many to count. A few of the males were fishing, the females were lounging in tents or spurring with each other, eating or talking in groups. There was a standing height dome tent in the middle of the camp. A latticework of wooden poles led up to the entrance with raw animal hides slung over the top gathering snow, and roped from pole to pole was a string of... Darrio swallowed hard. Paws.

Arro had also seen the atrocity, he snarled. "How many do you count?"

"Thirty-six."

"Nine dead wolves. Enough. Return now to den." Arro turned and skulked away.

***

Lurra's scouting party told a similar tale. They had seen another two dead wolves hanging from the trees, but no sign of humans.

"Never seen anything like this," Lurra said. The pack was resting in the den. All were listening to the alpha pair.

"Believe we caused this," Arro retorted. His head resting in his front paws.

"By attacking the camp? They took Zirrio! What did they expect, we would not retaliate?"

"Yes, Lurra. Don't think humans expected us to take revenge. They kill a wolf like they kill a fly. With no thought."

"We are not flies, Arro! We are a powerful, ancient race. These our mountains. They mock us. The natural order is off kilter. They prey on lone wolves and murder them. They wouldn't dare attack a pack of wolves."

"It is a warning, Lurra. A power show. Dead wolves along the river bank, the humans on the other side. They mark their territory. Other side of river is theirs and we crossed it when we attacked their camp."

"They cross into our territory, and territories of neighbouring packs, to hunt us. You saw paws of nine wolves in their camp. Who will be the tenth? One of your own fur and blood? A matter of time."

"What would you suggest, mated female? That we attack again? No. We do not know how many are at that camp. Too many to count, too many to take down."

Lurra glanced down at her newborn pups, shuffling around between her legs, climbing up on her belly, taking their first tentative steps. Yesterday they had opened their eyes to see for the first time. She gave the nearest to her snout a big long lick and it yapped happily.

"Can't take humans alone." She leaned her head back and rested it on Arro's hunched shoulders. "Need numbers, great numbers of fierce angry wolves."

"We are five adults, five yearlings, five pups. Not a great number."

"Those dead wolves were loved, part of a pack. Packs which mourn their loss as we speak. We must unite against a common foe. How many packs in this vast wilderness, in the mountains? How many wolves in those packs? Many thousands. A force to be reckoned with."

"Unite packs," Arro mumbled, as his eyes closed. Lurra had planted a seed of an idea and it was starting to take shape in the black wolf's mind.

Is it possible to bring all wolves into one pack? Who lead? We would kill each other before we even mounted an attack, mused Darrio. His three pups were asleep next to him, a tangled mass of limbs. He moulded himself around them, nestling his head next to Sarrya. Drowsily she sniffed at his face before settling down to sleep again. *Fear our peaceful lives about to change, sweet daughter.*

***

"Darrio. Important task," Lurra announced after they had all eaten their fill of a young elk the following evening.

He slunk over to her, back low, ears down. She had not forgotten his hesitation to kill the human at the camp attack, and had treated him with hostility since. This was the first time she had spoken to him.

"Time has come, Darrio, to repay our kindness at keeping you and pups alive."

He bowed his head. He had been waiting for this moment.

"Humans laugh at us, slaughter our kind with no worry of reprisal. Think we are weak race, closer to base animals than to them. But our males run on two legs like they do and we have a female now standing on two legs. Perhaps she is the only one, or she is one of many. We do not know. It is time to bring isolated packs together as one. Your task – find every pack in mountains and unite to common cause. Understand omega?"

Darrio flinched, approaching other packs usually ended in death, asking them to unite was an impossible task. "Understood, Lurra."

"Your pups stay with us, awaiting your successful return," Arro added and he arched his back, stretching out shoulder muscles before turning away from Darrio, dismissing him. Darrio noted the sharp tone in Arro's voice. *If I dare to return unsuccessful, my children will suffer.*

Darrio left the den to find his pups, Harro, Warrio and Sarrya. He would leave at first light and he needed to talk to them. The yearlings were not far from the entrance of the den. They were playing with a pine cone, bouncing it on their noses to each other and catching it in their front paws. His three along with his daughter's shadow Ricarro and his brother Berrio. They barked and yapped, enjoying the game.

Darrio watched for a while until Warrio noticed his father. "Pappy! You want to play, old wolf?"

"Not this time, son. Must speak with you and siblings."

The yearlings ignored him and carried on messing around. He shot forward and snatched the cone out of the air with his teeth, dropping it on the floor and snarling, "Now, pups!"

Harro slinked towards his father and Warrio followed.

Sarrya stood with paw on hip, pouting. "You always ruin our fun! Can't this wait?"

In a flash Darrio sprung on Sarrya, clamping her throat in his jaws and pinning her to the floor. She struggled and then submitted, ears flat. He was still bigger than her, but her strength surprised him. *Too feisty, that mouth get her into trouble.*

He let her go and jogged away to a secluded cliff overhang, away from the den. His two sons at his heels, his daughter lagged behind.

"Dear pups…" he started before Sarrya interrupted.

"We are not pups anymore, Pa! We are four seasons old."

"Shut up, Sarry." Warrio smacked his sister's nose with a paw.

"Shut up yourself!" Sarrya yelled as she jumped on him,

the two tussled back and forth.

Harro rolled his eyes. *At least I have one sensible one,* Darrio thought as he lunged between the bickering duo, breaking up the fight and holding both by the scruffs of their neck before pushing them to different corners of the hollow.

"Listen. I leave the pack at sunrise. I might never return. Tonight we say goodbye."

Three bawling voices started up at once asking why, why, why. They rushed at him, getting as close as possible, rubbing up against him and bumping their heads to his. He told them his orders from Arro and Lurra, deciding to be honest. The last thing he wanted to do was to leave them with another lie. One about their mother was enough.

"Bitch Lurra! She can't do this to you, Pappy. Will rip out her throat," Sarrya snarled.

"Those words to never leave your mouth again, daughter. I want you alive if I return," he soothed her. "Harro, Warrio, look out for your sister. She is unique. Many outside pack will want to harm her."

"I can look after myself, don't need help," his fiery daughter grumbled. Warrio snapped his jaws at her.

"I know, Sarry, you all can. Stay close. Trust each other, no one else. Not even Ricarro." He prodded Sarrya with his snout and she dropped her eyes to show she had heard.

"We love you, Pa," Harro said.

They slept that night in the hollow, curled up against the freezing wind and snuffling in each other's ears.

***

Darrio decided it was time to rest. He slumped down against a tree, panting. He had been running fast, trying to get as much space between him and the den as possible. He'd left at first light, leaving his pups asleep in the hollow to avoid an emotional goodbye, and the sun was now bright in the sky. He didn't have a plan and he needed to think. He had run up the mountain, away from the river but still within his own pack boundaries. He didn't want to be caught as a lone wolf by the humans, but other than that he had no clue where to start.

Can't think on an empty stomach. He caught a rabbit and settled down to gnaw on it beginning to formulate a strategy. He would begin with packs who were linked somehow to his own. Arro and Lurra's offspring. Norra. Arro had thought they were on her patch when they had seen the human camp.

He fought off the urge to take a nap after filling his belly and instead scampered with head low, to pick up the Xulr-Aaen odour.

It was near the end of the day when he caught the same tang in his nose. Darrio followed it sprayed on trunks and shrubs and knew he was on the Xulr-Aaen territory outskirts. He decided to spend the night on the edge, approaching a den in the evening risked disturbing the pack whilst eating their day's hard-earned kill, the time when wolves are most dangerous, sparring over their dinner and the choicest cuts of meat. The best time would be in the morning, before the hunt.

Darrio roamed for three days, but was no closer to finding the pack's den. In the end, they found him. Three grey wolves jumped him late in the evening of the fourth day. Viciously taking him down and drawing blood with their sharp teeth.

"You stink," a large male growled. "We have smelt you for days, brown wolf." *He must be the alpha.*

The alpha pinned Darrio's neck to the ground, another grey wolf held his snout between his drooling maw and the third dug his claws into Darrio's back. All were male. *Where is the alpha female?*

With an effort through a mouth clamped shut and throat crushed, Darrio whimpered, "Norra." The pressure eased from his mouth and he repeated, louder this time, "Norra. Please."

"What do you want with Norra, stinking wolf?" The

alpha's shoulder hair stiffened but he dropped Darrio's neck.

"Pawless dead wolves in trees. Humans," he managed. His throat was in agony.

"Bring him," the alpha told his two betas.

They allowed Darrio to stand and he followed the big grey wolf whilst the two others nipped at his lowered tail.

The den had been dug into the earth, the entrance hidden behind huge moss-covered, twisted tree roots. A long tunnel led into a wide, but low, cavity. Grubby, hairy roots from the vegetation above dangled along the tunnel and tickled Darrio's twitchy fur. His entry reminded him of when he had approached the Wulhor-Aaen carrying his newborn pups. This time, however, the den smelt of blood and the rest of the pack was wailing, paying him little mind. He was brought in front of a female laying on her side, her ribcage heaving. *Laboured breathing, something is wrong.* The alpha male went to her and licked her face, whispering in her ear.

The alpha female slowly rolled over to face Darrio. She had a huge gash in her chest with a broken spear sticking out, the head of the spear lodged partway in her flesh.

Struggling with the pain, she rasped, "I am Norra. Talk."

"Norra, I am from Wulhor-Aaen. Alphas are your parents Arro, Lurra."

"Yes, recognise your scent. You should not be here, but strange times. Tell me of humans and the pawless wolves."

"Humans kill wolves and hang them along the river bank. We have seen four, but there are more dead. Humans keep paws as trophies in their camp."

"We know," the alpha male cautioned, licking his mate's head again. "Tell us what we don't know, brown wolf, or you die. Norra owes no allegiance to her parents."

Darrio hesitated, recalling a lesson once taught by the mother of his pups, and then replied, "I know how to take out that human spear and heal the wound."

"Touch her and I tear out your throat!" The alpha male lunged at him growling and once again Darrio felt sharp teeth around his neck.

"Sinarro, mate. I am dying, I am in pain. What harm to hear what he has to say, I die anyway." Norra struggled with the words and the wails of the wolves in the den got louder.

Sinarro stood over Darrio, allowing him to speak.

"Need to gather clean water, fresh pine sap, pile of large flat leaves from the black berries, vine cord, a big wad of spider cobwebs. Are those things close at hand?"

"Need to go to stream. We are not able to bring water here," Sinarro said.

"Cannot move Norra. There is another way… urine," Darrio replied.

"Urine? You mad, brown wolf?" Sinarro shouted, but Norra's agonised whine stopped him short, and he decided to cooperate. Sinarro barked orders at the beta wolves, who scurried out of the den to forage.

"Permission to approach you, Norra?" Darrio asked.

She huffed in response, too weak to talk. He moved close and inspected the wound. It was not deep, the tip of the spear in her flesh. She had lost a lot of blood, but it was not spurting so had missed the artery.

The other wolves returned and Darrio set to work. "First pull out spear, quick and clean. It will hurt you, Norra. We need to hold you down." He looked at Sinarro for permission to touch his mated female.

Sinarro snarled but nodded. He gestured to two other wolves and the three of them held Norra. She took a deep breath as Darrio positioned himself over her and yanked out the spear with his teeth. The piercing howl that came from Norra rumbled around the den. Sinarro yowled in despair as his female lost consciousness. But she was still alive.

Darrio pushed the leaves down hard on the wound to

stop the blood flow, he told another wolf to apply pressure and he indicated to Sinarro that it was time.

"Clean it inside and out; need a lot of water when I remove the leaves. Now."

Sinarro angled his bulky body over Norra. "I'm sorry mate," he murmured as Darrio moved the leaves and a steaming stream of urine saturated the wound.

Darrio used some clean leaves to pat the area dry before applying the wadded cobwebs to seal the wound, next he smeared pine sap over it to ward off infection and then he bound fresh leaves over the top using the cord. When he was done, he looked up at Sinarro. "Check on it and change it every day, see how wound is healing."

Sinarro stared at him and then at Norra, who was breathing laboriously. They would know in the morning if this had worked.

"Guard him, do not let him escape. I do not trust this brown wolf," Sinarro told his pack, and then he wrapped himself around Norra, licking her head and nuzzling his snout into her shoulders.

The pack moved away to find their resting positions for the night and a female told Darrio to follow her. He hunkered down in a cold corner, hemmed in by pack wolves, and fell into a fitful sleep.

***

For the following two days Darrio was kept prisoner by the Xulr-Aaen. He checked on Norra's wound and did what he could for her. He found a crude way to bring her water using the skull of a long dead deer. No one spoke to him and he was given the end scraps of the day's hunt. Sinarro was waiting to see if Norra lived and if she didn't, then neither would Darrio.

On the third morning, as Darrio tended to Norra, she woke. Her eyes blinked open, startling Darrio. She glared at him, and then mustering all her strength, she attempted a snarl. She did not remember him, he was a stranger in her den.

"Friend. I will get Sinarro. Rest," he told her and then sprinted to find the alpha male. Darrio knew he would be nearby, staying close to his injured mate.

"Sinarro," he shouted. "Norra has woken!"

A rustle in the undergrowth and then the big grey wolf appeared, leaping over a bush and diving through the tree roots. Darrio and excited pack wolves followed at his heels.

Sinarro licked Norra's face and nudged her muzzle with his own. "My mate, you live."

"Sinarro," she spluttered and tenderly licked his face in return.

The pack, delighted that their alpha mother was alive, jumped and ran about in circles, rattling the earth walls. When chunks of dirt started to shake free from the hanging vegetation roots and fall on their heads, Sinarro yelled, "Everyone out!"

The wolves piled out. Darrio found a quiet, mossy nook near the den entrance and lay down, exhausted, and relieved that his wound healing had worked.

Later, a beta wolf roused him and told him he was wanted by the alpha pair. Darrio didn't know how long he had slept for, but the sun was dipping in the sky. He felt hazy as he climbed to his feet and stumbled into the den. Norra was sprawled on the springy moss that her pack had ripped up for her to recuperate on, and still looked frail, but she would live, Darrio was certain. Sinarro sat next to her.

"Your name, brown wolf?" Sinarro asked.

"Darrio."

"Darrio, we owe you our gratitude." Sinarro stood on all fours and wagged his tail.

Darrio shadowed the friendly gesture by wagging his own. They sniffed at each other and then sat upright.

"How did you know to do that?" Sinarro demanded.

"I was injured a long time ago, another showed me."

"Another wolf?"

"Yes," lied Darrio.

"It worked. Now, why are you here?"

Darrio swallowed and decided to come straight out with it. "To unite wolf packs into one army to fight humans, to take back the Lost Lands and to take revenge for the pawless corpses."

"The paws of our son Arro hang from the poles of those murderers," Sinarro choked.

"Sorry."

"We named him after Norra's father. A yearling. He went off for a run, never to return. Norra wanted revenge and we went after the humans. Found them in Xulr-Aaen territory, in *our* lands, on *our* side of river. They fought hard and Norra took the spear in her chest. They are strong and clever. After, we understood. No chance to take them with our small number. There are eight of us, three are newborns."

"Why," Norra croaked, she was listening, but not yet well enough to speak more than a few words.

Sinarro laid a paw on her. "Want to know why they kill wolves and string from trees. Most of our kind have never seen a human, only heard tales of the Peqkian invasion of south Wul-Onr valley hundreds of years ago."

Do I tell truth? That my pack started this brutality? A few heartbeats passed as he weighed up his options.

"I know..." One secret to keep was enough for him. So, with a knot in his stomach, Darrio told Sinarro and Norra the tale of the deer hunt gone wrong and the human camp massacre in the Lost Lands.

"Appreciate you telling us that," Sinarro said.

Norra jutted out her chin and Sinarro leaned in close to her mouth. She spoke a few words to her mate and then he turned to Darrio.

"We want humans destroyed. We will help you form wolf army."

Darrio leapt to his four feet and ran in a circle chasing his tail in a display of joyful thanks.

Sinarro yapped and then said, "My father Kurro and mother Jerra lead Maarr-Aaen. I will take you to them."

12

GANNI

There was a huge crowd for his sermon in Parchad holy square and he was pleased. Since the Crown Prince Ammad had declared he would be cleansed, High Priest Ganni had spent every day stirring up the Affarah hordes, reminding the peasants of the upcoming cleansing and ensuring enough sacrificial blood was gathered for the occasion.

The cleansing was tomorrow and today he had something special planned after his sermon.

"Children of God, it is now the time for personal reflection. Think on the sins you have committed and ask God for forgiveness. Sacrifice and give Him blood, pray and give Him your devotion. The wrath of God is coming and we must all be pure or face His doom," Ganni boomed, the lid of his lazy eye spasmed.

He turned his back to leave, his holy helpers echoed his words, "Wrath of God… Sacrifice… Devotion…"

Then came a shout from the mob, "My holy High Priest, holiest of holy in all of Drome, I beg you, I beg our great God, to heal my ruined legs!"

Ganni swung around and watched as the filthy audience parted to allow a bedraggled man on his belly to crawl up to the platform, using his arms to propel himself forward, useless legs dragging behind. The Affarah always beseeched Ganni for miracles and he ignored them, but today he would oblige.

"Please, my High Priest, please… My legs have not worked for many scorch seasons, I cannot work and only beg… I want to stand again, to be useful to God again…" the crippled man implored.

"Heal him! Help him! Fix his legs!" came the cries from the mass in front of him.

Ganni held up his hands for silence and an immediate hush descended. He nodded to his holy helpers to pick up the cripple and bring him onto the platform. Ganni wanted everyone to see what would happen next. The man was laid in front of the High Priest. He grabbed at Ganni's robes.

The High Priest kneeled and held his arms up to the sky.

"My all powerful, all seeing God, grant me the holy strength to fix this broken man and make his legs work again," he thundered.

Ganni shuddered and a beam of light shone down on him, illuminating him in a golden haze. He brought his hands down and laid them on the legs of the man. The man shrieked out in pain, clutching at his legs and there was a collective gasp from the crowd.

Ganni repeated this movement three more times and on the final time he bellowed, "Arise, for you are whole again. You have been redeemed. To serve our God. Every Dromedar man, woman, child must cleanse and they too shall be redeemed!"

The man wriggled his toes, his feet, his legs. He then turned painstakingly onto all fours and gradually stood upright. "A miracle! A miracle! My legs," he exclaimed and rose his arms up to the sky as Ganni had.

The throng cheered, screeching, "A miracle, a miracle! God is great, God is powerful!"

They rushed forward and Ganni heard pitiful voices

entreating him to heal their son, mother, husband. The High Priest gently shook his head.

He held the bedraggled man by the shoulders and proclaimed, "The power of God is unknowable and I am His vessel. He wanted this man to know His power, to devote his life to Him. This is a miracle! Tomorrow we will see our beloved Crown Prince cleansed of his sins, we can only pray that He will grant us another miracle. Now sacrifice and give Him blood!"

Ganni left the stage whilst the man whose legs worked again walked through the square basking in glory and allowing people to touch him and kiss his cheek. He was shadowed by two holy helpers. The other holy men continued to preach and Ganni knew that the mass would peter out as they went back to whatever it was they did in their worthless lives.

The peasants with spare money rushed forward to the marketplace to buy sacrificial animals such as rabbits, goats, pigs, dogs and cats. The poor trapped strays and sometimes rats, and the poorer still bought incense or butter candles. Then, loaded up from the marketplace, they made their way to the holy temple.

Ganni followed the crowd and paused awhile outside, taking in the grand structure with domes and arches. The temple had been built thousands of scorch seasons earlier to honour God. Many Dromedars, both rich and poor, had volunteered to be built into the walls. They huddled together and were sealed in, stood upright, their worshipful howling and prayers to God had gone on for days until one by one they succumbed. The stench of the rotting bodies seeping out from the mortar lasted for months. Now, it just looked like a wall, the skeletons dust within it.

In the first room of the temple the noise of the animals and the smell of their excrement mixed with smoky cheap incense, repulsed the High Priest. He watched as low class women gave their animals to the holy helpers to slit their throats, pouring the blood into the vessels. The blood flowed into a huge vat in the centre of the temple to be blessed and inconspicuously mixed with a little water to keep it flowing, and then gushed into channels surrounding the outside of the temple. The dead animals were slung to the sides of the room, the clean animals in one pile and the dirty strays on another. Royalty, the genteel families and his holy helpers would feast on the clean meat later. The dirty would be burned. The Affarahs believed that all the animals were burnt for additional sacrifice, they never asked for the dead animal back to eat and feed their starving families.

The poorest women with the ugliest humps could not afford an animal and instead lit incense and candles and pricked their fingers over the vessels adding a few drips of their own blood. Women menstruating went behind a screen, lifted their skirts and squatted over a vessel. Some women had caught their monthly blood in cups tied between their legs and brought it to the temple to pour in. All blood for the God was welcome but secretly Ganni found this particular custom disgusting. After giving blood, the women then prayed. He noted that there were no high class Tamadeen women there. Women were not allowed any deeper into the temple and the Tamadeen preferred not to mix with the low Affarah clan, often sending female slaves to deliver their blood sacrifices. The practice of sacrificing children as the highest honour to God had long been outlawed, but he suspected the blood that the slaves poured into the vessels on behalf of their mistresses was that of orphans and slave offspring.

He walked through to the second room, seeing a similar scene. After his miracle, there was a crush of men sacrificing animals or slitting their flesh to give their own blood. He picked his way through the stinking, sweaty men into the third room. It was ornate and luxuriously furnished for male members of Wakrime, Qacirr and Tamadeen clans. It was empty apart from three of his holy helpers. *Disgraceful*, thought Ganni. *The higher classes think they are immune to God's wrath.*

He nodded to his men and then walked into the centre of the temple. This grand area was sacred to God's speakers – him and his holy men. There were a number praying and Ganni joined them to chant in the old language, and not the heathen tongue Dromedars now spoke. Then, he cleansed. He took off his robes and slipped into a communal immersion bath with his holy men, full of the blood gathered in the temple. Ganni tried not to think of the women's monthly blood, tasting vomit in his mouth when he did.

Ganni dried himself off and walked up fifty steps and entered the fourth and final room. His room. It was forbidden for anyone else to step foot inside other than the High Priest. He cleaned it, slept in it, ate in it, prayed in it. Did whatever he wanted in it. When he had first been selected by the Qacirr holy families as the High Priest he was ecstatic and couldn't wait to have this room to himself. He imagined riches and luxury more exquisite than the third room. All High Priests were sworn to secrecy as to what this room contained and he took the vows before he could enter.

What a gigantic disappointment. Instead of the gold, marble, lush velvet and comfortable furniture he was dreaming about – and was accustomed to – the room was bare. A wooden floor and not even shutters on the windows. Nothing. He had laughed to himself for hours that first day and then slept on the hard floor.

Over time he had sneaked in a few cushions, a blanket and a few other small comforts from the house of his parents. He settled himself down on one of the floor cushions and started to unwind his hair from the long plaits that pulled tight against his scalp and made his head ache. He felt a pleasurable release as they came loose.

His parents would be pleased with him. The Deraasi family was one of the most powerful of the seven holy families. Holy family members married other holy family members and today there was so much intermingling that his father had married his first cousin, but this kept the blood pure and holy. Ganni was the eighth Deraasi High Priest in the family's ancient lineage. They controlled most of the sacrificial animal merchants in the marketplace and business was booming, the upcoming royal cleansing sparking a rush in blood giving.

His brother had managed today's 'miracle', finding a poor fool outside of Parchad in the harsh desert with a big, thirsty family. To help his loved ones, the fool agreed to secretly enact a miracle in the city in return for a pay-out. After, he would die. The family would then come into a sudden, unexpected cartload of food and water and never know where the fool had disappeared to. This farce happened rarely but always worked to prompt a surge of devotion from the peasants.

The fool had been left in the city for the past week, dragging his pretend useless legs, making sure to spend time in the busy holy square and the marketplace so people would notice him and he would not be a stranger on the day. The fool would be dead by now, his blood added to the vessels in the temple and his body burned. God didn't often dish out miracles, so on occasion they had to put on a show. The light beam from carefully angled mirrors had been his brother's idea, and Ganni had to admit, it was a perfect touch.

The High Priest was excited about the royal brat's cleansing in the morning, that promised to be a good show too. He had wanted Our Ruler Mastiq to cleanse, the sins of Drome ultimately resting on his shoulders, but the Crown Prince would do. Such a loathsome, arrogant boy, Ammad was the embodiment of ungodliness and such an appalling role model for the public. Ganni was certain the cleansing would frighten the brat into behaving, never wanting to go through the pain again. It was the first royal cleansing Ganni would perform and he wanted it to be perfect, they didn't happen often and it would be the pinnacle of his tenure as High Priest. Enough blood had been collected and there was a buzz amongst the people. Our Ruler's soldiers kept a close watch on his sermons and the damn Khumarah Assassins hadn't so much as sneezed anywhere near. Ganni was certain the underground group would not show their faces at the cleansing.

Ganni ran through the cleansing procedure another time in his mind. What he would say, how he would stand, the potent incense burning in wispy smokes behind him. He drifted.

He was awoken from his nap by a soft knock on the door. He sat bolt upright, it was forbidden for anyone to walk up the stairs to this room apart from him. *I must be dreaming.* The knock came again and he jumped up, trembling.

The door opened. Ganni gulped down a yell. In swept the most beautiful woman he had ever seen. A Peqkian. Black, sheeny skin. Fine, cat like facial features. Hair in long braids down her back and wrapped with bright orange material. A white, gauzy dress hugged her tall, slim body. She turned to shut the door and the thin material stretched across her round, plump buttocks. A sandstorm of long-repressed lust swirled in Ganni's loins.

"What are you doing here? No one can be here! No woman is allowed past the first room," he managed as she glided over to stand a few steps from him. She tilted her head to one side, winked and smiled. *I must still be asleep; this cannot be real.* He tried to ignore his erection.

"Are you a vision from God? Who are you? You need to leave immediately!" Ganni started to panic, he could not call for help as no one would hear him. Could he forcefully take her down the stairs? But what would his holy men think seeing a woman in the temple, seeing him touching a woman? He was still a virgin; he'd taken a vow of celibacy.

She moved closer and held out a hand to him, long fingernails with a small delicate wrist. She smelt of lavender. He backed away from her, this was sacrilege. She kept moving towards him and he soon found his back against the wall. She slipped straps off her shoulders and the dress slithered down to the floor. Ganni drank up her nakedness and felt dizzy. She reached out and took his hand and brought it to her cheek, to her lips. She sucked on his fingers.

He knew he needed to get away from her, get her out of his room but he couldn't move. The orange haired woman was offering herself to him and he wanted her. *God must have sent her to me for a reason, to show His pleasure in my relentless commitment to bringing His word to the heathens. It must be a gift.* She brought his hand down her neck and placed it on her perfect breast.

He squeezed her flesh and then tweaked her nipple. Then he violently pushed her away. *This is a test! I must not falter in my vows of celibacy.*

He pointed to the door. "Get out! Leave now!"

Instead, as quickly as he had pushed her away, she was kneeling in front of him, her hands finding his penis through his robes and putting her mouth around it. Ganni let out a little groan and shoved her shoulders to get her off but she was strong and wrapped her arms around his body, keeping her mouth clamped around him. Passion overwhelmed him and he pulled off the robe from his head, she took his bare flesh in her mouth. He felt an almighty wave of desire, holding her head tight onto him. She pulled away at the moment he thought he would explode and pushed him to the floor. She straddled him, grinding hard. He grabbed at her buttocks as he spilled his seed. He felt euphoric and looked up at this vision from God.

The woman stood.

"What are you doing? Come here and touch me some more…"

He sat up to reach for her, but then she punched herself in the face, leaving a livid purple mark under one eye. She ran her long fingernails down her arm drawing blood and as he watched his seed dribbling down her thighs, she pummelled between her legs. Then she started screaming, a noise so loud it shook him from his stupor.

"Shut up!" He leapt up and slapped her face, she shrunk back into a corner of the room and continued to scream. He bent over her and she started to kick at his shins, he grabbed at her legs, trying to get near enough to close her mouth.

It was in this position that his four holy men found him.

"High Priest," the eldest one wheezed, as they all panted with the exertion of running up the stairs. He looked up from the battered, naked woman on the floor who started to snivel pathetically.

"A woman! What in God's name is this?" the eldest said, horrified.

"She forced her way in here, she forced herself on me. She is evil!" Ganni insisted. But he knew they would not believe him. *I have doomed myself.* He collapsed on the floor.

***

On the stage in the holy square that he had so lovingly commissioned for Crown Prince Ammad's cleansing, Ganni stood naked and bleeding. The Cuttarrs had whipped him mercilessly all night. This was meant to be his big day, his first royal cleansing, but instead it was his shameful demise. He looked down into the swarm and saw the leering faces of the heathen Parchaders, enjoying this spectacle. Only yesterday they had worshipped him. Over to the left stood the Qacirr holy families. Between the cold stares of his father and brother, his mother wept silently. She couldn't look at him. In a haze, he saw Our Ruler come forward with Ammad.

"High Priest Ganni Deraasi has been stripped of his most holy title in disgrace," Ruler Mastiq yelled. "He abused his holy vows of celibacy and copulated in sin with a woman in the holiest of holy temple. This poor woman was taken by force to satisfy his blasphemous desires. Instead of the cleansing you were expecting to see today, we will be beheading this vile creature instead."

A cheer went up as soldiers came forward to get Ganni ready for the execution. His bowels gave way and he defecated down his blood-stained legs. The stench reached the front row who jeered and pointed.

"The sinner has shat himself!" a wiry old woman exclaimed. Laughter rung in Ganni's ears.

Our Ruler continued, and the crowd quietened down to hear him. "I have consulted the holy families and we have appointed a new High Priest. Let us all hope this one is pure and true to his holy vows. High Priest Zeead, please step forward," Mastiq ordered.

Zeead Medra stepped forward. A limp looking man with stiff, jerky movements and a fat bottom that made him waddle. The Medra family was the lowest of the Qacirrs and Ganni forgot his looming death for a moment to wonder how Zeead had been chosen.

High Priest Zeead gestured to the sky, his heart and then to the multitude, who cheered and followed with the answering motion. His voice was high pitched like a woman's, but forceful. "Children of God. He has chosen me to be His messenger, to speak with His voice, to do His bidding. The wrath of God is coming, but He is pleased with our devout faith in Drome. His eyes look north. God wants us to free the Peqkian people from their bondage! They have no God! They must take on the only faith, they must worship our God or we will all burn."

The mob was confused, this was a new message. They weren't to blame for God's wrath, but the northern hisspits were. It took a few moments for the peasants to process the new priest's words and then they hollered eagerly. Zeead nodded and stepped back.

"Now, my people. The end of this monster's life," Ruler Mastiq roared and he nodded at the executioners holding Ganni down over a block of wood.

Ganni said his prayers and glanced up. He saw Jakira, Our Ruler's whore and mother of the Crown Prince brat. She was out of place. Instead of standing behind Mastiq with the rest of his court she stood with the Medra family, her hand on the shoulder of Zeead's mother.

His last thoughts, before cold sharp steel lopped off his head, were, *Laetitia Medra is wearing new jewels... The brat's whore mother did this! May God's wrath fall on your head Jakira and wreak havoc on you and your family…*

13

RAMYA

The Melokai entered the assembly hall and sat on a wooden bench on a platform at one end, Gwrlain next to her. Her counsellors and court flowed in and perched around the outside of the room on benches like hers. In the middle was placed a large circular bed covered in orange cushions and soft blankets.

Gwrlain was humming, picturing who was in the room. She took his hand and grinned. There were a few glares and tuts from her court, usually the only males in the room were Chaz and the PGs picked for the occasion, but the Trogr came with her everywhere, as certain as her own shadow. *Change is good, nothing stays the same forever.*

"Welcome to this Deflowering Ceremony! Let's begin," she announced.

First the musicians started up, a pulsing drum beat, bells and pipes. In came the dancers in huge skirts that spun out as they whirled. They took each item of clothing off until they were seductively entwined in each other.

Then walked in five naked girls, sixteen-year-old virgins who had experienced their monthly blood, who had volunteered and been picked by their Mothers for this traditional ceremony. They walked past Ramya and bowed low and stood to her right. They were beaming, blooming in their youth and excited to start their pleasure journey in front of the Melokai. They each announced their names to the clapping audience. The girls moved to the centre of the hall and positioned themselves on the bed.

Five blindfolded PGs were led in by the new Mother of Mothers Naomya, who placed them in front of each girl. Ramya loved to watch the faces of her girls at this point, when they saw a peon naked for the first time. And not just any peon, the finest of Ramya's pleasure givers.

She remembered her own deflowering ceremony, at the pen and not in front of the Melokai. She hadn't been selected for that honour, but she had enjoyed herself all the same.

The experienced PGs took charge of satisfying the girls. The sensual moans quickened Ramya's pulse. She noticed some members of her court starting to kiss each other. Hanny fondled the courtesan Marya's huge breasts.

Ramya couldn't help herself, she stood, tore off Gwrlain's loin cloth, stepped out of her shorts and still facing the middle of the room, sat down on him. A gasp went up from those around the room and Ramya realised that this was the first time this had occurred. Her female court members would either watch, satisfy themselves or each other, but never indulge themselves with a peon.

"Call more PGs! Let's all celebrate pleasure like these beautiful girls of Peqkya who leave today as women," she shouted at her court.

Bevya, who had been preening her tail, sprinted from the hall to the PG set at the Melokai's command.

"Yes," Hanny cheered. She stripped off her clothes and those of Marya.

One of the girls moaned in delight as a PG emptied into her. He was shiny with sweat and exertion. Ramya watched as Hanny, impatient now to have a peon and not wanting to wait for the fresh PGs, claimed him, hauling him to the floor. He obliged, vigorously using his hand on himself, preparing to indulge the Head Courtesan.

Another twenty PGs arrived, not blindfolded, and were pounced on by her now rampant court members. Chaz claimed his favoured PG, Martaz, and refused to share.

Ramya glided on Gwrlain. She was having fun seeing this orgy unfold in front of her. She noted a few of her court members leave the hall, not appreciating this deviation from the usual ceremony. Two of her counsellors also left with disgust on their faces, warrior Gogo and teller Omya. *Oh well! Their loss!*

The PGs were hounded by her women, as soon as one woman was sated the PG was seized by another. This was the ultimate test for the pleasure givers, they had to quench the desire of every single woman, a weak performance meant an excruciating death.

Ramya spotted the PG Ferraz staring at her whilst he took the courtesan Marya from behind. He wasn't picked to deflower and had come in later. His face was screwed up tight and he yanked back the courtesan's hair. She moaned in delight, her huge tits bouncing. Marya's bliss tipped Ramya over the edge and she leaned back on Gwrlain, with a squeal.

The Melokai surveyed her court, some were still rutting but most were satisfied and smiling.

The warrior Lizya slapped at a PG's limpness shouting, "Get hard now. I want that piece of meat!"

The PG's face tensed as he willed himself to stand up after pleasuring so many women. It was Slim Stavaz, Ramya had savoured him, years earlier. But it was no good, he was completely spent. Lizya pushed him away, shaking her head and grabbed another PG. Slim Stavaz sank to his knees, clutching his face.

***

Ramya lounged in a shady area under the trees watching as Gwrlain worked to put the finishing touches to his upgraded nesting house. It was a tall, square roofed structure with a small opening on one side and no windows. Inside was rough wood, good for the birds' saliva nests to grip to.

The first design hadn't attracted any birds. Gwrlain had waited, his excitement waning each day that passed. Soon he realised that something was wrong. Rather than getting angry at the failure and giving up, he started again from the beginning, planning a new nesting house, inspecting the materials and location. Then he had ordered a rebuild, tweaking his strategy. He was adamant that this second design would encourage swifts to build their nests there and Ramya believed him, admiring his unwavering devotion to the task.

"One or two will come at first. Then more," he had told her in his thick accent.

Riv had calculated that they could make a lot of money selling these, which pleased Omya, but that it would take time for the industry to establish itself. First this tower needed to be finished, then the birds would come and then more could be built. Ramya adored watching Gwrlain direct the peon workers and flex his muscular arms doing heavy work.

"The first nest is for you my love, I will make best soup," he had said that morning as she smothered him with clay to protect his white skin from the sun. A huge tent had been constructed over the building site to block out the rays but she was careful. Sun exposure roasted his translucent, delicate skin.

She had summoned a council meeting here, under this tree, so she could stay close to Gwrlain. Her counsellors had arrived, some annoyed at the journey out of the city centre but others delighted at the change of scenery. She had told them, "We only live once, so let's enjoy ourselves."

They had given her the latest news, asked for her approval on various points, and left. Hanny had lingered. They were friends once again. After the first council meeting that Gwrlain had attended, Ramya made a conscious effort to find time for her courtesan, but her soulmatch was never far away.

Council meetings had once been Ramya's life, but now she had other priorities. She watched Gwrlain working on the nesting tower. He was talking to a swift that sat on his shoulder.

A cat landed in Ramya's lap and started purring. Ramya stroked its chin as she recalled the meeting. Gogo: thirteen wolves slaughtered, same number as was taken from the Peqkians, no further wolf sightings, warriors remain heavy for now. Chaz: situation in Troglo remains the same. Zecky: second Fert female envoy sent back to Fertilian with verbal message to send the Queen, not carved in chest or mutilated. Omya: not enough money left, can't keep scrimping and moving coin from pot to pot.

Only Head Trader Riv had a surprise. She had proposed opening a new trade route at the north-west border with the pygmies, one of her traders there having made contact and managing to exchange a few vegetables for some spices of sorts. The two stumps on Ramya's left hand itched and she brought it up to her mangled left ear at the thought of the conniving, evil, little creatures. Ramya had reacted viciously to the suggestion, and Omya had baulked at the cost, but Chaz had insisted. Ramya had told herself, *change is good, it is time to forgive and move on,* and approved the expedition. And, as Chaz had said, "Nothing ventured, nothing gained."

Gwrlain and his workers started to ease down for the day. He put everything in order and waved his peons off. The warrior Violya, his personal guard, stood to one side, observing his every move. His work finished, the Trogr jogged over to Ramya, V following at a distance.

Ramya beckoned her forward. "V, you have new orders. You will be leading a trading exploratory party into pygmie land. Please leave us and report to Gogo."

The warrior bowed and headed back to the barracks.

Ramya was reluctant to see the capable warrior leave her soulmatch's side, but Gogo insisted. "My trusted senior warriors are dotted around the borders," Gogo had grumbled earlier, "and Violya is skilled, trustworthy and fearless. The pygmies will not intimidate her. I'll assign another to Gwrlain, the threat to his person is not as great as sending Peqkians into unknown lands."

Ramya had cringed, as Gogo spoke the truth. The Melokai was being overprotective of her white giant, but he was now her life, her everything.

The pair stood in the shade of the trees watching the magnificent red sunset. He was behind, his chin resting on her head and arms wrapped around her.

Ramya whispered, "Gwrlain, my love, my soulmatch, we have made a baby. I'm pregnant."

14

JESSIMA

"Let us bring forth a baby boy!" he hollered when he realised he was semi hard. She hitched up her nightdress and straddled his bulk with her doll-like frame, moving back and forth. He closed his wrinkled eyes and concentrated, clutching a handful of her knee-length, blond hair. She stared at the stain on the velvet wall hanging, wondered for the umpteenth time how it had come to be there, and shook out her achy wrist, tired from an eternity of rubbing his limp manhood. Seconds later he cried "Jayne!" and spent his seed in her. Just as quickly, he fell fast asleep. Snoring louder than a hunting horn. Honk, honk, honk.

"My name is Jessima," she murmured at her husband Hugo, the King of Fertilian. She felt suffocated in the airless room, crushed by the weight of his beloved second wife's ghost and Hugo's desperation to quicken Jessima's womb. He was running out of time. Now in his early sixties he had still not produced a male heir. Jessima was one of eleven children, and the marriage match was made in the anticipation that she would be as fertile as her mother. Hugo hadn't wanted to marry again, inconsolable after Jayne's death but his advisors had been adamant. He needed to sire a boy. But in nine years of marriage she had not gotten pregnant.

Jessima needed some air. She pulled on her robe, slippers and shawl and crept out of the stuffy chamber. In recent years Hugo felt the cold more, and hated to have the windows opened, even now in the warm spring months. All drafts had been meticulously sealed.

"I'm going for a walk," she told the two guards posted at the King's door. The tall one followed her at a distance. They were used to her night time wanderings around the well defended castle. She sought out the deserted, dark corridors. She did not want to meet anyone. This was her time for silent reflection.

She approached a door with a thin strip of candlelight flickering underneath and paused outside.

"Oh boys, you are naughty!" a female voice yelled, followed by a fit of giggles and the grunts of a number of men.

"Where would it please you to put *me*, Princess?" one man with a gruff voice asked.

"Why, you swain," the female said, and then more giggles and then silence, as Jessima guessed the gruff man's member had found a pleasing home.

Jessima moved away. *I'm sure every man in Cleland Castle has ridden Princess Georgina.* Hugo had married his daughter to Lord Hadley Smyth in her eighteenth year. Hugo, against all advice about arranging a strategic marriage, had given Georgina a choice of three men. Georgina had selected the most attractive, they had wedded in a lavish ceremony and Hugo refused the bride nothing. The Princess was happy, but soon Hadley bored her, and she had persuaded her father to send him away on important missions out of the city. As her husband rode out of the castle gates, Georgina stood on the castle wall to wave him off whilst a guardsman kneeled hidden under her skirts with his tongue between her legs. The entire castle knew of her infidelities, most of the able men had been entertained in her bed, but not a soul dared tell Hadley or allow any whispers to reach King Hugo's ears. When Hadley returned after a mission, she was the perfect wife.

Odd that I'm her stepmother but we are similar in age. And my other stepdaughter is ten years older than I am.

Princess Matilda was Hugo's eldest daughter with his first wife Gracie. He'd been married young, a match organised by Hugo's parents and it was a loveless, short marriage. Gracie died in childbirth and the baby was given to nannies to care for. He didn't visit his first child for many years as he devoted all his attention to finding a way to wrench back the Kingdom from the false King Benjamin. When he finally found the time, there was no fatherly love. He married Princess Matilda off at the earliest opportunity, at fifteen, to Lord John Iddenkinge. A stuffy, middle aged man with lots of land, and men, in the south of Fertilian, including the lucrative salt flats. Iddenkinge had remained loyal to the Clelands, defending his land from Ben Thorne. The bride was his reward. Hugo never saw her, didn't attend the wedding. Jessima knew Matilda had two children, but otherwise heard little about the Princess.

Jessima reached the door to the garden and swung it open. The fresh gust of wind made her loose curls flutter. Her hair was usually gathered up in grand styles but Hugo preferred it down in bed as it was similar to Jayne's tresses. He stroked the lengths and his face glazed over. As Jessima stood in the doorway taking long gulps of air, the heavens opened and heavy rain bounced off the flagstones and splattered her ankles.

"Guard, I shall bathe in the garden pool," she told her tall shadow. "Do not allow anyone else out here."

He grunted his agreement.

She stepped into the noisy downpour, turned a corner out of the guard's sight and hearing, kicked off her slippers and discarded her clothes. She dashed about, stamping in puddles and chuckling to herself. She was already soaked when she slid her naked body into the raised pool, her skin the creamy pale brown of a chicken eggshell. She felt revitalised, as the raindrops sploshed around her. The breeze smelt fresh and of the scent of roses that surrounded the pool. She started slapping her palms on the moonlit water and ducking under trying to hold her breath for as long as possible.

She popped up. *I can hold it for longer!* She inhaled deeply and was about to go under again when a man's voice whispered from the shadows.

"Jessima?"

"Who goes there?" She tensed and sunk in the water, up to her chin, hoping it might conceal her nudity.

"It's me Jessima, Toby. What in all Fertilian are you doing here?" Toby's face came closer, parting the drizzle. His blond locks tousled in the rain. *So handsome.*

"Toby! What are *you* doing here?" She relaxed, it was not a murderer lurking in the gardens, but a man she knew. The King's brother and army general no less, with access everywhere in the castle. A man who should not see her without her clothes however. She glanced around for where she had flung her robe and hoped that he could not see her body beneath the silvery sheen of the water.

Through the deluge, he had to get close to be heard. He moved to stand behind her, with his nose over her shoulder. She could feel his hot breath.

"I required some air, came for a stroll in the glorious gardens and it started to throw down apples and pears. Then I heard all this delightful splashing and it was the Queen, no less, frolicking in the pool."

"Yes, here I am. And, alas, I should probably get out..."

"How about I get in!" In a flash, he had whipped off his sword belt and climbed into the pool still dressed, sitting opposite her, his bright green eyes sparkling.

"Your clothes," Jessima exclaimed.

"They were wet anyway."

"Yes, well, mine are on the ground. This is not wise. Please will you remove yourself and gather my clothes for me so I can dress. I'm not decent, Prince."

He went to get out and then changed his mind. He took off his own shirt and then struggled with his boots and trousers under the water and threw them over the edge of the pool. His torso glistened.

"There is no one around, Jessima, no one can see us and no one can hear us. And now we are both naked." He grinned mischievously and then squirted water through his fingers at her.

"Toby, please!" She kicked water at him. They edged around each other and he dived at her, pushing her head under the water.

"Why you little rascal," she gasped and pushed at his chest. He caught her in his arms and pulled her to him. They stared at each other. She could feel his heart pounding.

"Oh, Jessima." The words caught in his throat as he held her gaze.

Every inch of her skin felt hot and cold at the same time.

"We shouldn't be here, Toby." She tried to wriggle free of his arms.

"No we shouldn't, but here we are. I love you, Jessima." He loosened his grip, but she didn't move away from him, no man had ever said those three words to her. Her husband Hugo loved the wife before her and couldn't bring himself to lie.

Toby sensed her hesitation and lifted her chin and touched his lips to hers. A jolt of energy rushed through her body and she pressed back. The only man to ever kiss her was Hugo, with his coarse whiskers and onion taste, it was never more than a dutiful peck. The slight pressure urged Toby on and he kissed her passionately. Caught up in the moment, Jessima forgot to breathe.

She pulled away spluttering.

"Are you well? Have I hurt you, Jessima? I'm so sorry. Jessima?"

"I've never been kissed like that before." She caressed his cheeks and brushed droplets off his lashes.

"Ha, well you need to remember to keep breathing." He kissed her again. He tasted of mint. She wrapped her legs around him under the water, her breasts breaking the surface.

Toby pulled her hips close and she felt it. Strong, erect. Hard for her. *Hugo never wanted me, he is never like this.* She started to nibble at his ears and then curiosity took hold and she crept a hand down his body to explore. He groaned. *This is what it should be like! This is what it feels like to be desired!*

Slowly, he put his hand between her legs. "I bet no one has ever touched you like this either."

"Never," she managed.

"Relax," he whispered and she submitted fully to his caresses. A heat built and then she felt a sudden rush between her legs.

"Oh my!"

"May I, er, go further?"

"Yes," she whimpered.

He entered her and she moved on him, like she did with Hugo, who lay on his back like a corpse whilst she did all the work. She had been a virgin when Hugo wed her and she had no experience of love making. She was astonished when Toby took charge. He picked her up, and turned her round, so she was leaning over the edge of the pool, facing the roses. He moved her sopping hair to one side and kissed between her shoulder blades. He thrust and grunted behind her. The water fell in waves over the side of the pool, smacking on the paved slabs.

"I'm ready Jessima," he moaned.

"I consent. I want you to, I do!"

With her permission, he let go, panting in her ear.

"I love you too," she whispered.

He made love to her another two times, their bodies in positions she never thought possible. The clouds cleared and the sky started to lighten. Both knew it was time to leave, but couldn't bring themselves to part.

Her shadow guard had fallen asleep at the door and she snuck past him and back up to the King's chamber. She threw her wet clothes in the bath tub, wrapped a cloth around her sodden mane and sidled into bed with her husband. Toby's seed leaked between her legs, until a wet patch formed on the sheets. She worried the thumping of her heart would wake up the King.

That was the first time she had ever been alone with Toby, and perhaps the last. They had known each other since her wedding to Hugo at the majestic Cleland City Cathedral when she was introduced to three of the King's four brothers. As the youngest, Toby was introduced last and a spark flashed between them. *A connection*, Jessima always called it. *Love at first sight* insisted Toby, but it had taken her a while to get to know him, to trust him, to fall for him. At the beginning they always gravitated towards each other at feasts or special occasions. Then, when his estranged wife died, he would search Jessima out in the gardens or on trips outside the castle. She laughed so much in his presence that her cheeks ached for hours afterwards. Their meetings were always in the company of many others, even King Hugo. *Our friendship has been consummated tonight. My entire body is glowing, Hugo will think I have swallowed the sun!*

Hugo woke with a start. "Jayne?" he asked blinking. "Ah, Jessima. Yes. Of course. Good morning, dear. Ask the servants for my breakfast. And some well brewed tea."

"Shall we pray and thank God for this beautiful morning?" Jessima asked, knowing already what his answer would be. It hadn't changed in nine years.

"Later, deary, later," he said in his deep, scratchy voice. He'd taken an arrow to the throat in the battle with false King Benjamin, he'd lived to tell the tale but his vocal chords had suffered.

He wasn't particularly committed to prayer, but then, neither was she. They both found it a chore, but she felt she should ask anyway. She believed in God, but was trying not to think about Him too much this morning. *What must He be thinking of me for breaking my marriage vows?*

The breakfast was swiftly laid and King Hugo heaved himself from his bed, threw on his robes and sat to eat at the table with Jessima, pulling towards him dishes and plates piled high with food. Jessima selected a small sweetcake with pink icing and placed it in the centre of her plate.

"Do you know what today is, my dear?" he asked.

"No, my dear husband, do tell, what day is today?" Jessima replied, panicking that she had forgotten something critical.

"Today is my grandfather's birthday. The great King Edward. He would've been one hundred and twelve years old."

Hugo chomped on a fig angrily and washed it down with a slurp of tea. She nodded, willing for her husband to continue, he never mentioned his family. He barely talked to her at all. She nibbled at the icing on her cake and then placed it down again, pushing her plate away.

"I was twenty-four when that bastard Benjamin Thorne's rebellion slaughtered King Edward, my grandmother, Queen Amy, and my two uncles, Simon and Timothy, plus Simon's wife and babe. I was desperate to travel to Cleland City and fight Benjamin, but my mother kept us hidden in Lian, vowing the time would come for revenge. She was devastated, her parents and siblings so brutally murdered. I remember her crying at night. She'd just given birth to Toby and rejected the baby, too distraught to care for him in those early months. My brothers and I tended to him as best as we could and in due course mother's grief subsided and the babe became her everything."

Jessima flushed at the reference to Toby and picked up

her cup and held it to her lips blowing on the tea as if to cool it, in an effort to hide her cheeks. She hoped her husband wouldn't remember that she drank it iced.

Oblivious, Hugo beckoned for a servant and pointed at a steaming pot. The servant ladled the porridge into a bowl for the King and placed it in front of him. Hugo wafted a hand over it, impatient for it to cool and, as if locked in battle with his breakfast and to show the porridge he was the superior side, he scooped up a searing spoonful and swallowed. His cheeks burned a deeper red than Jessima's and he fanned at the air in front of his open mouth, making 'ahh' sounds as the porridge burnt his throat on the way down.

He swigged freshly squeezed orange juice and then continued, "It was fifteen years before I was powerful enough to avenge the deaths of my family. To claim back my rightful title of King of Fertilian and put the Clelands back into power. My dear mother Olivia and father Ernest worked tirelessly to build up my armies, to turn Benjamin's supporters to our cause. I hope I have made King Edward proud." Hugo turned his eyes upwards to the heavens as if asking his grandfather.

When no answer came, Jessima said, "I am sure you have made him very proud. You claimed your birthright, you overthrew the false King Benjamin, you have ruled Fertilian for twenty-four years."

"I have been in power for nearly a quarter century, aye, but I have *not* reigned Fertilian. It is split into three, it is not whole. In all these years I have not healed the wounds. King Edward governed a peaceful, contented country, I rule over a broken, unhappy one. I have failed him."

Hugo is disappointed in himself. Jessima pinpointed the reason for his frustrated mood that morning, but she had no idea how to respond, what to do to ease the pain of her old husband. So she stayed silent and offered him the plate of fruit. He picked an apple, took a large bite and ripped the juicy flesh away from the core with a wet crunch.

Then, whilst chewing, he shouted to his servants to get him bathed and ready for court, leaving the teeth-scarred apple on the table to go brown.

King Hugo left his chambers regaled in his finery and crown, resplendent and formidable. His jaw set in dogged determination once again and all traces of the self-doubt wiped away. Jessima called her maids in to dress her, ready for her miniature portraits.

"I shall not be bathing today, please bring my silver dress with all the net underskirts and the train that shimmers like water," she told Marcy whilst Tina started to tidy the room and make the bed.

"No bath, my Queen?" Marcy queried, brows furrowed. This was the first time Jessima had ever foregone a soak in the tub.

"Oh," Tina exclaimed, pointing at the damp patch on the bedsheets. She held it up to Marcy. "I do believe our Queen has been busy making babies with the King!"

Jessima blushed, nothing was sacred from these two handmaids. They had waited on her for the past nine years and fretted worse than her mother.

"You are absolutely right not to wash, my Queen! Keep his seed in there as long as possible." Marcy patted Jessima's red cheeks, grinning. Her maids wanted Jessima's womb to quicken as much as she did, perhaps even more.

"You should lay on your back with hips higher than your head. That's the best way to make a baby, so I've heard." Tina pulled the cushions off the sofa and before Jessima could disagree she was being ushered to the cushions, hips lifted and feet up on the arms of the sofa.

"You truly believe this will work?" she laughed, as Marcy massaged oil into her feet and legs and Tina kneeled behind her brushing her tresses, twisting and twirling strands into an elaborate design.

"Well, we can but try, my Queen." Marcy kneaded her face, dusted on white horse bone powder, applied charcoal to her lashes and then dabbed beetroot stain to her cheeks and lips.

The maids finished their tasks and escorted her to the room set up by the painters. Jessima stood admiring her dress in the mirror, it reminded her of the moonlit pool and it was about to be immortalised in these pictures. Her crown felt as light as a feather, but she knew after a few hours of wear its heaviness would dominate her thoughts.

The master painter manoeuvred her into his desired posture and then his eight miniaturists commenced their portraits. The miniature paintings were sent around the country to hang on castle walls and in churches. Some Lords liked to carry the Queen's picture on their person, believing it brought good fortune. There was a great demand, Jessima's beauty was renowned. The people of Fertilian expected little more of their Queen. Her job was to be like an ornament, silent and pretty to look upon.

She enjoyed sitting still for hours, being pored over, every line copied so precisely. She had perfected her innocent expression after so many sessions. Behind the row of painters, various ladies-in-waiting mulled about, chattering. She ignored them. There came a knock at the door, and a messenger appeared.

"His Grace requires your majestic presence in court, my Queen," he stated, waited for her to nod and left.

She sighed and the master painter sighed with her. It would take a long time to arrange her in the same pose again later. The ladies-in-waiting came forward and together they swished to the court hall.

Jessima was announced, she waited for the scraping of chairs as everyone stood for her entrance and then swept in and took her seat next to the King's elaborate gold throne. The ladies-in-waiting fussed about arranging her train and skirts until she muttered through clenched teeth, "Enough!"

"My Queen," Hugo proclaimed. She played her part, delicately bowing to King Hugo and fixing a slight smile on the corners of her lips.

"My King," she replied sweetly and he turned back to his advisors.

The noise picked up again. People took their seats and she was forgotten. She perused the hall. All the usuals were there plus a number of people Jessima had no clue as to their names. Her gaze caught *his* and she felt her lungs constrict. She blinked at Toby and then continued to scan. She settled into her placid expression, her role to be seen and not heard, and zoned out, daydreaming and fighting the urge to slump in the chair.

The King was listening to a report about this season's crop. Lord Walter Berindonck was blathering on about how the weather was optimal for a healthy harvest and that the lambing season was in full swing. *Blah blah blah. The crop is always good, no change there.* Fertilian was blessed with fertile soil, good rains, mild winters and not too hot summers. Every year was the same, oft they had too much food even after trading with neighbouring Peqkya. Lord Berindonck droned on. Jessima discreetly picked at a thread on her dress.

Up stepped Lord Zachary Macune, one of Hugo's generals and the change of voice startled Jessima. Lord Macune talked of the situation in the north east of Fertilian, the area held by the false Prince Arthur Thorne, Benjamin's son. Awful Arthur, as Jessima had nicknamed him. Awful Arthur was up to his old tricks again. Hugo waved at Lord Alon Sumner to give him a report on Arthur's twin sister Mary who also claimed the throne, being the older of the twins, but a female. Miserable Mary was causing trouble in the south east, and the threat of attack was imminent.

The first few years after Hugo claimed back his Kingdom had seen fierce battles and huge losses. Massacre and mayhem. Hugo had forced both Thorne armies back into their respective lands and a stalemate had ensued for two decades. Jessima didn't understand what had happened but all of a sudden Mary and Arthur Thorne had decided to stop fighting each other and join forces to launch an attack on Hugo. *The Gruesome Twosome.*

Hugo's forehead scrunched up with deep worry lines like the folds in her dress. The Gruesome Twosome's army posed a formidable threat, and scouts had reported that the joint army was now gathered in Rotchurch City, a few weeks' march from where they sat. It had taken a month or two for Mary's force to traipse up to Arthur's lands from Edester City, and there had been plenty of doubt that their truce would last, all expecting Awful Arthur's army to turn on Miserable Mary's men. But it had happened – they were as one and preparing for battle.

"What of Peqkya? Will they support us?" King Hugo asked.

"The cats have sent six emissaries back to us minus manhood and tongue with the same message carved into each man. We have since found and sent three competent women who returned unmutilated but with the same communication," said Toby. "They still ask us to send our Queen to negotiate with them. And I maintain that is folly!"

Jessima had an inkling of why she had been sent for and sat up straighter.

"I agreed with you, Toby, of course we cannot send our Queen," King Hugo croaked. "But our time is running out. Without Peqkya's support we do not have enough men to meet the Thorne's joint force. We lost thousands to that raging pestilence a year past and now we are outnumbered. I cannot go to Peqkya, I cannot be away from here and it is unknown how they will react to me as a man, even though I am the King." Hugo paused and turned to his Queen. "With the right men protecting her, I believe we can send Queen Jessima as our envoy. Plus, I want her away from Cleland City when war breaks out."

"*When* your Grace?" Lord Sumner said. "You seem sure that war will happen."

"Why would they be amassing soldiers so close to our borders, so close to our capital if they do not plan to attack. Are they sat there throwing dice and drinking wine? No, they mean to attack! And soon, as they know we are weak. That is what I would do." The King shouted as loud as his broken voice would allow so that no one in the hall could be mistaken, "War is coming! Brace yourselves for it my lords, my ladies. This pretend peace is done; bloodshed will soon be upon us."

"Conflict is coming, I agree, your Grace, but surely we can find more men rather than get *women* from Peqkya," Toby retorted.

"We have no more men. You know this, we have exhausted our people. All boys, men, grandfathers are armed and ready. Lian has sent as many able-bodied men as they can. The Peqkian warriors are disciplined and deadly. We need these *women.*"

"The cats will not support us. We have tried to communicate with them and it has proved fruitless!" Toby was exasperated and the tips of his ears turned beetroot, like the shade of Jessima's lipstain.

"We have not tried everything, Toby," Hugo said.

"We cannot send Queen Jessima," Toby persisted. "It is too risky, your Grace. What happens if they choose to mutilate or maim her? Or worse, take her life?"

"They stipulate that we send the Queen. I believe they will treat her with the courtesy that is due to her. They are a nation ruled by women, the Melokai wants to deal with another woman."

"No! We cannot endanger her life," Toby shouted, a little too fervently and everyone turned towards him. Hugo glared at him and started to raise out of his throne. He allowed his brothers to get away with more insolence than his lords, but Toby had gone too far and was in trouble.

"I will go," Jessima blurted, standing up from her chair. Hugo's attention turned from her love and to his Queen. "I shall venture to Peqkya and I will do everything in my power to get the Melokai to support our noble Kingdom and send warriors to fight alongside us."

All were silent. *What am I saying? I have no idea what I'm doing.* Toby looked horrified. Jessima smiled broadly, as if she had everything under control.

"Exceedingly brave, my dear," said the King, patting her hand. She sat back in her chair, floating stars twinkling in her vision.

"Prince Toby." King Hugo turned to his stricken brother. "You shall have the pleasure of accompanying my Queen and return her to me unharmed, leading a host of Peqkya's fiercest warriors."

15

FERRAZ

A gentle tap on Ferraz's cell door and Mikaz entered. Ferraz sat up in bed, alarmed. They had not agreed to go out that night.

"Ferraz, I must see him. I have to say goodbye," Mikaz whispered.

"It is not wise, Mikaz."

Mikaz sniffled, then his breath started catching and Ferraz knew that before long the sobs would start. Mikaz had been sobbing for three days, since Slim Stavaz was taken away. The love of Mikaz's life was in the marketplace suffering the slow, horrific death of an unsatisfactory PG. The warrior Lizya had reported Stav as failing to pleasure her at the deflowering ceremony so Stav's cock had been cut off, stuffed in his mouth and a stake had been rammed up his anus.

Just as a fresh bout of sobs gurgled up from the old PG's chest, Ferraz said, "We can go, but be silent or we will be discovered."

Mikaz quietened and in the moonlight that crept through the window shutter, Ferraz saw him nod.

They left the cell through the secret passage, jogged from the bank of the stream into the city and to the marketplace. It was deserted, everyone in Riaow asleep.

But there was Stav. In the middle, for all to see, serving as a reminder to all peons of women's dominance.

Mikaz ran to the stake and pulled back his hood looking up at the broken body, tears streaming. "Stav, my love, oh Stavaz. What have they done to you." He stretched up and touched Stav's toe.

Stav opened his eyes and squirmed against his bindings, desperate to reach out one last time to Mikaz but instead pushing the pole further up. Stav tried to speak through the gag, but all Ferraz could hear was muffles and distressed groans.

"Oh, my love, my love…" Mikaz repeated, choking.

The life drained out of Stav and he went limp, his head flopping down. Mikaz dropped to his knees and started to wail, flailing his arms and ripping at his hair.

Ferraz ran to him. "Be silent! You'll have the entire city's patrol warriors on us."

But Mikaz wouldn't stop.

Ferraz glanced about the square for any sign of movement and then shook his friend. "Quiet! You cannot avenge Stav's death if we are caught."

That did it. Mikaz silenced immediately and clenched his jaw. He took one last look at Stav and they ran back to the cells, tears streaming down the old PG's cheeks.

At lunch, they met in the PG communal area and sat in a dark corner. Mikaz was bawling, with raw eyes, snot streaming and spittle hanging from his mouth.

Ferraz kept a tight arm around the old PG's heaving shoulders. "Come on, you need to pull yourself together. If a call comes for you tonight and you're like this, you'll end up like Stav on a stake."

Ferraz glanced over to the set administrator. She was ignoring the commotion in the dark corner. For now. She liked Mikaz, he'd been in the set for a long time, and she was bending the rules for him. Anyone else making such a disturbance would have been reprimanded by now, but

Ferraz wasn't sure how long her patience would last.

"Come on now," he said again and gave Mikaz's shoulders a squeeze.

Mikaz entered a trance and he sat very still and silent. Ferraz rubbed his back.

"Ferraz, a call for you," the set administrator shouted.

Ferraz gave Mikaz a kiss on the head but the old PG didn't seem to notice. Ferraz pulled on his cloak and then followed Rivya's clevercat to the Head Trader's apartments.

"Ah, Ferraz, come in. Sit," Rivya said when he entered her bed chambers. "Tell me."

"Rivya, I have enlisted the support of another PG as well as several peons. I meet them again in a few days."

"Good. At this stage, we need numbers. The rebellion will not work unless we are supported by the masses. We have time. Get them riled up, Ferraz, get them recruiting every peon in the city."

"Yes, Rivya… any news of Irrya?" Ferraz was anxious to be reunited with the courtesan. He wanted to talk to her about the recent deflowering ceremony where he had seen the repellent creature Ramya now favoured.

"Irrya hasn't called for you? She returned from Drome days ago. It was a successful mission, she was perfect. She is the spark that will fire up the cammers! Because of Irrya, there is a new High Priest who backs our cause. Drome's support is swelling, soon the whole desert nation will rise up to overthrow the Melokai in the name of their made-up God."

Ferraz forced a smile. *Irrya has been back for days and not called me?*

"I'm sending back Ashya and Toya to carry some critical messages to our cammer friends under the guise of trade negotiations. I just need the Melokai's approval for another delegation to Parchad, but that won't be hard, she trusts me implicitly. Ha!" Rivya cackled and then with a flick of a bejewelled hand, dismissed Ferraz.

***

A few days later, in the dead of night, Ferraz and Mikaz slipped out to meet the peons in the city. Ferraz had told Mikaz not to come, but the PG was adamant.

"I hate Ramya. I want her destroyed. We need to free *men* from this sexual bondage." Mikaz's sorrow had transformed into fury, his teeth clenched and hands balled in tight fists. Ferraz had been shocked by his boldness, for using a forbidden word, but then admired his courage.

The two PGs snuck down an alleyway in a quiet part of town inhabited by peons and avoided the marketplace. Ferraz found the right drain and lifted the cover and lowered himself down, tailed by Mikaz.

"Friends," a nasally voice croaked from the shadows.

"Friends," Ferraz replied.

A candle was lit and the peon led the PGs along a low, stinking tunnel. Splashing through the city's shit and kicking the few rats that had escaped the cats, out of the way. The smell reached Ferraz's stomach and he doubled over and heaved up his dinner.

They climbed a few stairs and came out on an open, dry platform with the shit river trudging beside it. There sat two other peons. Several stools and pallets had been organised around a small fire. A cosy, but putrid, meeting place.

"Wevo, Steely, good to see you." Ferraz nodded to them both. His voice echoed down the tunnels.

"Take a seat," Steely rasped, a short, squat metal worker with ginormous biceps. "This is Shit-pick, he knows these drains 'n sewers. His job is cleanin' our streets 'n making sure the shit doesn't stagnate down 'ere. He showed us this place 'n this is where we'll meet from 'ere on."

Shit-pick took a seat and eyed the PGs suspiciously. He had a gaunt look and his nostrils had been sewn shut to block out the stench.

"Right, now we's all introduced, let's get started,"

Wevo began. He was a skinny weaver in Glendya's goat hair works, that produced Riat's best carpets using some new technique that Wevo complained put the peon weavers at extreme risk. His hands were cracked and swollen, lined with scabs and calluses. These peons had been selected by their fellow workers to deal with the PGs. They preferred not to reveal their given names, using monikers they had chosen based on their profession.

Wevo continued, "We 'ave been workin' 'ard and got more peons. From different industries like stable 'ands 'n' farmers, carpenters 'n' masons, slaughterhouse workers 'n' candlemakers. All sorts. We 'ave near one hundred peons."

"All willin' to rebel against the Melokai and way of life." Steely slapped his bulging forearm for emphasis.

"One hundred peons, that is not enough," Mikaz spat.

The thick voice of Shit-pick snarled, "We're workin' on it, pretty peen. How many peons you got?"

"My job isn't finding a few peons, shit face." Mikaz got to his feet, and Shit-pick stood to meet him.

"You wouldn't know nothin' about jobs or 'ardship! You don't work err'day in the city's shit. You zhaq PGs live a pampered life."

"Enough! We are friends here." Ferraz indicated for them to take their seats again. Mikaz's rage was going to cause issues if he couldn't channel it. "That is excellent news, Wevo. What is your plan to find more supporters? We have time."

"Err'day peons pledge their support," Wevo said. "We will reach two 'undred in a month or two. 'haps more."

"Good. At this stage, we need numbers. The rebellion will not work unless we are supported by the masses. Drome's support is swelling, soon the whole desert nation will rise up to overthrow the Melokai," Ferraz repeated Riv's words. He wasn't exactly sure what was happening in Drome, but the Head Trader seemed certain it was going to plan.

"We will be equal to women, *men* will be powerful

again," Steely shouted and pumped his huge arm in the air to roars from the others.

Mikaz clapped him on the back. "That's the spirit!"

"We will meet again in one week's time," Ferraz said as the cheering died down. "I will pass on your news that we should have two hundred peons on side in the next month or two and that this number is growing fast."

***

That evening Irrya's clevercat came for Ferraz. Her room smelt of lavender, too strong, as if the courtesan had doused herself and everything about her with the oil. Deep lines creased her forehead and she had plucked most of the orange thread from her braids. She sat absently picking at the frayed edges.

"My love, what has happened?" Ferraz dropped at Irrya's feet, holding her ankles and kissing her knees.

"My task was… shameful. I am despoiled," Irrya stuttered and she sunk to the floor next to Ferraz.

"No, my love, your task was a success! You have joined Drome to our cause."

"I… I had to give myself to a cammer. If I had known that would be my task I would have refused. I scrubbed myself for hours afterwards, but I feel his seed is still in me. It is repulsive. I am repulsive."

Ferraz's brows furrowed as he considered this. He was used to giving himself to another without question or thought, but she wasn't. "You are beautiful, you are strong, you are kind and passionate. We will have a new Peqkya because of you. Do not be sad, my love." He kissed her, but he could not raise a smile. He picked her up and carried her to the bed.

"Let me make you feel better, my love." He moved his palm up her thigh, doing the only thing he knew he could do well that might cheer her up.

"No, don't touch me! Don't ever touch me down there. I reek of that revolting cammer priest."

She spun away from Ferraz and hid under a pillow. He

lay behind her and put his arm around her, pulling her back into his chest and holding her tight.

16

VIOLYA

ଔଓ

The tall bamboos swayed in the wind, random gusts pushed the hollow stems sideways for a few moments before they sprung upright again. The warrior Violya loved the bamboo forest, a short hike out of Riaow. The endless rustling soothed her. She lay in the usual secluded spot, her long, lean limbs stretched out. Watching the towering grass as she waited for Emmya, for their weekly *whine and wine* get together.

This place held many memories for the warrior, imprinted on her soul.

"Run!" Emmya had yelled, when they were seven years old, and her friend couldn't hold off V's attackers any longer. Emmya had opened the cupboard door where V cowered, and shouted. V had run, with the bully Sianya on her heels, but V had kept going long after Sianya had given up. Out of the city, deeper into the sentry-like bamboos, away from the pen. She'd stumbled to a stop in a small clearing, the very place she now sat. The tall stems had stood watch over her, the swishing hiding the sound of V crying.

Sianya was vicious, broad, mean. Taller than V but still insisted on mocking V's height. V hadn't filled out, her gawky, long limbs flapped off her skinny frame. Her reddish hair another trigger for taunts. Matchstick, they used to call her. Or pole, or gangly arms.

"Sianya's just jealous that you're nearly as tall as her," Emmya would say. V's loyal, fearless friend. Half the size of Sianya, but twice as quick.

It had been dark in that cupboard. V shrunk into the shadows, terrified, as she heard Emmya scrapping to keep back the bullies, kicking, punching, poking. That's when V's magic first ignited, a surge of frothing lava that travelled from V's toes to her head and out her hands. It produced a ball of light in V's palms that illuminated the dank shelves that she hid under. Then the door had opened, the light fizzled to nothing and V had bolted.

"Welcome, Violya, to The Sight. I am pleased to make your acquaintance," Sybilya had said in V's mind, when the tears had dried. The Stone Prophetess's voice was firmer then, smoother. It seemed to hang in V's skull, long tendrils seeking and caressing every unfathomable corner of her being. "You must show others your signs of magic, learn your craft."

"No!" V blurted. *Not another thing to be picked on for.* "I hate being different to others, I hate standing out."

Sybilya purred, calming V's distress. "I respect your decision, Violya, but one day your magic will prevail. When you are ready, come to me and I will teach you."

V rebuffed the magic that tickled beneath her skin, itching to get out. Ignored its incessant chattering, its constant thrashing against her every decision, her every movement. "You could shrink to the size of a pebble if you wanted," it would tell her when she was in the midst of an escape from Sianya. "Shut up," V would reply.

Eventually, V silenced the magic. Denied but not forgotten, it bristled in her blood. Her teenage years were filled instead with crippling self-doubt. She was the best young warrior in the city but racked by voices, so many voices, that told her she was no good, that her instructors had made a mistake, that she should request early elimination and stop embarrassing herself by showing up to warrior training, and so on.

In those days, she crept out to the bamboo forest in the dead of night and secretly cut herself with her dagger, first on the soles of her feet and then, when all the flesh there was marked, on her upper thighs. The release of blood dulled the voices and eased the magic's pent up frustration.

After a particularly vicious session, when V was seventeen, she passed out and Sybilya came to her again. All the voices stopped, to be replaced with one.

"Believe in yourself," the Stone Prophetess had told her. "Go north east, past the Melioks, explore the world, explore yourself. Go on your eighteenth birthday and return to Riaow on your nineteenth birthday. Not a day less, not a day more."

The next morning, when V hadn't arrived for their daylight dances, Emmya had found her in their place in the bamboos, carried her back to the city and straight to Gogo. In a daze, V had told the Head Warrior of her vision and what she must do. Gogo gave her approval, and a few days later, on V's birthday, she went north east. She never harmed herself again.

Emmya called it 'V's Lost Year' and didn't ask what V had done or where she had gone, Emmya simply accepted it. V arrived home with a new aura. Her skin had always been darker than the average Peqkian, so black that in sunshine it seemed to shine silver, but Emmya insisted that it now had a gleam to it, like oil on water. V's hair had turned a vivid red. She kept it closely shaved, hating the attention it drew.

As if keeping her magic at bay wasn't torture enough, V returned from her Lost Year with another secret. It ashamed the warrior, certain she had let Sybilya down. V didn't explore and didn't find herself. She had found something, some*one*, and stayed in the same place with him. V pinched her wrist. *Keep them buried.*

"Boo." Emmya jumped out of the bamboo, pouncing on V.

"Zhaq! You cockface," V cried, her heart thumping. They hugged tightly.

"Right, let's get drinking. I've got so much to tell you, seed sacks." Emmya tied up her long, thin braids in a bow on top of her head and pulled out a flask of wine from her pack. She filled the two cups that V had brought. She handed one to V.

They tapped cups and V took a huge swig. "And I have so much to tell you!"

"You first." Emmya guzzled down her wine and then lay back and stared up at the swaying forest.

"I won't be babysitting Ramya's bedthing anymore."

"Hurrah!"

"Yup, his droning was starting to do my head in." V hummed in her friend's ear. Emmya swatted her away.

"But I hear he has a huge cock, like his hands and feet. I still say you should've had a go. He's blind, he would never have known it was you and not the Melokai."

"I would've eaten him alive, Em. The Melokai would've come back to a pile of bones and a hole in the bed."

"True. You and your big appetite. You are a right fatty." Emmya prodded V's belly. There was no fat to be found, V's muscular stomach was the envy of most of the warriors in the capital, as was her height. She still towered over the average Peqkian, but was no longer bullied for it.

Emmya asked, "So what will you be doing?"

"I'm being sent on a trade mission. I'll be leading nine warriors."

"Issee, Vee Vee, that's brilliant. I knew you'd make Captain soon. Well done you."

Emmya's praise reassured V, supressing her worry that Gogo had made a mistake.

"Where are you going to?" Emmya refilled their cups.

"Pygmie land."

"Issee, I thought Ramya hated them?"

"Yup, she does. But there is money to be made and some contact has been established. Anyway, what's your news?"

Emmya put down her cup and announced grandly. "While you are going to see the little people, I am going to see the desert cammers."

"You are going to Drome?"

"I am also accompanying a trading party, to the capital Parchad. There's been a few trade delegations heading there recently but there's been some religious weirdness since the last visit and Peqkians aren't particularly well liked at the moment."

"That doesn't sound good, Em."

"Nope, which is why they are stepping up the number of warriors. I'll be led by old Ashya, a few of us are joining her usual warriors."

"I'm not keen on that stinky cat, never have been."

"Me neither," Emmya agreed. "Ashya is brutal but her warriors love her. That's why Gogo allowed her to keep control of her company. Ashya's warriors all threatened early elimination otherwise."

"Look after yourself, Em, most of Ashya's warriors are cockfaces too. And make sure you stay clean, it's rumoured Ashya hasn't washed in forty odd years."

"Don't worry about me, Vee Vee, I'll keep it clean. You are the one heading off into uncharted territory!"

"True. And guess what? I leave tomorrow." V threw her arm around Emmya's shoulders, kissing her friend's cheek.

"Tomorrow! No weekly whine and wines for a while then. How sad. I'll just have to find me a new pal. Perhaps one of Ashya's cockface warriors or maybe a humpy cammer. They'd probably make a better friend, I don't know why I've put up with you for this long anyway."

V stuck out her tongue and pretended to pour her drink on Emmya's head, and they fell about laughing.

***

The trading party marched for three weeks on the meandering West Way, through forest, open grasslands, over hills, through busy towns and small villages, past farms and vast herds of sheep, cattle and goats. V enjoyed passing along the side of lush valleys, with enormous trees, ferns and vivid green moss everywhere. The low, fluffy clouds and tinkling of streams relaxed her. She had been tense since leaving Riaow, fretting that some of the warriors she led were older and more experienced than her.

The procession consisted of ten warriors riding bareback on horses, four traders on donkeys, a scholar on a tiny pony, three hulking yaks hauling carts, two clevercat messengers, ten donkeys laden with trading goods, and fifteen serving peons on foot. Six days before they reached Ashen Valley, they were the only ones on the road. At the valley, they turned north but V stopped the group.

"We will take a detour to visit the hallowed place where the stone army has stood for one thousand years and pay our respects to the birthplace of Peqkya. Any who do not want to come, wait for us here."

All in the group wanted to visit, none had been before, and even the peons were keen, so they picked their way through an overgrown path that hugged the side of a low mountain peak. The slopes were dotted with alpine buttercups and the vibrant yellow glowed bright against the grey rock. Jozya was beside herself with excitement and V could hear the assistant trader chattering behind her.

"I do adore those two, so in love. The Melokai has found her soulmatch. It is beautiful. I know some find it odd as Gwrlain is not a Peqkian, but I think it is wonderful. Do you have a soulmatch, Robya?"

"No," the shy, bookish, apprentice scholar mumbled. Robya was tall and thin and seemed to bend with the slightest gust of wind, as if she belonged in the bamboo forest. Although tall, V still loomed over the scholar.

"Oh, you will one day, my dear, I'm sure. Look at you, a beauty. I always wanted to be long limbed, but look at me. I'm sure I'll get along well with the pygmies, being so small myself." Joz laughed and V joined in.

Noticing V's laughter, the assistant trader urged on her donkey so she rode alongside the warrior. Joz was small and slender with twig like arms, and constantly buzzed, like a bee. "How about you, darling V? Do you have a true love?"

"No," V answered. *My soulmatch is long gone.*

Joz beamed brightly, her almond shaped eyes looking kindly at the warrior. "Well it is tough with all those delicious PGs to pick from and not many options otherwise. I, too, am without a companion. I'm rather choosy…"

The path came out on a low, wide valley. The air had a sharp chill and a gloomy fog hung over the middle of the valley, hiding the floor.

Joz's mouth stopped working and she shivered.

"We are here," Robya announced in a barely audible voice, staring down at her pony's honey coloured mane.

V split the group to ensure the animals and trading goods were well guarded. Her warriors did as she bid. It still felt strange to be the one giving commands as the captain and not taking them. She ordered the peons to tend to the horses. Horses were rare in Peqkya and most warriors rode ponies or went on foot. It was an indication of the importance of this mission and the rank of the warriors that led it, but the horses made V feel awkward. *Surely another warrior is more deserving of my mount.*

In the first group, V, apprentice scholar Robya, assistant trader Joz plus the two senior warriors Laurya and Finya climbed down the valley, leaving the others guarding, or resting, behind.

Deeper into the murkiness they descended, the white fog shrouding them completely, until they could barely see two steps in front. They crept along the valley floor in single file, each with their hand on the shoulder of the person in front, next to an angry river that thundered around huge boulders in its haste to get away from the place. There was no other sound, nothing dared to live here. The earth the armies stood on had also been turned to stone by the Stone Prophetess, as well as every living thing.

V led the group and stopped to allow everyone to catch up. She pointed. "There."

To her left was the first stone man. On the valley floor the mist cleared, and stretched out in front of them, as far as the eye could see, were Xayy men and beasts in the throes of battle, swords in hands, horses reared up, tigers with fangs bared, chariots turned over.

"Sybilya save us," Joz muttered, hugging herself tight. "This place is eerie."

The group stumbled and climbed over stone bodies and stray limbs towards to the front line, where the two armies had crashed into each other. A creaking echoed throughout the stone men.

"We should find the two Melokaz. They were locked in battle when Sybilya cursed them," Robya whispered.

V looked left and right along the line. *"That way,"* Sybilya's faint voice spoke in V's mind. V turned right and made her way through the twisted faces and broken bodies to the warring male rulers. Locked forever in an angry clinch, swords crossed and mouths snarled, the pair had a clear circle around them.

"Which is which, Robya?" V said.

The apprentice scholar studied them. "This one in armour is Melokaz Ashrav. This one without, is Melokaz Shavanaz."

Ashrav's army was dressed in primitive armour and had shields, whereas Shavanaz's men were dressed more like her, with daggers strapped to their arms and in leather. V walked around the two. Melokaz Shavanaz's face drew her attention and she stared, leaning in closer.

He blinked.

Startled, she grabbed her sword hilt poised to fight. The face was stone. *A trick of the eye only.*

"Let us find Sybilya's hill," she called to the others and marched away briskly. Her magic, dormant for years, tingled in her toes. The rest of the group jogged behind.

The Stone Prophetess had been watching the Battle of Ashen from a nearby hill, and they soon found the location through the tall grass. There was a large scorched circle, blackened by the magic. It stank of burning and the air was stifling with ash motes floating aimlessly.

V dropped to her knees on the hot ground and took a handful of the charred earth, clenching it in her fist and then letting it spill through her fingers over her forehead, leaving a small red mark. Her warriors copied her. Robya and Joz did the same.

***

"V, why did you do that in the scorched circle?" Robya asked when they had set up camp for the night at the start of the North West Road. The scholar touched her finger to the burn mark on her hair line.

V's magic had taken control on Sybilya's hill, stirring and then erupting so intensely that V couldn't deny it. But she wasn't about to tell Robya that. "I don't know, thought it was the right thing to do."

"I think it was. Thank you for showing us." Robya moved to her crude bed under a sheet of greased felt that hung between two trees. When possible, the scholar liked to sleep outside rather than in a dome tent. She pulled out a wad of parchment and a pencil and started to jot down the day's adventures. Robya documented everything, as was her task, and occasionally smiled to herself at some funny moment or memory.

It was a clear, warm night and Violya looked up at the stars in the sky. Robya had spent a similar evening a few days back teaching V and Joz the names and the formations. Two warriors were on guard, patrolling the perimeter of the camp. V did not think they would face any trouble, but huge lizards the size of a pig called this part of Peqkya their home and they had spotted a nest of the reptile eggs close by, so V decided to be cautious.

V's watch was a few hours away and she found her mat, the entrance to her tent facing Riaow as was custom. V never had problems sleeping, Emmya was the opposite and spent hours tossing and turning before she nodded off. But tonight, V fidgeted. For the first time since the cupboard, her magic, that *other*, had overruled her, had become her.

***

A pinch on V's face woke her and she sat bolt upright dagger drawn, ready to attack. It was Fin, who had her finger to her lips.

"V, there is something in the woods," she whispered. She pointed to her ear. *Listen.*

An owl hooted. V hoped it would be a giant lizard, she'd always wanted to see one of the elusive creatures. But then came a sharp cracking noise, the sound of heavy feet on the undergrowth and a deep, fractured groan from the distance.

"Wake the warriors, Fin." V tiptoed like a cat towards the noise, spear in hand.

It was not the reptile.

In the moonlight, she saw a lumbering figure. A hideous noise accompanied each move the thing made, like stone grinding on stone and bright sparks flew from its body. Moving seemed to be a massive effort.

She sensed the presence of her warriors to each side and could hear hurried movement as the rest of the camp prepared for a potential attack. The warriors skulked forward, moving to form a semi-circle around the creature. V's magic crackled in her fingers. *Danger.*

The creature let out a roar that split the night in two. It sounded like a stone wall crashing to the floor.

V ran forward screaming at the creature and her

warriors charged. It roared again then turned and smashed through the forest away from them. Sparks flew with each step and a burnt smell lingered. V ordered her warriors not to pursue.

"Must've been a forest demon, like the shepherd we met on the West Way told us," Laurya said.

"Must've been," V said, but her instinct told her otherwise. *No. That was a stone man. Wearing Ashrav's armour.*

17

AMMAD

Wheezing after sparring with four of his guards, the Crown Prince of Drome rested on one side of the sandy fighting pit to allow the next group to train and to catch his breath. Ammad watched his brother. His mother Jakira had been insisting for months that he bring Selmi along, and Ammad had finally relented. Sel was tall and wiry, friendly rather than ferocious. He was a decent camel rider but not in the slightest bit competitive. He had been riding since he was three, and Jakira affectionately joked that "Selmi could ride before he could walk," but Ammad doubted it. *I am definitely a better rider than he is.*

A guard broke Sel's defence and stabbed him with a wooden sword. Instead of getting angry and forcing his opponent back, his brother shouted, "Great shot!". *He'll be eaten alive on a battlefield.* Ammad's men mocked Sel to his face – a son of the Ruler no less – but Sel didn't care.

"Crown Prince. Come and fight the calfling, I'm bored of his feeble jabs," Qabull shouted, Ammad's brutal guard with an angry scar from ear to mouth. Sel dropped his practice sword and rubbed some dust from his eye. Qabull spun around and with one foot, took out Sel's ankles. Sel fell to the floor and landed hard on his rump. The guards howled, Ammad shook his head but Sel joined in.

"I guess I deserved that," he chuckled.

"Get up you fool," Ammad growled as he took a start position in front of his little brother. Sel clambered to his feet and into position.

Ammad lunged. He went on the offensive, slashing and stabbing but Sel's ingratiating smile never left his face. A face that looked so much like Ammad's own. The Crown Prince was so aggressive with his assault that the guards stopped to watch. But Sel held him off, meeting every swipe calmly. *Baby brother is concentrating on the fight and he is... good. Very good.* Soon Ammad was exhausted and had no desire to lose face in front of his men.

"Enough," he howled at Sel and beckoned to his men. "Let us eat and drink."

Quick as a flash, Sel stabbed Ammad's chest. A steel sword would have split Ammad's heart and pierced through his hump.

"Gotcha," Sel exclaimed, grinning.

Ammad dropped his sword and went for his brother with his fists. Two guards dragged him off as Sel cowered in the sand, arms covering his head.

Qabull hauled Sel to his feet. "Don't piss off your brother, runt."

Ammad marched across the pit towards the palace kitchens, followed by his ten guards. Sel trailed behind, the grin wiped off his face.

The merciless sun was high in the sky, and the sand was scorching. There was no one around, most choosing to take a midday nap, staying inside the cooler rooms within the shuttered air towers.

"Over there," the guard, Onhirid, said.

A lone woman stood by the stables, admiring the camels and feeding one from her hand. A Peqkian warrior with long thin braids tied up in a pile on her head.

"Let's go lads, I want that hisspit," Ammad ordered, a grim glint in his eye. *She's no Jozya but she'll do.*

The warrior noticed the group of twelve men stalking towards her and she grabbed both daggers, ready to brawl. She fought savagely, slashing and hissing but they closed in around her and pushed her into the pen with the camel.

"Ammad! What are you doing? Stop this. She is a guest in Drome, staying at the women's quarters. She arrived here last night with Toya's trading party. Toya is staying with Mama. Ammad! What will aunty Riv think when she hears. Ammad, stop," Selmi shouted, trying to wrench men off the black skinned fighter. Qabull turned and punched Sel so hard in the face that he collapsed. The guard looked down at the motionless boy and then up at Ammad, worry crossing his face, but Ammad nodded his approval.

Ammad and his guards overwhelmed the warrior and five men shoved her down in the hay. One guard seized her head and covered her mouth but she muttered the same words over and over. Ammad did not understand the Shella. Men grappled with her arms and others spread her legs. She was freakishly strong and would not stay still. Another guard restrained the agitated camel and the others kept watch on the courtyard.

"You're going to love this. I've always wanted to fuck a hisspit," Ammad told her sweetly as he cut off her leather shorts with one of her own daggers. He shunted himself into her. She thrashed wildly, and he flopped out.

"Hold her down," he screamed at his men. One of the guards on watch came over to help.

He thrust into her a second time. He laughed in her face but her stare was so full of loathing that he had to look away for risk of losing his erection. He spurted in seconds and rolled off.

"Lads, help yourself."

He soothed the prized camel, stroking its smooth neck, whilst his men took turns. She still fought them fiercely, but watched Ammad. He could feel her eyes burning the back of his head and her mumbling rattled in his ears. Her repulsion etched in his memory and rather than feel satisfied at finally having a Peqkian, he felt... peculiar.

When they were all done, Qabull punched her in the head and she passed out like Selmi.

"Leave her. Find a stable boy to blame. Bring him." Ammad kicked Sel's slumped body.

***

"What happened to your brother?" Jakira dug her long nails into Ammad's arm as they took their cushions for dinner. Ammad had been avoiding his mother all afternoon. Sel sat opposite, he was sullen and had a dark welt around one eye.

"He is covered in bruises, he slept all afternoon and refuses to speak," his mother insisted, tightening her grip on Ammad's bicep.

"He took a tumble when we were training, it's dented his ego. That's all, Mama." Ammad took a slug of chilled camel's milk. "Isn't that right, Sel?"

Sel peered at his lap, the corners of his mouth turned down and didn't utter a word. He had woken in Ammad's quarters and immediately started blathering about the hisspit. Ammad had slapped him and told him that if he breathed another word about it, his friend Baghadd, the son of the cook at his mother's craterside villa, would be trampled to death by Sel's favourite camel. Then that camel would have its legs amputated and be left to bleed to death, not understanding why it couldn't move anymore. Sel had not said another word after the threat, about anything.

Everybody noticed the absence of his brother's usual cheery demeanour, including his father. Ruler Mastiq didn't have much time for Sel, he had more important children than his sixth son, but enjoyed a quick chatter with the boy when Jakira brought him to the palace. Sel usually went bounding up to his father to say hello like a puppy, but today he had loitered behind his mother as Our Ruler had entered the room. Selmi's sulk wafted off him like a bad smell.

"Of course this has nothing to do with the dead hisspit warrior found in the camel stables, does it, Ammad?" said his mother, keeping her voice low. Sel's eyes flicked up, but his mouth remained firmly shut.

"What dead warrior? What are you talking about?" Ammad casually popped a piece of watermelon in his mouth.

"She was found slashed from vagina up to belly button and her insides spilling out. She'd bled to death and the dagger was in her hand."

"Sounds like she killed herself, Mama. Who cares?"

"I care. She had been beaten to a pulp and there were clear signs she had been taken against her will."

"Must've been a stable hand. Anyway, what's for the first course? I'm starving." He clicked his fingers to get a slave's attention, attempting to jerk free of his mother's grasp.

"The poor girl had etched something in her arm with the dagger."

He reached for another chunk of fruit. "This melon is delicious, especially with a squeeze of lime…"

"Three Shella letters."

"So what, Mama." He made a point of huffing loudly. "Let's talk about something else."

"She was trying to spell Ammad."

Ammad's hump prickled. Jakira knew, she always knew. He dropped the chunk on the table and put his hands in his lap, eyes cast down, cowering under the blaze of his mother's golden eyes. If they had been alone she would have taken off her slipper and whacked it around his ears. The busy dining hall saved him from that humiliation.

"Do you know what happens to rapists in Peqkya, my son? Any man who dares force himself on a woman and is caught, has his penis flayed. The woman, if she is still alive and can name her attacker, slowly peels off the skin. Then she cooks it however she chooses and the man is forced to eat it. He is then stripped naked and tied over a box in the marketplace, his mouth filled with mortar that sets solid to stifle his screams. All and every person who so fancies can then rape that man by poking sticks or poles or knives or anything they choose up his backside. They can throw stones at him or degrade him however they choose. Eventually this pathetic creature dies from his wounds or from starvation or both, and he is cut down and fed to hungry pigs. Riv tells me that pigs fattened with male flesh taste the best."

"Sounds nasty. I do hope there's pork served later, roasted with camel's milk cheese."

"Riv also tells me that a woman who knows she will not live to identify her attacker calls to the stone lady, their witch mother, to put a curse on him."

Ammad swallowed and shifted on his cushion. Jakira put an arm around him and pressed him close for a kiss on the cheek, but also to bring her mouth next to his ear. She did not want Sel or anyone else to hear what she had to say next. Her sweet smell of aniseed and nutmeg swilled in his nostrils.

"She was here with Riv's trading party, you stupid boy," she snarled. "Always ruled by your damn penis. You let her know your name! Sometimes I think you cannot be my child, so reckless. I should've allowed you to cleanse, perhaps that would've scared some sense into you. What are we going to tell your father? What will Riv tell her Melokai? This draws unwanted attention to Drome. I have requested an audience with you and Our Ruler after dinner to fix this."

Jakira clacked her teeth in his ear, slid her arm away and started a cheerful conversation with the woman sat on her other side. Ammad sighed with relief. Sel glared at him across the table. When no one was looking their way Ammad picked up the dropped watermelon and threw it at Sel's head. It bounced off his bruise, leaving a wet smear. Sel picked up his meat knife and threw it at Ammad. It skimmed Ammad's ear and stuck into the wall behind with a thunk. Ammad felt a tiny trickle of blood run down his neck from the nick. He frowned at his little brother. *When did he learn to throw a knife like that? That must have been sheer luck.*

Sel touched his fingertips to the tiny scar beneath his right ear. A reminder of the wound that Ammad had inflicted when they were both boys, when Ammad had thrown a knife at his younger brother in a fit of rage over a larger portion of mashed chickpeas. *He got me back, after all this time.*

A slave edged past him to place dishes on the table. Ammad dabbed a napkin to his ear, not taking his eyes off Sel. Jakira turned back to them, oblivious to the spat, and the first course began.

***

Ammad plucked the legs off a caught spider in the humid evening heat whilst his mother amused his father within.

"Mastiq, my love!" Jakira had exclaimed and kissed the ruler full on the lips when they had been admitted into his chambers for a private audience after dinner. "It has been so long!"

"Wait outside on the terrace a moment, son," Mastiq had muttered as he tugged Jakira down into his lap snuffling at her cleavage and prompting peals of fake laughter.

Ammad flicked the spider's limbless body over the balcony. *A moment has come and gone and still I'm out here sweating.* He imagined the Peqkian warrior, rubbing at himself to try to pass the time. Seeing fear in a woman's eyes aroused him, but the hisspit had not been frightened. She was disgusted, like Ammad was a worthless piece of camel shit on her sandal. He could not get hard. *Did she curse me?*

A loud groan followed by an over-the-top shriek came from inside. Ammad juddered. *Grim.*

Jakira shouted for her son to enter. Back inside, his

father's cheeks were rosy but Jakira was all business. Before Ammad could sit down she had broached her subject.

"Our Ruler, I don't believe we should tell the Peqkians about this dead warrior. Dead at the hand of a Dromedar. It will inflame them and could damage our trade partnership. I believe we should tell them that the warrior has gone missing, she decided to sample the delights of Parchad and never returned, perhaps falling into the perilous hands of the Khumarah. We will get the High Priest to bless and burn her body."

"Hmm, well maybe…" Mastiq muttered, baffled by the sudden seriousness of the conversation. He coughed up phlegm and stored it under his tongue, mouth hanging open, until a slave ran over with a pot for him to hawk in. He missed and the spit sagged over the side of the pot, attached by a string to his lips.

Jakira waited patiently for the green goo to be dabbed away by the slave and then turned to her son, "What are your thoughts, Crown Prince?"

Ammad, always nauseated by his father's grim spitting habit, took a moment to reply. "I agree with you wholeheartedly, Mama. It would not go well to anger the Peqkians. Our relationship with them is already thorny, we trade but we are not friends."

"Yes, yes, but honesty is favoured by the God…"

"I agree with you, Ruler Mastiq, truth is honourable and pleases our God. But the truth could spark retaliation and many innocent Dromedars will die because we were honest about this one woman. Save Dromedars, they are of the utmost importance to you. What is one hisspit?" Jakira insisted, she knew what to say to manipulate this man.

"I do not want to harm any Dromedars! I am their protector! I will tell the Peqkians that she has vanished."

"Excellent idea, Our Ruler, you always put your people first." His mother patted Mastiq's elbow like an obedient pet. She changed the subject. "Sel was in the fighting pit today practising with Ammad. He's getting strong."

"Sel?" Mastiq said.

"Your sixth son and eleventh child and *our* second son, Selmi. He is the image of Ammad, a little taller. They could be identical twins."

"Ah yes. Good. Strong like his father." Mastiq turned to Ammad. "Son, there's been some reports of our people helping the thieving Fert occupiers in the north. I'm sure it can't be true, but sometimes there are sinners. I have told the Minister of War, Whaled, that you will oversee this. He is in the capital and expects your visit in the morning."

"In the morning? But I'm meant to be…"

Jakira cut him off sharply. "Crown Prince Ammad is honoured to take on this mission, Ruler Mastiq. Thank you for the opportunity."

***

"Shut up, sit down and listen." Whaled placed his large hairy hand on Ammad's shoulder and pushed him down onto a chair.

Drome's Minister of War was in his early fifties, a bear of a man whose hump was covered in a heavy black fur, unlike Ammad's smooth mound. Ammad was mesmerised by the man's nostrils. Long tendrils of hair hung almost to his top lip which resembled the string-like, clumpy weed that clung to rocks in the palace lake. The nose hair swayed back and forth when he breathed, like the weed swaying with the current of the water.

The furry man continued, "My men have been patrolling and managing the northern borders and dealing with the damn Ferts for many scorch seasons. The blond haired, blue-eyed pieces of shit are skilled and capable. And now Ruler Mastiq sends me you, his suckling calf. Tell me, boy, how much experience do you have in dealing with Fert tunnel runners? In finding and shutting down the tunnels that run from Fertilian under the desert to ancient Vaasar, the place they call Lian? In sniffing out the

Dromedars who are betraying their nation? Tell me."

A vivid image of Whaled sniffing all that long nose hair back up into his skull came to Ammad's mind. Then he felt his body withering under the weight of Whaled's hand, his lungs felt constricted and his voice came out in a whine. "I have been trained to fight by the best guards, I can ride camels like no other, I…"

"Answer my questions or stay silent, calfling."

Whaled's shadow cast a cold, menacing darkness across Ammad's face. *Mama told me to learn from this man. She said, "Whaled is Mastiq's right arm, they love each other as brothers."*

"None, I have no experience. I hope to learn from you, Minister Whaled. I heard you are magnificent at your job."

The Minister of War took Ammad's chin between thumb and index finger and squeezed it like a lime. "You are a slimy worm. Your words mean nothing here. Keep your mouth shut or my men will feed you to the chickens. Understood, worm?"

Whaled walked over to where an extensive map was laid out on a table. Whilst his back was turned, Ammad rubbed his sore chin.

"Wriggle over here, worm."

Ammad obediently trotted to Whaled's side and gazed out over a beautifully painted map of Drome and the surrounding countries. Whaled pointed to a village on the Northern border, close to the mountains and in an unruly area notorious for Fert tunnels to ancient Vaasar.

"We patrol all this area, and my men found a tunnel air hole here." He tapped the map. "Where there's an air hole, there's people living nearby. Some of our people betray us by keeping the hole open, covering it up in dust storms or helping to keep the tunnel clear by removing the sand build up. The Fert thieves pay them with water and food. My men destroyed the air hole, blocking up the tunnel. You need to find the desert maggots who were helping the Ferts and deal with them."

"Can't I get down into the tunnel and deal with the

thieving occupier Ferts?"

Ammad's question was met with a slap around the ear.

"You are a worm, worms don't think. I gave you an order. Follow it or be hung for insolence. The Ferts would chop your slippery body into pieces."

"Yes, Minister of War." Ammad's ear stung from the slap.

"Ruler Mastiq wants you to lead this mission. God knows why. You will take twenty of my experienced soldiers. Listen to their counsel, they know more than you."

***

The Drome desert was harsh outside the crater. The sand scorched the camels' feet and the wind bit at Ammad's face. The dunes were relentless and climbing up and down, up and down, was slow going. After a few hours, Ammad was bored.

He had brought twenty of his own guards and two of Whaled's men. Twenty of Whaled's soldiers had presented themselves for departure that morning and Ammad dismissed them apart from the two youngest who would be easy to bully, a short one and a spotty one. Ammad would likely get another slap around the ear for that when he returned, but he trusted his men and trusted in his own judgement. *I'm the Crown Prince after all, I make the orders.*

They made camp for the evening and Ammad watched as his men trapped scorpions, assembled a pen and then took bets on which would be the first scorpion to perish. The men released the opponents and cheered as they stung each other to death. Ammad was desperate to join in, but sat to one side, maintaining his royal indifference. Whaled's two soldiers sat even further away, keeping their own company.

Ammad went to his tent and crawled onto his sleeping mat, listening as the men hunkered down. And then, a deathly silence. It unsettled him. He lay, eyes open, longing for the familiar din of Parchad and the comforting smell of his mother's aniseed and nutmeg oiled hair. Qabull's snore started up, faint. Ammad sat up. *I'll ask Qabull to sleep in the tent with me, so I'm not alone.* Ammad lay back down. *No! The men will think I am weak.*

He closed his eyes.

I'm an ugly worm buried deep in the dry desert. I'm stuck, not knowing how to move without any arms. I try but just bury myself deeper, deeper in the scratchy sand. It fills my mouth and I'm suffocating, desperately choking for air. Death is imminent…

"Mama, Mama!" Ammad shouted and thrashed, heart thumping in his chest. He stifled a scream when he realised where he was. He could hear his mother's voice, "*A childish night terror, that is all. Go back to sleep, flesh of my flesh.*" But he couldn't and his eyes stayed resolutely open.

In the morning, he scrutinised his men to determine if they had heard him. They could not hold his gaze and when he turned his back to prepare his camel, he heard laughing. *I need to stay awake tonight, I cannot have them thinking I'm scared by my dreams.*

They hadn't even packed up their camp when a mighty sand storm was spotted in the distance.

"Hunker down," Qabull yelled, "that fucker is heading straight for us!"

Ammad's men dug into the side of a dune and they bedded down with the camels.

For two days and two nights the storm raged over them. When it had cleared, and they had excavated themselves out of the pile of sand, the landscape was different, all blown into new dunes and peaks.

The fine dust still in the air blocked the sun and they spent four days going in the wrong direction.

***

Three weeks went by and still Ammad, his twenty guards and two of Whaled's soldiers trudged through the blistering sand, the tinkling charms and God-blessed bells that crisscrossed their camels' necks, the only noise. Their water and food was now on rations. Ammad had told them to leave half their provisions behind when they had set off, as the pack camels would slow them down. At the time, Whaled's spotty soldier had protested and Qabull had delivered him one of his famous punches. Ammad knew, as his men knew, that they were now in desperate need of those left behind provisions. But Ammad did not mention it and neither did the men, no Dromedar was permitted to publicly criticise the actions of Wakrime royalty.

They came across a small gathering of tents, occupied by wandering nomads of the Eqmadeh clan and their camels. Ammad introduced himself and demanded they give him water.

"We have none, we last drank four days ago. Our humps are running dry," a nomad rasped, his face like crumpled old leather. Ammad's guards took the nomads' scant food and rode off.

"We will get water at the village we are heading to," Ammad said.

His guards' tempers were starting to fray. Ammad was the only one drinking now. Whaled's soldiers brought up the rear and distanced themselves from the guards. They, too, had no water left. It seemed to Ammad that the pair were full of disdain for him and he resented their presence.

"I think we are here, Crown Prince," his guard, Nuurad, said.

"Think? Or know? Is this definitely the place?"

Nuurad shrugged. "I'm not an all knowing wiseman am I."

A sunken hole marked the location of the Fert tunnel air hole and Ammad peered down into it. The tunnel was bigger than he had imagined, but there was no way down. It would take weeks to clear out the sand.

"We need to find the traitors who helped the thieving scum occupiers! There is a village nearby, we will start there." Ammad raised his arm and kicked on his tired camel to run.

His men cheered and pushed on their mounts. The two soldiers exchanged a glance and followed at a walk after them.

Two days later they came upon the village.

"Here we are lads," Ammad bellowed as he spotted the village, made up of a shambolic collection of half-finished huts and animal hide covered hovels. *Further than I thought. On Whaled's map it seemed nearer.*

His guards gathered around him on the outskirts of the pitiful settlement, awaiting orders. They were gaunt with parched, cracked lips. The soldiers were still on the other side of a high sand ridge.

"First we find water. Then we find food. Then we find the Fert fornicators. Be as brutal as you must. Let's teach them a lesson!"

Their presence had caused a commotion, women and children screaming and men gathering together on the main pathway.

"Who goes there?" a wiry, elderly man shouted. These villagers were of the Yuurnan clan, the lowliest of Drome's people. The wiry man had a wide flat nose and large, low hump. A huge, ugly tattoo covered his face, a mark of importance for this clan. But it was the big, sloppy lips that sprayed slobber that revolted Ammad the most. Even though he was sat up on his camel, Ammad felt tiny wet specks on his cheek when the old man spoke.

"I am your Crown Prince and these are my men."

The ancient man bowed, and a wave of excitement passed through the fellow villagers. "Crown Prince Ammad! It is an honour! What brings you to Urakbai?"

The courtesy puzzled Ammad, he was expecting defiance. His guards bristled behind him, they wanted blood.

"Water and food is what we require. Immediately!"

"Of course, Crown Prince. We will gather as much as

we have and lay out a meal for you and your men." The old man clapped his hands and started to give orders. "Let us care for your camels, Crown Prince. Please, come and rest in our humble village community hut."

The sweltering hut was in the middle of the dwellings, the one distinguishable landmark in the ramshackle village. It stank. The Yuurnan wore scratchy camel's hair cloth and never washed as water was so precious in the desert. Ammad and his guards huddled inside the hut, along with the old man and a few other village men. A camel dung campfire was lit and the pungent, thick smoke made Ammad's eyes sting and each blink became an effort. He could barely see through the wisps that rose languidly from the flames and hung heavy in the hut.

"I am Samma, appointed chief of Urakbai. I've seen eighty scorch seasons," the old man declared proudly. "It is rare to see a Parchader this far out and in all my days I have never heard of a visit from the Crown Prince to this part of Drome. I feel truly blessed."

"Bring the water," Ammad grumbled.

"Yes, magnificence, here it comes." Samma ushered in two women holding a small wooden bucket each. Both had amputated the sides of their large flat noses. A small nose was a sign of beauty in Drome. These women's mutilated holes made Ammad taste bile. He was grateful for inheriting Jakira's petite, idolised nose.

"Here is our water, Crown Prince, gathered from each home in the village. We are delighted to share this with you."

"Is that it?" Ammad nudged a bucket with his foot and water splashed over the side. The old man winced at the loss.

"Water is hard to come by, Crown Prince. Our well has been dry for many months. This is more than we usually have as God blessed us with rain a few weeks past."

"We will take this but it is not enough. Find more."

Ammad's men lurched forward, filling cups with the water and slurping it down greedily. Ammad's guard Onhirid gave him a cup.

"My magnificence, we… we do not have any more." Samma lowered his eyes.

Qabull whacked Samma around the face. "The Crown Prince said get more water! If you disobey I will remove your head from your puny shoulders."

Samma put a hand to his face and hurried out of the hut. A few trays of meagre food arrived, carried by women. Ammad's men squinted at the paltry meal and the frustration of the past few weeks erupted.

Nuurad grabbed at one of the women and pulled her into his lap. "That food will not satisfy my hunger, so I'll take you too, my pretty."

She screamed and the village men jumped up to protect their wives and daughters. They met the sharp ends of his guards' swords. Carnage ensued. Ammad was swept up in the butchery and rape and soon the violence spilled out of the hut.

Scrawny village folk gathered as Ammad held a blade to the chief's throat. "Who here helped the thieving occupiers? Who are the traitors? Show yourself and your village will not be razed to the ground!"

"Ferts? We have never helped Fertilian! They stole Vaasar from us, we hate them. Take pity on us, we are honest Drome citizens. We love Our Ruler, we shed blood daily for the God," Samma pleaded.

"Show yourself, traitors," Ammad boomed, the power making his head swim. His men rushed at the people, who wailed and ran.

"Only the guilty run! You are all guilty, take them down, lads." Ammad slashed the blade across Samma's wrinkled neck and blood spurted. He threw the limp body on the sand and leapt after his guards, cutting down men, women, children. Nuurad had taken another woman, a dagger point at her neck. His youngest guard Khasar found the kitchen and yanked the hovel down onto the fire, setting it alight. A boy ran into the dunes followed by one of Ammad's guards who slashed the child's calves, bringing him down screaming.

The fire was spreading and bloody bodies lay on the sand. Women became playthings for his guards and one of his men came charging out of a hut brandishing two gold cups.

Urakbai was flattened and soon the only movement was his men, the camels and village livestock. Ammad savoured the destruction. His guard Haibal was clutching his side, where a lucky villager had landed a cut and Khasar had a bloody nose. The old chief had been telling the truth, no more water was found.

A whimper came from by Ammad's foot. A toddler still breathing. Ammad stamped on the child's mouth and crushed her face, squishing it into the sand, made soggy with villagers' blood.

Two camels came tearing into the village. "What the fuck have you done," the short soldier yelled. He jumped down from his camel and ran towards Ammad. The young pimply one followed his comrade.

Ammad waited for the short soldier to reach him, and then lunged forward, stabbing him in the belly. Pimples stopped short, aghast. Ammad's guards fell on the soldier.

The spotty soldier fought bravely and with his dying breath yelled, "This is the wrong village… Urakbai has always helped the army…. you have murdered the wrong people. You turned left at the tunnel… we should've turned right!"

Ammad's face flushed and in that instant, he saw his beloved camel stumble and collapse in the sand, dead from exhaustion. Yoyo had been bred for polo and was not as hardy as the other camels. *I so wanted you to graze into your old age, dear friend, not fall here amongst these Yuurnan maggots.* A small tear fell at the tragic loss of such a fine animal and landed on the toddler's smashed skull.

18

DARRIO

Darrio paused to take in the summer view across the Zwullfr. Rolling alpine plains swept down to a cluster of small, turquoise lakes that dotted the landscape like a deer's spotted coat. The crystal clear water reflected the fluffy clouds that broke up the blue sky. He had been running all morning and was exhausted. He had one more jagged ridge to navigate before he came upon the furthest edge of the Wulhor-Aaen boundary. He filled his lungs and pushed on. He couldn't wait to see his pups after many moons away.

The male alpha Sinarro had taken Darrio to see Sinarro's parents Kurro and Jerra, who in turn took him to see the Vierz-Aaen led by Jerra's brother Temrro. The Vierz-Aaen's alpha female Xocorra took Darrio to meet with Dregil-Aaen, led by her parents, Rrio and Varrya. On and on it went like a swelling snowball hurtling downhill. Some packs were missing a member and after Darrio had told his story, they knew to blame the humans.

He had met so many packs that he had lost count and travelled distances that he never thought imaginable. The Zwullfr was endless, his mountain homeland spilled out into vast snowy wilderness, weather-beaten rocky terrain and grassy plains that went on for as far as the eye could see.

Made first step to unite wolves against the humans. Arro and Lurra will not harm my children. Hope they will be satisfied with my effort.

It took him longer than expected to climb the ridge. The shards of broken stone gave way under his four paws and with every second step forward, he slid backwards. Progress was slow and the slate cut into his pads and sliced through his thick fur to stab at his skin. He reached the top and hunkered down behind a large boulder out of the wind, and fell into a deep sleep.

Darrio awoke refreshed and bounded down the ridge towards the forest, ignoring his bleeding paws. He howled with pleasure as he picked up the Wulhor-Aaen scent.

He ran into the den, ensuring he was upwind so they sniffed him in advance. His three pups were hopping about, tongues lolling and yapping happily when he arrived. They leapt up at him, trying to stand on his back and licking his snout. He seized them in a huge embrace, and entwined they bounced in a circle. He breathed in their smells and released them, smiling at their perfect faces.

"Pappy, we missed you," Harro yapped. Darrio's sensible, serious boy.

"Old wolf! Where have you been? Licking your balls for moons," Warrio joked.

"Cheeky," Darrio nudged Warrio's underbelly.

Sarrya didn't say a word, her brow furrowed. She fretted around him, pawing at his ribs and making high pitched whines to get his attention. But before Darrio could ask his daughter what troubled her, Arro grunted at him.

"You return like a hero, but what have you accomplished?" the black wolf demanded.

Darrio pushed his pups away and crept forward to the alpha pair.

"Packs will send a wolf to meet under Aaowl Peak, when moon is full again," he told them.

"How many packs?" Lurra asked. She glared at him suspiciously and smelt his fur.

"I met near fifty, those met with another fifty and so on. Hundreds will come."

"Hundreds. We will see. I await the full moon." Lurra showed her back to Darrio.

"Norra?" Arro asked.

"Yes, I met her."

Darrio told the alpha male of his daughter's injury and who Darrio had met and where his journey had taken him. Arro listened with head tilted, fascinated. Behind him, Darrio's pups eavesdropped.

The next few days were spent preparing for the gathering. The Wulhor-Aaen hunted and amassed meat, Arro ensured that the meeting place at Aaowl Peak was well scented and easy to find, and Lurra scouted out resting sites for the guest wolves. Darrio was kept busy, he wasn't granted a moment to speak with Sarrya. Her brooding worried him. *Wish to go back to normal, simple lives. Hunting, eating, sleeping.*

The night of the pack-meet came, the moon full in the sky. Darrio couldn't eat, his stomach in knots. The Wulhor-Aaen sat in the middle, the alpha pair flanked by their pack. The location was a flat, barren area surrounded on all sides by glaciers and snow-capped mountains. Aaowl was the highest peak in the vicinity, shaped like a crescent moon and was an easy landmark to find. Mounds of elk and deer meat were piled high.

The waiting seemed endless and it took a lot of effort for Darrio to sit still. His fidgeting annoyed him but he couldn't stop his legs from quivering. *What if no one comes?*

A wolf barked to announce his arrival and crept forward from the boulders. Darrio went to meet him. They sniffed at each other's behinds and stood wagging their tails. It was the grey wolf Sinarro from the Xulr-Aaen. Darrio introduced him to Arro and Lurra.

"Sinarro, welcome," Lurra said, "Daughter Norra, is she well?"

As they conversed, another tentative bark sounded from the rocks. Darrio greeted the owner. Zemrro from Dregil-Aaen, a young beta. Then Jerra from Maarr-Aaen, Sinarro's mother, arrived.

Zemrro gnawed at an elk and chewed hunks of meat whilst Jerra snuffled and licked her son.

The night got cooler, and Darrio's tail tremors betrayed his nerves. *Three, only three.* Lurra's simmering anger felt hot on his whiskers.

"What happens now?" Zemrro huffed, bored.

"Wait," Lurra snapped. Although from different packs, Lurra was still of higher status than the beta. Zemrro lay down, muzzle resting on foreleg but still alert. He didn't sleep, he did not know or trust these wolves to close his eyes.

A sudden blast of barking announced the arrival of more. Darrio ran out to meet them. A steady stream of wolves came through the moonlit boulders. Too many for Darrio to greet individually. They gathered in groups, smelling each other. Assessing who was a friend and avoiding territorial dispute rivals. The pungent mix of scents made Darrio lightheaded.

Lurra howled for their attention. "Arroooooowwww! Welcome friends, please eat your fill of meat. We have much to discuss."

Glowing eyes turned towards Lurra, twinkling like stars in the night sky.

"For the first time in my knowledge the packs from across the Zwullfr unite to fight a common enemy – filthy Peqkians! Together we smash them down and avenge the deaths of our family, our ancestors, our race. Together we take back the Lost Lands." Lurra's passionate address sparked howls of approval, but some were not convinced.

"I am Verra from Zegr-Aaen. We have never seen a human. We have never had any trouble from humans. Why should we join? Why invoke the wrath of these creatures?"

It was Sinarro who answered, "Friend Verra from Zegr-Aaen. I am Sinarro from Xulr-Aaen. My son was captured, slaughtered, mutilated and strung from a tree by humans who dared to leave the Lost Lands and cross into Xulr-Aaen territory. Wolf territory. These are our lands, our mountains, forests, rivers. We must protect them. Now, you have no human issue but if left unchecked they will push further, deeper into our lands. Into Zegr-Aaen patch. We must keep them out, we must fight them."

"Sinarro of Xulr-Aaen, an interesting point. I am Xocorra of Vierz-Aaen. We know nothing about humans, we know nothing of their desires. How can you say they will invade our lands?"

"I am Alurro of Gurr-Aaen. Peqkians stole our lands in south Wul-Onr valley, what is stopping them from stealing more of our homelands? Killing more of our kind? We have all no doubt heard the tales as to why we can do this." He stood up on his back paws. "We developed this ability in order to fight back against the two-leg humans when the time was right. Great Mother Wolf has shown us that the time is now!"

"I heard that Wulhor-Aaen pack wolves crossed into the Lost Lands. That is what brought the humans across the river. It is not a sign from Great Mother Wolf, that was pure stupidity!" the beta Zemrro piped up.

Many voices filled the night as the debate spilled over into smaller groups. Tension was growing, Darrio could hear jaws snapping and claws scraping on the stones. He glimpsed a few dominance displays.

Lurra shouted, "Friends. Debate is healthy, let us put aside anger and discuss peacefully!"

Her shout went unheard as noise levels increased. Male wolves were starting to stand on two feet, trying to make themselves taller than a challenger. Arro stood and howled, but no one paid any heed.

This will turn into a massacre! He glanced at Lurra but caught Sarrya's eye instead. His daughter was crouched with the rest of Wulhor-Aaen, sensing the danger.

"Aaaahhhhwoooooooo!" Sarrya bellowed.

She stood on her two feet, raising up to her full height. Taller than many of the male wolves. She yelled again, a deep booming sound that dislodged pebbles and made them clatter down the nearby slopes.

When she was certain she had the attention of every wolf she said, "Stop arguing. What will that achieve? Nothing."

The gathered wolves stiffened, staring at her in astonishment. Any standing males dropped quickly to four feet.

"Yes, I stand on two feet. Our ancient race has evolved. More powerful! But if we evolve then the humans evolve. Nothing stays still, all is movement. Enemies are coming. Let us agree how we stop them."

Sarrya walked forward to barks of surprise, dropped to four paws and nudged Lurra's side. "Listen to Lurra! Let us organise ourselves." Sarrya slunk back to take her place next to her brothers.

Lurra blinked her thanks to the yearling and then said to the stunned wolves, "This female is the first to stand and there will be many to come!"

Awed silence filled the hollow. *Nothing will ever be same again*, Darrio thought sadly.

Arro shattered the stillness, his voice rousing the wolves. "Now, friends, we discuss uniting against the Peqkians. It is time."

The wolves talked and howled through the night, clouds floated past the moon and it started to drizzle. Darrio listened but did not get involved. He sat with his pups, guarding Sarrya. She hunched low behind him with Harro and Warrio to each side. Although the majority of wolves were curious and excited, some were wary, viewing her as an unwanted abomination of nature. Throughout the night wolves made their way over to gawp at her, take in her aroma and some even offered males for her to mate with. Darrio swatted them away as respectfully as he could.

"That was a big risk, Sarrya," he scolded her when the visitors had dwindled, facing forwards and not looking at her.

"I know, Pappy," she whimpered behind him.

He was expecting a fiery response and softened. She sounded miserable, frightened. "Well, it would have been known sooner or later. When this is done, let us talk, daughter."

"Yes..."

"Sarry, it will come good," Harro soothed.

Darrio heard him move to comfort his sniffling sister. Her crying broke Darrio's heart, and he willed for this meeting to end.

***

Three days later all the visiting wolves had left and the Wulhor-Aaen got back to a semblance of normality. Sarrya led her father to a gap under a bramble thicket and they crawled through into a snug, hidden space free of the thorny bushes.

"How did you find this place?"

"With Ricarro, some time past," she replied and padded in a circle before lying down.

Darrio settled himself, and watched his daughter cleaning between her toes. Her shoulders relaxed for the first time in days. He started to nibble at the cream pelt around her neck, he hadn't groomed his pups for what felt like a lifetime.

"Pa, get off!" She wriggled, but then lay still and half closed her eyelids, secretly enjoying the preen from her father.

"Tell me, daughter," he urged between licks, "why stand at the pack-meet?"

It was a long time before Sarrya spoke. Darrio knew not to push her.

"I have weird dreams, since you left. Same thing over and over. Same… creature."

"Creature?"

"It is silly. Don't worry, Pa." She clammed up and turned her back on him.

"Not silly, Sarry, I have dreams too."

She inhaled and exhaled slowly. "A stone creature. Female, like me. She speaks and I wake up with the same words rattling in my mind."

"Words?"

"They make no sense."

"Try me, old Pappy might help."

"She says 'to face the enemy, unite your foes'."

"To face the enemy, unite your foes," Darrio repeated back.

"Yes. When everyone was shouting something in me went, 'Now! This is how you will unite your foes'. I jumped to my two legs and spoke. Don't remember what I said. Then felt embarrassed that everyone stared at me."

"You did well, Sarry, it helped to unify us. But brought unwanted attention on you as first standing female. Some wolves happy, some curious, some frightened about you and what this could mean for our race."

"I know." She turned back to face him and snuggled into his chest.

"Any other words?"

She nudged at him and mumbled into his fur.

"What do you say, pup?"

She raised her voice, "She tells me to 'trust only your father.'"

"Ha! This dream creature sounds sensible," he chuckled and snorted in her ear.

"Ew! Pa!"

"I'm very trustworthy you know."

"I know… There is one more thing."

"*Trust* me."

She sat up abruptly. "What happened to mother?"

Darrio's nose heated up, his good humour gone. He hated to lie. "Died whilst whelping you and your brothers."

"I know, Pa. That's why the dream creature's last words make no sense."

"What are they, daughter?"

"She repeats, 'find your mother'. How to find her if she is dead?"

"Can't help you," he faltered.

She raised her brows at him and clawed the thick mane on his neck, imploring him to tell her more. Darrio shifted away from her gaze, showing her his back.

19

RAMYA

"I am so, so sorry, my Melokai, she took her last breath moments before you arrived."

Naomya wrung her hands and fretted. She had not yet eased herself into Ramya's council as the new Mother of Mothers. Ramya did not doubt her abilities but she was awkward and unsure of herself. A pretty, little woman marred by her greasy skin and painful-looking acne, that had left deep craters in her cheeks.

"Take me to see her."

Naomya led Ramya through the hallway of the pen and into a small bedroom. There was only one cot in this room, many playthings and a chair for the mother left in sole charge of the baby. Luxury for a Peqkian child. All others slept in dormitories, shared their toys and their mothers.

In the chair sat an anxious mother, her nervous energy was palpable and eclipsed that of the Mother of Mothers. In the cot, a dead two-headed baby from the village of Qipaz, who the entire nation had pinned their hopes on to hold The Sight. Both of the child's faces were twisted in agony. Ramya turned her back on the cot and its grotesque contents, to look at Naomya.

"The baby arrived yesterday morning, my Melokai,

after a long journey to the city with mother Carrya here, who has taken such diligent care of her. Chaz presented the baby to the Stone Prophetess in the afternoon. Sybilya did not speak or make any indication that this child might hold The Sight, however we were hopeful. But, despite our best care, the girl… died." Naomya's voice trembled. Carrya slumped in the chair and held her head in her hands. Her body rocked and her legs jiggled.

"Do not be upset, it was not meant to be. I have no doubt you both did all you could to keep her alive. I am hopeful we will find a child with unique powers any day now. Naomya, please instruct your mothers across the country to continue to test all children, including the peens, for The Sight, and not just those who look or act differently. There has to be one out there. And please work with Zecky to convey this news of the child's death to the people. They will be as disappointed and saddened as us."

"Yes, my Melokai." Naomya shrunk back, but then seemed to change her mind and cleared her throat. "This is hard for me to say, but I must. Sybilya's power is waning and if we cannot find a new prophet or prophetess to take her place soon, we need to prepare for a world without her, without her magic."

Carrya's body stilled and she looked up in shock. "I cannot imagine what will become of us with her gone," she said, voice wobbling. "Peqkya exists because of her."

"It is unimaginable," Ramya agreed. An unbearable sadness came over her. She shook her head, trying to cast it off and noticed the two mothers waiting for her response.

She took a deep breath and repeated to herself a favourite saying from the Stone Prophetess, 'What comes next is based on solid plans and solid action in the present'. Then she thought, *yet another problem for me to deal with,* and immediately felt guilty.

"We must consider and plan for Sybilya's withdrawal

from our world. It will be painful for us and for our people, and we should be ready."

Carrya started to sob and Ramya left the room, the Mother of Mothers on her heels. In the hallway, Ramya said, "Please inform the counsellors at your next meeting to consider what is to be done. I shall also reflect privately and we will reconvene to formulate a plan at a suitable time."

***

Inaly Lake glistened. Ramya and Gwrlain lay on a blanket under a shady pavilion listening to the gentle waves lapping on the shore. She could smell the ginger from their pot of tea, now cold. Gwrlain stroked her hair. The image of the dead baby's twisted faces from that morning had shaken Ramya and her hand rested protectively on her swelling belly.

Nearby, Riaow's residents were also enjoying the lake. Splashing and laughing in the water, kicking balls, playing instruments and eating picnics. Many had rowed boats out to a tiny island in the centre of the lake where the ashes of the first ruler of Peqkya, Melokai Rominya, were scattered and a huge carved wood statue stood in her memory.

The natural reservoir was filled by five rivers bringing fresh water from the mountains and surrounded by high forested hills. Sybilya's was the highest, affording an incredible view over the water and city, but the prophetess couldn't move to appreciate it. Through the pines Ramya glimpsed the blue arches that snaked up the hill to her hut. Every now and then the summer heat haze broke and the majestic snow-capped mountain peaks caught the sun and shone a bright white in the distance.

Ramya watched as log gatherers floated a massive, felled tree across the lake and heaved it up on to the shore. It was covered in green slime and had been submerged for a long time. The log gatherers started to scrub it down and prepare it for use. It would become the basis for new huts for her people, perhaps a boat or maybe a beautiful carving to be hung on walls for decoration. The Peqkians hated to cut down trees, and so trawled Inaly Lake for those that had fallen naturally. For every tree they had to cut down, another three were planted in its place.

Her guards stood a few paces away, the citizens posed no threat, they kept a respectful distance and never encroached. *They still adore me. I am one of them and always will be.* Gwrlain had been accepted as a permanent fixture in the Melokai's life and to see him was now normal for Riats, the whispers and pointing had subsided, although there was still the occasional head shake or disgusted look.

And besides, the people of Riaow now had other things to think about as Omya's cuts to the public spending budget were starting to be felt. Ramya had given permission to the Head Teller to halt the building of a new healing centre until further notice and for the city trading times to be shortened to daylight hours only, to save on candles and the tinder needed to light the streets. There had been some grumblings, Peqkya thrived under Ramya's rule and prosperity was all anyone could remember, but she was confident that her people understood that this cutting back was necessary and for their benefit. Ramya and Head Speaker Zecky patiently listened at public assemblies to those who failed to understand, who continued to gripe, and then reiterated amiably that there was no other choice.

A waft of roasting meat hit Ramya's nose and her stomach grumbled. She was permanently hungry. Her previous three pregnancies had been hateful, especially the last baby, the peen. Nine months of sickness and feeling uncomfortable, but this one was different. She felt like a flower blooming.

Gwrlain was ecstatic, singing every morning to her belly and massaging it every night. He delicately made love to her and would not let her do anything strenuous. He tended to her like she was a precious being.

He shuffled himself down on the blanket and chanted

his own language in hushed tones to the swelling bump. Ramya didn't know the words, but she knew they were full of love. He then put his cheek on her and started humming. She felt the delicious vibrations through her body and then gasped.

"Issee, she heard you. The baby moved!" Ramya positioned Gwrlain's hand on her side.

"She kicks," Gwrlain marvelled. "Beautiful girl wants to meet her beautiful mother." He gazed at the movement beneath her skin.

"And her handsome father." Ramya pulled Gwrlain's face up to hers and kissed him. Her gut gurgled again.

"Mother is hungry, baby is hungry." Gwrlain rifled through the basket of food.

As Ramya was gobbling down Gwrlain's delicious homemade birds' nest soup, from nests harvested in his successful redesigned tower, Bevya meowed and picked her paws through the pebbles. "Gogo, Omya and Riv approach, they requesssst a moment of your time for an urgent issssue."

Before Gwrlain, Ramya had wanted to know the intricacies of everything that was going on and be involved in all decisions that impacted her people, but now she had assigned the trifling tasks to her counsellors, instructed them to meet without her, to only involve her in urgent matters, so she could spend as much time as possible with her soulmatch.

Gwrlain squeezed her ankle, shielded his skin from the sun with his cloak and wandered down to the shore. Ramya adjusted herself on the blanket. "Call them over."

Gogo squatted, Omya stood perfectly still, but Riv lowered her heavy frame down onto the edge of the blanket and leaned awkwardly on her elbow. She was out of breath from the exertion of a short walk from the city. She was getting fatter, which made Ramya wonder who was going without in order to feed her. Basic food and water was distributed evenly throughout the realm. No

Peqkian went hungry or thirsty. *I've spoken to her about this before, and she denies her gluttony.*

Gogo rolled her eyes in her hairless eyelids at the Head Trader's cumbersome movements. She said, "There is an issue with Drome, my Melokai."

"An issue with *Drome?* We have traded peacefully with Drome for years. What's happened now," Ramya groaned. *Recently the news is always bad. As soon as I fix one problem another bares its fangs.*

"There is a new High Priest who is stirring up hatred against Peqkya. He asserts that we are Godless heathens that must be punished."

Ramya pursed her lips in disgust. "Religion is such a waste of time. They could use all that time and effort to improve Drome, to help their people in the desert, to stop thirstation and starvation. Ruler Mastiq treats his citizens despicably. What does this mean for us?"

"I would say it means nothing for us, my Melokai. Trade is booming, this will pass as quickly as it started," Riv said.

Gogo tutted, she flicked her cold stare from Riv to Ramya. "My Melokai, our warrior Emmya did not return with the last trading party. *That* is the issue, not this zhaq priest."

"Why not? I know Emmya, she used to guard me. A good warrior if I recall."

"An exceptional warrior, my Melokai," Gogo said. "It is inconceivable that she did not return. Ashya led the campaign and insists Emmya vanished. According to the cammers, that happens a lot in Parchad. It is a wild place, there are great pleasures to be had and the ruler has many enemies from a rival clan called the Khumarah who lurk in the city gutters. They say they will send Emmya back if she shows up."

"Utter nonsense." Ramya was a warrior before she was the Melokai, warriors are loyal and disciplined, they don't disappear.

"My Melokai, I do not believe the Dromedars would lie to us," Riv said. "Perhaps this warrior was not all she seemed. Parchad is a city full of temptations."

"*This warrior* is called Emmya. *This warrior* is not the kind to be tempted away from her duties, away from her people, away from her nation." Gogo bristled at the suggestion and raised her voice. "We need to go and find her, she is either being held against her will or she is dead. We leave no woman behind, that is warrior code."

Riv shrugged. "We can't go marching in to Parchad to find her. That would impact our relationship with Drome, damage trade agreements and lose us money. I'm sure Ashya did all she could to find Emmya before returning to Riaow. I say we forget about her. What are your thoughts, my Melokai?"

Ramya scanned Inaly and watched as a Peqkian woman showed a friend how to swim in the tranquil lake, as three women ran around after each other on the grass whooping in some game, and as one sat fishing in a bobbing boat. *Can I risk peace with a neighbouring country for one Peqkian?*

The Head Teller Omya was stood bolt upright, her fingers clasped tightly together. "My Melokai, trade with Drome is an important income. The cammers buy the bulk of our poppy seed crop and keep half the medicinal quarter in business with their obsessive consumption of creams and ointments. We cannot afford to aggravate Drome. I agree with Riv."

"Gogo, we cannot attempt to find Emmya." Ramya's voice was low. "We must trust that Drome is telling us the truth and that Emmya will be returned to us if possible."

Her Head Warrior's nostrils flared and her chin jutted but she stayed silent.

"Is that all, counsellors?"

Omya and Riv both dipped their heads. Riv shambled to her feet.

Gogo didn't move. "No, my Melokai."

Ramya waited for the Head Trader and Head Teller to

leave. "Tell me."

"The wolves have been quiet, none spotted near our borders. But the last report states that there was a night of howling so loud that it echoed around the mountains. My captain believes it came from hundreds of wolves gathered in one place. Ominous."

"How so?"

"Chaz has finished rummaging around the two wolf bodies preserved from the camp massacre, and has had his nose in all available materials on the race in the library. His verdict? The wolves are now intelligent, over the years growing closer in kind to humans. My Melokai, a gathering of hundreds is a significant occurrence as wolves tend to stick to their small packs."

Ramya pinched the bridge of her nose. *Yet another problem, can't the world just run along smoothly?* "Increase our warrior numbers on the border and stay alert. Recall a company from Troglo, all seems quiet there, and send to the north-west border."

Bevya's frantic meowing rung in Ramya's ears and the clevercat landed on the blanket at her feet, jumping about like a bucking horse.

"Melokai," she hissed, "there issss a messssenger from Fertilian!"

Ramya puffed out her cheeks and blew out the air in a rush. "*Another* messenger. When will they get the hint? Please tell Zecky to deal with it."

"No, no, nooooo!" Bevya leapt into Ramya's lap, clawing at her to convey urgency. "The messssenger, it isss the Queen! Queen Jessssima of Fertilian hasss come, Melokai."

20

RAMYA

"You are such a darling little kitty cat," Queen Jessima told Bevya as she tickled the messenger's chin. Bevya was stretched across the Queen of Fertilian's lap and the clevercat's loud purrs thrummed off the walls.

"She doesn't usually get this much attention," said Ramya, concentrating hard to understand Jessima's southern Shella accent. The Ferts, thousands of years before, taught the Xayans their language and it had become the primary tongue in Xayy, and later, Peqkya.

The Melokai watched as the small, pale woman fussed over the cat. Her long straw coloured hair was curled and intricately folded on top of her head. Her potent fragrance wafted about her in a cloud and she wore a long, heavily layered dress that someone else must have put her in.

After all the introduction formalities, tense discussion and arrangements for the Queen's entourage, it was Gwrlain who had suggested that Ramya speak directly with Jessima. And that only he and Prince Toby Cleland, the Queen's guard, be present. "Fair," the Trogr had said, "Two female, two male." So here they were, in the walled garden.

The southerner had chosen a bench surrounded by

sweet smelling plants and next to a raised pond covered in lilies. The males stood at the entrance to the garden, within sight but out of earshot. The Queen was enthralled by Bevya, stroking her and asking her questions. When the cat replied Jessima squealed in delight.

"We do not have talking animals where I'm from," she cooed at the cat, twirling her tail and nuzzling her face. Bevya mewed and licked the Queen's dainty chin.

"I will need to dismiss her from our presence so we can talk. Bevya, you are no longer required."

"Oh, what a shame. Good bye, kitty." Jessima burrowed her nose into the messenger's neck and Bevya jumped down and sauntered away.

"So, Queen Jessima. Tell me, what is it you want."

"May I be so bold as to say your skin is incredible, so smooth and… dewy. As if you are illuminated from within," Jessima gushed.

The compliment took Ramya by surprise, her physical appearance never drew praise. "Umm, yes, thank you."

"I know this is a shocking question to ask, but I must know… do you ever get pimples? I'm twenty-nine and I still get pimples! It's so annoying, especially when you have everyone staring at you, nit-picking about your appearance. Am sure you can appreciate that the Queen must look her best at all times. On one important occasion, I woke up with a dastardly red spot in the middle of my forehead! I was mortified, truly. And no amount of horse bone powder or clay paste could cover it up."

"I look like everyone else, I wear a warrior's outfit."

"Yes, you do look terribly fierce! And so comfortable with your body. I'd hate to have so much flesh on show, I'd feel exposed. Your figure is incredible, so… robust. Mine is all skinny with bones jutting out everywhere. I've tried to put on weight but just can't. My mother used to say I eat like a horse, but look like a bird," Jessima giggled.

"All that cloth on you would get in a warrior's way. And all that hair. I would not have the patience to brush and braid all that." Ramya reached out to touch the blond mass, suddenly curious about the texture.

"Oh yes, it is a pain. But the King likes it long, and that's the fashion back home. It's one of my best features, I'd say."

Jessima started pulling out clips and pins and her hair tumbled down. She tipped forwards and messed her hands through the roots, shaking out the curls. She flipped her head and her hair whipped backwards. "Oh, that feels quite wonderful. Give it a good feel, I entreat you!" Jessima gave the ends to Ramya, who smoothed it in her fingers.

"Soft, like silk. I prefer it down. Here, feel mine." Ramya tilted and Jessima touched her tight, coarse curls.

"Oh, I love it! So different to mine."

They sat back on the bench and took each other in. Ramya felt immediately at ease with the diminutive woman, like dear friends meeting again after a long time apart. Her relationship with Hanny had been the same at the start, bypassing formalities and wariness and launching straight into intimacies. And also with Gwrlain, although that was deeper, each recognising a kindred soul in the other.

"I've never left Fertilian, I had not a clue as to what to expect of Peqkya. Toby filled me with dread about this mysterious realm in the mountains, but really, this is lovely," Jessima swept her hand to indicate the garden, "and you, my dear, I think you are lovely."

"That is very kind of you."

Jessima's tone changed to serious and she leaned in close. "May I ask you a question, Melokai Ramya?"

"Go ahead, Queen Jessima."

"Are you pregnant?"

"Yes." Ramya smiled and patted her bump.

"I knew it. I saw that little mound and just *knew*. Like a glow coming from you or some such thing." Jessima clapped and then reached out with both hands and cupped

Ramya's stomach.

Ramya flinched at the contact but then laughed. "If you were anyone else you would have your hands chopped off for touching the Melokai uninvited."

"Truly? Oh my." But Jessima did not take her hands away, instead she brought her face close.

"Baby doesn't want Jessima's hands chopped off, does she? Baby girl will love her Jessima. Oh, she's moving!"

They watched the wriggling and when it stopped Jessima sat back again.

Ramya shifted position and asked, "Why do you think it will be female?"

"I've got a feeling. What do you think?"

"We also think it will be a girl." Ramya glanced towards where the males stood. "Gwrlain is desperate for it to be a girl."

"How fabulous. Can I tell you a secret?"

"Sure."

"I'm with child too!" Jessima jumped to her feet and hopped about like a little bird. The sudden movement caught the attention of Gwrlain and Toby and they started moving towards them.

"We're fine," Ramya shouted and held up a hand to stop them, turning back to the giddy woman.

"It's the first time. I'll be a mother. I'm beyond thrilled!" She whirled around and then took Ramya's face in her hands and kissed her cheek. "I haven't told anyone else yet. I wanted to be sure, but I can't keep it a secret anymore."

She pulled Ramya to her feet and attempted to twirl her about. Ramya resisted, but the delight of the woman was infectious and she joined in her little dance.

Jessima skipped over to some grass and reclined on her back, patting for Ramya to join her. "My sincerest apologies but I just needed to let that out. I was about to burst, but we need to talk about important things don't we."

"That can wait. Let's enjoy the sunshine for now, Queen Jessima."

"What a tremendous idea! God is shining down on us today." Jessima entwined her fingers with Ramya's and sighed contentedly.

"Gemya, tell us. How did the Fertilian Queen arrive in Riaow with absolutely no prior warning?" Ramya said later that evening. She sat in the council room with Gogo, the border warrior Gemya stood by the window.

"My Melokai, we watched from the mountains as the Fertilian party approached and detained them at the border. The Queen, her personal guard the Prince Toby, fifty peon soldiers and ten female attendants. I immediately dispatched a fast warrior to deliver a message to Riaow. Over a high, icy path we discovered the messenger's body. She had slipped, broken her ankle and frozen to death, so no message arrived to announce the Fertilian Queen's coming."

Ramya nodded. "Only the Prince is here with eleven women. Please explain."

"I gave the order to refuse entry to the fifty soldiers, my Melokai. I did not think a small force was necessary to accompany the Queen into *our* lands to deliver a message. I accompanied the Queen and her group with four other warriors on the journey from the border to Riaow. The fifty Fert soldiers are camped below the South-Eastern Meliok mountains under the watchful eye of my border warriors."

"You made the right decision, Gemya. And the Prince?"

"The Queen was adamant he remained at her side. I did not believe one male posed any threat. He is clearly a fighter, but I do not believe he has the skills to better a Peqkian warrior."

"Thank you, Gemya, you are dismissed."

The warrior bowed and left.

When the door was shut, the Head Warrior said, "The sudden arrival in the city of this party has exposed a vulnerability, my Melokai. Our defences are not formidable enough."

"Peqkya is not vulnerable, Gogo. We have never been attacked, and I doubt we ever will be. This was a one off. In future, two fast warriors are sent to deliver urgent news."

"Yes, my Melokai, but we should increase our border forces. If this group can arrive in Riaow unannounced then so could…"

"Gogo, you are overreacting. Queen Jessima poses no threat whatsoever. She's actually quite amusing."

"But, my Melokai…"

Ramya held up her hand and then stood. The vein in Gogo's head throbbed but all Ramya could think about was getting back to Gwrlain and attempting to recreate the same bliss she had felt earlier that day by the lake. As the Melokai left the council chambers, she said, "Promote Gemya to captain, she showed good initiative."

***

The entertainment in the dining hall was in full flow, although most of Ramya's court watched the exotic yellow-haired, pale-skinned southerners. The Ferts had been in the city for five days and only the Queen and the Prince ventured out. The ten ladies-in-waiting, as Jessima called them, preferred to stay in their rooms. But tonight, a feast had been prepared and they were obliged to attend.

Jessima was sat next to Ramya as a guest of honour and leaned in close, nodding at her women, who sat wide-eyed and worried at all the novelty around them. "I don't like one of them," Jessima confessed with a grin. "My two favourite handmaids are back in Cleland City."

Ramya smiled.

"I've had such a wonderful time, Ramya. Your dancers, your city, your people! Incredible. Oh, and when the Riats reach out and touch my hair! It makes me laugh so much."

"They have never seen anything like it," Ramya replied.

"It's a shame I have run out of Fertilian gifts. I've so enjoyed handing those out."

For the past few days, the Queen had insisted on personally distributing small tokens from Fertilian to Riats, and her and Ramya had wandered the city streets for hours. Jessima was fascinated by everything, and to Ramya's surprise, she thoroughly enjoyed the Queen's company.

Great platters of spicy goat stew streamed out of the kitchens. Jessima clapped her hands. "Oh, and I *love* Peqkian food."

Wine was poured for Melokai Ramya but Jessima whispered, "I have heard that wine is bad for the baby. I don't know for sure, but I'm going to stick with water."

Ramya had the cup removed and water brought in its place. "That's good advice, Jessima, thank you."

Prince Toby was stood behind his Queen. Although he was the King's youngest brother, Ramya would not allow any male to be seated at the table apart from Gwrlain. Toby was reserved and watchful but doted on his Queen. Jessima openly adored him back, and Ramya noticed the entourage gawping at them and gossiping to each other.

Ramya watched as Toby stooped at Jessima's side and spoke in the Queen's ear.

"Yes, yes, I shall, Toby." Jessima pouted and then nibbled on some goat's cheese. She went to take another chunk but changed her mind. She sat up straight and fixed a stern expression on her delicate features. She pulled her long blond hair over the opposite shoulder, gathered her hands together in her lap and leaned in to Ramya. "Toby thinks it's time for us to talk seriously about why I'm here."

"Go on, Jessima," Ramya encouraged her friend.

Jessima shifted in her chair. "I believe I've mentioned to you about our predicament in Fertilian and the Gruesome Twosome Thorne twins. Well, we require some assistance to defeat them and to put an end to this mindless war once and for all. I would humbly like to ask you to…" Jessima paused.

"To what, Jessima?"

In a rush, the words tumbled out of Jessima's mouth. "To lend us three thousand warriors please."

"*Three thousand!*"

Jessima's eyebrows shot up and she put a hand to her cheek, frightened by Ramya's venom.

"Zhaq, Jessima! Do you honestly believe I have three thousand warriors ready and waiting to send to Fertilian? Are you mad? Or stupid? Or perhaps both," Ramya shouted in the Queen's face, then stormed out of the dining hall.

A few hours later Ramya's guard announced the Queen of Fertilian. Ramya beckoned to let her in. She could hear Jessima with Toby in the corridor.

"I'll be fine, Toby! Leave me be. Please wait for me back at our quarters. I'm sure one of Ramya's guards can escort me back."

Ramya overheard some muttering and then a little face appeared at the door.

"May I come in?" Jessima asked timidly.

"Yes, come in."

Gwrlain stood, kissed Ramya's forehead and then walked through into the adjoining room, leaving the two women. Jessima took a few steps closer. As Gwrlain closed the door behind him, Jessima spoke at once.

"I'm so sorry, Ramya!"

"Come here, Jessima." Ramya patted her sofa and waited for the Queen to sit. Jessima perched on the edge, poised to take flight.

Ramya took a deep breath. "I overreacted at dinner, I'm sorry. I… I can be hasty at times."

"It is my fault. I'm terrible at this sort of thing, Ramya. I'm repeating what the King told me. It's too many to ask for, he is being greedy. You don't need to send anyone if you don't want to."

"I have grown fond of you, Jessima, and I will help you. I will help Fertilian. I can offer a third of your demand for warriors."

"Thank you, thank you!"

They embraced and the Queen trembled in Ramya's arms. As they pulled apart, Jessima clutched Ramya's hand.

Ramya said, "There is one thing that you can do for Peqkya in return."

"Of course, sweetling, anything."

"We, as a nation, are…" the Melokai paused and swallowed. "I'm a little embarrassed to admit this…"

"Go on, Ramya, I will not repeat it. I am good at keeping secrets that need to be kept."

Ramya nodded, wondering what secrets this dainty, innocent looking woman held, and said, "Peqkya is struggling with a lack of… funds. Public funds."

"Oh," Jessima exclaimed. "You need money. That is one thing we Ferts have plenty of!" She laughed and then winked at Ramya. "I have an idea and it involves King Hugo's favourite food."

***

"One thousand warriors! My Melokai, that will leave Riaow exposed and our force diminished." Gogo stood and banged her fist on the council table.

"The Ferts are our biggest trade partners and Queen Jessima has agreed to take plenty more of our homegrown birds' nests," Riv replied.

"Paying *triple the value* in coin no less, and paying *upfront* for every consignment," Omya chipped in, a smile on her thin lips. "A welcome arrival of coin to our dry coffers."

Avoiding Gogo's scorching stare and leaning as far away as possible from the Head Warrior, Riv pushed on, "We have always had a peaceful, abundant relationship with them since before Peqkya, even in the time of Xayy, where our then rulers sided with the Ferts to help take

Lian from the Dromedars. The Fertilian salt flats provide an endless supply of salt, and most of our vegetables and fruit come from them as they excel at agriculture. Fertilian in turmoil is bad for Peqkya."

But Gogo was not convinced. "Let the zhaq southerners fight their own war! We can offer a few warriors to train their pathetic male soldiers, but not one thousand women."

"Do you defy my order, Head Warrior Gosya?" Ramya said calmly. Her counsellors took a collective intake of breath, waiting for Gogo's response.

The skin on Gogo's hairless head pulsed with fury as she bowed too low and for too long, an insult, and seethed, "I will make the preparations to send the warriors to Cleland City, my Melokai."

Ramya thanked her counsellors and rose to leave. She noticed that Riv was smirking. *No doubt dreaming about her dinner.*

21

VIOLYA

The trading party was weary when they finally trudged into the north-west border village that had made contact with the pygmies. *One step closer to the unknown*, thought V. Passing the north westerly Melioks had been a dangerous slog. On a narrow, icy pass they had lost two peons and a donkey carrying precious trading goods. The donkey had lost its footing and fallen over the precipice taking the peons with it. V had given strict instruction for humans to stay upland of the animals to prevent this exact situation, but the stupid peons had not listened.

V hadn't seen the stone man again. She had toyed with the idea of sending one of her clevercats back to the capital with a message, but decided against it. What could V say? That the stone army seem to be coming alive with one warrior roaming about nearby? They'd think she had gone mad, nothing of the sort having ever been reported before. She would check on the stone army on her return journey. For the time being, she allowed her warriors and trading party to call it a forest demon, and forget about it.

An old warrior jogged out to greet them and show them to their beds.

***

The next morning, they sat on carpets around a fire. The rain hurtled against the large hut's dome roof and fell in sheets past the open doorway. The village was set at the foot of the mountains, in a clearing of the dense forest, close to a stream. The noise of hooting birds, squawking monkeys and unidentified animals howling and calling to each other, seemed to intensify with the downpour.

The old warrior, Parzya, introduced V, Joz and Robya to the Mlaw village leaders: scholar, teller, mother and speaker, who reported into the Melokai's counsellors. "And this is trader Wistorya." Parzya motioned to a wizened, old woman.

Joz bowed low. "We are delighted to be here Mlaw leaders, I am the assistant trader Jozya. This is apprentice scholar Robya, who excels in languages, and this is Violya, our warrior captain. Personally, I am extremely excited by this opportunity."

"Dear, you will have to speak slower for us village folk. You Riats all speak so fast," the old trader, Wistorya, grumbled. "Did Rivya not come?"

"Unfortunately, she was not able to attend and sent me in her place. I have been learning from Riv for the past six years, accompanying her on numerous trips, drawing up trade deals and re-negotiating contracts as well as assessing the quality of specific goods. This is my first solo trading mission and I'm confident that we will be able to strike a hugely beneficial deal with the pygmies. Riv is a skilled negotiator and a real inspiration to the trading profession. I do hope that I suffice." Joz articulated each word and flashed her endearing smile.

"Pity, she is excellent. I'm sure you will do just fine, Jozya." The old lady patted Joz's arm.

"Tell us, Wistorya, how did you come to make contact with the pygmies?" Joz said.

"The huge, natural sinkhole that marks the end of our country and the start of theirs, stretches thousands and thousands of paces in both directions, the west leads to the

Sarenky Sea and the east towards Jagged Canyon. It is why it was chosen as a Peqkya border, easy to defend. Peqkians have never attempted to cross, as what was the point? We don't need to push our borders any further and we haven't, until now, had any interest in trading with the little people. We attempted to establish a trade route north by venturing through the Jagged Canyon and we all know how that ended." Wistorya held up her left hand with two fingers bent down and then pointed at her ear, indicating their Melokai's disfigurement.

V's apprehension churned in her gut. *These dangerous half-people bested our Melokai, an exceptional warrior, and we are about to venture into their lands.*

Wistorya continued, "This village is situated at the narrowest point of the sinkhole. Opposite, the pygmies have a village. It has grown as ours has. We see their fires at night and they see ours. Occasionally their voices carry on the wind, and I imagine that sometimes they hear us. This is such a remote area, that the presence of that village across the black, deep gash in the ground is strangely comforting." She stopped to take a drink of pungent tea, concentrating to control her shaky hand whilst bringing the cup to her lips. V noticed her blackened, ruined teeth.

"When I was a young girl, I tried to communicate with the village across the pit. The village leaders allowed me, believing it a harmless, futile endeavour. I used sounds, smoke, fire and for a long time I had no response. Then, all of a sudden, when I was banging a drum, I heard a reply. The same beats I played were copied. This went on for a long while, and the village leaders decided it was friendly. One day an arrow was fired with symbols I could not understand, and after that an arrow came with a vine rope affixed to it. We secured it our side and we were joined. Years passed and we built a pulley system which fed a small basket from one side to the other. We passed them small items and they passed us things back. This is how trade started."

"Amazing," Joz exclaimed. "What did you trade?"

"They sent us a plant, we sent them vegetables, goat's cheese, grains."

"What kind of plant?" Joz asked. Robya scribbled notes frantically.

"We call it pitfire, I do not know what they call it. You cook it with water and then drink the potion. It gives you a burning feeling when you first drink it." Wistorya rubbed her belly longingly. "After you drink it you start to feel… altered. Your mind creates colours, shapes, distorts what you are seeing. You feel euphoric. Like drinking your body weight in wine, but better."

"I want to try some!" Joz clapped her hands.

"I do not recommend it. It is powerful. Once you have a taste of it, it consumes you. I have weaned myself off pitfire but it has claimed many years of my life and I do not know what it has done to my insides, they are likely as ravaged as my teeth." She curled her lips back and Joz's eagerness drained from her face at seeing the dark stumps. "Some who tried it could not cope with the hallucinations. We have had three incidents of women hurling themselves into the sinkhole after drinking too much."

Joz's shoulders slumped.

"I suggested to Riv that it is sold as a pleasurable drink, but watered down. The next wine. Potentially very lucrative. But after seeing its effects on the villagers, we need to ensure we keep it away from our people. The Peqkians need to trade it, not take it. Come, let me show you the sinkhole and our pulley system."

The huge black hole was a short walk from the village. The rain hammered down relentlessly.

"Here's our ropes." Wistorya proudly patted the knots and baskets that were intricately tied to various trees and stumps.

"Impressive engineering," Robya remarked, examining it and sketching some of the apparatus.

"Thank you, that's down to young Urya. Our village

apprentice scholar." Wistorya smiled with closed mouth, hiding her ruined pitfire teeth and beckoned forward a woman who had been trailing the group with others from the village. Urya gave them a shy wave.

"We haven't tested our latest update to the system," Urya murmured, in a voice smaller than Robya's, "but I am confident it will work. All my calculations show that this width of rope and these pulleys will hold the weight."

"Hold what weight?" Joz asked. She stood a long way back from the edge, clutching a tree trunk. V could just make out the village on the other side.

"The weight of two humans or one animal, such as a cow or donkey or horse." Urya beamed. Robya regarded her with awe.

"You mean to send us across this giant hole on these little ropes?" Joz stammered.

"Absolutely," the village scholar mumbled. "That is the only way across."

***

"Will this rain never end?" Joz scowled at the sky and then at the hole. She was shaking. They had been paired according to weight and V stood next to her. V insisted on going first, in case of any trouble on the other side, which meant the trader was joining her on the maiden voyage.

"Are you *sure* they are expecting us, Wistorya?" Joz fretted, the third time she had asked her fellow trader. This time Wistorya stayed silent, and Joz wrung her hands.

V and Joz were strapped into rope hoists around both thighs. Robya's pencil scratched an illustration of them for the record.

"Smile, Joz," V said.

Joz buried her face in the crook of her arm and let out a little wail.

"Hold the rope in front of you tight and don't lean back," Urya said. "Slowly walk forward and then at the same time sit in the ropes, and take your feet off the ground."

"On my count, Joz," V said.

"Zhaq," she replied.

"One, two, three!" They both raised their feet and the rope took their weight. V's bottom brushed the dirt. Parzya's warriors heaved the rope and V and Joz jerked forward. Joz screamed.

"It will be fine, enjoy the ride," V soothed, but as she advanced closer to the brink her face contorted and she chewed at the inside of her cheek. She tried hard to believe her own reassurances, but her body refused and sweat oozed under her armpits.

On the second heave, they were hanging over the darkness. Both looked down. Joz fainted, letting go of her rope and flopping backwards. V caught her before she tumbled into the abyss.

V spent the rest of the journey with one hand holding her rope and one holding up the tiny trader. The warrior's arm muscles screamed, but the exertion distracted her from the unfathomable nothingness below. It took twenty minutes to cross. V felt helpless dangling, as if the earth's cavernous mouth would soon snap shut and swallow her whole.

"You could've leapt across, flown, disappeared and reappeared. You chose the hardest option…" The magic said.

Be quiet! V snapped.

As they drew closer to the pygmie side, V could see a flurry of activity. She took in the bizarre little people. Their hair was blue, shaped in monstrous horns, antlers, spikes or buns, making them seem taller than they were. Their bodies were a pale pink colour with intricate markings covering their torsos and huge rings hung from nostrils, eyebrows or ears.

A number of muscular fighters stood in a semi-circle around the pulleys. They clutched spears but were not poised in a fighting position. *Puzzling, I was expecting hostility, but they seem… inquisitive. Stay alert, this could be a trick.* Although the pygmies were little, there were many and V imagined them swarming her at speed, fighting fast and vicious. *That is how I would fight if I was their size.* V counted the number and formed a plan for taking them down, if it came to it.

The blue haired natives pulled V and Joz in and V's feet touched the ground. Still holding up Joz, she stood to her full height. The creatures stared up at her in silence with beady black eyes. They were as tall as V's hip and she felt like a giant. She eased Joz onto the ground and then stepped out of her own hoist, a hand on her short sword, and placed herself between the trader and the pygmies.

A few words were spoken in a singsong language and the hoist was propelled back towards the other side.

Joz groaned. Dozens of beady eyes rolled towards her. She rubbed her temples and propped herself up on her elbows. "Oh!" She recoiled under the weight of black stares and blue hair. Recovering, she turned on the charm. "Hello, my name is Jozya of Peqkya." She clambered to her feet and then smiled, turning her palms up in a friendly gesture.

A pygmie stepped forward and said something in the singsong and then mimicked her smile by awkwardly baring his teeth. They were as black as old Wistorya's, but had been filed to a sharp point. Joz gasped and lurched backwards. The pygmie turned its palms up and Joz forced a warm smile again. V could not determine if the pygmie was male, female or something else entirely and saw three hooked fingers. *I sense curiosity and intrigue, still no threat.*

Joz continued chattering away, and the pygmie continued in its language. It seemed a perfectly enjoyable conversation, but neither had any idea what the other was saying.

Wistorya shouted from the hoist, almost upon them. Joz turned to welcome her and the warrior Laurya but V continued to face the pack of fighters, she would never turn her back on them. She watched their every move, every breath, for the smallest hint of violence. Laurya came to stand next to her as Joz and Wistorya communicated with the pygmies. The old village trader's blackened teeth endeared her to the pygmies who cooed and clucked every time her lips parted to show them.

The rest of the group arrived, then the trading goods and lastly the animals. V left one clevercat and the yaks behind at Mlaw village, as well as their tents which were too bulky to carry. The beady orbs turned to look as the docile donkeys were manoeuvred across the void, then Robya's twitching pony and finally the warriors' horses, thrashing and kicking. V's warriors called out to their mounts trying to calm them.

The last to cross was Fin's horse. The dappled brown and white male reared and lashed out as soon as his feet hit solid ground again. The harness was unleashed and he bolted, slipping in wet mud and struggling to find his footing. A back hoof slipped over the edge and he stumbled backwards, plummeting into the sinkhole. The fraught whickering echoed pitifully from the depths. Fin hung her head for a few heartbeats before returning to her warrior's stance.

"You could've saved that horse…"

Go away!

"I am you, we are one."

No, we are not.

"It is time to come out of the shadows."

V clenched her teeth.

The pygmies led them away from the sinkhole and into dense rainforest. They walked on a dirt track that wound its way through small huts interspersed with tall, orange barked trees and towards a little village. Other pygmies came out to watch the procession of black giants and strange animals, crowding the muddy path and soon making it impossible for the party to move onward.

The crowd pitched forwards and the Peqkians and their animals squeezed tightly together. The pygmies jostled them, getting amongst them and under the horses' legs, reaching out to touch whatever they could with a high-pitched grunting that grew louder, ack, ack, ack.

"Push them back, warriors," V shouted, alarmed by the menacing stares, bared teeth and grabbing, claw-like fingers. "Be ready to fight but don't attack unless I say so. Priority is to move this crowd back peacefully."

She unsheathed her sword, the swooshing metal startling the pink swarm in front of her. She crouched low, opened her arms wide and stepped forward, the crowd in front melting away. Her warriors, stationed around the group, did the same, and soon the Peqkians had some breathing space.

The grunts intensified but the pygmies kept their distance. The Peqkian party started to walk again, eventually stopping at an undercover area formed of unknown animal skins laced together to keep out the rain. V stooped to get under. Pygmie fighters stood around the outside, looking in at them, but did not venture any further, and behind them loitered the crowds.

V ordered half her warriors to guard the three trader helpers, the trading goods, animals and serving peons and the other half with her at the other end of the tent, to protect Robya, Joz and Wistorya. The trio sat with fifteen pygmies who moved in unison. If one looked left, they all looked left. V couldn't tell if these were the same ones who had met them at the sinkhole, they all looked alike, but they clearly held some importance. Hours passed as the scholar and two traders tried to converse with them and the crowds outside the tent dispersed, the novelty of the strangers fading.

Food was brought out and Wistorya tucked in. "This is a favoured dish here, roasted frog meat. You should try it." She pushed the leathery white meat towards Joz.

"This must be why they have sharp teeth," Joz chuckled as she took a small morsel and attempted to chew before discreetly spitting the piece back onto her plate.

Cups of red water were distributed.

"This is pitfire," Wistorya said. "Do not overdo it, they like it strong here. For them it is a great honour to be drunk." Wistorya took a huge swig. Joz and Robya both had a small sip but V and her warriors abstained, they could not lose focus. *I will take some back for Emmya and I to try at one of our whine and wine nights.*

The pygmies drank heartily, turned and vomited behind them and then drank some more. Wistorya fell backwards, writhing around on the floor, groaning. A small dribble of sick ran down her chin. On V's command, a warrior stepped forward to check the old trader, and as the warrior bent down, a squeal shot from Wistorya followed by hysterical laughter. Joz and Robya had a similar turn, groaning followed by uncontrollable laughter. They grabbed each other in a swaying embrace. The pygmies broke their unified movement and joined in, and the rolling howls were peppered with broken chatter.

This is like guarding a bunch of excitable kittens! V stifled a smile. Soon the revellers grew tired and fell asleep where they sat.

***

"My brain hurts," Joz whined the next morning as they made their way on foot away from the village, deeper into pygmie land. The trader clung to V who lugged her along the path. "Like you've cleaved it open, V..."

"If you don't stop whinging I will cleave it open," V said, and she ruffled the trader's untamed hair eliciting a groan in return. Unlike Joz, Robya had managed to get up onto her pony, but was retching over to one side as it plodded. Wistorya sipped at water. The pygmies seemed fine.

The night before, Robya had established the names of some of the pygmies that accompanied them, Amjin (front horn), Oghril (antler protrusion) and Moqtoa (two buns above the ears). V could tell them apart by how their hair was shaped, otherwise they were identical and they moved as one. Robya was picking up words of the pygmie language and had figured out the plan. They were travelling down river to the capital.

There were two wooden boats with rowers sat waiting at a river bank. Each boat had a covered deck. V ordered her warriors, the animals, trade goods and peons split into two. Joz and Robya came with her, the three novice traders on the second boat. She did not know how long this journey would take and she had grown to enjoy the tall one and the small one's company.

Wistorya waved from the bank as they pushed off, turning to travel back to Mlaw.

The river soon widened into the biggest expanse of water that V had ever seen.

"Issee," Robya exclaimed, too awestruck to tear her eyes away to write her scholarly notes. "We are the first Peqkians to ever see this!"

V couldn't manage a reply, the magnificent sight rendering her mouth useless.

***

Four uneventful days later, they arrived at their destination. The river flowed into a wide, shallow lake dotted with jutting rock islets, covered in lush green rainforest. The water was crystal clear and brightly coloured fish darted in and out of coral. Surrounding the biggest island was a network of floating houses, markets and walkways. The boat landed on this central island and V wobbled off. She felt uneasy on the solid ground after so long on the water and focused on containing the queasiness in a compact ball in her stomach. If she let it spread, she would keel over.

V turned her attention to her surroundings. The nearby market was bustling, teeming with pink skin and singsong chatter amongst buckets filled with fish of all colours and sizes, wooden tubs of vegetables and unknown animals hanging from wooden stalls. It reminded V of the busy Riaow market and a pang of longing for home rung in her chest.

The wooden walkways and huts were unpainted and the earthy tones contrasted with pale skinned pygmies and the bright fish. The pygmies who were not on foot bounced about in little circular boats, woven with reed, like a cat's ball cut in half. The boatmen held on to the walkways, doing business or shopping from the water. Then they pushed off and with one paddle turned in rapid circles making progress in the direction they wanted. V could not understand how this worked, and watched the boats flit about, mesmerised. The place stank of fish, but was scrupulously clean. The wood was old and faded, but well maintained. It pleased V to see that the pygmies cared for their capital, like the Riats.

The trading caravan traipsed through rainforest and hordes of pygmies with whacky blue hair lined the path. They watched silently, no cheering or jostling like at the village. V perceived no threat. Amjin Front Horn and Moqtoa Two Buns led the way, Oghril Antlers stayed with the boats.

"If I understand our hosts correctly, this is their capital Ujen. I believe they are taking us to whoever rules them, in there," Robya said, pointing towards the mouth of a cave. On the journey she had thrown herself into conversing with the pygmies and learning their language. "Judging by the boats, the well organised village and now this floating city, this is a civilised society. More advanced than I was expecting."

"Isn't this exciting." Joz clapped her hands.

V peered at the cave opening. As they entered the cave, the pygmies thinned out. Her eyes adjusted to the darkness and she could hear Robya communicating with either Amjin Front Horn or Moqtoa Two Buns. The two pygmies both sounded the same.

"We need to dismount and leave the animals," Robya relayed the message. "The rest of the way is on foot."

V led the Peqkian group, walking behind Moqtoa Two Buns. The cave was lit by torches attached to the wall, the flames flickering. The passageway narrowed until V was forced to crawl on her hands and knees behind the blue-haired buns. It took all her strength of mind to convince herself that she was not suffocating, that she would not get stuck, although the rocks scratched her arms and legs. With an effort she burst through a slit into a massive cave crisscrossed with gigantic, glistening crystals. Some bigger than the boat she had arrived on and longer than Inaly Lake in Riaow.

"Issee," she managed to say as Robya popped out onto the cave floor.

"Incredible," Robya uttered. Moqtoa Two Buns ushered them to keep moving, but both were rooted to the spot, awed by the dazzling pink and white marbled crystals in front of them.

As the passageway spat out more of the group, they continued deeper into the cave, walking on the crystals and hopping from one to the other. Passing under an archway covered in tiny twinkling crystals and into a larger cave with a throne fashioned from the glowing gemstone.

Pygmies lined the length of the cave, V counted less than one hundred, and on the throne sat three pygmies, all in the same position and with the same expression. In front were armed fighters with spears aimed at the Peqkians, the first aggressive position V had seen. She indicated to her warriors to be vigilant as she stood to one side to allow Joz and Robya to approach the throne. Moqtoa Two Buns introduced them.

"It is an honour to meet you," Joz said, treating them to her captivating smile and bowing. "My name is Jozya of Peqkya. We come to trade with you."

Robya tried a few words in their language. The middle pygmie replied, tapping his chest and repeating the same word until Robya echoed it back to him. Robya had worked out on the boat that the males had markings on their arms and the females had markings on their chests and shoulders. The other two, females, introduced themselves.

"Utuli, Soogee and Yehep. It is an honour." Robya bowed and they brimmed with delight at her precise pronunciation of their names. There followed a disjointed conversation about how both sides were happy to be in each other's presence and the trade goods were brought in by the peons, helped by pygmies, and laid on the floor. Joz talked through each item very slowly, as if that would make the pygmies understand.

The three rulers jumped from the throne at the same time and beckoned for the scholar and trader to follow them. V went to follow but was held back by pygmies brandishing spears. Her warriors sprung to action and took up a defensive formation around the Peqkians. V plucked two spears from the fighters in front of her and turned them on their owners. They felt like twigs in her hands. More fighters came forward, but would never break the Peqkian warriors' circle. V snarled at them. *Come on then! You've lured us this far but I've been expecting violence. We will destroy you all, and you know it.*

V stared at the little creatures and all she could hear was the magic fizzing in her fingers. Then the lightest touch on her shoulder from the trader.

"It's fine, V, honestly, we'll be fine," Joz said.

"I think we need to go with them," Robya added. "I don't think they will harm us."

"We are not leaving you," V snapped.

Robya turned to the throne and tried to communicate using broken words and her hands to convey her meaning. The three rulers spoke in whispers to each other and then replied to the scholar.

"They say that two warriors can come and the others must stay. You must give up your weapons."

"Fin, with me. Warriors stay here and guard the novice traders, goods and peons. Give them your weapons."

The warriors gave up their swords and arm daggers. Spears were untied from their backs and dropped on the floor. V and her warriors were lethal with or without weapons, the pygmies were fools to think otherwise.

The three rulers led the way into a dark passageway. Robya and Joz followed, with V and Fin behind. Grunting fighters jabbed spears at the two warriors' backs. The black swallowed them up, like Fin's horse falling into the sinkhole days before.

22

FERRAZ

"Yes, yes, right there, baby!" the Head Trader Riv shouted.

Mikaz grunted.

"Harder," the old warrior Ashya exclaimed.

The courtesan Irrya tittered and the assistant trader Toya shrieked, hiding her yellow stained teeth behind a hand as was her habit. Ferraz let out a long groan.

Then they got back to business. The rebellion leaders, as Riv had taken to calling the assembled group, continued to meet at Riv's apartment, in her bed chamber, under the pretence of an orgy. Riv insisted that her housekeeper and serving peons were simple of mind and wouldn't think about such things, but it was best not to take the chance. Every once in a while, they peppered their hushed conversation with shouts and Ferraz and Mikaz would push around some furniture, grinding it along the floor or jump on Riv's bed so it squeaked. Ferraz didn't feel much like a leader, he did what Riv told him to do, but he felt like a critical piece of the puzzle, and these secret meetings made his heart race.

"Mikaz, please give us an update on your peons," Riv said.

"We have gathered near eight hundred supporters from

the city. Peons who want equality in Peqkya and who are unhappy with their lot in life. Peons who want to know their children, and who want to be free to choose who they love. Peons who are willing to fight against the Melokai and who are willing to die for the cause. I feel like we have only scratched the surface, and many more will come forward," said Mikaz, back straight and voice proud.

Since Stav had died, Mikaz had thrown himself into the mission of building, what Riv called, an underground army. He would slip out Ferraz's secret passageway most nights and meet with groups of peons, give rousing speeches about why the time was ripe to overthrow the current order and bring down the Melokai. He caught up on sleep in the communal area between calls and welcomed the taunts from ignorant PGs that his age was getting to him, it dispelled any suspicion.

"Excellent, excellent," Riv replied. "Our allies in Drome are keeping up their end of the bargain. It is taking time to garner support for a holy war against Peqkya, but everything is moving in the right direction and all the threads of this rebellion are weaving together."

The group cheered and raised their cups. Ferraz took a swig of wine. He looked at Irrya, who did not return his gaze. She stared vacantly at the floor. She had been miserable since her return from Drome months past. Ferraz suggested that she not take part in the rebellion anymore, but she was determined. She wanted to destroy Ramya. She called for Ferraz most nights and he desperately tried to pull her out of herself, but the Irrya he knew was buried deep beneath the gloom. Since their reunion, they hadn't had sex, Irrya was repulsed by the idea, muttering about the cammer still being inside of her. So Ferraz patiently cuddled her and whispered his love into her hair.

"We have work to do in Riaow," Riv continued, twisting a large, glinting ring around her finger. "Two of the Melokai's closest supporters, who pose the most threat to us, are Chaz the eunuch and the Head Warrior Gosya. Ashya, can you explain."

Ashya's hair was whitening around the temples and her skin sagged off her muscles, but when she spoke Ferraz shuddered. She frightened him. He was pleased that she had never called for him to pleasure her, the pressure would've made him crack and undoubtedly fail. Her voice was deep, and her smell was deeper. Ferraz tried to position himself as far away from her as possible, the stench made his eyes water.

"Gosya's force in the city is thin. Warriors are in the north and the east. And Melokai Ramya has done us a favour by sending a further one thousand troops south to Fertilian. Gosya is training up the junior warriors, fifteen years old and straight from the pen, to boost her numbers. Education that usually takes two years is being condensed into six months. These novice warriors are weak and inexperienced. Easy to overthrow." Ashya's eyes narrowed into evil slits. "Our problem is Gosya. We need her out of the way, she is too strong. We cannot get close to the Melokai if Gosya is at her side."

"By 'out of the way' do you mean dead?" Irrya said.

"Yes, ideally. Or out of the city when we choose to attack. She will die when she returns."

"More death," Irrya muttered. Ashya sneered, disgust at the courtesan's weakness palpable. Irrya shrunk into herself, folding her arms tight around her body.

"We are working on a plan to remove Gosya, and it will involve our PGs," Riv said, nodding towards Ferraz and Mikaz. "I will give you instructions when finalised. In the meantime, we can weaken Chaz."

Riv turned her cumbersome body in her chair to face Irrya and plastered an enormous grin on her face. She leaned over and squeezed the courtesan's knee. Irrya flinched at the touch.

"Irrya, dear, this is a job for you since you so excellently performed your last task."

"Yes, Riv," Irrya mumbled, her chin on her chest.

"Chaz is in love with the PG Martaz. Martaz needs to be *out of the way* so Ferraz can get close. Irrya, you will call for Martaz and he will *not* please you," Riv said gently, ensuring the instruction had been received by the courtesan by staring at her until she responded.

Mikaz grimaced, tears welling in his eyelids but not falling. This is how Stav had died, how many PGs died, when they failed to please a woman. Ferraz put a hand on his friend's forearm. Riv was oblivious, not knowing Mikaz's feelings for Stav or understanding that this horrific, painful end is what all PGs feared.

"You want me to kill again, like that cammer priest," Irrya whispered when she had grasped the instruction.

"Well yes, but indirectly! Just think about how happy we'll all be when Ramya is gone, you don't want to let us all down do you? And you don't have to do any of the killing yourself. Are you clear on your assignment? Yes? Good. The sooner the better please. Then you will come into play, Ferraz. Now, let us wrap up this… orgy."

Ashya and Riv continued to talk as Ferraz led Irrya onto Riv's bed. Toya pulled Mikaz over to the wall next to the door, she let her plush fur cloak slip from her shoulders and gathered up her exquisite silk dress. Riv was adamant that there had to be sex smells and stains around her bedroom for the deception to be believable, plus, she joked, that she enjoyed getting into freshly laundered silk sheets after her serving peons took the dirty ones away.

Irrya perched on the end of the bed with her head in her hands. "Oh, Ferraz, my darling, why do I have to end another's life with my actions? Why must this always be my task?"

"It is for the rebellion, it is to destroy Ramya, it is for us to be together for the rest of our days. Sadly, there must be death so we can have a new life."

Ferraz stroked her orange-braided hair and slipped his hands under her dress. Rather than stop him, as she had done for months, she submitted meekly and lay back on the bed. *She must be ready to have me again!* Toya was yelping in delight behind them as Ferraz pushed himself into Irrya. The courtesan tensed and turned her head to one side. Silent tears ran down her face as she mumbled, "I can't… I can't…"

Zhaq. My love is not enjoying this. He moved off Irrya and she curled up into a ball. He closed his eyes and brought himself to climax with his hand, ejaculating over Riv's bedsheets.

He whispered, "I love you, Irrya."

She smiled weakly at him. "I love you too, with every part of my being."

***

The next night Irrya did not call for Ferraz, she called for Martaz. Martaz obediently went, a look of surprise on his face as he was never called by this courtesan.

***

The following evening the set administer shouted, "Ferraz! A messenger has called you."

Ferraz hoped to see Irrya's clevercat but it was Riv's. He followed.

"I am taking you to the apartment of Head Sssscholar Chaz. Riv gave me a messsssage for you. You are a gift to Chaz from Riv, the Head Trader. Riv is ssssorry for the lossss of PG Martaz, for not fulfilling hisss duty to give pleassssure to the courtessssan Irrya. Riv hopessss that you will bring Chaz ssssome amussssement."

Ferraz was admitted into Chaz's light-filled chamber. There was little furniture and the walls were painted with various ancient symbols in a bright blue colour. Mounds of books and manuscripts were everywhere. The eunuch sat on a simple sofa surrounded by pencils and parchment. Pencil shavings were scattered around the floor. He was sketching a face. He glanced up at Ferraz, his eyes puffy and bloodshot.

"What are you doing here, PG? I was told I had a

message from Head Trader Riv? Where is her cat?"

"I am her message. I am Ferraz." He fell to his knees in front of Chaz. "What is your pleasure? Tell me and allow me to bring you delight. Riv sends me as a gift to you in this sad time."

"What? Outrageous. I do not want any company. You may leave," Chaz ordered, the white patch on his face flushing red.

In normal circumstances Ferraz would obey the order, but this was not a normal circumstance.

"But, my handsome master, Riv ordered me to please you, do you not recall me from the pen? We grew up together, you are a brave peon. Heroic for what you did to yourself."

"No, I do not remember you. Go away."

"I'm here to distract you from your pain."

"My pain? What do you or Riv know about my pain? Martaz and I were intimate, affectionate with each other, we conversed and we laughed and we enjoyed life. Tell me, Ferraz, about loss. About that excruciating emptiness that comes from losing someone you love. Go on, speak."

Ferraz opened his mouth but no words came to his tongue. His mind was empty. *I could tell of losing Ramya, but she is still here, she just didn't want me. I could speak of my son, but he is not lost to me either.*

Chaz grew impatient and then nodded as if Ferraz had confirmed what he was thinking. "You look like a fish out of water gaping like that. You have a pleasurable appearance but up here," Chaz tapped his head, "you are insipid. No personality or substance, no wonder I have no memory of you from my childhood. Close that unpleasant hole and leave."

Ferraz made no move to go. Chaz stood and flipped his drawing materials everywhere. He shouted over the clattering, "Go on, get out and I will forget your insolence, PG."

Chaz pointed to his door with his mottled hand and a

knock sounded. "Yes! What is it?" he shouted at his second interruption that evening. Ferraz got to his feet.

Bevya entered and looked from one peon to the next. "Ssssorry to dissssturb your entertainment, Chaz."

"The PG is just leaving." Chaz gave Ferraz's back a little shove and Ferraz edged towards the door, defeated. *What will Riv say? What will she do to me? I'm meant to get close to him.* Ferraz slunk past Bevya who watched him leave with glowing eyes, she knew him well, from the days he was Ramya's favourite. As he stepped out of the room the clevercat continued, believing she was alone with Chaz, but Ferraz lingered a moment out of sight.

"The Melokai hassss called a meeting," she hissed. "A courtessssan hassss killed hersssself with a knife sssstolen from the kitchen. Sssshe cut a baby from her belly and sssstabbed it and then cut hersssself. The baby wassss deformed, it had a hump on itssss back. The courtessssan Hanny issss devasssstated. Sssuicide issss an exceedingly rare occurrence and one which our Melokai issss deeply ssssaddened by."

"Sybilya save us! Which courtesan?" Chaz replied, Ferraz could hear him shuffling and collecting his things.

"Irrya."

Ferraz's knees buckled and he slumped against the wall. He could hear the scholar and the cat coming towards the door and he hauled himself away and back to the PG quarters. He snuck into his cell rather than go back to the communal area and curled up in a ball on the cold stone floor.

Irrya.

A baby with a hump. A cammer hump…

He felt as if he had been punched in the stomach, a dull, overwhelming ache. His chest heaved and his face screwed up into a tight ball. Tears forced their way through his clenched eyelids. He could not risk a sound but an agonised intake of breath caused a sharp groan that echoed in the void of his cell.

I want to disappear with my son, away from this madness, this sadness, this horrible life. He sat upright and leaned against the wall. *My son is all I have left now, but he doesn't know my face. I don't even know his name. Where would we go? How do I even care for him? I'm useless, a useless piece of meat.* He cradled his head in his hands and wailed, suddenly not caring who heard. *Irrya. Now I know about loss, Chaz, now I know.*

23

JESSIMA

"It'll be too cold," Jessima exclaimed.

"Come on! The water will be refreshing on this warm day," insisted Ramya.

The Queen of Fertilian and the Melokai of Peqkya were wandering on the shore of Inaly Lake, outside Riaow. Gwrlain sat nearby, under shade from the trees and Toby stood a few paces behind the women. The sun sparkled on the water, temping Jessima in.

"But what will we swim in?" Jessima said.

Ramya started pulling off her leather shorts. "Nothing, of course."

Jessima stared, open mouthed at her friend.

Ramya grinned. "Peqkians are not ashamed of our bodies, we are proud of them. No one cares what you look like under all those skirts."

Jessima looked around at Toby, who was keeping a close watch on her, and then shrugged. "Oh, why not! We are leaving tomorrow, and I'll be stuck with my stuffy ladies-in-waiting for weeks."

She pulled off her dress, then stepped out of her underskirts. Ramya, already undressed, came to help. Toby, when he realised what was happening, turned his back with a smile on his face.

The two naked women took a few tentative steps into the cool water. It nipped at Jessima's ankles, then her calves, then her knees. She hugged her arms around her. "It's freezing!"

Ramya took her hand. "Take a deep breath and we go under."

Before Jessima could argue, Ramya had tugged her down under the depths. The chill pricked Jessima's skin and she shivered. But then they started to swim and as her body warmed, so did the water.

"You are in love with Toby," Ramya said, as they bobbed in the lake, out of earshot of the Prince.

"What?"

"I see how you gaze at each other. Is Toby the father?"

"Absolutely not! King Hugo is the father."

Ramya did not answer, but an exaggerated wink suggested she knew the truth.

"You are a funny one," Jessima said and she dipped her head back in the water, her hair spiralling around her. *This is Toby's baby.* The thought kept hovering at the front of her mind and she kept pushing it away. For nine years Hugo's seed hadn't taken root inside her, and now, after one night with his brother she was with child. *A boy.* She felt certain.

"I think your ladies-in-waiting have the same suspicion, Jessima."

It was true. Jessima had overheard her ladies wittering on about her and the Prince and knew they were eager to get home to spread rumours around the castle. Jessima and Toby had not been alone since the night in the pool and she yearned for his touch. He made sure they were always on public display, two friends talking and laughing, always a respectable distance between them.

"They are such terrible gossips. They have no proof and we do not give them any reason to suspect a thing, we act entirely properly around each other at all times."

Ramya laughed and splashed Jessima. "You don't need

to convince me."

Jessima splashed back and then dove under, heading back to shore. *I need to be careful around Toby, and everything will be fine, just fine.* No one would dare to suggest such a thing to the King, that his Queen had fornicated with his brother, for fear of what Hugo would do to *them*. The King would never believe it.

***

One thousand Peqkian warriors gathered in the courtyard and training grounds the following morning. Jessima stood with Ramya in the council chamber surveying the ranks and watching Toby talk with the broad-shouldered, mannish captain, Denya.

"They look formidable, Ramya. Thank you." *The terrible Thorne twins won't know what has hit them! Hugo will be pleased with me. I bring back a baby and an army.* "Where are their mounts?"

"We do not have many horses and we cannot spare any ponies. They go on foot."

"When we get home, I will send you one thousand Fert horses. They will be the finest stallions and not like your short, stocky ponies that have such an ungainly gait when they trot. Our Fertilian steeds can gallop at a pace three times that of your ponies."

"That would be a welcome gift, Queen Jessima." Ramya hugged her friend close. She nodded at Toby, who was beckoning Jessima. "You had better get going."

"I will also send you some saddles, riding bareback is not at all comfortable, no matter what you say."

***

At the Peqkya and Fertilian border, they met Toby's fifty soldiers, who stood at a distance and looked on in wary admiration at the lines of meticulously organised warrior women.

"Captain Denya, would my men be able to train with you in the morning?" Toby said.

Denya grimaced at the Fert soldiers. At sunrise every

day the Peqkian warriors danced through a series of movements, stretches and positions in unison before training. Then Denya directed the women, simulating battles or splitting them into groups and pairs to fight. Their focus was unrelenting, not a sound passed their lips. After the training, they broke their fast, talking and laughing whilst devouring their food. "I detest *men.* Undisciplined. Lazy," the Captain sneered at Toby.

"Ah, yes, well… I'd like you to discipline them, Captain Denya."

Denya snorted. "We start tonight. When training, you and your males are under my command, and under the command of my women. If any male so much as breathes heavily, I will cut out his tongue. If any male falls and does not get up, I will chop off his legs at the knee and leave him for dead. If any male breaks formation when we dance, I stab out his eyes. Focus and you and your males will learn."

After they made camp Denya split the Fert men into five groups. Each group stood behind a warrior who patiently taught them the movements. Denya coached Toby one to one and Jessima watched as her handsome man sweated and contorted his body into poses and stances he found awkward, worked hard by a woman whose muscles were twice as large as his own. He had let his beard grow on the journey and the dark stubble made his green eyes sparkle even more than usual.

Commotion drew Jessima's attention. A warrior was walking around her ten Fert soldiers adjusting their bodies into the correct posture and tweaking their technique. One man on the back row was pulling faces and ridiculing the warrior, playing the fool for the men closest to him. Faster than Jessima could comprehend, the warrior was on the man, her dagger against his throat. The warrior whistled at her captain. Denya replied with a nod.

The warrior sliced off the disobedient soldier's lips and threw them to the ground like two fat slugs. He wailed like a baby. Toby bounded forward shouting and his men rounded on the warrior. To train, the soldiers had dropped their swords but the cats still had their daggers strapped to their arms. In seconds, Toby and his men were surrounded by a wall of women. The Ferts stood no chance.

Denya stalked towards Toby. In one swift movement she had him pinned to the ground with his arm behind his back and pressure on his shoulder. Jessima exploded off her chair to dash to his aid but was held back by her frightened ladies-in-waiting. Her heart thrashed against her ribcage.

Denya shouted to the men, "I do not tolerate disrespect. My warriors do not tolerate disrespect. That soldier would be dead if he was a Peqkian. I have spared his life."

The captain released Toby from her grip, shoving him forwards. "And I have spared your life, *Prince*." She spat the last word in disdain.

Toby's face scrunched in on itself, and a vein bulged in his neck as he clenched his jaw. He took his time to stand, rolling his shoulder and slackening his face. He squared up to the Peqkian and replied smoothly, "We *appreciate* your valuable instruction, Captain Denya. Elmgard, get back to the tents and staunch the bleeding with rags. Take your… lips as they could be sewn back on when we reach Cleland City. Men, listen and learn. I implore you, Captain Denya, please continue."

The men moved reluctantly back into their groups and continued their practice. Everyone ignored the chastised soldier. Elmgard was sodden with blood, a huge gaping hole from under his nose to above his chin exposed gum and teeth. It was repulsive and Jessima gagged. He patted around in the dirt, found the slugs and then stumbled away.

The next morning, the soldiers danced with the warriors. They kept their heads down with concentration. When it came to the mock skirmishes, the Fert soldiers were annihilated. Jessima was mortified, these were some of the most skilled fighters in King Hugo's army. Even Toby spent most of the time on his bottom, knocked down repeatedly.

After, the Fert soldiers slumped on their horses whilst the warriors jogged behind them, unrelenting.

"You never seem to tire," Jessima said to Captain Denya as they made camp for the night.

"Breathing is easier here. There is more air than in Peqkya so the warriors feel flooded with energy," Denya replied with her deep voice.

"Oh! That explains why I struggled for air when we first climbed the Meliok mountains on our way to Riaow."

The Captain grunted and strode off. *She has no time for me, a woman with no fighting skills.* Jessima looked around for Toby. She was desperate for conversation, her ladies-in-waiting bored her. She spotted him asleep in his tent, and sighed in disappointment.

***

"Lords and ladies, my heir grows in Queen Jessima's belly!" King Hugo proudly shouted to his court.

Jessima beamed as Hugo's rough hands fondled her swelling bump, snagging the fine material of her dress. She had picked a tight fitting outfit for the occasion, ensuring the little lump was prominent. She enjoyed the clapping and cheers and swept her gaze across the crowd, fleetingly landing on Toby. He stared back for a moment too long before looking away, a small trace of a smile playing at the edges of his lips. *Lips that have touched mine.* She reddened and glanced down to arrange the cushions on her grand chair next to Hugo's throne, dithering before sitting and hoping to conceal her burning cheeks.

Lords were shaking the King's hand and ladies were congratulating her. Through the hive of activity, she spotted Toby smiling at her. No one paying him any mind. He mouthed the word *beautiful* at her. She resisted the urge to whoop and twirl in circles. *He loves me!*

The merriment continued, but the talk soon turned to the looming Thorne conflict. As Jessima listened to the chatter, the jubilation of a new royal baby was overtaken by fear of war. Smiles faded on faces and frowns replaced them. The atmosphere in the hall became tense, serious. Jessima's happy mood soured. *My babe will join a world full of destruction and despair.* The stark realisation felt like a slap in the face and she sat on her hands, trying not to bite at her nails.

The ladies were dismissed for King Hugo to talk warfare with his trusted Lords and advisors. Queen Jessima did not move. He looked at her and she leaned in close to him, pleading, "I would stay my King, my husband, my love. I will not interfere, only listen."

King Hugo considered her, scratching his coarse beard. She made a show of rubbing her belly, smiling warmly at him. She knew she had been a good wife, getting pregnant and bringing the warriors back from Peqkya and he decided to oblige her. He nodded curtly, his mouth pursed into a thin line, as if to say, "don't embarrass me," and turned away.

Captain Denya was summoned. The Peqkian warriors had received a warm welcome and were settled in a makeshift tent city outside Cleland City walls. That morning, Toby had taken King Hugo to watch the training and on the Prince's advice, the King had accepted the Peqkian captain into his war council. But not all were pleased and as they waited for Denya to arrive, the grumbling started.

"Are you certain we can trust these cats, your Grace?" Lord Simion said.

Plump Lord Duggenham added, "Would it not be better to agree our plan of attack and to send them out into battle with specific instruction. They do not need to know the full picture. They are pawns that we will play first."

"We don't involve every Fertilian army captain in our deliberations, why this Peqkian captain?" Lord Berindonck bleated.

King Hugo silenced them with a sweep of his hand and he rumbled with his abrasive voice, "Never question me. If I want your counsel, I shall ask for it."

The Lords squirmed at the rebuke and darted loaded looks to one another, their mouths puckered. The broad, muscular Captain walked into the room and Toby indicated for her to stand by him as he announced, "Gentlemen, this is Captain Denya from Peqkya."

Denya nodded at the King. Her intimidating presence triggered a nervous ripple amongst all those in the room as Lords straightened their posture, crossed arms and jutted chins, never having seen such a woman before. Jessima hid a chuckle. *I can't wait to tell Ramya about this! How one of her beloved warriors petrified a bunch of whinging old men.*

King Hugo rasped, "Welcome. Let us begin."

There followed a long discussion that Jessima half understood, the King asking each of his Lords and advisors their opinion, and questioning their tactics or probing for more strategic thinking. Denya listened and watched as the men pointed to locations on a map spread on a table. When all had spoken their piece, the hall went quiet and King Hugo turned to Denya and bid her to speak.

She pointed at the map and said, "You should attack here. From height. The enemy's army will be squeezed to pass through the valley and vulnerable. They will not expect it. This is the only place they can pass into your lands to get to Cleland City. Otherwise they must travel a long way south. After, we push them back and meet them in battle on the plains here. We will outflank them and attack from all sides, forcing them back to Rotchurch City, and then we lay siege."

"But that is the Yettle valley, that is in Arthur Thorne's land," an ugly Lord exclaimed, whose name Jessima had forgotten.

"It is dishonourable not meeting them on an equal footing. We have to meet them on Yettle Bottom plains," fat Duggenham blustered.

Denya stared at Duggenham, sizing him up. "Those are the words of a man who does not want to win the battle."

"What in all Fertilian are you suggesting, woman?" Lord Duggenham turned to the King, and wagged a hand in the Captain's face. "How dare she insult my loyalty! This is a Fertilian battle and it is simply not proper or respectable. This smacks of cowardice. We have to meet them face to face, as equals. Just think of the impact this kind of underhand tactic will have on our soldiers. These Peqkians might blindly follow baffling or abnormal orders, but not our men. They have honour and decency."

"We want to win the battle, Lord Duggenham," Toby said. "We all know that King Edgar took Lian from the Dromedars by complete surprise, and that encounter was one of our greatest achievements. An unexpected assault would shred the Thorne Twins' army to pieces. It is *our* land, Lord Littlehales, *our* valley and it does not belong to Arthur Thorne. Captain Denya is right. We need to weigh honour with victory. I choose victory."

Toby was impressed with the Peqkian warrior. An uncomfortable prickle made its way down Jessima's spine, until she remembered that Denya liked women. Most nights on the journey from Riaow the captain had a warrior, or many, in her tent, sating her desires.

A surge of voices started up as Hugo steepled his fingers, contemplating.

"I have no desire for a long drawn out war, I do not want men to die needlessly." His razor sharp voice silenced the squabbling men. "Attacking at Yettle will end this twenty-four-year feud swiftly and decisively. It is honourable to save Fertilian lives and not to squander them."

He thumped his fist savagely down on his throne, a

noise that made Jessima flinch. He bellowed, his voice as loud as a thunderclap, "We *crush* the Thornes once and for all!"

Jessima sat against the stained wall hanging waiting for her husband to finish his noisy ablutions in the washroom next door and come to bed. She was exhausted, but as the dutiful wife, could not rest until King Hugo was in bed and asleep in case she needed to service him or listen to his grumblings about the day.

He shuffled under the bed clothes and propped himself next to Jessima.

"Do you think I'm doing the right thing, dearie?" he asked.

She was stumped by the rare request for her opinion. "Um, in what way, cherished husband?"

"By ambushing the Thornes rather than meeting them on equal terms, on equal land."

"I think, that whatever you think is the right thing to do, is the right thing to do," Jessima stumbled. She was useless at this kind of thing.

"I'm getting old, I will not be here much longer I fear. My health is ailing and I need to see this thing out. I must unite Fertilian before I die." He examined his hands back and front, tutting at the prominent veins and thin skin, the wrinkles and age spots.

"Oh, darling husband, you will be around for many years to come! You have a son on the way who needs you to take care of him, to teach him all you know and to love him unconditionally." Jessima took one of his papery hands and placed it on her bump.

He snatched it off and crossed his arms. "Yes, yes. A son," he sighed, "and what will I be leaving my son? A broken Kingdom that in all this time I have *still* not healed? What kind of a legacy is that? I've failed."

"You will heal it, cherished husband. We will win this battle and get rid of those nasty, terrible Thorne twins once and for all."

"I truly hope so, dearie. You know, my biggest regret was leaving the false Queen Charlotte and her brat twins alive. A moment of weakness."

"I would say that was a moment of mercy," she said, feeling like she had given a clever answer, and kissed him on the cheek but it was the wrong answer and he glowered at her, shaking his head.

"You are young, you don't understand." He rolled down the bed and turned his back to her.

The tension between them sizzled. *He is frustrated and I seem to be incapable of saying the right thing.* Jessima held her breath and waited for the heavy breathing to start. Instead Hugo's body started convulsing, gently at first and then heaving so that the bed shook. It took her a moment to understand that this bear of a man was weeping. Jessima reached out a hand and gingerly placed it on his shoulder. He jerked forward out of her reach and she recoiled, laying still on the mattress like a log of wood, willing it to be morning. A sudden wave of guilt at her infidelity made her head spin on the pillow and she closed her eyes tight, trying to block out God's disappointment in her.

24

AMMAD

They were in high spirits as they set off on the return journey back to Parchad. Ammad was impatient to get home and didn't care he had attacked the wrong village. His men joked about the *village pillage* and they feasted on the plundered livestock, including a pig and many goats. There seemed sufficient water in the pouches to last them a good few weeks, but this ran out quicker than the food and in days they were down to rations and then there was none.

His guards started to dig holes. They went down thirty feet to find a damp bit of sand where the scant water pooled briefly. It was gruelling work and Ammad loafed against a camel and watched, his men bringing him the first palmful of liquid. They had to keep moving, so had to dig every three days.

"Crown Prince," Qabull said, out of earshot of the men, "I think you should help to dig the well today."

"What are you talking about? Preposterous!" Ammad replied as he hunkered down in a shady nook beneath a high dune. He pulled his hood up, crossed his arms and rested his chin on his chest. He planned to doze.

"Crown Prince, you must dig the well today," Qabull insisted.

"Go away and bring me water when you find it."

A huge fist grabbed Ammad's raggedy cloak and yanked him to his feet. Ammad's hood whipped back as Qabull pulled him close, so the tips of their noses touched.

"Ammad, if you don't fucking dig you will not live out this night. The men are angry that not *all* on this journey are pulling their weight. If they decide to vent their anger, I won't be able to stop them."

Ammad at once understood his guard's warning. He shuffled over to the patch of sand the men were attacking and held out his hand for a makeshift shovel. The men stared at him and no one gave him any tool, so he knelt and started scooping out the fine powdery sand with his once soft hands, panting with the exertion.

Eventually their extreme fatigue ended the digging and to survive they started to drink their camels' blood, making a small incision in a vein, sipping a few drops and then sealing up the wound with wax. When each weary camel's neck was lined with waxy deposits and there was no more vein to see, they gave up on this and started to drink their own urine.

After a month of solid camel riding, and with Parchad barely a week's ride away, the beasts started to flounder.

"The longest camels can go without a drink is thirty days and that time is upon us," the guard Nuurad muttered as he stroked his seated camel's emaciated rump. It had refused to stand and no amount of coaxing by the men could bring it to its feet.

"This is a sad day." Nuurad unsheathed his sword, kissed the camel on its shaggy forehead and sliced its throat. He caught the blood in a flask, and once full, put another under the gush until no more blood ran out.

Nuurad drank his camel's blood but refused to eat even the smallest morsel of sacred flesh. In Drome, mistreating camels brought severe penalties and eating of their flesh was an abomination. Three further men refused but

Ammad ordered a fire made and gorged on roasted camel meat, more concerned with filling his empty belly than with upholding traditions.

Every day that followed they lost at least one camel, until there were none. The men lumbered through the undulating dunes. A week's camel ride turning into three on foot. At night, Ammad picked through his clothes and inspected every inch of his body hoping to find fleas and ticks to eat.

Three of his men died of thirstation, one dropping dead whilst walking, the other two dying in their sleep. Ammad tried not to sleep for fear of not waking up. The dreaded night terrors now a distant memory.

They trudged on. The stifling scorch season heat draped itself over Ammad. Each step he dragged through the deep sand felt as if a man clung to his ankles. He could barely close his mouth and every grain of sand that blew in stuck to his tongue, the grit grinding between his teeth.

One day, Qabull said, "There is Jhabia." No one looked up and no one picked up their pace.

The great ridge of rock signalled they were near to Parchad. It took days to climb up and over Jhabia and soon the massive sand sculpture of a hand reaching to the sky loomed in the distance, marking the way in to the city. Behind it the crater wall shimmered in the heat haze.

His men insisted they give blood at the sacred sculpture, to give thanks to God that they had not died in the desert. Having no energy in him to disagree, they schlepped the extra distance, about the length of his polo field, and jostled through throngs of Parchaders to the Hand of God.

A boggy ring of blood-blackened sand surrounded the sculpture. When it started to squelch under foot they stopped and using their blunt swords, nicked fingers, palms and wrists to shed blood. Ammad pricked his little finger and held it over the bog. It took an age for his water-starved blood to form a droplet, and getting impatient, he shook his hand. A tiny red bead flew up and dropped, disappearing into the blackness.

Ammad's men waded in knee deep to the blood sodden sand, chanted prayers and waited for their blood to clot. He stumbled back from the crush and took in the crowd. Merchants had stands selling all kinds of goods, food and water stalls as well as entertainment including snake charmers. A lot of coin changed hands and Ammad knew the Qacirr holy families would be raking it in from their business here. A fat holy man, dressed in all the holy finery, was repeating blessings for anyone who threw him a coin, but behind, people clustered around another preacher, engrossed by his words. Ammad moved closer. This second preacher's thin frame was dressed in a simple, collarless tunic and his voice was soft.

"This is not the true God," he said, pointing at the sculpture. "This is the true God," he tapped his chest, "in your heart. He does not ask for your blood or pain or animal slaughter. He loves all things, He loves you and He loves peace. God is in your homes, He is everywhere. You do not need to go to the extravagant temple to pray to Him. He does not want slaves, everyone is equal in His eyes. He does not want war with our neighbours, the Peqkians, He wants friendship…"

A Khumarah preacher, in the open, brazenly questioning Drome religious teachings and, by association, the rule of his father. Ammad had never seen one before and determined to wipe the city clean of the Khumarah clan as soon as he got the chance. He stared at each of the pitiful Parchaders listening to this filth, vowing to hunt them down too, until he came across a pair of beautiful female eyes. The rest of her face was wrapped in a tatty shawl apart from a slit that exposed an obviously high-born brow and the top of a tiny nose. Next to the owner of those dazzling eyes, a face Ammad knew, half hidden behind a hood… his own.

"Selmi," he yelled and the face jerked from preacher to the direction of the voice.

Qabull's hand on Ammad's shoulder pulled him away. "Time to go."

Ammad wrestled out of his guard's grip and looked back, but the face was gone. *What is my brother doing sneaking outside the crater walls to listen to Khumarah preachers? And who was that Tamadeen girl with him? Was it even Selmi? I'll interrogate the little runt later.*

He beckoned to Onhirid and sent him ahead to inform the palace of the Crown Prince's imminent arrival. The guard grumbled but obeyed when Ammad promised him ten of the finest whores when they returned.

They shambled through the slums outside the crater walls and the dark stares and urgent whispers from men with covered faces frightened Ammad. This was the stomping ground of the Khumarah Assassins and it would be just his luck to get murdered here in filthy rags and stinking like a slave latrine. He glanced back at his shattered men. *If we are attacked now, no one has it in them to fight back*. He took a deep breath and tried to pull his shoulders back and walk tall, but his insides felt hollow and he slouched back down. He wrapped his shawl around his head and put a hand on the hilt of his sword. He was relieved when they reached the wall unscathed.

They took the peasants road over the crater wall with the city scum, the royal road being too far away to walk to in their exhaustion. They stumbled through the streets to jeers of Parchaders who recognised the Crown Prince from his polo matches and who had never seen him on foot or so dishevelled. He was too proud to ask them to spare a few drops of water. He noted High Priest Zeead's holy men dotted about the city, stirring up hordes against the Peqkian hisspits and he managed a smirk.

Ammad arrived at the palace expecting a fanfare for his return. But only Onhirid waited for them with slaves carrying buckets of water and food. Ammad gulped a bucket down and then poured another over his head. His cracked lips stung. He wanted to wash away the desert and have his slaves massage his sore body. Then he would be preened, his facial hair was out of control and his once glorious, black hair was matted and grey from the dust. After, he would make his damn cock work and find a woman or two.

He was furious with his mother for insisting he led this mission. *"The people respect a man with military prowess," she'd told him. I'm the Crown Prince, I should not be subjected to such hardship! I nearly died.*

He grabbed a flatbread and tore at it hungrily, and strode off in the direction of his apartment but was stopped by one of the Ruler's slaves. "Our Ruler demands an immediate meeting with you. Come now."

Shit, he thought as he bellowed orders to his guards, gobbled more food, and tried to smooth down his decrepit clothes.

***

Ruler Mastiq sat on floor cushions in a cool chamber. He was joined by the new High Priest Zeead and the Minister of War, Whaled. Behind the ruler stood several Cuttarr cutthroats, teeming with danger. Everyone looked annoyed at Ammad. Whaled rubbed his massive nostrils with thumb and first finger, his nose hair casting strange shadows on his chin.

"Son, you disobeyed Whaled's direct order and did not take his men on your mission! This insolence must be punished," Mastiq boomed.

"Father! I am *so* pleased to see you too. I have been away so long and I've missed you *terribly*." Ammad bowed low and then kneeled onto a cushion. Whaled's rage rumbled like steam off a boiling pot and engulfed Ammad. He started to sweat, salty trickles gathering dust as they rolled down from his temples.

"Well yes, of course I'm pleased you have returned, Ammad, but really you need to obey Whaled if you are to excel at army affairs..." Mastiq's tone softened, he had no backbone for scolding.

"Tell me, Crown Prince, was your trip a success?" Whaled cut in.

"Yes, it was a success. I thank you, Father, for allowing me to lead such an important mission." Ammad bowed again to Mastiq. He clicked his fingers at Qabull. The guard brought forward a bag and upended it on the floor. Three festering heads tumbled out. Mastiq pinched his nose and Zeead leaned back from the stench.

"These are the heads of the villagers who helped the Fert occupiers," Ammad declared.

Whaled stood and nudged at the putrid fleshy balls with his foot.

"This one with the tattoo is Chief Samma from Urakbai village. He is not a traitor. He would never betray us to the occupiers. Samma was one of my most trusted men in the north." Whaled moved his huge bulk towards Ammad. "You have murdered innocent people you fucking idiot! The maggots who helped the Ferts are still out there!"

"Horrific," Mastiq exclaimed, a tickle in his throat turning into a wet, lump-filled cough.

"I assure you, Father, that these are the men that betrayed you. I questioned them thoroughly. It is sad that their apparent loyalty was turned by the thieves." Ammad gave Mastiq a long, mournful look.

"Lies," Whaled snarled in Ammad's face.

"Now, now, Whaled, if my son says he questioned them…"

"Our Ruler, my dear friend, he spouts lies," shouted Whaled, and grabbed the rags at Ammad's neck.

Ammad went limp, and reached pathetically for Mastiq. "Dada, I swear! I've had such a dreadful time, look at me, I'm skin and bones. I nearly died, Dada, can you imagine it? If I had not returned? I swear these are the traitors, I swear! It's so upsetting…" Ammad started to sob, hanging pathetically from Whaled's grasp. He glanced up to check his performance was having the desired effect on his father. It was.

Mastiq placed a hand on his heart. "Very sad, son, very sad. Don't fret about it, I'd hate for you to be upset. Whaled, release him and let us talk of other things. We must trust what he tells us, he has my blood in his veins after all..."

The Minister of War glared at Mastiq and flung Ammad to the floor.

Mastiq said, "High Priest Zeead is insisting that we free Peqkya from its bondage. Its people are lost and need to be delivered to God. How can we save them?"

"We send our army?" Ammad ventured, composed again. Being bold was the only way to influence Mastiq. His father did not pick up on subtleties.

"Send our army? Are you mad? The Peqkians are vicious fighters, this is known. Ruler Mastiq, we do not want to initiate a battle when they have not attacked us or given us any cause to attack them." The hair on Whaled's face stiffened in anger.

Mastiq nodded, swayed in his friend's direction but then Jakira's puppet, the big-bottomed High Priest, chipped in, his stiff arms jerking to life. His woman's voice squeaked, "Do you, Whaled, deny the desire of our God? He has spoken and we must obey! Any denial of God's will is sacrilegious folly."

"Ridiculous, you blinkered fool," Whaled exclaimed and glared at Zeead who shrank back, intimidated.

"Are you saying, Whaled, that us Dromedars are not strong enough? That we kneel to hisspits? Ruler Mastiq, Father, we are a powerful nation, we should liberate these heathens and set them on the right path. We need to bring God to them. You, my father, can bring God to them! We must act. We can't sit back like Ruler Wahakbi whose dithering lost us Vaasar. Who lost us our link to the sea, to trade, to fortune."

"Yes, yes, son," Mastiq mumbled, retreating into his cushion. The accusation that he was similar to the much-loathed ruler of thousands of scorch seasons past, stung. *I am winning this tussle. Mama will be proud.*

"I will not send the Drome army to Riaow. If that is your desire, *friend*, then you will need to find another Minister of War," Whaled fumed.

"Oh no, that is no good, Whaled, no good at all." Mastiq wrung his hands. "I will think on this some more, we can talk again another time. Now, I need to deal with some issue with my harem, a daughter does not want to marry as instructed but for love, the usual trivial nonsense. Then I must dress for dinner, that headdress takes an age to put on. High Priest Zeead, will you stay and bless me. You are both dismissed. Slave! Clear these reeking heads away."

The minister stomped out the room and Ammad followed him. Out of earshot of his father, Ammad grabbed Whaled's arm. The hairy monster of a man turned on him and for a moment Ammad feared for his life.

"What is it you desire, Whaled?" Ammad whimpered. His mother had always taught him that every person could be swayed if you found their deepest desire.

"What are you talking about, lying worm," Whaled growled. He took Ammad around the throat and smashed him against the wall, a fingernail away from a tall coloured glass window depicting a lotus flower that rattled with the force.

"To change your mind. To attack Peqkya. Once we have them in hand, we will use their warriors to take back Vaasar and smite those thieving Ferts once and for all. What… do… you… want?" he coughed out as Whaled's grip tightened. Sunshine poured through the glass panes and a glowing red light hit the minister, turning his facial hair a menacing purple.

"Nothing will make me change my mind. It would be a slaughter. Perhaps you can go and invade with your dim-witted guards under this false holy cause. I would happily watch you being torn to shreds."

"Gold? Women? Lands? Status? Power? What have you always wanted, Whaled?" Ammad insisted. Whaled lifted the Crown Prince off his feet and threw him down, a glint in his eye.

"Jakira," he said and strode off.

His laughter rang down the corridor and clanged in Ammad's ears.

***

Ammad burst into Jakira's chambers at her craterside villa, charging past slaves who tried to stand in his way.

"Mistress is indisposed, Crown Prince," Medi said, the slave guard who stood at her door. Jakira trusted him to run her household as well as her slave snooping network on the streets, bringing her all the latest incriminating news and wild rumours which she stored away and then used to her advantage at the right moment.

"Is she dressed?"

"Yes, Crown Prince."

"Well then, she can receive me!"

Ammad pushed past the hulking slave and into her back room. His mother was laying on a couch staring out the window, fanned by a slave. Her arm resting on a table with the palm up and a tube inserted into her inner elbow. On the other end of the tube on a high table was a child, pinned down with straps and with mouth and eyes bound. The girl was squirming but healers fluttered around trying to soothe her. Dark red blood flowed out of the child and into his mother.

"What the…?" Ammad exclaimed and stopped in his tracks.

"Oh, flesh of my flesh, welcome home! Come and give me a kiss." She smiled at him drowsily and beckoned him over. He obeyed and pecked her on the cheek.

"You look terrible, and you absolutely stink." She crinkled up her nose and swatted him away.

"What is all this?" Ammad pointed to her arm.

"When you conquer Peqkya there will no doubt be a drought on Peqkian ointments and potions, so I'm trying new things. I might have found the answer to eternal youth. Fresh young blood flowing through my veins helps keep me beautiful."

"Who is the child?"

"Oh, only a slave child, Ammad. She'll be fine. Every noble woman of a certain age is doing it. I'm thinking of hosting a party next week, where we can transfuse young blood for old and swap all the latest gossip."

"Can I give it a try?"

She pinched his arm. "No, you are still young! I should be taking your blood."

Ammad grimaced. "Urgh I don't think so!" Then he coughed. "Mama, I have something important to tell you. In private."

Jakira clicked her fingers and the healers stood to attention. "Unhook me and leave us. Tend to the child, keep it well fed and watered. Tomorrow we will transfuse again."

The needle was pulled out of her arm and she pressed a cloth to the prick. Ammad shuddered. He hated needles. The child was unstrapped and carried out. Jakira was more generous to her slaves than most masters, having been a slave once herself. Her story was legendary in Parchad, but never spoken about in her presence. At thirteen, Jakira's beauty had astonished Mastiq as she served him at a noble's villa. Understanding she was still a virgin, he claimed her for his harem. Her beauty was equalled by her wit and she became one of his favourites.

As soon as they were alone, Ammad relayed the meeting and Whaled's demands. Jakira was livid. She jumped up, grabbed the slipper off her foot and slapped at Ammad's head and shoulders. He held his forearms up to block her, but suffered the punishment. It didn't hurt him all that much and was more a show of power from his mother. She exhausted herself and then sat stony faced, her lips twisted into an ugly grimace.

To break the silence, Ammad tried humour. "Mama, you will get terrible wrinkles if you keep your mouth screwed up like that, not even fresh blood will help."

The teasing enraged her and she started whacking him again. He ducked the blows and waited it out until she wilted on the couch.

"I cannot. You know I cannot. Why couldn't he have picked jewels or gold or anything else."

"He is asking for the impossible to make a point, Mama."

"I know that, stupid boy!"

Ammad braced himself for another round of slipper bashing but instead Jakira sat still, deep in thought.

"I am bound to your father, the Ruler of Drome! I cannot be with another man. Any treachery to the ruler would see me die in the most horrible of ways. It would be impossible to keep secret, your father would hear of my betrayal and then where does that leave you? Where does that leave Sel?"

Ammad frowned, he had not considered the threat to his own position.

Jakira continued, "And regardless of if we were caught, could we trust Whaled to keep up his end of the bargain? Or perhaps he is doing this to remove you as Crown Prince."

Ammad shrugged. Jakira stood and paced the room, mumbling to herself. If anyone was going to work out an impeccable plan, it would be his mother and it was pointless interjecting in her deliberations. His stomach growled and he called a slave to bring some food.

A plate of spiced meat and mashed aubergine arrived and as Ammad was about to tuck in, Jakira spoke, "I must meet with Whaled immediately. Make it happen."

Ammad frowned and pushed the food away, his mouth watering, and he went dutifully to find Whaled.

***

"You have a daughter called Razanne," Jakira said to Whaled after a rapid conversation in which he haughtily responded to her questions. The Minister of War slouched in a chair, knees wide, arms crossed and smirking. But this statement stumped him and he sat up taller. Ammad watched his devious mother. She knew this would hurt him and up until that point had allowed Whaled to feel like he was the one winning this game.

"What of it?" he snapped.

She turned to her son. "Ammad, Razanne is *very* beautiful. Born to a high bred woman who was once Whaled's wife. She was a friend of mine, but sadly died many scorch seasons ago." Jakira turned back to Whaled. "Razanne is how old now? Fourteen?"

Whaled did not reply. Instead he started to pinch his nostrils with thumb and forefinger, pulling at hair and digging around with his nails.

"Yes, she must be fourteen now! The same age as Selmi. In fact, I think Selmi and Razanne learnt their letters under the tutelage of the same wiseman when they were little." She patted Ammad's knee.

"I do not know of her," Ammad replied, unsure as to where his mother was going.

"Of course not, Whaled has tried very hard to keep her away from the palace. However, she is now of marrying age. I'm assuming you will re-introduce her to court soon?"

Whaled stayed silent. *She's got you by your no-doubt-insanely-hairy balls! Go Mama!*

She continued, "I'm sure you know of the tradition that states a Crown Prince can pick any woman he chooses for his harem before he is married. And once picked, this woman is bound to him for life, never being able to marry the man she loves, growing old, lonely and never satisfied. It is a terrible life to be in a royal harem, often you are favoured for a scorch season or two if you are lucky and then completely forgotten when the next nubile concubine comes along."

Whaled maintained his muteness. Ammad grinned, he was not aware of this tradition and he very much liked the sound of it. His mother went on, like a snake delivering the deadly venom through its fangs after a vicious bite.

"Once in a royal harem you must do what your master tells you. Some women have been treated horrendously, given to other men, to guards, to slaves. Whipped or degraded. Anything the master desires. I have been exceedingly lucky. Our Ruler favours me and after all these scorch seasons, I still hold his attention. Mastiq is a kind man. Do you recall the stories about his father? He was not a kind man."

She shook her head sadly. She rose from the chair, swept her lustrous hair over her shoulder, around her neck and down over her breast, twisting it so it fell in one large curl and then glided to the window, gazing out. Whaled followed her movement with his eyes. She positioned herself behind the Minister of War and put a hand on his shoulder, digging in her long fingernails, painted gold and filed to a point. Her tone changed, cold.

"So, Minister of War, here is the deal. I give myself to you for one night in the utmost secrecy. If we are discovered, you will tell Mastiq that it is a lie. You will find a way to lead the Drome army into Peqkya and overthrow Melokai Ramya. If not, Ammad will select Razanne as one of his harem. If she refuses, then she dies."

Whaled was cornered. He whipped her hand off his shoulder but kept hold of it. He stood, so his full lumbering height towered over the woman. She peered up at him, brows arched. He crushed her hand but she did not flinch.

"Deal." He broke off the eye contact and spat on the floor, releasing his hold on her.

"Excellent." She gathered her gown and swept towards the door. Pausing to allow Ammad through. She turned back to Whaled and with a voice like honey said, "Oh, and I think I should warn you, my son is not as kind as his father when it comes to women. Such a shame, I have tried to teach him otherwise, but he has inherited his grandfather's nasty streak."

***

Ammad spent an inordinate amount of time under water poured by slaves, washing every crevice more times than he could count. *This is more water than most people in Drome drink in a scorch season!*

Once he was finished, he walked through to his chambers. A girl awaited him there, Laurie. She was his favourite whore. A Fertilian girl whose father had sold secrets about his country to the Dromedars and spied for many scorch seasons, until discovered and put to death. His family fled to Parchad, squandered the man's payment for services rendered to Drome and now lived in squalor. Other Fertilian snoops had double lives, living lavishly in Parchad and shrewdly in their own country, but Laurie wasn't the fastest camel in the race and could just about manage to spread her legs for a few coins.

Laurie had lush blond hair that fell in curls to her knees, pale skin and blue eyes, dulled by too much poppy. She liked to tell him with her ugly, stunted Dromedari that she looked like the Queen Jessima Cleland, but tonight she wasn't talking much.

She was tied down to his bed and was struggling to free herself, he'd never bound her before, choosing the cheaper, uglier whores to satisfy his more violent tendencies. He had never wanted to mark Laurie's fine body or exotic face, until now. When she saw him, her efforts increased and the leather drew blood from her bound wrists. As he approached the bed, she started to scream but the material around her mouth muffled it.

"Now then, Queenie, what shall we do with you? If only you were the real Jessima. Those Fert fuckers are the next for our massacre. Your vile, thieving people," he said as he crawled onto the bed, straddling her. He drank up the fear that flashed in her eyes, but he was still… flaccid.

Ammad grabbed his camel whip. He held it to her neck and she tried to call out again. He cracked it against the wooden frame, she flinched and started snivelling. He was still not hard. He yanked at her breast. *Perhaps torture will help.* It didn't. He looked at his limp member and willed it to stiffen. Then he grabbed it, rubbing vigorously whilst biting at her nipple.

"Shit." He sat back on the bed. The girl, sensing that her imminent suffering had passed, relaxed her body and then a noise started up. She was laughing. Through her gag. He slapped her but she didn't stop.

"Shut up, bitch!"

But she was no longer frightened of him, amused by the lifeless chunk of skin hanging between his legs. Her body convulsed in hysterics.

He took his knife from the table and held it to her cheek. "This will stop you laughing."

Laurie saw his threat as empty and didn't stop. He pressed the point harder and nicked her skin. She silenced and stared up at him as he showed her the blood tipped knife. She started struggling again, turning her head away from him as far as she could. He grabbed her hair, admiring the blond strands between his fingers, and yanked her head so it was still. Snot bubbles grew and popped at Laurie's nostrils as her breaths became more rapid. She started crying, her eyes popping from their sockets, petrified. But her terror did not arouse him.

Irritated, he extinguished the light in her eyes, running his blade across her neck and watching her life ebb away as the blood spilled out onto his fine silk sheets. Even the rush of power he felt at her death didn't stir his dormant cock.

25

RAMYA

Ꞷ

She missed Jessima. A vacuum filled the space where the Queen of Fertilian's joyous laughter had once been. Ramya moped and on some days, wouldn't leave her bed. She had never moped before and she had never stayed in her nightdress all day. Her irritable mood made her sharp with her counsellors and – worse – with Gwrlain. Every time she snapped at him she immediately regretted it, not understanding where the malice had come from and only recognising it when it was too late and already out of her mouth.

A few hours after she had fallen asleep Gwrlain gently woke her, smoothing her hair. "Follow me, my love," he whispered. "I will lead you."

He wrapped her fur pelt around her shoulders, guided her feet into warm boots and led her by the hand through her apartments, out into the garden and through into the forest. She could barely see, but Gwrlain hummed his way. They traipsed uphill through trees and soon left the bustle of the city behind.

They came out on a rolling meadow filled with flowers such as poppies, geraniums and rhododendrons. The sweet smell was heightened as the previous day's downpour had quenched the flowers' thirst after the long, dry summer. It was a clear night; the substantial rains and swollen clouds had taken an evening off and the stars twinkled in the sky. The light from the moon helped her to see what was in front of her. A makeshift tent, cushions and blankets. Gwrlain let go of her hand and lit the candles around the tent, singing. Ever since he had sung that first time in the prison, his harmonious sounds never failed to elate her. As if he sung just for her.

The flickering candles bathed the area in a warm glow. Gwrlain stood in front of her grinning. He had decorated it with flowers, ribbons and small strips of cloth. He took her hand again and helped her to sit on the cushions, organising them around her so she was comfortable. She listened to the grass and flowers rustling and allowed the aroma to wash over her. She snuggled into a blanket. Gwrlain leaned back and pointed up.

"Look at the stars," he said. "Look you are here and this is me and this over here is Jessima. She is still close. You can see her light and she can see yours. I know you miss her, my love, but you will see her again."

"Thank you, Gwrlain." She kissed him tenderly and he wrapped her up in his arms.

***

Ramya sat with Gwrlain sheltered from the lashing rain, watching young warriors train in chariot warfare. Her dark mood had lightened and she was exhilarated by the skills of these young women. One stood out from the rest. She was quick, precise, intelligent. Gogo was stood in the midst of the training pitch with dust swirling about her, shouting direction and keeping order. The Head Warrior was enjoying herself. Ramya beckoned her over.

"Who is the girl with the long, thin braids?"

"Her name is Monya, my Melokai. She is excellent, isn't she."

Gogo strode back onto the pitch and singled out Monya to leave the mock battle and fight with her. Monya handed the reins to another warrior, vaulted from her moving carriage, rolled on landing and then took up position in front of the Head Warrior, sword in hand. They sparred. Gogo pushed her hard and the girl responded well, conserving her energy with well-considered movements. She made a few mistakes, and each time Gogo told her where she had failed. Monya concentrated on Gogo's words and then did not make the same mistake again.

From the side lines the Melokai clapped, Monya turned to look and Gogo put her sword to her neck.

"Never be distracted, warrior," Gogo shouted, but she patted Monya on the back and sent her to spar with another novice.

Two horses came tearing onto the pitch, dodging the chariots with ease. The riders jumped off the bare backs and landed at Gogo's feet. A few words were exchanged and then Gogo ran to Ramya, followed by the two warriors.

"My Melokai, these messengers have brought news of the wolves."

Ramya stood and motioned to the warriors to speak.

"My Melokai, we have ridden hard from the north-east border. A week ago wolves were spotted. A great number, thousands. Our captain sent out two scouts, they did not return. Instead we found their bodies strung from a tree near to our camp. Their hands and feet had been hacked off. At night, the wolves howl wildly. Our Captain is readied for an attack with the five hundred warriors she has with her. It has taken us two weeks to get here, it might have already happened." Raindrops streamed down the messenger warrior's gaunt face, clinging to her eyelashes.

"Thank you. Any other message?" The warrior gestured not and Ramya dismissed them. "Go. Rest and eat well. We may have need of you later."

Gogo's joy at training her new warriors vanished and her brow furrowed.

"Zhaq," she muttered under her breath.

"So, it has begun," Ramya said grimly and Gwrlain placed his palm on the small of her back from his seat behind her. "We need to send reinforcements. How many warriors can go?"

Gogo thought a moment and then replied, "We have one thousand to send, my Melokai. We cannot spare any more. The capital will be left with these young warriors."

"So be it. Who will command in your absence?"

"Ashya will stay behind."

"Good. Have my horse prepared. We leave on the morrow."

Gwrlain erupted from his chair. "No, Ramya, the baby!"

"I'm pregnant, I'm not an invalid! I will see these standing wolves for myself. I'll pet them and then I'll flay their skins to adorn our beds."

Gogo raced away and Ramya turned to Gwrlain. He clenched and released his fists.

"I know what you are thinking." Ramya put a hand to the Trogr's cheek. He remained stiff and did not return the touch. "I'm the Melokai and I must do my duty for my nation but I must also protect our baby. I can do both, my soulmatch. I can, I know I can. I must. They need me there."

26

DARRIO

Two thousand wolves howling in unison made the air vibrate. It was a formidable sound and Darrio knew it would intimidate the enemy on the other side of the river. It terrified him. The wolves stalked up and down the river bank in view of the Peqkians, flashing their glowing eyes at the camp.

After the full moon pack-meet at Aaowl Peak, thousands of packs had sent between one and seven wolves to fight and take back the Lost Lands. A momentous occurrence, but it bothered Darrio that the wolves were disorganised and had no leader. They had gathered in small groups, working out who they wanted to be around and who they didn't, and sticking to these newly formed packs. Darrio took comfort in the fact that all were united in one aim – to slaughter the humans sat on the other side.

The wolves estimated that there were around five hundred humans and at first, the humans had responded to the howling with spears and arrows, but all fell short and were washed away. To the east was the birthplace of the Great River, high up in the Zwullfr mountains, deep in wolf territory. From its source, the river flowed over a steep waterfall and then into the Wul-Onr valley where they now stood, at its narrowest and calmest point. To the west, it angrily flowed downhill as huge rocks frothed up the water in raging rapids before it broadened so wide that it was impossible to see the other side. The reason for the river's name. The wolves had not ventured that far west for many generations, preferring to stay in the mountains.

Neither side had made a move and for six nights they had eyed each other across the water, the wolves howling at sundown and into the night. Both wolves and humans knew that crossing the river to attack would leave them open and vulnerable, so the fight had become nothing more than a stare off.

"Got an idea," old timer Benrro rasped. He had come back after the full moon pack-meet with four wolves from his Karracht-Aaen to fight.

"Go on," the grey wolf Sinarro urged, ears pricked.

Benrro stood on back paws so all nearby could hear. "We take half our number and track up river, cross upstream of the waterfall. I know a path. Humans cannot get further east; mountains are impassable for those creatures. We enclose them and attack from sides and behind, pushing them towards river. Rest of our number then swim across. We will have them circled, as we surround prey. Then we go for their necks. They will not expect an attack from their side of the valley. We are stronger in a circle than in a line."

"Good idea, Benrro," said Darrio's alpha Lurra, moving closer to the old wolf and sitting in front of him. "How many nights to climb, cross, descend and surround the humans?"

"Seven if we run night and day and take few rests."

"We have half our strength for seven nights. Leaves us weak if humans attack," Lurra replied.

"Will they? They wait for us. They do not want to cross the river," Sinarro said. "We continue howling each night and stalking the river bank. They will not know that we split our numbers."

"Agreed. How do we know when wolves are in place on south side?" Lurra asked.

"We return the howl and then attack," Benrro responded. "You hear our voices, you swim."

"I like it, let us tell the rest." Lurra stood and gave orders for her pack members to take messages to groups along the river bank.

***

Darrio remained on the north side with around one thousand wolves, awaiting the signal from the other thousand. The wolves were baying for blood and all accepted Benrro's suggestion, to have something to do other than look at the enemy. Sinarro and Lurra left with the south side attacking troop and Darrio knew they would have a hard journey ascending the mountains, avoiding icy crevasses and avalanches. He had no idea what the river was like before it tumbled over the waterfall ledge, and hoped for the troop's sake that it was a small, passable stream. All the wolves left behind kept up the howling each night and waited, impatient for the return cry.

Seven nights passed, and then eight and then nine and no return howl came from the other side. Darrio started to worry and he noticed the general mood become agitated with some wolves insisting they attack anyway. Scraps broke out and the disorder turned dangerous. He sent his pups back to Wulhor-Aaen den and told them to stay there until he came for them.

On the tenth night, the wolves on the north bank howled and a few heartbeats later there was a reply. It was a fierce sound; the wolves were in position.

Cries of "Now!" echoed along the bank and wolves plunged into the river. Darrio slipped into the icy water and paddled as fast as his paws would take him. Sounds of chaos started up from the other side. Wolf wailing and human screaming. Flashes of light as torches were knocked over and flames licked up the sides of tents. Human warriors crowded along the bank and threw spears and loosed arrows at the mass of dark fur steadily advancing across the river. Many found their mark and the water turned red as blood seeped from wounds. The dead floated off downstream.

As the first wave of wolves started pulling themselves out of the water, the warriors attacked with spears and then blades, chopping down many. The initial surprise at the attack was quickly forgotten as the Peqkians aligned themselves strategically and fought as one, listening to commands from one leader and moving with a graceful, controlled precision. Years of combat practice making them, by far, the superior side in terms of discipline and skill. But the sheer number of wolves overwhelmed the humans and forced them back, the wolves taking advantage of the rough ground and the human's unsteadiness on their little feet.

Darrio attacked warriors, ensuring their death was swift. He knew Peqkian warrior weaknesses after hours of training, but had chosen not to relay that information to any other wolf to avoid inevitable questions about *who* had coached him. That was best left unknown and unsaid.

The five hundred warriors along the river bank were soon herded together and surrounded by the wolves. They formed up in a circle kneeling with spears out, and behind them crouched warriors with swords, poised to fight. The archers in the centre. The wolves howled and scratched at the earth with sharp claws. The Peqkians hissed and snarled, eyes wild with fury at being trapped.

This will not end well.

The male wolves unfurled to their full height on two legs. A menacing display of dominance. The warriors responded by hunkering down, holding their positions.

The first wolves sprinted forward into the spears, any that broke through were stabbed. A volley of arrows sprayed them and for a while the only sound was the yapping of dying wolves. But more wolves came, pressing the humans closer together as they backed up into each other. The wolf attack was relentless and the Peqkian formation fractured, with wolves swarming through the crack into the midst of the warriors and tearing them apart from the inside.

Those wolves are braver than I. Darrio held back, he did not want to die and leave his pups behind. And deep down he did not want to destroy humans. He found half dead warriors on the ground to finish off quickly, so no one could say he wasn't committed to the fight.

Warriors cut down wolves, wolves tore out human throats. The mayhem went on for hours, and soon the sun rose on blood soaked, trampled ground and a blanket of tangled corpses. The destruction was complete and the surviving wolves panted and surveyed the carnage, searching out dead friends. A small group of warriors had managed to retreat into the Small Mountains, desperately scrambling up unstable glaciers. No others remained alive.

In the daylight Darrio picked his way over bodies and found Lurra. Her head was snapped and she had lost most of her rump. He could not find Sinarro and slowly lost hope that the grey wolf was still alive.

"Victory!" Xocorra of Vierz-Aaen exclaimed, her tail wagging. "Wul-Onr valley is ours again. Let us feast on human meat and assign new packs to settle here."

A small cry of agreement went up from the surviving wolves. Perhaps half of their number still stood, but they were exhausted. Darrio licked his injury, his back haunch had been slashed with a knife, and he volunteered to cross the river to spread the news of the humans' defeat. In truth, he wanted to get back to his children.

***

Darrio limped for days from den to den telling of the victory and how the wolves will stay on the south side of the river to hold it and make sure no further humans come. He flinched at every step, a jolt of agony from his wound shooting through his back, his body telling him to rest, but he pushed on. Every wincing shuffle forward took him closer to his pups. Celebratory howls and yips could be heard across the mountains. Many asked after their pack wolves, but Darrio could not say who survived or who died, he simply did not know. He delivered the message and swiftly hobbled away.

Finally, he lurched into the Wulhor-Aaen den, to deliver the news that Lurra was dead. Arro wailed when he heard of the passing of his mated female, clawed up great clods of earth, slashed livid gashes in the bark of trees. He had wanted to go and fight by her side, but she had insisted that he stay behind and guard the den and their young, telling him that she wanted "a home still here to come back to."

"Home still here," he growled at the sky, at the woods, at the den, at the rodents he viciously hunted and pulverised with one snap of his jaws, spitting out the mess. "But you not come back, Lurra. Not come home." The pack shrunk back from his rage, into shadows, out of sight.

That night, Darrio pulled aside his pups and the four of them cuddled up in each other. He licked his wound.

He was awoken by Sarrya nudging at his face.

"Pa, can we talk?"

He nodded and padded around his snoring sons. Warrio's legs twitching as he hunted in his sleep. She led him to the secret thicket and once tucked away inside he spoke, "Sarrya?"

The words came tumbling out of her. "Pa, the dreams. Won't stop. And… worse. Stone creature appeared to me. She seemed… alive."

"*Appeared?* When? Where?"

"Few days ago, when we attacked Peqkians. Morning after the battle, running in forest with Ricarro, away from river, Pappy, before you ask, up mountain slopes. We lost each other. Ran about shouting his name but could not find him. Paused to catch breath and take in surroundings and… and…" Sarrya choked, finding it hard to catch her breath.

Darrio leaned on her and rubbed his head into her neck for comfort. "Go on," he said.

"Went dark, blacker than night. Could not see anything, thought had gone blind. All forest noises gone, and all smells. Could not feel the rocks under paws or rain on fur. Stood upright on back paws and could not move, something held me, pinned me there. Thought I had died. So frightened." Sarrya whimpered at the memory, and Darrio snuffled her fur. "But then noticed tiny speck of bright light, only thing I could see. Concentrated on it, willing it to grow. More I focused, bigger it got, until I was standing in middle of a ball of light. Could see the black beyond. Then a smell of pines and a pathway appeared, a tunnel covered with blue, and a faint noise of little wails and trills. Floated up the tunnel, like snowflakes float gently from the sky, and noise got louder, louder until it hurt my ears. Went in a wooden enclosure and stood in front of the stone creature. She seemed angry, but not at me. Little cats ran about, between my back paws, licked at my fur and massaged their claws in and out, humming, and I wasn't frightened anymore. She spoke to me, in a strange language that I understood. Then woke up, many hours later, in forest... She *marked* me."

"Marked you?" Darrio's voice raised in alarm. "Are you hurt?"

"Ssh, Pa," Sarrya replied and she rolled on her side so her four legs were facing Darrio. "Look at my pads."

Darrio pulled her nearest foreleg to his face and in the moonlight, inspected the bottom of her paws. He yelped when he saw. Her dark grey pads, the colour of every wolf's pads, were red. Bright like the redcurrants that grew near the river. He started to lick at them, determined to get the colour off. Sarrya giggled as his efforts tickled.

"Stop, Pa, won't work. Tried. All my pads red, like the

creature's hair."

Darrio dropped her paw and then stared at his daughter. "What did she say?"

"She's not happy about wolves fighting with humans."

"Not *happy*?"

"Sounds stupid, but humans are not our foe. Enemy we need to unite against is bigger, darker. This is a waste of wolf lives, a pointless battle, Pa."

Darrio considered his daughter. Every day she seemed to grow wiser as well as in stature. He was certain that if they both stood on two feet she would be taller than him now. She spoke like a sage old wolf, not a yearling, like the weight of the moon was on her shoulders.

"Daughter, this is a pointless battle. My feeling from the start. Wolves died and for what? More humans will come; we cannot beat them. As for our true enemy, I cannot comprehend who or what this could be. It terrifies me." He continued, with a sharp tone, "Never repeat that to anyone. Daughter, you hear me?"

"Of course, Pa." Her eyes darted up to his.

"There is more isn't there, Sarry."

"Yes." She rolled up, eagerly hoping for answers from her father. "True enemy," she said, "not from south. Danger comes from *east*."

He had no answers for her and could not meet her gaze.

Eventually he muttered, "Have you asked her?"

"Yes. But she does not answer. What lies to the east, Pa?"

"Mountains and frozen wilderness. Past that I do not know."

A rustling distracted them as another wolf edged under the bramble. Darrio and Sarrya hunched up, ready to fight if necessary. The wind was behind them, blowing their scent into the oncoming wolf but they couldn't smell any trace of who was approaching.

"Sarry!" Ricarro's face came into view.

Sarrya bounded over to her friend and they wagged their tails at each other.

"Hello, Darrio," the yearling said.

"Leave you two to it," Darrio sighed, eager to have some time to himself to think.

***

Darrio leapt into the chilly water and made for the other side. He heaved himself out and greeted the wolves stationed there, asking for one in particular. He was pointed in the right direction and soon picked up the scent.

"Benrro," he said and lowered his eyes.

"Darrio," the old wolf replied. Benrro's injuries from the battle meant he could not swim back or ever return to his pack. He had lost two legs, a front and a back, but remarkably he had survived.

"May I ask you a question?"

"Yes," Benrro croaked and propped himself up on his back leg as best he could.

"What lies to the east of Zwullfr?"

"Mountains and wilderness."

"Yes. Past that," Darrio said.

"When I was a pup, mother told me the tales that her mother told her and her mother before, that beyond our lands was nothingness. A vast nothingness, not hot, not cold, not flat, not mountainous, not green, not white. No animal lived there. If I was naughty, my mother threatened to send me to Nowhere. What she called the place."

"Nowhere," Darrio repeated.

"Could just be tales to spook pups, but that is what I know."

"Thank you, Benrro." Darrio kneeled on his front paws and said, "You want anything?"

"No, well-tended here."

Darrio set off back to the den. *Nothingness. Nowhere. What enemy comes from nowhere?*

27

JESSIMA

"Oh, Daddy, no!" Princess Georgina squealed in mock embarrassment as King Hugo told the tale of when she had accidently wet herself when she was a toddler. It was one of his favourites.

"She told her handmaid she needed to go, but old Bessie just wasn't hotfooted enough to get her to a chamber pot and she relieved herself right where she stood on the flagstones! There was a stain for weeks, it looked as if a hulk of a dog had pissed there rather than a tiny four-year-old moppet." He chuckled and the Princess cupped her cheeks with her palms.

Jessima was not keen on Georgina, but Hugo's youngest daughter and second child always cheered him up. She doted on him as he doted on her, a relationship Jessima resented. As a child, Jessima fought with her ten siblings for a minute of her father's attention. Eventually she gave up, realising painfully he preferred his sons. Her family lived in central Fertilian and she hadn't seen them since her wedding. She exchanged regular letters with her sister Geraldina, who kept her up to date on the Walter family shenanigans. She missed them.

"You are the exact double of your mother when you

laugh." Hugo's eyes glazed with the memory of Jayne. "I wish you could've met her."

"I know, Daddy, I wish that too." Georgina turned down the corners of her mouth in upset. "Anyhow, did I tell you what that wicked Lady Mudgway has been up to?"

He laughed again, shaken from his reverie. "Go on then, tell me, sweetling."

She started to prattle on as Toby walked in to the sitting area. A heat flamed between Jessima's legs and she shifted her dress to cross them tight underneath, scared that others in the room would feel the warmth that wafted from her.

"King Hugo, Queen Jessima, Princess Georgina." He bowed courteously and sat on the sofa next to Georgina. She turned her exposed cleavage towards him and pecked him on the cheek, batting her eyelashes at him. Jessima resisted the urge to fly at the princess and rip out those lashes one by one.

"Toby, for what do we owe this pleasure?" King Hugo said.

"I do apologise, your Grace, for disturbing your leisure time with these two fine specimens of the female kind, but I need your guidance on an urgent matter. I promise to detain him for a few minutes only, ladies." He patted Georgina's knee and stood.

"Of course. Do excuse me, I shall return henceforth." Jessima's husband stood and led his brother out of the room.

Georgina leaned in close to Jessima and lowered her voice. "He's gorgeous isn't he! I bet he has a huge manhood."

Jessima leaned away from her stepdaughter, they were not friends. In her most disapproving and mature voice she scolded, "Don't be ridiculous, he is your uncle. And my brother in law."

Georgina cackled and her chest heaved so energetically that Jessima was sure a breast would pop out.

"So! I would ravish him if given half a chance. Wouldn't you?" Georgina winked and Jessima stood abruptly.

"Excuse me, the baby is making me feel nauseous." She hastened away from the woman, seething.

Jessima ran to her bedroom and flung herself on the bed thumping her fists on the pillow. *Would he want her? She is beautiful and willing. He did pat her knee so casually and he definitely ogled her breasts. Definitely. They were hard to miss. Perhaps they have already done it. Oh, I want him for my own.*

***

Queen Jessima sat like a statue at the back of the war room, hands on her swelling bump. King Hugo had allowed her to be present as she had kept her promise to remain silent. At first he was adamant that she need not worry her pretty little head about such things, but she insisted that she would worry *more* if she didn't hear what was happening and that stress was bad for the baby. Her husband relented and now her presence was accepted and all but forgotten by everyone else in the room.

In truth, she just wanted to be close to Toby, most of the battle chatter swept over her head. He had been preoccupied with the impending war and they hadn't had a chance to speak for many weeks. She observed him from afar, soothed by his voice and daydreaming about his touch.

A large map was spread out on a table and the King and his council positioned themselves around it talking tactics, preparations and logistics. The Peqkian Captain Denya joined them. She had proved her worth with shrewd strategic thinking and had been accepted as a valuable advisor.

"The training of the army by Captain Denya is proceeding well, your Grace," Toby said.

"Excellent," his brother, the King, replied.

Denya instructed Toby each day and Jessima noticed that his body had changed. He was still slender but now his muscles were honed. When he rolled up his shirt sleeves to point over the map, she caught flashes of his bicep and quivered inwardly. She wanted him to make love to her again, and the thought consumed her.

"So, we are ready," King Hugo rasped, stroking his beard. "And now we wait for the Thorne army to make a move. What is the delay?"

Lord Zachary Macune answered, "Our scouts tell the same story. The Thorne twin army is camped out and the soldiers laze about and eat. There is no training, the men are not disciplined. There is still a divide between each twin's host. There is much movement in and out of the main pavilion where Arthur Thorne resides with Mary Thorne's husband, Lord Clement Pullman. Mary does not appear to be there, and neither is false Queen Charlotte. We have no information as to where they are, as yet. Pullman is in charge of Mary's men and speaks for her. There are ample provisions, horses and weapons. It is not clear why they tarry."

"I imagine they are arguing about how to attack. After all, it has taken them more than two decades to agree to join their armies," Lord Alon Sumner snorted.

The men all guffawed and then the King asked about the salt flats.

"The situation remains constant, your Grace," Lord Gregory Doddy replied, who was in charge of salt processing operations. "The eastern salt flats are still controlled by Mary Thorne and the west by us. Each keeps to its own side. Princess Matilda and her husband Lord John Iddenkinge have top notch control there. Iddenkinge's men are loyal and work hard. There have been no skirmishes for many years. It is safely in our hands. Defeating the Thorne twin's army will of course mean we can take the lot. Although our spies tell us that far in the east the salt is starting to dry out to a useless wasteland, which is slowly advancing. Nothing to worry about our end. In terms of production, we have plenty.

More than we need in fact."

King Hugo saved his scratchy voice and nodded his thanks to Doddy.

"Your Grace, shall I call in Lord Andrew Chattergoon for an update on the Lian tunnel situation?" Toby asked. The King nodded and the lord was summoned.

Chattergoon strode in. He was tall and his clothes were rugged and functional, an air of danger clung to him. Jessima knew he had a tough job, keeping the tunnels from Cleland City to Lian open. He spent much of his time under the desert in north Drome, dodging the desert rats.

"Your Grace." He bowed to King Hugo.

"Tell us of the tunnels." The King eased himself into a chair.

"We have opened tunnel nineteen after tunnel eighteen was discovered by the Dromedar rats and destroyed at airhole D. T19 is now operational and the movement of goods has begun with tunnel runners already making return journeys. So far we have no issues."

"Good. Anything else, Chattergoon?"

"Yes, your Grace. At the present time, we have a glut of desert rats wanting to help us. A village near T18, airhole D, known locally as Urakbai, was brutally annihilated by guards from the capital. I believe it was a pointed message to those that help us, but, since the massacre, many villagers and nomads have come forward, disgusted with the treatment of their fellow clan desert dwellers. We pay them with water as the bastards in Parchad let their people outside the crater walls go thirsty."

"Well we have plenty of water, it's like gold to these poor desert people," Toby added.

"Yes," Chattergoon replied. "And every year there is less and less rain in the desert. But there is more, your Grace."

"Go on," the King said, taking a swig of wine.

"Drome soldiers are amassing in the northern desert. It is… *odd.* Where they are gathering is in the north *east.* If they were planning another attack on Lian, they would gather to the west."

"Are they planning an attack on Cleland City?" Toby asked.

"I cannot say. We are watching them closely. It might be a ploy, or they might be gearing up to strike the tunnel network. I have increased our men along the tunnels, and upped the watch at Lian. However, the rat army is positioned here." Chattergoon jabbed a finger at the map.

"That is near to the Peqkian trade route through the mountains, that is the route we took." Toby drummed his fingers on the table as he considered this.

"The desert rats could not possibly think to invade the mountain cats?" Lord Macune asked.

"It is a possibility," Chattergoon replied. "There are around ten thousand rats and more arrive by the day. The brute of an army general, Whaled, is with them. His presence is significant. They are making suspicious forays in the direction of the Peqkian border. I believe they are looking north to Peqkya."

"Ramya," Jessima yelled and shot to her feet. All faces turned to stare at her, it was as if a chair at the back of the room had spoken. "We must tell Melokai Ramya!"

***

Jessima sat in the sunshine, twisting strands of hair and attempting to control her shaking legs. She was wrapped up in itchy blankets against the cool breeze, trying to enjoy the crisp autumn day but her mind kept returning to Ramya. Her brow ached. The men had gone out hunting, and the women sat waiting for them to return, servants hurrying to lay out the picnic and get a fire burning under the spit to roast whatever the hunt caught.

Jessima had a craving for salted tomatoes with basil and a special order was positioned in front of her, the castle cooks having excelled themselves in perfecting the ratio of ingredients. Her mouth watered and she resisted the urge to dive in and devour the lot before the appropriate time.

"The hunt! They are returning," Lady Berindonck blurted, relieved. It was well known that her husband Walter was a terrible horseman and she fretted for his safety on every hunt.

They came tearing up the hill towards the women, King Hugo in the front in high spirits. Toby was a few horses back, a beam of light seemed to shine down on him. Jessima scanned the women to see who was staring at him. She was certain they all were; he was the most fetching of the lot. Her lips puckered. *Back off ladies, he's mine.*

Hugo reined in his horse and came to a halt a few paces away. A stable hand held onto the bridle as he dismounted. He came striding up the hill and in that moment Jessima thought he looked strong and virile, half his sixty years. His cheeks flushed with the effort of the hunt. She sat upright and waved.

He saluted back but then his face turned into a grimace and he stopped, clutching his chest. His legs buckled and he dropped to the ground, groaning. Lords, ladies, servants all rushed forward. Jessima bumbled around in the cushions trying to break free from the blankets and cursing her cumbersome belly. She stood to see Toby yanking off the King's tight cloak from around his neck, putting an ear to his heart and then holding a hand over his mouth to check if he was breathing.

He rolled the King onto his side and started to yell orders, "His heart is faltering but he is still breathing! Fetch a medic!"

A rush of panic swelled and crashed against Jessima's skull and her vision blurred. She fainted.

***

King Hugo lay in their marital bed, surrounded by fussing medics and praying clerics. Servants scurried about obtaining whatever the King or his healers needed. Jessima sat to one side, watching the coming and going helplessly for she too was tended by healers checking her pulse or feeling the baby beneath her flesh. Marcy dabbed at her temples with a cool compress and Tina rubbed her ankles.

Toby had explained to her that the King's heart had over exerted itself on the hunt and had struggled to keep up with itself causing him great pain. They had administered poppy and he was no longer in pain, but his heart was still recovering. Her husband's already gruff voice was now a whisper as he slipped in and out of consciousness and mumbled, asking for Jayne. Always Jayne. It made everyone in the room uncomfortable, and every time the name of his dead wife passed his lips, Jessima felt nervous glances in her direction. *I wonder if I called out for Toby when I fainted. Oh God, I pray not!*

"I feel the need to retire, please escort me to another bed chamber and allow the King to rest." Jessima mustered the energy to push herself up out of the chair and felt Marcy's sturdy hands under her arm to help guide her.

Lord Macune marched into the chamber, followed by most of Hugo's war council, including her love, Toby. Jessima paused.

"Your Grace," Lord Macune said from the foot of the bed at the drowsy King. "We have had report that the Thorne army is on the move. We must ride out to meet it on the morrow to reach Yettle valley in time."

The King grumbled and indicated to a servant to prop him up in bed. Dried spittle gathered at the corners of his mouth and made his beard clump. His dishevelled hair and crumpled bedclothes gave him the air of a madman, rather than the King.

Hugo beckoned the men forward and in a barely audible voice replied, "Get the army ready then, we leave in the morning."

"Yes, your Grace," Macune said. "We will organise for something more comfortable to carry you to battle."

The King coughed his consent and then with extreme effort croaked, "Send the Queen and Princess to Lian. At dawn. Keep them safe."

Jessima's gaze lingered a moment on Toby and she longed to run to him, to be comforted in his arms. Instead she walked to the bed, placing her hand over her husband's and said, "My King, my husband, my love. I will make the preparations to go to Lian tomorrow with Princess Georgina."

***

Georgina droned on and on as their carriage lumbered through the castle gates into the city towards the tunnels. The Princess was excited about this adventure and all the new men she would soon make the acquaintance of, claiming she was bored of every single man at the castle. Jessima turned her attention to the streets whilst the two ladies-in-waiting tittered at the Princess's lame jokes and insinuations.

Cleland Castle was sat atop a hill in the centre of Cleland City. It was surrounded by a moat and one drawbridge was the only way in and out. The city sprawled around it and a huge stone wall marked the first boundary. Since that first wall, the city had expanded and a second stone wall marked the latest boundary. So, to attack, any force needed to break through two walls and then cross the moat. Jessima felt nervous leaving the castle behind. She rarely ventured past the moat and had never been to Lian. *I have travelled to and from Peqkya and I was just fine. No harm will come to me now either.* But the difference was that Toby was not with her, and instead she had to travel with her tedious stepdaughter.

The sun was rising and the city was coming to life. It was relatively orderly, the great fire during the Thwarting of Ben Thorne, when Hugo had reclaimed his crown, had razed much of the city to the ground. Hugo had rebuilt the area, paying much care to the street layout and building tall townhouses with small yards for animals. Hugo had also demolished much of what False King Benjamin had built across the city, including sound buildings, saying he could never love a place that had Thorne's repulsive mark left all over it.

The carriage passed through an area called Little Drome, inhabited predominantly by Dromedars. Jessima was fascinated by their strange back humps and stared shamelessly at a passing woman whose nose had been amputated at the sides. These settlers had helped the Ferts somehow, either by espionage or by helping to maintain the tunnels. Hugo ensured they were well watered.

As they neared the tunnels, the huts and merchant stands grew haphazard and chaotic. This part of the city was nicknamed the Sea Shore due to the number of Lianites and island peoples who lived here. The strong smell of fish nauseated Jessima and she reached for her vial of lavender oil. All trade that passed through the tunnels and under Drome came in and out here and there was a thriving market, as well as eateries, guesthouses and many brothels. Tunnel running was a dangerous job and the men needed to let off steam before a return journey.

Georgina blathered on, but at the mention of Toby, Jessima's attention pricked. She continued to look out at the streets, but monitored the conversation.

"Since his wife died, I hear he's savoured the delights of hundreds of women. He's an absolute sex maniac, utterly obsessed. I've never ridden him though sadly, us being related. It's rumoured he's sired offspring with half the women in the castle. Have you seen all those brats running around with green eyes? Toby must be the father." The Princess roared with glee, hugged her waist and doubled over in her mirth.

In Jessima's mind she roared *Liar! He loves me, only me.* She turned towards her stepdaughter and glared and in a matronly tone said, "You should not speak such lies about the King's brother, your uncle no less."

"Oh, Jessima, do cheer up. You must've heard the gossip. I also hear he's lain with most of the Peqkian warriors, apart from the captain. Everyone knows that wily cat is more into women. She was flirting up a storm with

Lady Cynthia Sumner the other night. Cynthia was a beauty once but is now so old! Everyone has their own tastes I suppose. I wonder if Cynthia spread her legs for Captain Denya? Now that would be a sight to see!"

Jessima leaned across the carriage and slapped Georgina. "Do not say such horrid things! Mind your tongue, Princess."

Georgina touched her hand to her face and then lunged at Jessima. They tussled about until the two ladies-in-waiting wrenched them apart.

"You wait until I tell Daddy," Georgina whinged.

"It will be a long time until you speak to him again, and whilst he's not here I'm in charge," Jessima replied in her strictest voice.

Georgina folded her arms and stuck out her tongue. Jessima pursed her lips. Her ear lobes felt like they had been scorched on a hot iron.

The carriage came to an abrupt stop. Lord Andrew Chattergoon was waiting for them with a group of his men. The tunnel entrances gaped wide and ladders poked out the top, with men toiling to unload and load cargo into them.

"My Queen." He bowed low as Jessima peered out of her carriage and gave him her hand to kiss. "How is King Hugo, I pray he is well?"

"Our Grace is recovering well, thank you, Lord Chattergoon. God has chosen to hear your prayers," Jessima replied. In truth, she had no idea what state of health her husband was in. He had refused to see her that morning before she left and his medics were cagey in answer to her enquiries. If Hugo died, her unborn baby, if a boy, would be heir to the throne. If a girl… then Hugo's eldest brother Prince Ernest. She vowed to do everything in her power to keep the babe safe.

Georgina hustled her out of the way and leaned out the carriage to give Chattergoon her hand and to give all his men a grand display of her bust.

"My Princess." He bowed. "May I come in and brief you on the journey."

"Oh yes, please *come*," Georgina teased and she shuffled over the seat to allow him room next to her. He climbed up into the carriage and squashed in, his hair tickling the ceiling of the carriage. Georgina rested a hand on his knee. He ignored her.

"I simply can't wait to see the Sarenky," she declared, squeezing the Lord's knee.

In a severe voice, he said, "I will be accompanying you with twenty of my men and with your twenty soldiers and delivering you to the Lord and overseer of Lian, Prince Ernest. Lian is the safest place you can be when war breaks out, separated from the mainland of Fertilian, self-sufficient, easier to defend. If it comes to it, we can destroy the tunnels and any Thorne attackers would need to come above ground, through the desert of Drome and through their army. You do everything I say on this journey, do you understand? If you don't, then we die."

He flicked his attention to each woman and held the eye contact for a few uncomfortable seconds. Lastly at Georgina, whose jaunty smirk turned into a petrified frown. She removed her hand.

"Currently there are four operational tunnels," he continued. "Three are used for fast running food and various other products. The fourth is used for running people and horses. I expect we will travel at a slower pace than usual, so it will take us six to eight weeks to get to Lian. You will feel suffocated, you will sweat more than you ever thought possible, you will be exhausted and you will be frightened. Be under no false allusions, you will suffer on this journey. There are no luxuries, not even for royalty."

"Oh my," Georgina exclaimed, clasping a hand to her mouth.

Chattergoon went on, "The tunnels are not high enough to ride a horse and most animals do not cope well with the confined space. Due to your condition, Queen Jessima, you will be pulled by one of our trained donkeys on a sand sled. The rest of us will be on foot. Down in the tunnels, there is no day and night, we walk six hours, we sleep six hours and we keep this pattern up until we reach the other end. Understood?"

The women managed to murmur their agreement.

"To conclude, there are many dangers in the tunnels. We will protect you."

"My Lord, what dangers?" Jessima stammered, her gut gurgling.

"My Queen, we may come upon sand scorpions, snakes and other poisonous creatures. There is a constant possibility of collapsing walls as well as detection by the Drome rats, especially as we near Lian where they direct most of their attacks. We have plenty of provisions with us including ample water, but in the event that we lose our supply, there is no water to be found. We will be the only party travelling within this tunnel, there is strict instruction not to enter the tunnel from either end until we have passed through, however on occasion we encounter illegal smugglers and bandits who manage to sneak in and lay in wait for prey like us. There are also many dead ends and old tunnels, and in some places it is like a maze. Not everyone who goes in the tunnels comes out. As I said, follow my instruction and we will protect you."

Jessima's legs started to shake and her dress rustled.

Chattergoon eased himself out of the carriage. "Wait here," he said.

Jessima stared at Georgina who stared back, their earlier altercation forgotten as they processed this information about their imminent journey, one they had only known they were going on late the night before.

"Shit," the Princess swore, sharp intakes of breath making her chest heave for all the wrong reasons.

The profanity filled the carriage like a gust from a hot oven. Jessima felt an urgent twinge in her bowels and shouted at a lady-in-waiting, "Find me a privy immediately!"

28

RAMYA

The Melokai rode at the front of one thousand warriors north west from Riaow. To her right was Gogo and to her left, her beloved Gwrlain.

Although uncomfortable with the baby pressing into her ribs, she enjoyed the journey through the rugged countryside and across the majestic Melioks. She greeted every Peqkian they came across and welcomed their chatter and news of the harvests or of the animals they tended. One group on the road were honey hunters and they had a huge vat of fresh honey still in its combs, cut from a bee nest on an overhanging mountain cliff. They were taking it to the nearest village market. Ramya swapped meat and wine for a pot of the sweet stuff and spent days savouring the sugary goo.

The Zyr Peq pass was stunning but treacherous, the season was changing and getting cooler. They camped at the base and paid their respects to the highest peak, the point jutting into the blue sky and surrounded by clouds, but didn't attempt to summit and did not linger longer than necessary. They had brought plentiful provisions including warm garments and tents to avoid any frostbite and illness from over exposure to the cold, but were relieved when they started their descent into Trequ valley.

Half way down the steep slope a Peqkian hobbled forward. She was scrawny and underdressed for the inclement weather, her nose, cheeks and chin eaten away by frostbite. The tips of her fingers had already fallen off and Ramya suspected from her bearing that her toes had succumbed too. The warrior shivered and her bottom jaw juddered.

"My Melokai, I am warrior Kiya. Welcome," she said.

"Thank you, Kiya. Let us set up camp and get you and your warriors warm and fed and then you can enlighten us as to what happened here." Ramya removed one of her cloaks and leaned from her horse and wrapped it around the scrawny warrior's shoulders. Kiya bowed.

Gogo shouted orders and the serving peons set about erecting the camp, digging the hard ground to level it for the tents. The cooks brewed honey and ginger infusion and started to prepare a nourishing meal. Ramya ordered all spare furs and boots to be distributed to Kiya and her freezing warriors.

Once they were all seated in the Melokai's pavilion, covered with blankets and with a hot drink warming their insides, Ramya gestured for Kiya to speak.

"My Melokai, five hundred warriors were stationed here after the camp massacre. At night the wolves paced up and down the north bank of Trequ river and howled. Then, one night, that howl was met by a howl from our side. They had surrounded us. Our eyes were on the river and we only had a few on patrol to watch our backs, a fatal mistake. The wolves from the north bank swam across the river and attacked. We fought our way through and up into the mountains. Eighty-two survived the attack but we have suffered huge losses in this weather. We had only the clothes on our backs, no tents or food. We are now thirty-five warriors. The serving peons were either slaughtered by the wolves or ran into the mountains to fend for themselves. I was nominated as leader due to my rank and experience."

"Tell us of the wolves, Kiya," Gogo said. "How do they fight? Weaknesses, strengths?"

"They are disorganised, but single minded in their desire to kill us and ruthless in their assault. They have no care about risking their life or the lives of fellow wolves. They took us by surprise and encircled us, which was clever. But they do not seem to have a leader, it is very much a pack mentality, making decisions on the go by majority agreement. They have no weapons, the males stand to fight on two feet or on four feet, whichever gets results. Since the battle, we have been spying on them when the wind is in the right direction, otherwise they can smell us. They have gathered up the weapons from our fallen and are learning how to use them."

"How hard would it be for us to attack them?" Gogo said.

"The wolves have established a border along the edge of the valley forest and are carefully guarding it. They know where our camp is, they cannot see us but they can sense us and smell us. It would be hard to take them unaware, but with numbers we can overthrow them. I imagine they would be near to useless if we met them in a line. They know how to fight as a pack, surrounding their prey. If they can, they go for the neck."

"How many are down there, Kiya?" Ramya said.

"I think one thousand, my Melokai. And I estimate that one thousand died in our battle. We were five hundred against two thousand." The warrior choked and briefly showed her sadness before taking a breath and composing herself again.

"I have no doubt that you and your warriors fought bravely," said Ramya. "We will cut these cockfaces down. Go and rest. Eat and keep warm."

Kiya withdrew from the tent and Ramya turned to her Head Warrior.

"I need to see this pack for myself and then we can

formulate a plan, my Melokai," said Gogo.

"I was thinking the *exact* same thing."

The next morning, they scrambled down the mountain towards the wolves, Kiya led the way. Gogo did not care about heeding the wind direction so the wolves knew they were close. The beasts started snarling and crowding together. Stalking back and forth along the forest tree line. They were bigger than Ramya expected and when a male stood with a Peqkian spear in his paw, her breath stalled at the menacing sight.

Gogo crept nearer, taunting the wolves. Arrows were loosed haphazardly and one skimmed past the Head Warrior's knee. She snapped it in half and hissed at them. The trio withdrew back up the rocks to their camp. The sound of howls at their backs.

***

Gogo decided to attack in daylight, when the wolves seemed less alert. The warriors lined up and crawled forward with the ambition to encircle the wolves and play them at their own game. It was hard going over the scree and boulders, but they had time and Gogo ensured the line advanced as one down the barren slope.

The wolves were enraged, snapping their jaws and scratching at the bark of trees to create a sound that made Ramya shudder. They were armed with Peqkian spears, daggers and swords, but as Kiya had informed them, were not in any way disciplined. Strutting chaotically rather than establishing units or even defensive stances.

Ramya watched from afar with Gwrlain humming at her side. She wanted desperately to lead her warriors into battle and fight alongside them, but she could not fit the breastplate armour over her pregnant bump and her movements were sluggish. Plus, Gwrlain had told her that if she went in to battle then he would join her and he had no idea how to fight. *I cannot risk his life.*

Her warriors reached the tree line and faced the

snarling enemy. Gogo yelled and like a pincer, the outer flanks streamed forward. The wolves vaulted and the two sides clashed in a tumult of steel and claws. The wolves blocked her warriors from forming a circle and ferociously pushed them back into a line and then started to flank them at the sides.

Ramya watched as Gogo stabbed her sword through the throat of a wolf, withdrew it and stabbed at another. The woman's skill was remarkable and soon a circle of beasts built up around her. Ramya scanned her eyes down the rest of the line and saw razor sharp fangs rip out brave Kiya's throat and she slumped, her attacker spitting the gory, mangled flesh on her dead body. It was a similar story wherever Ramya looked.

"They are evenly matched," Gwrlain observed from her side.

She stared at the tangled stew of skin, fur and blood in front of her. "Zhaq."

This is not going in our favour and there is little point wasting more lives. We need a different approach. She banged on the drum, calling her warriors to retreat. Backs straightened as they heard the signal and they edged back up the slope.

The wolves let them go and did not give chase. A fact that Ramya found strange, any normal enemy would chase down opponents until the death and gain as much ground as possible. These wolves wanted to hold their land, and didn't put a claw further than the tree line, as if it was their boundary. *Land that once belonged to them,* she realised, *before Melokai Tatya's Wolf Expulsion. But it is Peqkya's now, and we will reclaim it.*

The next few days were spent formulating a second attack plan. The wolves ate the cold bodies of dead warriors until a heavy snowfall settled over the corpses and froze the flesh solid.

Ramya groaned, "Gogo, let us walk and talk, we have been deliberating for hours. My back aches and I cannot stay in the same position for too long."

She stood and stretched out her legs. They set off around the camp. It was slow going as Ramya lumbered along, not being able to see where to place her feet over her protruding belly.

Two messengers astride panting, drooling ponies hastened into the camp. Bevya sat on the rump of one pony, her claws sunk into its thick hide, clinging on as it made its bumpy descent. The warriors dismounted and the clevercat jumped down, sniffing and then bounding over rocks and skidding on ice to arrive at Ramya's feet.

"My Melokai, I have newssss from the Head Sssscholar," she puffed. Gogo picked her up and tucked her inside her cloak. They continued to walk. The cat rested against the Head Warrior's shoulder, thankful for the warmth.

"Go on, Bevya," Ramya urged.

"There issss trouble with the Trogrssss, my Melokai."

Ramya stopped, rooted to the spot.

"Bevya, go and find Gwrlain and bring him to us. He should hear this."

The cat sprang down from Gogo's arms, nose in the air and then set off in the direction of the main tent. Gogo tutted, she still did not trust the Trogr, maintaining he was a spy. Ramya ignored her. Moments later Gwrlain came sprinting over with the cat. Bevya jumped back up into Gogo's arms.

"I thought the baby was coming!" he exclaimed, his chest heaving.

"Not yet, my soulmatch, but there is news from Troglo."

At Ramya's signal, Bevya continued her message, "Five Peqkian tradersss have been kidnapped by the Trogrssss at the trade point, my Melokai. Trade has ceassssed. Warriorssss attempted to ressscue the women but the Trogrssss defend the cave entrancessss and there wassss a vicioussss battle. Our warriorssss thwarted, many dead, warrior numberssss are too low. Chaz requestssss more warriorssss ssssent to the easssst. He awaitssss further insssstruction."

"Warriors dead! Zhaq those cave creatures." Gogo shot an impaling look at Gwrlain and then grinded her teeth, jaw pulsing. "We have no more warriors to send, my Melokai, all that remain in Riaow are the novices."

Trouble from the east. This is the start. The blood of Peqkians has been shed... Ramya turned to her white giant. "Gwrlain, why would they take five women?"

He sighed sadly. "It has begun."

"What has begun, my love?"

In his thick accent, he replied, "Our species is slowly dying. It has been for many, many years. Gradually females stopped being born and those who were born were fought over by the men. Some conceived and bred more males. Occasionally a girl was born. It became dangerous for families with female members. There were kidnap attempts and rapes, the men becoming increasingly more desperate to breed a female child."

His clear skin turned a sallow yellow and Ramya held his shaking hands. It tore at her to see him in such agony.

"My father was part of a group tasked with finding ways to ensure the Trogr race does not die out. One of which was to steal females from other races, that are similar to us, to procreate with. Humans. It was to be triggered when there were only five breeding age females left in the nation, this number being considered critical. This time must've come."

Gogo frowned at Ramya with repulsion. "We need to get them back, my Melokai."

"Without question," Ramya said. She glanced at Gwrlain and knew that there was more to his story, "Gogo, Bevya, please leave us. We will speak later."

As the warrior and clevercat departed, Ramya clasped Gwrlain in a tight hug.

"Issee, my love, what is it? What happened to you?"

she asked gently. *He is ready to tell me of his banishment.*

Hesitantly he said, "I have a sister, Lulac, she is rare and attracted much attention. My father, instead of protecting her, claimed her as his own, against her will. He insisted that he had impregnated my mother with a female baby and that he could do it again with Lulac. I was sickened by this and rebelled against him. There was a fight and I... I killed him."

Gwrlain dropped to his knees in the snow, his head in his hands. Ramya reeled with the revelation and for a while did not move or speak. *A murderer, my soulmatch is a murderer.* A wave of horror crashed over her. But a tiny voice broke the surface. *I am the Melokai, I was a warrior, I have taken many lives in my time… and for less noble causes.*

She pulled his face towards her belly and stroked his head. "Oh, Gwrlain, my love."

"I was sent out of the cave to die in the daylight. But my friend, Bance, was in charge of the disposal, and I think he left me close to the Peqkian camp hoping I might survive or be killed swiftly rather than suffer under the burning sun. Lulac and Bance were in love. I don't know if they still live, but at least my father cannot do any harm to her. Can you still love me?"

At last Ramya knew what haunted him and for a moment she thought it might haunt her. She grasped his shoulders. "You protected your sister, it was an honourable thing to do. I do not love you any less, in fact, I think I love you more."

***

The Melokai and Gogo sat in the main pavilion facing each other, Bevya waited outside. Gwrlain huddled behind Ramya in a dark, melancholy corner. Ramya was tired, the baby was restless and pushing on her bladder. Although she was wrapped up in her fox fur cloak and sat close to the fire, she was cold to the bone.

"I know we have only just arrived and our first clash saw a defeat against an enemy we underestimated, but we must send warriors to the east, Gogo. We cannot take this threat from Troglo lightly. Although it pains me to say it, I think we must reduce our number here and send five hundred. And I think you and I must return to the capital, we cannot direct our forces on two fronts from here."

"Yes, my Melokai. I am concerned about our warrior numbers. We are stretched thin; our number will be split in three if we send a company to the east. We cannot leave so few here. Do you agree to withdraw Violya and her warriors from pygmie land and call back the trade delegation?"

"Agreed."

"We must also recall our company from Fertilian, my Melokai."

"I cannot do that, not without risking severe repercussions. We need the southerners' money."

"We *need* to increase our force, my Melokai."

"You are doing that, Gogo, you have trained hundreds of novices in record time."

"I need fighters, not inexperienced youngbloods.

"I know, Gogo, but what can we do?" said Ramya, exasperated.

Her Head Warrior rubbed her chin and for a while the only sound was crackling, burning wood and warped Peqkian voices carried on the fierce wind outside.

"There is a way, but we will need help from great Sybilya."

"What are you talking about, Gogo?"

"We need our Stone Prophetess to call up her strongcats."

"They are volatile, uncontrollable. We haven't used tigers in battle for thousands of years, they are wild."

"Perhaps, my Melokai, but they will destroy the wolves."

***

Bevya and the two messengers were sent back to Chaz to inform him that the Melokai and the Head Warrior plus five hundred warriors would return at once to the capital. Ramya also sent two warriors as messengers to Mlaw, to recall the pygmie land trading party.

A garrison of five hundred remained in the Trequ valley, to hold back any wolf attack and maintain their position. Ramya hoped that the wolves would not attack, the Peqkians would be sorely outnumbered, and she also hoped that Sybilya would grant her request to galvanise the tigers. *She has to, for the sake of Peqkya, she has to.*

Two days later they were ready and set off back to the capital.

29

VIOLYA

Violya, Joz, Robya and the pygmie ruler clambered onto a nearby floating walkway and into a hut that bobbed on the angry waves. The rain fell fast and the dirt track on Ujen's central island where they had just been walking, turned quickly into thick mud.

"I have never seen rain like this," V said.

"We spend half the year on the water because of rain like this," Utuli replied, one of the three rulers of the country Majute, called a Potenqi. He had learnt the Shella language as he taught Juutayan to Robya. His accent was impeccable and he was always smiling, a big toothy grin that showed off his pointed stumps, filed down to eat tough meat rather than to look menacing. His blue hair was fashioned into three spikes. "The mud is impassable, but it is also dangerous."

"How is mud dangerous?" V asked, amused. She found this strange, new world curious and, although she remained wary, every day that passed revealed the Jutes, as they called themselves, to be friendly.

"Look." Utuli pointed as the mud became a mass of slithering bodies, entwined in each other.

"Giant snakes," the scholar Robya cried.

V watched a group of pygmies who were still climbing

onto a walkway. Several fighters stood ushering the group of Jutes forward. A snake shot up and took a pygmie in his jaws. The fighters sprung to life, holding on to the victim and attacking the snake with knives, catapults and spears. They managed to wrestle the screaming pygmie from the scaly beast. *Strong little fighters, these Jutes.*

Buckets full of pitfire water were chucked on the writhing snakes. They wormed around each other and then were still, any movement becoming laborious. A monotonous hissing started up and V glimpsed an occasional black forked tongue.

Huddling in the hut, Joz continued her trade discussion with the Potenqi, which had been going on for weeks. The crystal caves were used for ceremonial and formal occasions and after the Peqkians had been greeted, they had not returned. It was a sacred place for the Jutes. The three Potenqis had either nominated Utuli to deal with them or, as V suspected, Utuli had volunteered himself. He had taken a liking to Joz.

Robya was now almost fluent in the language and Joz had negotiated product swaps for various goods from Majute, including their clevercat who now followed Potenqi Soogee around learning Juutayan so it could do the ruler's bidding. The Peqkians ate fish from the lake and meat from frogs the size of donkeys, which Joz knew that the Ferts would like, having a taste for exotic foodstuffs. The trader also agreed to take pitfire to trade with the Dromedars who were obsessed with pleasure seeking and decadence.

"I have animals for you," said Utuli and beckoned to an assistant to uncover a wooden cage. "These are our pet caterpillars."

The caterpillars were the size of a kitten with a pale orange eyeless head, five berry red feet, a black body with yellow spots and a stripe of turquoise along each side. And from head to bottom they had furry, twig like hairs sticking out in lilac. Joz was dubious, scrunching up her forehead.

Utuli let one out and it dashed about and sat on the trader's lap making a trilling noise. Joz reluctantly fussed it and it made a sound like purring.

"It's soft," Joz exclaimed. "Come and fuss it Robya! V!"

Both the scholar and the warrior reached out a wary hand to pet the caterpillar and it jumped onto V's arm and crawled its way up, twittering in her ear and rubbing its colourful body along her neck. V stifled a laugh as its hairy feet tickled her shoulder.

"It likes you, Violya. That is a female, you should name her," Utuli said.

"Get off you weird little thing." V went to flick away the creature, but found she couldn't. It had settled on her shoulder, it's orange head nestled under her ear. It smelt earthy and its presence was a comfort. Utuli gave her a bunch of pitfire leaves to feed it and V held one up to the creature. It chomped and chewed, swaying happily.

"I think I'll name you Emmo," V whispered to the caterpillar and it gave her cheek a long lick with its tiny scratchy tongue. This time V did laugh and it snorted and bumped its nose to hers.

The Potenqi continued, "It will live up to twenty years and is compelled to find a master, making it a loyal pet. Legend tells us that under the right conditions it turns into a butterfly, but that hasn't happened for many hundreds of years."

"Does it become a beautiful butterfly?" Robya said.

"No, actually, it is an ugly thing, a dull grey. We are all pleased it stays as it is, colourful and pretty."

As V listened to Joz haggle hard with Utuli, Emmo snuggled in a ball in her lap, nibbling at her red feet to clean them, making a munching noise.

"I think that the Ferts will like these, but I cannot commit to taking that many at this stage. Perhaps a few to see the uptake and then we can order more. I can't tell you the value until we have tested the response," Joz said with a huge smile. She was irresistible.

Utuli smiled back. "Agreed, dear trader. All we have done since you arrived is talk business. And I am bored already of muddy Ujen. Have you ever seen the... Robya, what is the word for…"

The Potenqi spoke a word to the scholar in his language and she thought for a while.

"It means sea," Robya announced.

Utuli took a moment to form the word. "*Sea.* Let us go to the *sea* tomorrow."

"Ooh an adventure. What a fabulous idea, Utuli." Joz clapped her hands.

The noise startled Emmo who snuffled indignantly in the small woman's direction, making V laugh again.

Another sound caught V's attention as two Jutes scrapped with each other on a nearby walkway, which bounced precariously in the rain spattered lake, sploshing water. She knew what this was, and had seen it before. *How wonderful, drunk snakes to my left and drunk pygmies to my right!* The Jutes were peaceful, usually moving in unison and speaking as one, but occasionally too much pitfire juice saw a skirmish break out between tribes and then they went berserk, fighting in a frenzy until wrenched apart. *Imagine turning pitfired-up pygmies loose on an enemy!*

The Potenqi's gaze had also been drawn by the squabble. "A Qaziik and a Janugah. They are always at odds. We have done much to stop tribe wars and unite Majute, but history runs deep. It was a rogue faction of the Qaziik that attacked the Peqkians many years ago on our Eastern border. A shameful episode and one which you must relay our apologies back to your Melokai."

V's interest was piqued; this episode had not been mentioned until now. Joz and Robya were under strict instruction not to bring it up and risk the trade deal. But since he had mentioned it, V wanted to know more. "Utuli, our Melokai Ramya was at that clash, before she became Melokai. She was reluctant to trade with you."

Utuli brought his three fingers up to his face, mortified. "Oh! How awful. We are a passive people and respect and honour all creatures. We train fighters to protect us against attackers, but these tend to be animals such as snakes or river eels. If your Melokai is ever in need of our support, we are willing allies."

"This rogue faction, do they still live?" Robya asked, pulling out her notebook.

"Yes, I believe so, in the remotest part of north east Majute. Near the place you call the Jagged Canyon. We hunted them to bring them to justice, but they evaded us and scurried into the darkest jungle in the deepest ravine, never to emerge again."

"What tribe are you from?" V asked and saw Robya cringe at her nosiness.

He glanced over at the snakes flopping about in an intoxicated stupor and a flash of misery passed over his usual cheery countenance. "I am a Qaziik. The leader of that rogue faction was a family member."

Then he grinned up at his Peqkian guests. "Let us retire. We have an exciting day ahead of us tomorrow."

***

"Hold on tight," Utuli shouted.

He sat at the front of the giant, white-legged centipede, V behind him, followed by Joz and Robya. Two fighter Jutes at the rear. A second centipede behind them carried more little Jutes. The Potenqi kicked the centipede and loosened its reins and they set off in a jerky, rolling movement. Clacking legs made light work of the thick mud and they kept to higher ground away from the snakes.

It had taken hours to cross the lake to the western shore, their little boat skilfully dodging rocky islets that broke the surface of the water, unseen until the last minute due to a heavy fog. As they landed on the shore, the murkiness cleared and they had been greeted by these gigantic creatures.

The leggy beasts clacked along and they passed Jutes

who lived in giant snail shells hung from trees and cleared rainforest that now held fields of frogs and other livestock, as well as endless rows of the pitfire plant. The farmers rode huge beetles like ponies.

At each bump Emmo dug her little claws into V's scarred thigh and gave an irate snort at the inconvenience. The little thing amused her terribly. *So many new experiences, the world is bigger than I could ever imagine with some strange things in it!* V considered the crazy hair shapes of the Jutes on the centipede next to her and then touched her own. Her hair had grown from a short crop to a cloud of frizzy curls, the colour of poppies. *I'll get Emmya to cut it when I get home.* For now, Emmo liked burying herself in it, shaping odd partings and pushing it into strange angles. *I fit right in with the Jutes!*

V settled into the rhythm of the centipede, lulling her into a trance. A vivid image formed. No sound, or movement, still like a painting, capturing a moment in time. She saw Jute fighters in the Melokai's courtyard in Riaow. Then a second image of the House of Knowledge on fire. Then a third, the stinky warrior Ashya readying for a fight. At first these were faint but they flashed one after the other, on repeat, the colours getting brighter, brighter until V wanted to raise her arms to shield her eyes.

She jolted back to the present.

Joz laughed behind her. "Not like you to nod off, V."

V raised a hand, but did not look back. The assistant trader would've seen the alarm in her eyes. *What was that? Not a dream, too real. A premonition, a forewarning of things to come?* She wondered if it was a vision from Sybilya, but V could not feel the Stone Prophetess's presence. V touched ear to shoulder on both sides, stretching out her tense neck, and pushed the… *premonition…* to the back of her mind. But an awareness pulsed through her veins, once understood it could never be forgotten. *I must return to Riaow.*

As they got closer to the Sarenky Sea, the rain eased off

and the wind picked up. The trees became sparser and those that stood had massive, gnarly trunks gripping into the earth. The centipedes came to a lurching stop at the bottom of a hill and a briny smell enveloped V.

The Jutes strapped Utuli and the Peqkians into rope contraptions and then hooked each onto a large rope that had been laid up the hill and tied around various trees.

"It is extremely windy up the top," Utuli cautioned. "These are to ensure we do not blow away." He tapped the rope and chuckled. "Do not be frightened, dear Joz, it is an incredible sight!"

Emmo crawled into V's cloak and hunkered down as they climbed the hill and pulled themselves up using the rope. As they neared the top, the few trees had been blown sideways and the crashing sound of waves boomed. The pummelling air made V's eyes water.

Utuli shouted something, but it was carried away by the wind. At the top, a huge expanse of angry water spread out in front of them. Grabbing the rope tightly, V's long arms allowed her to peer down over the edge of the steep sided cliff, to see a sheer drop with rocks jutting into the sea and white waves the height of four of her, smashing into them. The rolling surf kicked up a wild foam and V could feel the flying salt dig itself into the lines of her face.

As far as she could see was grey sky and grey sea, chalky cliffs and white tipped waves. The majestic openness thrilled her after months in tiny huts. Suddenly so much seemed possible to her, a vast sea of endless opportunities. In the distance, large fish were leaping out of the water, flipping and splashing back down. V sensed this was playtime, the joy of the creatures' acrobatics lifted her spirits. *I feel blown away, not by the wind but by this sight!* Her magic swelled and crashed against her bones. *"It is time to come out of the shadows."*

A sudden gust took Utuli off his feet, the rope around his waist stopping him from hurtling away. He desperately tried to reach the rope to pull himself back, his arms and legs flailing. Through the raging elements V could hear Joz yelling as he flapped like a flag. V hauled herself along the large rope, and with one arm holding it she leaned out as far as she could, grabbing at the Potenqi. She caught his foot and tugged against the force of the wind, as if it was her opponent. They tussled awhile. Then with a surge of strength she heaved him in and upright again. Shaken, he nodded at her in thanks. They descended back down the hill, V's protective hand on Utuli's back.

"Issee," Robya said as they crouched down behind the centipedes against the worst of the wind and caught their breath. "I have never seen the Sarenky. Peqkians can glimpse it from the highest mountain on our western border but according to our histories, not one has ever ventured to the sea."

"I wonder what incredible things are out there," V said.

"This is as far as we have gone," Utuli said. "We have tried on many occasions to find a way down to the sea, to work out how to launch a boat and to explore what is out there, but we have not been successful. The wind, the rocks, the cliff are unpredictable. But we won't give up until we succeed. Occasionally we see boats on the sea out in the far distance, but they never come close to the cliffs. We call them, in your language, Chaos Cliffs."

***

When they arrived back to Ujen a few hours later two remarkable things awaited them. No rain and a Peqkian warrior.

I must return to Riaow. This is a sign.

"Lizya," V shouted as she recognised the warrior. She jumped from the boat to embrace the warrior slapping her on the back. Lizya and V had guarded the Melokai together with Emmya in times past.

"Look at your hair!" The warrior patted the red mass that framed V's face.

V led Lizya to a quiet corner so they could speak without being overheard. "Issee! What brings you here, my friend?"

"V, I have an important order from the Melokai. I have travelled for weeks to reach you, through this bizarre country. Daya is at Mlaw village in case I never returned. But I made it, I found you." Lizya sounded exhausted and V found her a cushion and insisted she sit before carrying on.

"Well you have reached us and you are safe. What is the order?"

"Melokai Ramya recalls the trading party immediately. War has broken out with the wolves, the Trogrs have kidnapped five Peqkians and one thousand of our warriors are in Fertilian. We are low on numbers and need you to return to the capital. You will likely be deployed to the eastern border to lead a mission to find the taken women. We must leave tomorrow; the snows are nearly upon us and I suspect much will have changed whilst I have been on the road."

After V had spoken with Utuli, Robya and Joz and given orders to her warriors, she rushed back to Lizya, who had drooped on the cushion. V gently shook her awake, eager to hear news of home.

"What is *that*?" Lizya pointed at V's shoulder.

"Ha, this is my pet. Her name is Emmo." V picked up the caterpillar and put it in Lizya's hands. The weary warrior tickled under Emmo's chin and the colourful creature squealed in delight. "Named her after our crazy friend Emmya."

Lizya laughed and played with the pet, then sadly looked up at V. "Emmya has gone missing, in Drome. She didn't return with the rest of the trading party. It is said that she went out into Parchad and lost herself in the pleasures there. I don't believe this, not many of us do, but the Melokai has not sent anyone to Drome to find her."

The news was like a punch in the stomach, V's legs buckled and she slumped down next to Lizya. V knew, as

Lizya knew, that warriors didn't come home for one reason and one reason alone.

"Emmya is dead," V said. A black cloud sunk low and surrounded her, snatching at her breath, chilling her skin and sucking all the warmth from her veins. She shivered violently. The skies burst open and the deluge of rain drowned her silent tears.

***

"Ah, good morning, V, I was just on my way to find you," Utuli said.

The Potenqi beamed up at the warrior as they stood on a floating wooden walkway between huts. It bobbed languidly, the shallow lake still and misty. V waited for the Jute to continue, before she revealed why she was up so early and seeking him.

"The rulers have been thinking, and we must insist that an envoy accompany you, in order to apologise to Melokai Ramya for that unsanctioned attack years earlier. Brinjinqa is my personal guard and assistant, and is fluent in Shella. He will travel with you, if you are in agreement."

Envoy or assassin? V's suspicion sparked, but was soon doused. She had seen the Jutes in Riaow. Many, formed up in tight lines, not just one.

V dipped her head. "Brinjinqa is most welcome, Utuli."

"Good, good." The Jute edged forward, as if the conversation was closed, but V didn't move.

"I have a request of you, Potenqi Utuli of Majute"

"Oh, please, continue." He gestured with his claw hands for V to speak.

V hesitated, still unsure if this was a good decision. She was speaking on behalf of the Melokai, presumptuous, punishable by death. The warrior had gone to sleep clouded with thoughts of Emmya, repressing the emotion by resolving to find out what had happened to her friend, and if necessary, take revenge on any who had wronged her. But V had woken with her thoughts charred by the same three images as yesterday, one in particular.

"Peqkya is at war and has need of fighters." The words came out in a hot rush that swept over V's face and settled around her ears. They smouldered as she continued, "I humbly ask of you to send a company of Jute fighters with me to Riaow. As you know, we leave in a few hours."

Utuli's lips gaped to show his blackened, filed teeth. Recovering himself, he said, "We are a small, peaceful population. We are not in the habit of committing violence for others. However, I have not forgotten you saved me from the wind at Chaos Cliffs. I will consult with my fellow rulers, Soogee and Yehep. But you do not give me much time."

30

FERRAZ

Ashya was eating roast chicken, gnawing at the bones and dribbling juice down her chin. Mikaz was in the old warrior's bed chamber pleasuring assistant trader Toya for the orgy show. They were waiting for Riv, she was in a council meeting with the recently returned Melokai which seemed to be going on forever.

Ashya had taken advantage of being in charge whilst Ramya and Gosya were away, by secretly training the underground peon army in the hills outside the city, who she moaned was slow and stupid. But she was impressed by the number and by the leaders Shit-pick, Steely and Wevo who she said were single-minded in their desire to destroy Ramya.

Ferraz sat looking out onto the terrace in Ashya's apartment, he could smell the old warrior from a few paces away and his nose wrinkled. A range of equipment and weapons was dotted around the dusty terrace where the warrior pushed her body to fight off the deterioration of age. He sighed and slumped further down the chair. His body felt wrenched in two, a painful hole in the middle.

Irrya.

Since her death, he had sunk into depression, not eating, moving, speaking. His skin had reacted to her passing by erupting into raw, pus-oozing sores and flaky scales that bled if he moved too quickly. The medic had told his set administrator that he needed some time off from PG duties and he wallowed in his cell. Every day, Mikaz got him up in the morning, bathed him, carefully rubbed lotion on his body and dressed him, and slowly Ferraz's skin mended. Mikaz had snuck out to Ashya's training sessions as well as attended the rebellion meetings and afterwards relayed the information to Ferraz. Riv had sent her condolences via Mikaz, but her latest message had been that they shouldn't let Irrya's death impact the rebellion and she specifically requested Ferraz to be at the next meeting. He wanted to stay in bed, to sleep and forget, but here he was.

He could see the courtesan sat opposite him, where she should have been, her face twinkling and orange braids bright against Ashya's dank walls. But when he looked closely her form faded. He was frightened Irrya's memory would shrivel into nothing and he obsessively brought images of her to his mind and replayed times they had spent together over and over.

Mikaz and Toya finished up and bounded into the room, red faced from their exertion.

"May I?" Toya asked, one hand up to hide her yellowing teeth, and the other pointed at the glut of food laid out on the table.

"Help yourself, I'm done with the chicken," Ashya grunted and she pushed the meat towards the trader and then made a grab for the whole baked salmon, pulling the dish towards her. She gestured to Mikaz who hung back. "And you, PG, you may eat if you wish."

The assistant trader and the PG sat at the table with her and dug in.

"Ferraz, are you hungry?" Mikaz said.

Ferraz did not acknowledge the question. He could not bring himself to eat. He sighed again, that was about all he could do.

A pounding on the door announced the arrival of Riv. The Head Trader was beside herself with excitement, she slammed the door shut and shouted, "Fuck me, Ferraz!" Then quieter she said, "That damn Melokai kept us waiting as she insisted she visit Sybilya immediately for some urgent business with the wolves, which she wouldn't tell us about, all a bit bizarre."

Riv did a merry dance over to the table, twirled in front of them and then bowed low to Ashya.

"Make room! I am happy and when I am happy I am ravenous." She pulled up a chair and pushed it in between the three so that Toya and Mikaz had to shuffle around the table. Ashya passed her a plate and the Head Trader piled it high.

"And why are you so happy, Rivya? Has the Melokai keeled over of her own accord?" Ashya said.

"Ha! Not quite," Riv answered through a mouthful of buttered potatoes, "but everything seems to be going in our favour my friends. Ramya brought five hundred of her warriors home from the wolf war but has already ordered these out from the city again. The majority are to go to the eastern border to take on the Trogrs and a few are to go with that cockface Gosya to spy on the Drome army amassing in the south."

"But that is not good news, how do they know about the camel army?" Ashya snapped.

Riv chewed and swallowed a huge chunk of chicken, and her reply was a long time coming. Ashya's tension mounted.

"Zhaq, Riv!" the warrior erupted.

"This is delicious." Riv licked at her greasy fingers. "A Fert messenger arrived to say that the Dromedars are gathering in huge numbers by our mountain trade route, Ramya has ordered Gogo to go-go-go to check it out three days hence." She sniggered at her own joke and then stuffed a wedge of salmon in her mouth.

"I still do not comprehend why you are happy about

that?" Ashya's patience was running thin and she leaned into Riv and grabbed her chin so the trader was looking at her and not at her plate. Half chewed pink fish tumbled out the Head Trader's mouth.

Riv batted the warrior's hand away and flicked the fallen fish off her lap for the cats who lingered under the table waiting for scraps. Above the meows, she said, "Gogo will not reach the border, we will eliminate her tomorrow night. Donkey peon found me today whilst he was unpacking the trade train from Parchad and gave me these."

She pulled out of her cloak pocket a small vial of green liquid and an even tinier vial of red liquid and placed them carefully on the table.

Ashya's eyes glittered with malice. "Did he bring any other news?"

"Yes, the Dromedars are in position and have the soldier numbers ready to invade Peqkya. But there is no suitable route in for the army other than by using our trade paths over the mountains. As we all know, these are heavily guarded. They are scouting the best way in, and we are to hold tight for more news."

"It is nearly upon us!" Mikaz grinned. "My peons will be so pleased; they are itching to make a move."

"Indeed," Riv said. "With Gogo gone, Ashya will be called upon to advise the Melokai. Ramya thinks you are a skilled and experienced warrior and she trusts you. Ha! You can go and spy on the Drome army in Gogo's place and *ease* their entry into Peqkya whilst you are there."

Ashya winked at the trader, a grin on her thin lips. She put her elbows on the table and leant her chin on her clasped hands, thinking. Riv continued to eat.

When she was done, she called, "Ferraz!"

Mikaz scraped his chair back and came to help Ferraz to stand and walk over to the table. Ferraz could not meet Riv's eye, he felt ashamed, guilty somehow for Irrya's death.

"Dear, are you up to this?" Riv asked, her head angled to one side. Ferraz knew she did not truly care about him but he needed to be able to perform. For Irrya, for his son. To destroy the vile Melokai who had caused so much suffering. He stood up straight.

"Yes," he responded in as firm a voice as he could muster. "You remember your promise, to keep my son safe when this comes to pass."

Riv nodded brusquely and then gave him the two vials, handling them delicately.

"Go," she said and turned back to her food.

***

"Big order peons," the set administrator shouted the following night. "The Head Trader Riv is wanting *mass* entertainment."

She called for specific PGs and sent them out, leaving Ferraz alone in the communal area, but not for long.

"Ferraz, cat here from the Head Warrior Gosya. The PG she requested is with Riv, so you'll have to do. Do not disappoint her."

Ferraz followed the cat through the snow. He felt feverish, dizzy and his skin felt clammy. It was almost healed and he had smothered his body in lotion all day to be deemed fit to work by the set medic, and be presentable for callers. He loosened his cloak. *I failed with Chaz, I cannot disappoint again.* He entered Gosya's chambers and kneeled at her feet.

"What is your pleasure? Let me pleasure you."

"I'm leaving tomorrow on another mission and I need a good rut," she replied. Ferraz did not like her hairless head and protruding eyes. Hard, dangerous. Her skin was rough, strewn with scars and her hands were calloused. *Irrya's skin was soft, perfect.* The thought hit him hard and his throat constricted, which led to a spluttering cough. Gosya did not seem to notice and carried on chattering. He had heard from other PGs that the Head Warrior often liked to talk first, to get everything out of her head. Ferraz listened, head still bowed as she paced around the room. His knees started to ache.

"Issee, I need to forget about all the strange things that have been happening of late. The wolves, the crazy standing wolves! And the cave creatures kidnapping our women. Emmya, poor Emmya, whatever happened to her. And now the cammers are playing up and today, this half creature born to the Melokai…"

Ferraz's ears pricked and he dared to speak, "Half creature, mistress?"

"Yes, *half creature*. The thing born today of our Melokai Ramya and the Trogr Gwrlain. I am told she had a difficult birth pushing out that monstrosity, and now she refuses to give up the baby to a pen, saying she loves it and wants to nurture it! She is trampling our traditions; I cannot comprehend it. But alas she is Peqkya's Melokai, she can make or break rules. And she is my Melokai and I will always be loyal to her. But it all just seems so… wrong."

Another half baby. He reeled backwards and fell on the floor. Gosya turned to look down at him, dangerous eyes narrowing. Ferraz rolled over and righted himself back on his knees.

"Mistress, let me pleasure you, I will take your mind off these troubles." Ferraz grabbed for her hand and awkwardly started to lick and suck her fingers. Soon his PG skills kicked back in.

He picked her up and lay her on the bed, spreading her legs. Gosya groaned and pulled off her clothes and then pulled off his. She took his cock in her mouth. He hoped she wouldn't notice its abnormal red colour.

"Look at you," she grinned, "so pink and juicy."

She parted her lips and stuffed him in, sucking at him greedily. *Good*, he thought, *keep drinking deep*. Her face stretched as she parted her lips wide, making hmmm noises whilst moving up and down. He winced as he felt teeth and dared to peer down his nose. Her face had distorted and she started to gag. She couldn't comprehend what was happening, pushing him away and clawing at her neck. Her eyeballs bulged out of their sockets and her lips turned blue. A wrenching crack exploded from her chest and she keeled over onto the bed. Her body convulsed and then was still. He leaned in close to check her breathing. She jerked. He fell back on the bed, heart racing.

"Zhaq!"

He watched as a blob of blood welled in her nostril and broke free. It trickled down her face and seeped into the sheet.

Convinced she would not move again, Ferraz rushed to the wash area and splashed his cock with water, rubbing it vigorously to remove all traces of the snake venom. He gargled and spat down the drain. *Will the anti-venom wear off?* Riv had told him that the Drome snake venom was untraceable in the body, making the heart burst and appear like a natural death. Only the anti-venom could counteract it.

Earlier that night, before he had left his cell for the communal area, he had drunk the green vial first and then smeared the red liquid all over his cock and swilled it in his mouth before dropping both vials down his secret passageway to be washed away by the stream.

Glancing over at the warrior's sprawled body, Ferraz felt a sense of purpose again. *Something has gone right for me at last. Irrya's death was not in vain.* He dried himself off and then ran for the door shouting for her staff, for help, for her messenger like a crazed peon who had just witnessed a woman have a seizure whilst he was servicing her.

"Gosya is not well," he yelled running naked through the corridors of the Head Warrior's apartment. "The Head Warrior has collapsed! Help!"

31

TOBY

Prince Toby Cleland stared at the expanse of grass in Yettle Bottom Plains where a few hours earlier one thousand Peqkian warriors had stood, wrestling with his lower jaw to keep it from hanging off his face.

At some point in the night, whilst Toby celebrated their first victory with his brother King Hugo, Captain Denya and her company had snuck off and joined the Thorne Twins. She had been disgusted that the Ferts would get drunk on the eve of a battle and retired with her warriors to make camp. No one had paid them any attention, too busy slugging the fine wine that Hugo had ordered opened.

Toby wanted to scream, to fall on the grass and thump his fists and yell until his lungs gave out. *How could she betray us? Betray me? Abandon her Melokai's orders?*

He swallowed down the desire, he couldn't be seen to be bothered by this turn of events, not in front of his men, the commanders, squires and messengers who shadowed him. He reacted meticulously, any hint of disquiet would spook them. Toby rolled his shoulders, swung his arms from side to side to stretch out his waist, raised chin up to the sky to ease some tension in his neck, telling them indirectly, *I'm unperturbed by the missing warriors, we have our second battle in a few hours, and it'll be a doddle.*

"And that's not all," the scout continued. Lippy, they called him now. The soldier Elmgard had lost his lips for mocking a Peqkian warrior. Hideous to look at, but now one of Toby's best spies. Combine his facial disfigurement with some rags, a stoop and a limp, and he looked like your average army camp hanger on. He'd seen the Peqkians arrive first hand before creeping back and waking Toby. Elmgard spoke with a clacking, nasally slur through his exposed gums, words blending into one another. "Men come. New battalion. Four thousand I reckon."

More men! We were already outnumbered. And now with the warriors gone... "Where did they come from?" He asked, nonchalantly.

Lippy slurred, "Iddenkinge."

"Iddenkinge's men? Are you certain?"

"Aye. Rumour is Grace Iddenkinge betrothed to Jeremy Thorne."

Toby wanted to punch the lipless soldier in the face, rip off his eyelids to match his hole of a mouth, shred his nostrils, punch holes in his ruddy cheeks at this news. *Another fucking betrayal, as if one kick to the bollocks wasn't enough.* Instead he said, "Anything else?"

Lippy shook his head.

"Find out Denya's payment," Toby said and signalled the scout to leave. The Prince took one last look at the vast emptiness, which earlier had been filled with his guarantee of a victory, turned his back and made for the King's pavilion.

My niece, Princess Matilda, has betrayed her father, has betrayed the Cleland family. King Hugo's eldest daughter and her husband Lord John Iddenkinge have joined the bastard Thornes. Toby scratched his stubble. His damn, itchy stubble, which right now he hated, like writhing bugs crawled all over his face. He'd only kept it because Jessima had told him she liked it.

Queen Jessima. My Jessima. What will become of you? She'd be hunted, she carried Hugo's heir. If a boy, the new King.

The Thornes would not rest until she and the child were dead, to quell any future uprisings. *I pray she'll be safe in Lian.* There had been no message yet to say she had arrived, had survived the tunnel journey, but Toby trusted Chattergoon. He was resilient, shrewd, loyal.

I trusted Captain Denya, and look where that got me. Toby had insisted the Peqkian be included in the war council, be privy to the full detail on soldier numbers, strategy, logistics. The sneaky cat knew it all, and now the enemy knew it all too. And there was no time to reconsider tactics. *Shit.* Toby stopped mid stride, his squire skidding in the dewy grass to avoid bumping into him. Guilt hollowed Toby's chest and weighed heavily over him. He felt small, insignificant, stupid. As if he had shrunk to the size of the tiniest stone under his boot. *I persuaded the King to trust the captain, and now we are doomed.*

He shook his head, as if he simply dismissed a trifling thought, and continued to pick his way through the camp, the dawn mist clearing to reveal soldiers readying themselves, donning armour, sharpening weapons. A few paces from the King's pavilion Lord Berindonck intercepted him.

"I told you not to trust the cats," the lord bleated. "I told the King not to trust that damn woman. And now she has not only deserted us but taken all our secrets with her! A foolish, disastrous…"

Toby grabbed the blustering man's arm, twisted it around his back and pinned him to the ground. A move the turncoat cat had taught him no less. Berindonck whimpered. Toby could've snapped a few bones, Denya had certainly shown him how, but he dropped the lord. *Flawless reaction, impeccable. If my men didn't think I was rattled, they do now.* Toby held out his hand and Berindonck eyed him suspiciously before taking it. Toby heaved the man to his feet, patted his shoulders and smiled as if they were great friends.

Straightening his tunic, Toby nodded to his men, as if

the hot-headed grapple with a lord hadn't just happened, and entered the King's tent.

"Ah, here's the general," King Hugo rasped. He stood, wheezing, as servants dressed him for battle. He rested one hand on a squire, who stood patiently, alert to steady the King should he falter. Hugo's recent ill health had left him weak. It pained Toby to see. Hugo had journeyed here laying in a cushioned cart pulled by horses rather than riding his great, white stallion. Each night fussing medics attended him rather than his war council. But the previous day's successful ambush in Yettle Valley, and the Thorne army's retreat to the plains, had bolstered the King's resolve and he was determined to ride out at the head of his army to meet his foe.

Berindonck stumbled in, glared at Toby, and took his place with the other lords and advisors on Hugo's war council. They all looked grim-faced.

"Your Grace," Toby said with a small bow.

"What news before we thrash these false Thornes once and for all."

"Captain Denya and her company have skipped off to join the twins."

Hugo saved his ruined voice, and grunted in reply.

"But they've been training us for months, it will be a well-matched clash."

Grunt.

"And Princess Matilda has betrothed your grandchild Grace to Arthur Thorne's eldest, Jeremy. Iddenkinge's men have come up from the south."

"That little bitch." The King's scratchy voice didn't falter, Toby could detect no emotion. *He can't still think we'll win this?*

A horn sounded, enemy movement spotted on the plains. *They are lining up.*

The King thumped fists on his steel breastplate. "It is time," Hugo said to his war council, as loud as his croak would allow. "We will skin the cats alive. And a thorn doesn't frighten me. That army is full of little pricks."

His men laughed, echoes of "little pricks!" and "skin the cats!"

"Leave us." King Hugo gestured for Toby to stay.

When only the two men remained, Hugo slumped and Toby lurched forward to catch him. Hugo's fearless show of strength was costing him dearly. Every last shred of the King's will was channelled into this performance of his former self.

The King said, "We'll be annihilated."

Toby's mind formed a rebuttal, a no, a smooth "nonsense, we'll win this," retort. But he couldn't bring himself to lie to his brother, to pretend that victory was a given, that the Cleland army stood a chance. They were marching into a slaughter and both knew it.

"Aye," he replied.

32

DARRIO

꧁

The humans had been quiet for many nights, not leading a second attack or venturing close to the wolf front line at the edge of the trees. A blizzard the night before had thrown a white blanket over everything and now the humans' stench was faint. The whispers around the wolves was that the Peqkians had conceded and relinquished the Wul-Onr valley south of the river. Although none dared to declare it for certain.

"Too easy," Darrio brooded. They were huddled in the secret thicket near the den and could speak freely. His offspring were maturing fast, too fast, the war speeding up the process. "This is not the end, no matter the talk."

"It is not the end," Sarrya replied, no hint of doubt in her voice. She lay on her side with legs out flat, front paws crossed.

"How do you know? What made you so smart, little sister?" Warrio put his front paws on his sister and tried to stand on her. She allowed it, but Darrio knew she could topple her brother in an eyeblink. Sarrya's recent growth spurt meant she towered over all three of them, her muscles rippled beneath her fur and each day, her face looked more human.

"What happens if they attack again, Pappy? We do not

have the numbers to fight back," Harro observed, anxious. He was the eldest of Darrio's pups, but now the smallest. Everything he said was carefully considered. He was the thinker whilst his brother was the doer, full of energy.

"We call up more wolves from the packs," Darrio said.

"We have to fight again," Harro said, a morose expression on his face.

"Ahhhwoooo a fight! Let me at them," Warrio shouted as he skipped up and down, front paws to back paws and then leapt on his brother, who grappled with him briefly and then kicked him away. Warrio chased his tail in the confined space, stepping on all of them.

"Not a good thing, Warrio," Darrio cautioned. "Do not want you three to fight. Humans are lethal. Old Pa would not cope if anything happened to one of you."

"You survive, Pa," Sarrya said.

"Pleased to hear it, daughter." He laughed at her conviction, but it unnerved him.

A beckoning howl from Arro called them to attention and they padded away from the thicket single file, ensuring no one saw them, and made their way to the den.

"We have news," Arro announced to his depleted pack. Although his alpha female Lurra had died, he had yet to be mated to another, but the Wulhor-Aaen still considered him their alpha, in these strange times all natural ways of life had been distorted.

"Wolves holding our new land need support, from all packs. Reports that humans are stirring. Apart from pups, we all must go. Ricarro, stay here and mind the little ones."

Ricarro's eyes flitted to Sarrya and then he looked at the floor.

"Must yearlings go, Arro?" Darrio braved.

"Yes," Arro sighed. He was utterly defeated. As well as losing Lurra he had lost his child Marro in the last battle. His five pups wailed for their mother and his efforts to comfort them had been in vain. "We leave at sunrise, be ready."

***

The veteran wolves patrolled the front line south of the river and behind them the new arrivals loitered, waiting for some kind of instruction. The veterans had Peqkian weapons in their paws or strapped to their backs, but there was none left for the newcomers.

Sarrya sat alert, eyes towards the Peqkian camp and sniffing at the air, heavy with festering wolf urine and excrement.

"A new smell," she told Darrio. "A dangerous scent."

"You have a *dangerous* scent, sister," Warrio joked and he pounced on her, but she was not in a playful mood and like a lightning flash, Warrio was pinned to the ground. Sarrya stood on him, her jaws around his muzzle. He whimpered, startled by her show of power.

She released him slowly. "Shut up, Warrio."

Warrio slunk away and moped behind Darrio, cleaning his fur and glancing around to see how many had seen that display of dominance. It was dawning on him that his sister was now the strongest of the three.

"Pups! Not the time for nonsense," Darrio snapped and he put a sympathetic paw on Warrio.

A roar split the air. Darrio shuddered. All the wolves stood alert on four paws, facing the Peqkian camp. The roar became a battle cry as more voices joined in. It rebounded off the steep valley sides before an ominous silence fell upon them.

"Pa?" Harro whispered, frightened. His hind legs quivered.

Darrio shook his head, too stunned to speak and it was Sarrya who answered.

"Tigers."

"Don't exist stupid! Tigers are a myth," Warrio said, still angry at her aggressive behaviour.

"Do exist. You see soon enough," Sarrya replied as she skulked forwards. Darrio followed her and behind him came his sons.

"Look, stupid," she said to Warrio as they reached the edge of the forest where the veterans patrolled. "You believe me now?"

Up the mountain, glimpses of reddish-orange fur could be seen. Snow disturbed by the large paws crunched and creaked, echoing down to the valley floor. The dangerous scent was overpowering.

Warrio squinted and then gawped wide eyed at Sarrya. "Tigers." His voice trembled in terror.

"Move back from here, pups," Darrio said and he turned and jogged away, a sudden twinge in his injured leg shot pains along his back and he stifled a yelp. His children stayed close on his heels. They stood alert next to a haphazard group of yearlings who swayed and yowled in confusion and fear.

"Whatever happens, stay together," he told his three. "Fight hard, don't be reckless. Retreat across river if things don't go to plan. Understood?"

Sarrya and Harro mumbled their assent.

"Warrio! Hear me. Do not be rash."

Warrio blinked twice at his father, in a trance. The roars came again, and the brave wolves along the front line howled in reply. Darrio joined his voice to theirs, as did all of those gathered. They sounded formidable. The huge cats bounded down the mountain, with no sign of the Peqkians, and attacked. The howl dwindled and an ear-splitting cacophony of snarls, barking, whining and hissing came in its place.

Darrio stood on two feet, braced for the onslaught. "Get ready!"

The tigers swept aside the front line wolves and came at them, blood dripping down fangs and a vicious fight ensued. Darrio lost track of his children's scent as he fought for his life, the tigers pushing them towards the river. The first sounds of plops came to his ears as wolves fell or launched themselves into the water. *Must retreat to north bank.*

In a fleeting break from the tigers' assault, Darrio searched for his children, sniffing and calling their names. He caught sight of Warrio holding his own against an opponent with three other wolves. The distraction almost cost Darrio his life as a hulk of a tiger swiped a massive paw at his face. He ducked and missed the skull-crushing blow by a fur's width. A sharp claw connected and scraped down one eye, blinding him.

He toppled into the water and lurched for the other side. The river swarmed with frenzied wolves and with every stroke he caught fur and limbs and jostled to keep his nose above the surface. He wrestled through churned up, belly high mud, grunting with the effort. Finally on solid ground, he shook off his fur and turned back towards the southern bank, helping to fish out the wounded.

A few stragglers remained on the other side, courageously fending off the big cats. Darrio watched with horror as his kind were systematically destroyed, the corpses flung into the river to bob away. When none was left standing, the savages prowled, snorting and biting chunks of flesh out of dead and nearly dead wolves sprawled on the bank, making a show of chewing and swallowing. Growling after every gruesome mouthful. There was no more than a hundred of the beasts, and Darrio could see no tiger casualties.

An ugly brute stomped on a wolf, leaning in with slathering jaws to rip a bite out of its rump, but the wolf barked and tried to stand. Darrio staggered backwards.

"Harro!" he yelled.

He sprang forward, to dive in the water.

"No, Pa!" Sarrya screamed and leapt on his back, claws dug deep and yanked him back from the edge. Her strength overwhelmed him and he fell back, wrapped in her strong arms.

"Harro!" he bellowed again. The tiger was toying with his son on the other bank, swatting him and standing on his snout. Harro wailed pitifully.

A boom rumbled about the valley. Time stood still. Trees swayed in the wake and angry waves lapped at the southern bank, demanding attention. Darrio froze, not comprehending where the sound had come from. Then he felt the vibrations in his daughter's chest and realised it had come from her, as she roared again.

The tigers stopped their pacing and glared at the line of wolves. Rows of black eyes took in each other across the sloshing river. The monster taunting Harro paused to look, then he sniffed and shook his head and bit down on Harro's neck. An agonising pain stabbed in Darrio's chest. Sarrya thundered again and the brute stiffened at the noise.

But instead of eating his son, the tiger pulled him up onto his four paws. Harro stood on wobbly legs, head down, submissive. The tiger nipped at his haunches and he stumbled away out of sight.

"Pa, pa!" Warrio called, running up and down the river bank.

"Here, Warrio," Sarrya shouted. Darrio was mute.

"Did you see? They have Harro! Pa!" he cried.

"We know," Sarrya said and signalled to Warrio to be quiet. Darrio's body went limp and he couldn't move. He felt Sarrya's maw around the scruff of his neck and she dragged him away from the verge and lay him down in some mossy grass. Darrio panted, his chest heaving.

"Pa's eye…" Warrio muttered to Sarrya as they stood over his crumpled form protecting him from the surge of wolves retreating from the bank, pushing away any that came too close.

"One still works," Sarrya replied.

Warrio snorted in his father's ear, but Darrio did not respond. "Pa, will clean your wound." He started to lick around the bloody gash that sliced through Darrio's eye.

Sarrya bent low and said, "Harro will live, I go to fetch him back."

Darrio jerked to attention, finding his feet, but it was too late. Sarrya had bolted down to the bank and into the water, swimming across.

"Sarrya!"

"Stay there, Pa!" she hollered back, careful not to swallow water. Darrio fought against every bone in his body telling him to go after her but his mind said, *Don't move, listen to your daughter.*

A howl went up from the wolves as they saw her approaching the enemy. Tigers emerged from the trees and stared at the lone figure. They roared and assembled where she would climb out, a grim welcome. The roars became hisses and snarls as they bared sharp teeth at her. She clambered out of the water and they surrounded her, marching her away. She was lost to Darrio as the dense forest shadow engulfed them.

"Crazy sister," Warrio said, but he stared across the water with admiration. Wolves surrounded them, gabbling in astonishment at what Sarrya had done. Darrio sat and stared at the other side, trying to make out any movement. But the captors and their prisoner had vanished.

Arro approached. "Darrio, what is Sarrya doing?"

Darrio couldn't respond, his tongue slack in his mouth. Warrio answered with his eyes down and head bowed in respect to the alpha male, "To get Harro back."

"Will slaughter them both." Arro shook his head mournfully and slunk away.

Warrio sat close to his father. The curious bystanders dispersed, bored by Darrio's muteness, and the father and son watched. Daylight faded and at dusk, dainty snowflakes started to drift down.

"What is that?" Warrio pointed his snout at a dark shape stumbling out of the trees. "Harro! It's Harro!"

Harro plunged into the water and paddled, but he was either too injured or too exhausted to make any progress and the current started to drag him downstream. Warrio sprung into the water and swam frantically after his brother. Darrio's whining reached a high pitch as Warrio snatched at Harro's neck, latching on with his teeth and started to pull him back.

Darrio ran after them along the river bank and heaved their sodden bodies into the snow. "Harro?"

Harro's eyes flickered open. "Pa," he spluttered before coughing up blood.

"You'll live, son."

Harro gazed up at his father, his eyes glazing over. He tried to say something but retched up black bile.

"Rest," Darrio said.

"Sarry," he spat and then swallowed hard. He regained some strength. "She gave herself for me."

***

Warrio built a small den near the river for them. He was helped by a number of wolves, all eager to hear about the enemy from the freed captive. But Harro didn't speak, he concentrated his energy on recovering. Darrio stayed with him, comforting him and doing what he could to ease his pain. Warrio took up position watching the water.

"She's not dead, Pa," Warrio said. "I sense her."

The wolves were scattered, some had returned to their packs in the remote Zwullfr wilderness, some had stayed near the river, insistent that the battle was not over, and others lingered in a dream-like stupor unsure what to do. They gathered around Darrio, inquisitive about what might happen next. He was sick of their counsel, but reassured by their presence. He shut his ears to chatter that they should mount another attack.

Two nights came and went, and for Darrio it seemed like an eternity. A whole lifetime since he'd lost Sarrya behind a wall of striped fur. The noise of the battle paled into insignificance compared to the deafening silence that followed it. Valley life continued as normal, the carnage of days past forgotten with the onward march of time, and buried under thick snow.

His imagination horrified him with its depictions of the brutality and torture that Sarrya might be suffering. More than once he had resolved to cross the river and find her, but couldn't bring himself to abandon his sons. So he slumped, listless, and waited for something to happen.

On the third day, as he watched a slug pick an unhurried, slimy trail over a fallen branch, a yell went up from Warrio.

"It's Sarrya, Pa!"

Darrio darted to his son's side and watched as his daughter glided through the calm water, ripples spreading out behind her. The tigers crouched and mewed at her receding back.

She reached the bank, shook out her fur and turned to make her roaring howl in response. The tigers quietened and kneeled on their front legs, dipping their head at her. Then they disappeared into the trees.

Sarrya turned and ran to hug her father and brother.

"Harro?" she asked.

"Breathes," squeaked Darrio, his voice stuck in his throat at the mind-blowing display of submission from the tigers. Wolves surrounded her, their ears down. She raised up to her full height on her back paws and took in her audience with gleaming orange eyes.

"This is our side of the river. That is theirs. The tigers and the Peqkian humans will not trouble us if we cause them no issue. Understand? We are not at war. We are allies, we fight together against a common foe."

Heads nodded, mesmerised by her stature and the intoxicating authority in her voice.

"From herein, I command the wolf army. My name is Sarrya, daughter of Darrio. Anyone object?"

Darrio's uninjured eye watched as all present crouched down and averted their gaze. *She is their leader. My fearless daughter, only a year old.* He hunkered down beside her. *She is* my *leader.*

"Go! Tell your packs of this news. When I need you again I will summon you."

The wolves stood and started to back away, sprinting

into the forest in all directions back to their dens. Sarrya looked down at Darrio.

"Pappy, get up! So embarrassing." She dropped to her four paws and giggled, nudging him.

"You, little brother," she swiped at Warrio, "you can stay down!"

Warrio lunged at her and they tussled around on the floor yapping, as if they were carefree pups again.

Darrio stood over them dumbfounded. Struggling to shape the words, he sputtered, "How… What… Tigers… Sarrya?"

"It was nothing, Pa, tell you later. First can we hunt? Starving." Sarrya bounded off into the forest trailed by Warrio. When Darrio didn't move, she insisted, "Pa! Come *on*! Harro is good."

He set off after her, stumbling as he got used to running with one eye.

33

AMMAD

The Crown Prince of Drome rode his camel through the camp, admiring his battalions. Around fifty thousand Dromedars were gathered, in high spirits, invigorated after the great march north from Parchad. The numbers had swelled as nomad Eqmadehs and villager Yuurnans joined their ranks on the journey through the desert. The soldiers busied themselves making weapons or gathering large stones to use as catapult missiles. Some were enthralled by the holy men preaching and rousing hatred against the Peqkians, the infidel enemy they would soon thrash and deliver to God.

The preachers reminded Ammad that he still hadn't questioned Selmi about seeing him by the Hand of God sand sculpture. His brother had avoided him, and Ammad was too busy with this invasion to seek Selmi out. *I doubt it was him anyway, he isn't brave enough to leave the safety of his mother's skirts, let alone leave the city!* Jakira had forbidden Selmi to come to Peqkya, although Ammad suspected he didn't want to come anyway. *He's got no fight in him, the little runt.* Ruler Mastiq also stayed behind, Jakira insisting that Ammad's royal presence would endear him to the people as their "heroic, brave prince" and that Our Ruler was needed in Parchad.

The men were mostly Parchad peasants of the Affarah clan, or slaves. They avoided the Crown Prince's gaze and he revelled in the power, sometimes he bestowed on them the briefest smile or smallest nod. *I like being feared.* Behind him followed Qabull and his trusted guards. Whaled's soldiers did not like Ammad's men, they were outsiders since rumours had spread about how the two soldiers, their brothers in arms, had really died on the Urakbai campaign. Ammad's men camped together and shadowed him.

The Crown Prince dismounted at Whaled's tent, where the Minister of War convened with his various Tamadeen generals. Ammad threw back the flaps, bent low and swaggered in. His men waited outside. Whaled glanced up from his intense discussion with a Peqkian warrior, via an old feeble Dromedar translator, and rolled his eyes.

"Worm," he said.

"Who the fuck is this?" Ammad pointed at the warrior. She glared at him, not appreciating his tone or finger waving in her face.

Whaled stood and bowed towards the Peqkian. "This is Warrior Ashya of Peqkya, a friend of trader Riv, a friend of Drome. She entered our camp ten minutes ago."

"Why wasn't I called for?" Ammad stomped his foot.

"Shut up, sit down and listen," Whaled retorted, turning back to Ashya and taking his seat again.

Ashya's scowl bored into Ammad's skull as he scrabbled about for a seat. All were taken by Whaled's six generals who had no intention of moving. Ammad lugged a floor cushion over and perched on top of it, sitting as straight as possible. The embarrassment of being lower than everyone else in the room was excruciating, but they would not speak until he was sat.

Whaled slow clapped. "Finally." He turned to the translator and spoke a few words, which the old man relayed to the warrior and she replied.

"Warrior Ashya says she has a company of five

hundred loyal warriors stationed along the trade path. She convinced the Melokai to send Ashya's entire force in case of conflict with the Drome army. The warriors have cleared the way up the mountain, eliminating border warriors and messengers not part of the rebellion. For now, she holds the path and the Melokai does not know. Trading parties have been stopped by the Melokai until the situation with the Drome army is understood, so there is little chance of encountering any more warriors. Not many civilians live along the route as there are few grazing pastures. They will not be alarmed if they see Peqkian warriors accompanying our army, and if they do, are easily eradicated."

Whaled nodded at Ashya to indicate he understood her message and Ammad did the same, not wanting the old hisspit to think Whaled was in charge.

She continued and the translator repeated, "However, the path is not suited for an army to traverse. It is single file most of the way, hazardous for man and beast. To move the entire Drome army will take months and by that time, news will reach the capital of your advance, even with Ashya's warriors keeping messengers in check."

Ammad fidgeted, eager to ask questions, but as Whaled stayed silent, so did he.

The translator continued, "Once up the mountain, the route opens wide and it is an easy road east to Riaow. The best attack will be a swift one."

Ashya gestured for Whaled to ask questions. The Minister of War did not speak immediately, instead he poked at his nostrils. Ammad cleared his throat and started to talk but the hisspit's flat palm in front of his face stopped him short, she was waiting for Whaled. *How insolent! I am the one who has instigated this and got this man and his army on board.* He resisted the urge to slap away her hand, she was important and he couldn't risk offending the stinky bitch.

"What are the defences in the city of Riaow?" Whaled

asked. "We have planned for a long attack and have catapults and ramming machines for walls, and which can be used to cross moats."

Via the translator, Ashya replied. "Warrior Ashya says that the city has no protection from attack. The nation of Peqkya is a plateau surrounded by a belt of mountains. The Peqkians guard the mountains as their natural defences, an enemy on this side must cross the stretch of open tundra before reaching the southern Melioks and so are an easy target, as can be spotted from afar. No foreign army has ever passed into Peqkya, and there has never been an attack on Riaow from outside forces. Any fighting has been between internal foes, but not for many, many years.

"There are few warriors in the city, around eight thousand, most young novices with no experience. Ashya suspects you will be able to march in without much resistance. The Riats will not put up a struggle, they will have no comprehension about what is happening. Ignore them. The city layout is like a pebble dropped in water. The streets ripple out from the centre. We head for the Melokai's apartments and court buildings at that centre, warriors will defend these and protect her there. We will be assisted by a band of one thousand Peqkian civilian men who have joined our cause. Including your soldiers, we have a more than adequate force of fifty-one thousand.

"The time is ripe for attack, Ramya is vulnerable. Her Head Warrior is dead and she has no replacement. Most of her exceptional warriors are out in the field. She is weak, allowing a monster to manipulate her and keeping an equally monstrous baby at her side. The Melokai was once a formidable fighter but her body and her warrior's mind have dwindled.

"You must prepare for freezing weather; winter is upon us. You will gasp for air as we live at a higher level than you and breathing becomes difficult. Peqkians are adapted to it. You will find you are not as strong as in Drome, although Riaow is at a lower elevation which will ease the struggle. Warrior Ashya warns that this will not be an easy fight. Novices are highly trained. One youngblood warrior is worth five Dromedar soldiers. Don't underestimate them."

There followed an intense discussion about when they would attack, how many soldiers they would take and how they might strike, with Ashya drawing the court buildings and pointing out entrances and key rooms. Ammad lost interest. He was impatient to be there and cleave the Melokai in half with his sword. The logistics and intricacies of planning bored him.

He brought out his pipe and lit it. He felt the familiar fuzzy feeling and knew the poppy was taking effect. The dreamlike rush was fast becoming his only release, since his cock refused to function. He sunk deeper into the floor cushions and slouched on his side, one eye on the group.

Ashya grunted her approval at the plan and slapped Whaled on the back. Then she stood and strode out of the tent, kicking Ammad's buttocks as she passed. He jerked, and scrutinised her blurred form. He laboriously pulled himself up, ignoring the laughs of the generals, and followed her out of the tent. He watched as her pony galloped off and then felt fluid, stumbling into Qabull's arms.

"Come on, Crown Prince, let's get to our tent." The guard dragged Ammad away as respectfully as he could.

***

Nothing happened for days and Ammad wiled away the time in an intoxicated stupor. One evening, through his foggy haze he heard his guard Khasar shout, "What is that?"

Violent gales rattled their camp. The felt of their tent shook wildly although they had secured it with more ropes earlier that day. But Ammad soon realised that it was not the tent he could feel moving and it was not the start of an inevitable post-poppy headache.

"The earth is moving!" Ammad screamed as he clambered into the open, squinting to see in the twilight.

Soldiers gawped at the shaking dirt, trying to balance and stay on their feet. A huge splintering sound echoed off the land as it wrenched itself apart, massive erratic lines opening like glass cracking. Ammad jumped out of the way of a crack and watched as men floated away from him on islands of earth. Screaming and distorted shouts reached Ammad's ears as a pack of men, huddled together, plummeted into a sudden dark crevice.

The rumbling stopped, but a sharp crack signalled the start of movement again. Instead of pulling apart, this time the earth slammed together, closing the cracks, forming huge chaotic mounds of rocky earth and squashing men and camels. Ammad ran here and there, dodging the waves of dirt crashing down on one another, until all was still.

The flat plain, which had been so perfect for the Drome army to camp on, was now a lumpy mass of sprawling rocky hills and giant boulders, like shattered glass swept into a pile of jagged edges. Broken bodies, camels and tents dotted the transformed landscape. Dazed men slumped on the ground, covered in heavy layers of dust. One nearby was screaming, his ankle pinned under a huge rock. Ammad crouched down and wept, suddenly believing in His existencc and fearing the wrath of God was upon them. *I'm sorry for my sins, I'm sorry God, forgive me God.*

Qabull found him cowering and hauled him up. His guard had suffered a wound above his ear, bright red blood smeared down to his jaw. He too had wept, his tears drying black on his dusty face to form two V-shapes under his hollow eyes, like some horrific mask.

"We need to find Whaled," the guard said. And although Ammad would never admit it, the hairy man was exactly who he wanted to be with at that moment.

The Minister of War was busy checking for survivors and ordering the able men to recover what they could, light torches and catch the escaped camels. He told them all to calm down, he had heard of such a thing as the ground shaking but it had never happened in Drome, so they just had to accept it and deal with the aftermath. His practical reaction soothed Ammad's terror, and when Whaled shouted at him to carry injured men over to a makeshift medicine tent, he obeyed without a second thought.

Hours passed as they worked in the darkness and Ammad breathed a small sigh of relief as the first of the sun's rays touched them. But the respite was short lived as small aftershocks started to rumble. At each new judder the Dromedars braced themselves for another bout of destruction, but blessedly, it never came.

"Look!" a soldier shouted and pointed in the direction of the mountains.

A massive dust cloud rose and spread throughout the sky, blocking out the sun. A deep thundering noise followed the drifting darkness, but the earth under Ammad's feet did not shake. Soon a river of dirt and rocks came into view, surging down the mountain ripping up trees and consuming everything that lay in its wake. Shouts went up from the men nearest the mountains and all started to run as the moving earth touched the edge of their camp and advanced steadily. It slowly lost momentum and ground to a halt. Then a rain of stones fell on them forcing men to take cover.

When the debris shower eased, Ammad stumbled around searching again for Whaled.

"God is not happy with us! God does not want us to proceed!" He tugged on the minister's arm.

"This has nothing to do with God, Ammad," came the gentle response, whispered closely in Ammad's ear. "This is nature, changing her shape, bored of her current form and wanting to look different. Like your mother changing her gown. Pull yourself together. I swore to Jakira that I would keep you alive, and you are alive."

Ammad was bewildered by the mention of Jakira, his legs buckled and he clutched Whaled's arm to stay upright. The formidable man lifted him and set him back on his feet, patting his shoulders. Ammad peered at his filthy, bruised and bloody feet. *Whaled has not once spoken of her. He hasn't boasted of their night together or provoked me with lewd innuendos. And why is he calling me Ammad and not worm? What happened between him and Jakira? Are they now friends? Or… more?*

Ammad's mouth opened to speak but Whaled had switched back into directing the rescue, pointing and shouting orders at Ammad and the men who crowded around him.

***

The camp was cleared of rubble, dead Dromedars and animals, and resurrected in a shambolic fashion, far less impressive than before. They burned the corpses on a pyre, with holy men chanting prayers and blessings. Ammad cried and lamented the loss by shedding blood with his men, this time slashing his wrist. After, the Minister of War ordered a feast of the dead livestock, to help settle frayed nerves.

As the men were eating, Whaled walked to the edge of the pile of dirt and rocks that had flowed down the mountainside with Ammad and the four surviving generals. They stared at the loose earth, trees and rubble that led up into the mountains.

"The earth shaking and fracturing has given us a new path," Whaled said and trod boldly onto the churned-up soil. "We climb this into Peqkya. Tomorrow I will send out scouts to probe for a suitable route. This," he swept an arm around him to imply the devastation, "is our saviour."

***

Just short of forty-five thousand Dromedars tramped up the scree, it was slow going but the men fanned out and moved in droves rather than single file. The camels, cattle and catapults stayed behind along with injured men and bulky machinery. Only the essential supplies came with them. Whaled had told them that they would travel light and fast. They trudged on through the calf-high shingle, making their way around boulders or trees torn up from the roots and soon came upon a company of warriors with spears directed at them. Ashya stepped forward and greeted Whaled. She led the army off the dirt path and onto a flat plain, where they set up camp for the night.

Through the translator, she told Whaled, "You have crossed the border and are now in Peqkya. Two more days' ascent and then we descend deeper into the country, along the flat road. Ashya's company has suffered a few losses but they are still strong. Ashya cannot know if the earthquake hit the capital Riaow. She has sent a spy warrior ahead to understand the impact. We hope that the city too has been obliterated."

At sunrise, they set off with the Peqkian warriors leading the way. The old hisspit was on a dumpy pony, followed by ten of her more senior warriors on ponies. The rest were on foot. The Drome army followed at a steady march.

During the week long trek, they encountered few Peqkians. One roaming shepherd simply moved her small herd out of the way and waved at the hisspits, who waved back. The peasants trusted the warriors implicitly, believing they were loyal to the Melokai and did not seem suspicious in any way of the hordes of foreign soldiers that trailed behind. Ashya shouted to any who stared too long that this army was here to assist with the wolf war, which seemed to answer their doubts.

A few of Ashya's warriors had gone on in front, sweeping the way of potential messengers and keeping news of the Drome army's advance from the Melokai. Another advance group was instructed to seize the pony farm just outside the city, to supply mounts for the Drome army.

The roads were full of holes and fissures; stone walls and huts were rubble and ragged bulges of rock and grass jutted up where the land had smashed back together.

Ashya dropped back from her lead position and brought her pony alongside Whaled and jumped down so she was walking with him. Ammad shoved soldiers out the way to catch them up.

Whaled summoned the translator.

He repeated, "Ashya says the shape of her country has changed. We are a few days from the capital but these are new roads, these are new hills."

Ammad punched his arm in the air. "It is another sign, Whaled. A new Peqkya for a new ruler!"

34

FERRAZ

"It is time." Riv twisted her ring and beckoned for Ferraz and Mikaz to sit. The set administrator had collected them from the cells for the unusual early morning call, joking that the Head Trader was insatiable recently. The PGs had tittered nervously at the woman's joke, and they had followed the clevercat to Riv's chambers.

There a warrior stood, one hand on sword and the other clenched in a fist at her side. One of her muscular thighs was nearly as wide as Ferraz's chest and she towered over them. The PGs huddled together on the couch not daring to look her in the eye.

Riv said, "This is Sianya, she has come from Ashya. An earthquake on the border paved the Drome army's way into Peqkya and this evening, they will attack with their full force. It is a shame that the quake was not felt here… Anyhow, we have much to do. Sianya, do you have anything to tell these peons?"

The warrior grunted. "Make sure you and all of your peons have blue and yellow cloth tied around your upper arms, so we know who you are. Don't be late. Watch the courtyard and be ready when you see me leave. Which one of you is Mikaz?"

Mikaz raised his hand just off his knee, intimidated by the huge slab of a woman, and croaked, "I am."

"I will find you and give instructions. Don't screw up." She turned to Riv. "Head Trader, there will be an escort of two warriors and two cammers waiting for you by the Leqari bridge. Travel light."

"Of course, we will be back again soon enough once Ramya is removed and order restored. Sianya, you may go, I will see you again soon." Riv watched the retreating warrior's back and swirled her pink orb on the chain around her neck and then brought it to her lips. "This Sarenky pearl will be coming with me, ha, worth more than the whole of Peqkya!"

She chuckled to herself and then wriggled in her chair to get her squashed buttocks comfortable and turned to the PGs. "Mikaz, assemble your peons and prepare for attack. Ferraz, bring me your son before midday and that task you have failed once? Finish him tonight."

Ferraz and Mikaz embraced. Neither wanted to let the other go, both aware that this might be the last time they would see each other.

"Thank you for giving me this purpose. In our small way we will help to rid Peqkya of that rotten Melokai and usher in a new era where *men* are in control of their lives. I will see you again soon. Tomorrow when we celebrate our victory!" Mikaz held Ferraz's face and touched his forehead to Ferraz's brow.

"I will see you tomorrow, Mikaz." Ferraz blinked away the tears that threatened to fall and without another word, Mikaz jumped down the passageway and into the water beyond. Ferraz counted to one hundred and then followed.

Mikaz was going to meet Shit-Pick and Steely to rouse the peons and distribute the crude swords that Steely had fashioned out of steel leftover from making warriors' weapons. Skinny Wevo had been beheaded in the marketplace the day before as punishment for strangling Glendya, his female boss at the goat hair workshop, with rope he had just woven.

Ferraz was heading to his son's pen.

He had imagined this moment more times than he could count, but now it was happening he faltered, not taking a deep enough breath and swallowing too much water. He emerged by the river bank, spluttered and gagged, then lay on his back, chest heaving. *Pull it together! I don't have much time.*

He hauled himself up, threw on his rags and hurried towards the pen, slowing to a hobble when he came across another Riat. It was a cold day, but it was dry and he knew at this time the toddlers would be bundled up in warm clothes and outside enjoying the fresh air. They were always watched over by a junior Mother who was easily distracted when one child cried or fell. He crept towards the fence and scanned the children. His peen was there with another girl, trying to skip rope. They laughed as their feet tangled.

First, he needed to get into the records room. Ferraz had no idea what his son was called and to gain his trust he'd need to know his name. He pulled his shabby cloak tight and the hood low over his face and stumbled in through the wooden door, aiming to appear like a confused elderly peon if he came across anyone. A wall of noise hit him. Children squealed with delight or bawled, soothing voices came from the Mothers.

The layout of this wooden building was the same as his old pen, a small lounge area to his right with floor cushions and a low table where the Mothers took a break, further to his right were their bedrooms, a kitchen and washroom. In front of him was the door to the outside area where his son played, and to his left were the children's bedrooms, play areas and dining hall. The records room doubled up as the office for the pen's head Mother and was the first door to his left. Being back in a pen made him feel clumsy and unsure of himself, like he was a child again.

He heard two voices coming down the corridor and he ducked under the low table, curling up in a ball. He stank like Ashya. Sweat drenched his armpits and he fretted they would smell him. *Think, fool, think.* He focused on memories of his childhood. *They won't rest, this is the busiest time of day.*

"Yes, Mother Samya, I have taken note of that," a young voice said.

"Good. Let us visit the playrooms before mid-morning snacks," the older woman replied.

They passed him and entered the second room to his left, the noise of children growing and falling as the door opened and closed. *That was the head Mother, meaning the records room is empty.* He rolled out from under the table and ran into the first room on his left. It was devoid of people but full of shelves crammed with books. These noted every child that had lived at the pen, what profession they had entered and which peens had been ended.

A huge tome lay open on the desk and Ferraz ran to it, skimming through the entries. Mother Samya wrote a small entry about each child, every day. He found the peens, and scanned the words for anything that might indicate his son. He froze as the door from the next room opened and closed and the two women came back out into the corridor. They turned left and away from him, into the next playroom. He traced his finger down the page.

He read: 'A charming little peen, despite his physiological oddity, who shows great kindness to his peers and unfaltering obedience. Today, one girl asked him if she could have his blue eyes and he replied, "If Mother Samya lets me, then you can."'

Blue eyes! Ferraz found the start of the paragraph. Artaz. *My son's name is Artaz.* A warm flush spread across his torso. *Oddity?* He scrambled back through pages, searching out the first entry on Artaz. When he found it, he gasped and clasped his hand over his mouth. It stated: 'Male baby arrived today, but on closer inspection he had both male *and* female sex organs. Seems healthy otherwise. Rare blue eyes. We are watching closely for any hint it may have The Sight and will call it Artie for now, for either Artaz or Artya, depending on how it develops as it grows up.'

Ferraz dashed into the street. *My son may have The Sight!* He took a moment, focusing on calming his breathing and bringing his thumping heart back to a normal level. He skulked to the play area, grabbed a stone and when the young Mother's back was turned he threw it at a toddler's head. *I'm sorry little one. But it's necessary.* The child screamed and brought a grubby palm to his bleeding cheek. The Mother turned towards the child and rushed over to comfort him.

Ferraz leaned over the low fence and whipped up Artaz. The peen was too astonished to make a sound and Ferraz bundled him up in his cloak and ran faster than he had ever run before, to a quiet passageway where he had stashed a sack and ropes. The child started to squall.

"Hey, Artaz, how are you? Don't cry, I'm your father. Do you know what a father is?" He put the peen on his feet and kneeled so their eyes met. He stroked the child's head and hugged him. Artaz struggled.

"You don't know me, but I love you very much and I'm here to protect you. We're going on a little journey and you are going to a new country! There's lots of desert there and no mountains. Shush, don't cry, Artie. What's this?" Ferraz pulled a face at the child and then stuck his tongue out. Artaz's crying stopped for a moment at the distraction and Ferraz continued until the child quietened.

Artaz pulled two small carved figurines from his pockets, a bird and a cat. He held out his palms and screwed up his little face, intently focusing on the toys. The figurines twitched and, for a fleeting moment, floated above Artaz's palms. The child beamed up at Ferraz, eyes sparkling. Artaz grabbed the figurines out of the air and bashed them together, before giving them to a gaping, stunned Ferraz. *My son has magic!*

Voices drifted closer from the main road and Ferraz snapped to action.

"I'm going to need you to drink this. It's yummy. No one can see a lone child out of the pen, it will raise far too many suspicions." He pulled out a small bottle of white milky liquid, that Riv had assured him was safe for a child. It was a sleeping potion she took, from one of the finest medics in Riaow's medicinal quarter.

Artaz refused to drink it and squirmed in despair, pummelling Ferraz's hands away with his little fists. Ferraz held his head and pinched his nose, forcing the liquid down his throat.

"Forgive me, Artaz, forgive me," he whispered.

He kissed and hugged the peen as the potion took effect. He rocked him gently as the child wriggled and groaned. Artaz's eyelids sagged and he succumbed. Ferraz bundled him up in the sack and tied it to his back and headed for Riv's apartments, a route he had scouted many times in preparation for this moment.

He snuck in the back, past the caged animals, and waited for the Head Trader in the bed chamber. He heard her voice directing serving peons about the storage of her things. She came into thc bed chamber and closed the door.

"Riv," he whispered. She walked to him and stared at the prone body of Artaz, on her bed.

"Take it off there and move it to my couch," she sneered.

Ferraz did as told and stroked the peen's face. He was in a deep, peaceful slumber.

"How much did you give it?"

"I gave *him* the entire bottle. His name is Artaz." *This is a mistake, what have you done stupid peon?*

"Good." She walked to the door and yelled for Toya. A few moments later the assistant trader rushed in.

"Toya, this is for you to deal with on our journey. It cannot be seen or heard. It will sleep for the next day at least."

Toya moved over to the couch and smiled down at the child, lips closed so as not to expose her stained teeth. Ferraz took her hand, and she jolted at the illicit contact.

"Please, Toya, his name is Artaz. He is nearly four years old. Please tell him I love him and take care of him for me." He kissed her hand and then pulled it down so it rested on Artaz's cheek.

She softened and gently cupped the peen's tiny head. "His hair is dark red, like a plum."

Ferraz frowned. Artaz's hair had always been black, but the trader spoke the truth. It now had a reddish tinge. "He's a special boy."

"He's beautiful. I will look after him for you, Ferraz. I promise," she said.

"These are his." Ferraz handed her the figurines and she nodded.

Tears welled up and he sniffed repeatedly as snot started to form. The pain of uniting with his son only to be wrenched apart again was excruciating.

"Riv, can I not come with you?" he begged, knowing the answer.

"No, Ferraz, Chaz is still breathing! Say your goodbyes and leave. We have work to do, *you* have work to do. The child will be fine, you have my word. I will send him back to you from Parchad when it's safe, when all the fighting is over and we have taken control." Riv stood with one hand on the door, tapping her foot.

Ferraz bent down and kissed his sleeping peen, trying to scorch in his memory every detail about his little face and sweet smell. A tear dropped on his son's forehead and he wiped it away with his thumb. *Goodbye Artaz, I love you. We will be together again soon, and with your magic, you will be the most powerful peen in Peqkya!*

He inhaled deeply and walked to the door, stopping to

look at Riv.

"Let's kill this zhaq Melokai," he said. "For Irrya, for my son."

Riv clapped him on the back. "Yes, yes, Ferraz. For anyone you want, dear. Just remember to kill zhaq Chaz first."

35

RAMYA

It was late and Ramya sat in front of the fire, exhausted by motherhood. Hanny was cooing over the baby, cuddling her and planting sloppy kisses on her cheeks. The baby made a gurgling in response. She was one of a kind and Ramya felt overwhelmed by love for the little thing. Her skin was a beautiful pearlescent grey, a perfect mix of her mother's black and her father's white, translucent skin. A fine silky down covered her from top to toe. She had inherited eyes from her mother but they were pink like her father's two blind mounds.

"Issee, my Melokai, she is gorgeous. Aren't you my little Terya." Hanny nuzzled her nose into the baby's chest, but she screwed up her tiny face and then the bawling came. Hanny swiftly passed her back to her mother.

Ramya bounced the baby and tried to soothe her. She laughed. "I have no idea what I'm doing. Naomya has been giving me lessons in raising a baby. Usually they'd be in the pen by now."

"You are crazy to keep her, but I understand. Terya is precious."

Gwrlain came in from the next chamber drawn by the sound of Terya's crying, kissed Ramya's hair and took the baby from her arms. Terya settled immediately, comforted by her father's presence. He started to sing to her softly and her delicate eyes closed, content.

Hanny looked on in awe and then raised her eyebrows at Ramya, who smiled. "She loves her father, he only has to sing to her and she quietens down. He just seems to know exactly what to do." Ramya yawned. "I think I must retire to bed, my darling, I will see you tomorrow no doubt."

Hanny's tone became serious. "Ramya, before I leave, I need to tell you something."

"Go on."

Hanny glanced up at Gwrlain and he took the hint, wandering into the next room with the baby. The courtesan leaned in close to the Melokai.

"There are murmurs of discontent, Ramya, whispers in the wind have reached my ears. It started around the time of Irrya's suicide. People are unhappy about Gwrlain and now the baby, unhappy about the Fert alliance, unhappy about your rule."

Ramya gasped. "What *people*?" she asked, suddenly wide awake.

"I don't know, my Melokai, if I did I would tell you. But I hear that it goes as far up as the council. I think *something* is about to happen, I understand that they want you… *gone*."

Ramya's mind and stomach churned at once, as if she was in the medicinal quarter and had spent too long breathing the fumes. She forced herself to put her thoughts in order.

"Council sessions have been… fraught recently. I know Gogo, poor Gogo, was displeased with many of my decisions."

"Gogo is gone, it can't be her," Hanny replied. "Omya is never wholly in agreement with many of your actions either, my Melokai."

"True, but would Omya want to depose me? I cannot believe it. I will talk to her in the morning."

"I think that is wise."

"Did you hear what happened at the public assembly two days ago?" Ramya asked. Hanny shook her head. "There was uproar because Zecky informed the people that I am keeping the baby and not sending her to a pen. Warriors had to move in to calm everyone down and send them home. Zecky said it was most unnerving. I dread to think what might've happened if I had been present. I had to triple the number of warriors on the streets that night as Chaz cautioned it might spark a protest or some kind of unrest. Can you imagine! That has never happened in my rule."

"Well, you perhaps should consider changing the law, Ramya. I mean, it can't be one rule for you and one rule for everyone else. Maybe make it an option? If you want to raise your baby then do, if not then send it to the pen. I would definitely still send all mine to the pen! I have a tough enough time taking care of myself." Hanny chuckled and put a firm arm around Ramya.

"Yes, good idea. I'll deal with it tomorrow, and address my people. I always want to do the best for them. They know that, don't they? I do so much. Surely they see that?"

"I don't know… I guess they do. I think you are an excellent Melokai." Hanny squeezed Ramya's hunched shoulders.

Ramya stared down at her mutilated hand, scarred and pock marked. *Proof that I have given myself to the nation! Surely my people don't begrudge me my happiness with Gwrlain and our baby? After twelve years of devotion. Perhaps they don't love me anymore… even after all I've done for them...*

Bevya came bounding in through Ramya's door. "Melokai! A warrior hassss arrived with sssome disssturbing newssss. Come now to the courtyard!"

Ramya and Hanny ran down to the courtyard, which was taking a pounding from hailstones.

"My Melokai," the warrior said. She remained on her pony, the hood of her fur cloak shielding her face from the stones, and also from the Melokai. Ramya stood in the candlelit entrance.

Odd, thought Ramya, *she should dismount.* "Speak, warrior."

"I am Sianya of Ashya's company. They follow close at hand. The Drome army has invaded Peqkya and are in pursuit, on the way to the capital."

"Why were they not stopped at the border? How did they pass?"

"They overwhelmed us, my Melokai. There must be around forty thousand soldiers."

"How far away are they?"

"Within the hour, my Melokai."

"An hour! Why was a messenger not sent earlier, Sianya? Is this the reason why we have had no reports for days from our borders guards?"

The warrior faltered, "I… I do not know, my Melokai."

Ramya stared at the warrior, who shifted in her seat.

"Thank you, Sianya. Go and rest at the barracks. We will keep watch for Ashya, and ensure the gates are left open for her."

Sianya turned her pony away and went back out the gates she had just entered, rather than towards the training grounds that led on to the barracks.

"Bevya! Brief my counsellors and get them here at once. Then go to the barracks and get my warriors here. Tell them to prepare to fight. After go and tell Gwrlain to meet me in the assembly hall with Terya and bring me my daggers and sword."

"Zhaq, Ramya! The Drome *army* in Peqkya? *Forty* thousand soldiers… How has this happened?" Hanny was as stunned as Ramya.

The Melokai strode towards the gates and looked out, ignoring the hail clipping her bare skin. She turned to the gate keepers and said, "Keep these gates open for Ashya and her company. Then close them and keep the cammer army out."

She noticed lowly peons gathering outside the gates, holding fire torches. They huddled in small groups with more peons joining them, pouring out of the alleyways. In the distance, she saw a warrior on a pony giving orders to a peon. The woman, she realised, was Sianya and the peon was familiar. An old PG whose name she couldn't remember. *Something is not right here.*

A shout from behind drew her attention. Gemya, currently in charge after Gogo's death, was positioned in front of a line of warriors. More jogged in from the barracks and took up position in the courtyard and vast training grounds.

Gemya shouted again, "My Melokai! Get behind us, we are here to protect you."

Ramya ran back across the courtyard, gravel crunching underfoot. The line of warriors opened to let her through. Waiting with Hanny were her counsellors Zecky, Naomya, Omya and Chaz. Their presence made her feel stronger. Bevya bumped her thigh with her head. The clevercat held Ramya's weapons under one paw and her sword in her mouth.

Ramya took them from the cat. "Where is Riv?"

"Not in her apartment."

"Go back and ask her housekeeper and serving-peons where she has gone, find her and bring her here."

The clevercat bounded off whilst Ramya led her counsellors into the building and up the shadowy stairs to the council chamber. As she walked, she strapped her daggers to her arms and struggled to fasten her sword belt around her still swollen belly. There was no time to light candles so she felt her way around the dark table, in the shape of her beloved Peqkya, to reach the window. She opened the inside shutters, flung open the outer ones and peered out into the gloom. As she leaned on the windowsill a blast of icy air smacked her cheeks and a violent shiver shot through her body.

Warriors had positioned themselves by the gates.

"Ashya's company is fast approaching," shouted Gemya from the courtyard. "Let them in and then close the gates."

A silence fell. It was broken by the noise of the peons gathered outside the gates, who cheered and raised their arms. The old PG was stood in front of them shouting.

"That's Mikaz! What is he doing?" Hanny yelled, pointing.

Ramya heard snippets of his speech and her fists clenched.

"We are here to rebel against the vile Melokai Ramya! We want equality for *men*," Mikaz shouted. "We want to be free to choose our paths in life. To choose who we love. To choose where we live. To bring up our offspring. Now is our chance to topple the oppressor and bring back the glory days of Xayy where *men* held the power. This is for your sons. Your sons' sons. Kill the Melokai!"

Echoes of "Kill the Melokai!" and "We are men not peons!" came from the swarming crowd.

Ramya was crushed. *I thought they loved me.*

"After all you have done for peons! And they turn against you," Hanny exclaimed.

"A quenchless thirst for power is in every peon's nature," Head Speaker Zecky sneered. "As much as we wish it wasn't, it is, and always will be. That is why we must control them. You tried to be kind, Ramya, to control peons with care, but they have chewed up your generosity and spat it back at you. Peons have an insatiable greed like cats, you gave them a bone and now they want the whole carcass!"

Ramya was speechless. *Can't the zhaq peons see that they have it better now than ever before? Couldn't they be satisfied with that? They should be thanking me not threatening me!*

Gemya yelled, "Destroy anyone who enters that gate and poses a threat to our Melokai. Those peons are hostile!"

The peons paused outside the courtyard, stamping their

feet, yelling and brandishing their burning sticks. A bright flame sliced through the dark night, licking at the roof of the House of Knowledge. A glow from the steelmakers quarter brightened the sky and another in the direction of the wood carvers quarter. The peons cheered, a chant of "Fire, fire, burn the Melokai down!" started up.

"Gemya," Ramya bellowed from the window, "we must stop an inferno!"

Thankfully Gemya heard. She ordered, "Company B, leave through the barracks entrance and quench those fires! Do not allow them to spread, they will gut our precious city. Destroy anyone who tries to stop you."

A few hundred warriors hastened away from the courtyard.

Bevya sprung onto the windowsill and pawed at Ramya. "Melokai, Riv issss gone from the city, left earlier today. Her houssssekeeper sayssss sssshe issss gone to Drome."

"To Drome?" Ramya had little time to understand the implication of this information as a distant pounding sound was followed by Ashya and her warriors galloping up the Riaow streets towards the enclosure. As the old warrior neared, half of her company split off and headed for the barracks.

"She is coming too fast," Omya observed. The Head Teller had been in the middle of undoing her neat bun for bed when Bevya had arrived to summon her. Half her hair was still plaited into neat, orderly coils, the other a wild frizzy mass. "The cammer marauders must be right on her heels."

Through the torrent of hailstones Ramya watched in disbelief as old Ashya came flying through the gates, slashing at the warriors positioned there and ensuring the gates could not be closed. Her warriors poured in, jumping from their mounts and slaying their fellow warriors.

Gemya hesitated, as did all under her command. Peqkian warriors did not raise a hand to other warriors.

Ashya was breaking the ultimate code and the complete shock delayed their response.

As Gemya saw her women fall, she snapped to her senses. "Attack Ashya! All those wearing blue and yellow are our enemy. Do not leave one traitor alive!"

On her command, the Melokai's loyal warriors hit back savagely.

A bolt of realisation slotted into place and Ramya's body convulsed. "Riv has left the city and gone to Drome! She is behind this, with Ashya."

There was no reply from her counsellors, a shocked tremor stunned them all. The Melokai gulped for air, suffocated by Riv and Ashya's betrayal. She flailed around, forgetting momentarily where she was. She swallowed back sick, a taste of stew lingering on the back of her tongue. Omya ran to steady her, holding the Melokai's arms firm and keeping her from collapse.

"How has this happened? How did we not know about it and prevent it? I have failed…" Ramya rambled.

"Nobody is infallible, Ramya," Chaz told her. "None of us saw this coming. Riv…"

A white anger seared in Ramya's chest and she pulled away from Omya, moving to go and join Gemya. "I need to be out there fighting!"

Chaz stood in her path. "No, my Melokai! You must stay alive to avenge this despicable treachery. You are no good to anyone if you are dead."

She thumped both fists on the council table, letting out a snarl, but turned back to watch the skirmish from the window.

The peons surged through the open gates after Ashya's company, the charge led by the PG Mikaz. She saw now that they were armed with makeshift weapons, wood blocks sharpened at the end, some knives, clubs, shields fashioned from wood. Some even carried crude swords. What they lacked in weaponry they made up for in hatred, attacking in a fearless frenzy. They too had blue and yellow strips of cloth wrapped around arms, heads, legs. *The colours of Drome*, Ramya understood with disgust.

"Archers," Gemya yelled and a flurry of arrows pelted down from the warriors stationed on the rooftop. A wave of peons staggered and dropped to the floor. More teemed in to the courtyard, treading over their fallen comrades.

A resounding horn heralded the approach of the Drome army. The humped soldiers came bareback on Peqkian ponies, awkwardly jumping off their mounts outside the gates, and shoving their way to the front of the battle. In an undisciplined haste, the Dromedars cut down Peqkian peons on their own side.

Ramya watched as her courageous warriors encountered four or five enemies at a time.

"The cammer swords seem to be tipped with some poison! When it breaks skin our warriors are paralysed," Chaz shouted.

Her warriors started to fall back under the onslaught. The tang of smoke filled her nostrils as Riaow burned.

"My Melokai, it is time to move to the assembly hall," said one of the young warriors who had been ordered by Gemya to protect her and the counsellors. Ramya recognised her as Monya, the novice that had so impressed her during chariot warfare training.

Ramya ran into the bright hall, past throngs of her court members who were busy lighting torches, and into Gwrlain's arms. She paused there a moment, breathing in his musky scent. He stood on the platform, the baby sleeping on a cushion under the simple wooden bench that was her throne. The warriors herded everyone in the room and formed a protective line in front of them, facing the door.

"My love," Ramya said and she kissed Gwrlain passionately. "Give me Terya. I will strap her to my back and protect her. You do not know how to fight. I do."

"We must run and hide, Ramya. Protect Terya. Let us be away!" He grabbed at her arm. She shook him off.

"No, Gwrlain! I cannot turn my back on my people. I belong here, there is nowhere to run to."

Gwrlain nodded slowly. He picked up the baby, kissed her gently and gave her to Ramya. He ripped a blanket and tied Terya to Ramya's back.

"I know how to fight for those I love," he said, pulling a dagger strapped to Ramya's arm and taking up position beside her.

She touched his arm. *No harm will come to my soulmatch or my baby.* They stood together, waiting. Poised for combat.

Clashing steel and shouts came like distant thunder as the Dromedars forced their way into the building and progressed towards the hall. Soon the fracas was at the door and young warriors kept the cammers at bay for long drawn out minutes. Ramya was ready for them. *I will strike them all down to protect my little family.*

A shriek came from her left, she turned to see Chaz fall forward, a dagger lodged between his shoulderblades. Behind him stood a pleasure giver, with blue and yellow wrapped around his arm. He looked familiar but in the moment, Ramya couldn't place him. The PG pulled another dagger from his waistband.

His cold glare met Ramya's. He stepped forwards with weapon raised, ready to leap towards her and parted his lips to shout something.

Ramya flung her dagger and it struck him between piercing blue eyes. His mouth gaped comically before he fell forward on top of Chaz, who groaned under the weight.

"Zhaq, insipid Ferraz," Chaz hissed and nudged the dead body off.

Ramya yelled, "Stay alive, Chaz! Together we will avenge this treachery."

A cammer soldier forced his way through the door, then more soldiers streamed in, but none of Ashya's disloyal warriors or any pathetic peons. *Too cowardly to attack me.* Her counsellors and courtiers stood shoulder to shoulder in front of Ramya. They had taken up weapons and fought back. The clevercats had also joined the scrap, backs arched and fur stood on end.

A huge hairy cammer pushed his way in and Ramya guessed by his demeanour that he was in command. The Drome Minister of War, Whaled, she surmised from various reports she had read in the past. When Gogo had first been appointed Head Warrior, she had gathered intelligence on all Peqkya's neighbours with a network of discreet spies.

Bevya flung herself onto Whaled's hairy hump and started clawing his shoulders and biting his neck, clumps of his hair puffing into the air. With one big hand he flung her off, flecks of his blood spraying from the scratches she had inflicted. The clevercat slammed against the wall and crumpled on the floor. Then he shouted orders in the Dromedari language and pointed at the Melokai.

Behind him came a haughty male-child, his demeanour and clothes indicating he was royalty. Crown Prince Ammad el Wakrime, all grown up. He fixed his stare on Ramya and tore his way through the wall of warriors and courtiers that stood between them. *Come and get it.* Ramya bared her teeth and hissed.

Whaled followed in Ammad's stead, cutting down attackers at the Crown Prince's back. Monya stood firm in front of Ramya and engaged Ammad, he struggled to keep up with her blows and parries. An ugly brute with scar from ear to mouth came up to assist the Crown Prince, one of his personal guards, no doubt. Monya held her own against the two cammers. It was only when the hairy Minister of War joined his sword that the young novice was overwhelmed. Monya took a stab to the leg and fell, frozen by the poison.

The three turned their attention to the Melokai and in their rush, did not finish off the young warrior. *A mistake*, thought Ramya, *always ensure your opponent is dead before you walk away.* Gwrlain engaged the scarred brute, the Crown

Prince and the Minister of War turned to her.

Ramya beckoned the cammers to come closer with the two fingers of her left hand, a big grin on her face. Her right, holding her sword, came up to meet them. She crouched, hissed, and then leapt up, engaging Ammad, somersaulting and swiping at Whaled. She sidestepped their strikes effortlessly and counter attacked. They had clearly never fought together and were clumsy, breaking each other's flow.

She ducked and twisted, landing a kick on Ammad's shins. Then danced behind Whaled and smacked his hairy hump. She laughed out loud at their bungling. Both were adequate swordsmen. Individually they might put up a decent fight, but together they were pitiful.

Whilst Ramya was enjoying frolicking with the two kittens, she ensured she didn't move too far from her soulmatch and could hear him humming to see. He was fighting ferociously with Ammad's ugly personal guard. Her white giant towered over his opponent, his movements awkward but his sheer brute force kept the cammer at bay. She and Gwrlain slashed and stabbed side by side.

Time to finish these two humpy fools. Ramya feigned a lunge and twisted to the other side at the last minute, carving a line across Whaled's chest. The jerking movement woke Terya who let out a cry and wriggled on Ramya's back. *Stay still baby, I love you, stay still.*

Terya's wails seemed to bolster Gwrlain's determination and he sliced the scarred brute across the waist. The guard dropped to his knees, hands desperately trying to keep his guts from spilling on the floor.

Ammad let out a pained wail as the guard crumpled, not unlike one of Terya's cries. *Ha! That scarred brute meant something to him. Good, he can suffer as he's made Peqkya suffer.*

Gwrlain made one of his pulsing hums in celebration, it rattled the entire hall with its force. He pointed at Whaled, as if to say, "You're next". The Minister of War stepped up to cross swords with the Trogr.

Ramya winked at the Crown Prince, who suddenly did not look quite as cocksure and confident. He readied himself and bounced on his knees. Ramya attacked. She toyed with him awhile. Ammad was quick, but lacking in skills. His decisions were obvious, his thrusts lacked power.

Struggling to keep her balance with Terya squirming on her back, she'd had enough. *Now you die.* She attacked the Crown Prince viciously and knocked his sword out of his hand. It fell to the ground. She brought the point of her sword to his neck.

A blistering pain in her calf, and her leg gave way. The scar-faced guard, who Ammad had bleated for, had crawled across the floor, leaving a smear of innards in his wake, and, with his last breath, stabbed Ramya in the leg. *Gwrlain didn't finish him off, a mistake.*

Ramya attempted to stand, but tripped and stumbled over her throne, dropping her weapon and landing hard on her rump. Her sword clattered out of reach. She grabbed for her daggers, but both were gone. She dove for her sword.

But the Crown Prince seized his chance, he bent down, grabbed Ramya's sword before she could reach it and then, with a huge roar, he thrust it through her chest and out the other side.

Terya stopped wriggling and slumped against Ramya's back, the point of the blade slicing her little body almost in half. Her blood mixed with her mother's and seeped in a hot rush down Ramya's back.

Ramya tried to scream but nothing came out. The noise pinned in place by the sword in her chest. She sunk down, down, down. Gwrlain howled. *My baby. My soulmatch.* Suddenly all she could hear was her torn heart desperately trying to pump blood. *It cannot believe this is the end.*

Ammad took hold of his sword and held it high, he swiped it down and went to slice off her head. In mid swing, Monya's sword held his back and he turned to her and laughed, shouting in his language.

Melokai Ramya looked over at Gwrlain, fighting with Whaled in a wild fury. A gut-wrenching wail echoed around the hall from his mouth, as if his entire body was imploding.

I was blessed to experience love, the purest, absolute love. My people never loved me. This Trogr loves me. I was living a half-life until he made it whole, made me truly happy. My trouble, my wonderful trouble from the east.

As Ramya's life ebbed away, her nostrils flooded with the sweet smell of Terya's lotion, which, earlier that terrible night, she had lovingly caressed into her baby's delicate skin.

Melokai no more.

Lightning flashed behind her eyes, but she did not hear the answering thunder.

36

VIOLYA

V, eleven warriors and one hundred Jutes paused on the West Way, a few hours ride outside of Riaow, resting their animals.

The pygmies rode shiny blue beetles, that kept up with the horses. She kicked on her horse at a gallop, for the last leg into the city, and her warriors and the Jutes followed.

She did not think the horses would survive much longer, but she would not delay. Their journey from Ujen had been relentless. They had arrived at the sinkhole, and were swiftly hoisted across to Mlaw. There, under the protection of the village warrior Parzya, V had left Joz and Robya, the novice traders, donkeys, serving peons and the strange Majute foods, creatures and merchandise that Joz had traded for the Peqkian goods. Without rest, the warriors and the Jute fighters had set off for Riaow. Over the snowy Melioks and at speed along the North West Road and, before they turned on to the West Way, V had ordered camp set up and taken two warriors with her to check on the stone army.

The three warriors had stood on Sybilya's hill overlooking Ashen Valley. What they witnessed made Lizya drop to her knees. The stone men were still rooted to the spot, but were tentatively moving arms, heads, hands. The grinding of stone on stone and shrill crunching as knuckles moved or eyes blinked made V shake and quiver, like a mole was burrowing into her ears.

After, the warriors and the Jutes had barely stopped, the message they carried to the Melokai critical – the Stone Army, that has stood for one thousand years, is coming alive.

Sybilya told her, "My powers are failing, V. I can't hold the magic much longer. You must stop the stone army."

As they approached the capital, a pounding hailstorm hindered visibility and V slowed her horse to a plod. She could make out specks from torches clustered around the first huts at the edge of the city, next to the wood carved statue of Melokai Annya. Her stomach lurched.

"Wait here," V said. "There must have been some disorder for warriors to block the road and at this time most residents should be tucked up in their beds. I will investigate. Keep out of sight until I return."

V crept up the side of the road in the murky ditch to assess. Suddenly she was glad for the hail, as the strange males who hunched together at the entrance to the city had not seen or heard her group's approach. Foreign soldiers speaking in an incomprehensible language. Six city night patrol warriors lay dead at their feet. As she watched they touched a torch to Melokai Annya's wooden toes and laughed as the flames licked at her shins and then shot up. When the fire started to eat at the statue's face, V had seen enough and edged away.

She scrutinised the hills that surrounded Inaly Lake, but they were dark. The Mount of Pines was dark. *"I am safe,"* Sybilya whispered in V's mind.

"The city is overrun with strangers. There are Peqkians dead," V told her warriors. They nodded at her, grim-faced.

"Brinjinqa, stay silent and stay hidden. We will fetch you once we understand the situation," she whispered.

The Jute captain bowed. "I am yours to command, V."

They tied their exhausted horses to trees. V pulled Emmo out from her cloak and put her on the back of a horse. The caterpillar cowered from the hail and snorted to show her annoyance at being disturbed. "Stay here, I'll be back for you soon." Emmo reared up on back legs to watch V leave.

The warrior Fin led the way on foot through the undergrowth to an unused pathway into the city, a few paces away from the soldiers. The twelve warriors darted through the tiny streets and alleyways, avoiding the major thoroughfares that were clogged with soldiers shouting in accented Shella, "Stay indoors, stay safe!"

The small band watched in horror as soldiers slaughtered Riats who didn't heed their warning, leaving their homes to gawk at the hump-backed strangers.

"Sybilya save us," Lizya muttered. "What the zhaq has happened here?"

V quietly unsheathed her sword and held it ready, her warriors did the same. They pressed on in the darkness. Near the centre of the city was the House of Knowledge. It was on fire.

The sight, so familiar, singed V's breath. The air shrivelled in her chest and she gasped desperately. Lizya slapped V's back and grabbed her chin to look in her eyes.

"I'm good," V mumbled. *I foresaw the future.*

Many hundreds of soldiers surrounded the building and milled about in the square. Frightened ponies cowered together, skittish as the fire spat and crackled. The soldiers chopped down scholars who fled the inferno through the library's doors. Signs of a skirmish fought and lost by Peqkian warriors marred the square with bodies of young warriors strewn about.

"Zhaq!" Fin spat and made to stride out into the open, to assist the scholars.

V tugged her back and pulled her into the shadows. "No. Not yet. There are too many. Follow me."

They crept towards the court buildings and the Melokai's apartments, heading for the barracks. The noise of battle greeted them and V stopped. She peered around a wall at the scene.

She ordered her warriors to huddle behind the wall so they could speak.

"We need to fight!" Fin snapped.

"We will, but not yet, we assess first and then we make a plan. There are twelve of us and many thousands of them," V whispered. "The humps... I think these are Dromedars, the desert people. They have surrounded the city and attacked strategic locations. This is a tactical, coordinated attack, the same as we have learnt and played out in training sessions. It must mean a warrior is involved somehow."

A ripple of loathing went through the warriors.

Lizya said, "What do we do, V? There was a small number of inexperienced warriors in the city."

All eyes turned to V and she felt uneasy, in case she made the wrong choice. *"You can do this," Sybilya's familiar voice said. "You must."* V made her decision.

"Fin, fetch Brinjinqa, meet us at the courtyard. Take down all the cammers who block your way."

Fin thumped a fist to her chest and ran.

To the remaining ten warriors, V said, "The Melokai has guards and is a skilled warrior. We help these innocents first."

Grunts of agreement in reply.

They backtracked and at the House of Knowledge they each stole a pony. Raging through the city on the circular Tatya Highway, they banged on dome huts yelling, "Riaow is under attack! Peqkya is under attack! Our Melokai is threatened. Rise and fight against our enemy, the cammers. The Melokai Ramya needs your help. Only you can save your city. Only you can save your beloved Melokai."

The cammers charged them on foot, with some attempting to mount ponies, struggling pathetically to clamber on the bare backs. The eleven warriors eradicated all that came at them and then charged in return, picking off the fleeing cammers with ease.

"They are disorganised and undisciplined and yet arrogant, surprised to be beaten," V shouted to Lizya.

"Foolish males," Lizya replied.

Women started to leave their homes, armed with anything they could find. Brandishing small knives, tools of their trade and fire pokers, they fell upon the soldiers. Seeing their neighbours and friends fall under foreign steel incensed the Peqkians and they fought aggressively, recalling the combat lessons they had received at the pen. More and more brave women took to the streets.

V's band circled back to the House of Knowledge, followed by a heaving mass of enraged Riats and rushed at the soldiers, smiting a path to the burning building. The warriors slashed and destroyed the cammers, pulling them away from the door and freeing the scholars trapped inside. Riat women picked up the weapons of fallen cammers and turned them on soldiers still standing. A ferocious clash ensued.

When V was satisfied the Peqkians prevailed, she yelled with sword in the air, "Now we go to our Melokai!"

She led her warriors towards the back of the court buildings, fighting their way through the soldiers that crossed their path. They vaulted from ponies and ran to the assembly hall's hidden back door, near the platform, that only the Melokai's personal guards knew.

V pushed the door, but it was jammed. Screaming, a baby squalling, and Gwrlain's howling, boomed from within. The warrior Laurya shifted V aside and together with Daya, they rammed their shoulders against the door, sweeping aside the dead bodies that were blocking it.

"Thank you," V said as she ran into the hall, taking in the carnage and scanning for Ramya.

V's eyes found the Melokai, and saw her stumble.

A cammer male-child grabbed Ramya's sword and

thrust it through her heart, driving it through her body until the hilt. The point burst out of the little creature that was strapped to the Melokai's back. The baby. He moved to behead Ramya with his own sword. V bounded forward to save her Melokai but the male-child was blocked by… *Emmya? No, not her, a youngblood warrior.* The male-child laughed viciously and shouted at the youngblood who held back his sword with her own. He readied himself to fight.

V looked down at her Melokai, her ruler and protector, chosen by Sybilya and the people of Peqkya. Ramya was an inspiration to V, never satisfied with staying still, or fearing to break with tradition, always trying to improve the lives of her people. Ramya had always been kind to her, courteous, encouraging.

And here she was, dead.

I was too late to save her. V glowered at the killer who had spilled Ramya's blood. The young warrior who had blocked his blow lowered her sword and stepped back, offering V the male-child. He turned to face the tall, red-haired warrior and his laughter dried up in his mouth. His eyes darted about for support, but there was none. He shouted something in the Drome language and his soldiers formed up to help him.

"You murdered our Melokai," V snarled at him.

Beforc he could even take a breath, she amputated an arm at the shoulder, spun and hacked off the other one. He stood dumbfounded, staring at the first stump that sprayed blood. V raised up her sword to cleave him in two, but a hairy cammer soldier yanked him out of her reach, shouting what sounded to V like "Ammad".

Five cammers lunged towards her, whilst the armless male-child known as Ammad was dragged away. She took a deep breath and engaged the inept soldiers, taking minutes to flatten them all.

She whistled at the warriors she had arrived with. They finished off their opponents. Lizya pulled her sword out of the misshapen hump of a soldier and spat on his jerking body.

The ten warriors looked up at V for her direction. The youngblood stood with them. V stared at her, she was a mirror image of Emmya with long, thin braids tied on top of her head.

"I'm Monya," she said and dipped her head at V.

"Violya. V. You fight well."

The cammers were withdrawing from the assembly hall. Novice warriors finished off the stragglers and courtiers crowded around the body of the Melokai. Gwrlain hugged the dead baby to his chest with one arm and with the other, he cradled Ramya, rocking back and forth. His haunting, inconsolable screeching was the saddest sound V had ever heard.

She raced towards the door but heard her name.

"Violya," Chaz groaned at her feet. He pushed himself up onto his elbows, a huge blood stain on his back. "Ashya is with the Dromedars. Beware, their swords are poisoned!"

"Ashya," V repeated, confirming her suspicion that a warrior was involved. *That conniving cockface.*

Her small band cut their way through fights and over dead bodies and out into the courtyard. Ammad was slumped across the hairy male's shoulders and he jogged forward, one arm around a leg and one hand gripping Ammad's hair. He stooped under the weight but was moving fast. A circle of cammer soldiers surrounded him, pushing forward and bringing up the rear, attacking any Peqkian who approached. The hail had turned into a fine rain and thunder rumbled in the distance as V noticed the armed peons for the first time fighting chaotically… on the side of the foe. She sneered at their stupidity.

V bounded after the retreating cammers, her sight set on the armless murderer but she was blocked by a traitor warrior and V was forced to tear her gaze away from the male-child. The distraction angered her, she couldn't lose him.

It was the bully, Sianya. Now a hulking woman with evil slits for eyes and one of the few in Peqkya who was taller than V. Their swords clashed, Sianya smirking. She landed a blow on V's bicep. It was the first blood V had shed and she stared at it. Magic bubbled out. *How dare she!* The red-haired warrior flew at the huge slab. Sianya grunted as V clambered onto her back, wrapping her legs around the hulk's waist and her arm around the neck and squeezing. Sianya lumbered about, trying to shake V off. V tightened her grip and the woman fell to her knees. Resistance ceased.

Ashya and several more of her cronies readied themselves for an assault against V and her warriors.

"Well look who it is," the reeking warrior growled. "Gosya's favourite stray sheep has returned. She is dead too, did you know that?"

V's eyes widened. *No!* She loved the Head Warrior. Gogo had believed in her vision and had permitted her to leave for a year, and trusted her to return.

"You didn't know. Well, we got her," Ashya crowed and started to spin her sword around in a circle at her side. "You and me… I'm going to finish all of Gosya's mangy herd." Ashya readied herself for a fight, the exact same movements as in V's premonition.

This time V's breath remained steady and she raised her sword. Ashya charged. V dodged her, spun around faster than Ashya could blink and stabbed the old warrior deep in the shoulder rendering her sword arm useless. V kicked out her legs.

"You betrayed your Melokai. I will allow our people to decide what your fate will be."

V bent down to bind the traitor and a gurgling cackle bubbled up from the leathery face.

"Emmya was your friend wasn't she."

V froze.

Ashya snorted. "She was raped by the cammer prince Ammad and many of his guards. Then she committed suicide, slashing herself from vagina to belly button. The shame of it, she couldn't defend herself. Pathetic!"

Ashya heaved herself up and kneeled on the gravel, sniggering.

I will decide the fate of this stinky cat after all! A fiery, frothing upsurge raced from V's toes to her head and then out of her fingertips. They glowed crimson. She dropped her sword as shards of red light shot from her palms, piercing the old warrior like bolts of lightning. Ashya's body jerked as if stabbed by multiple blades, her eyes popping from her skull.

"Zhaq you!" V shouted. A sizzling flash scorched the courtyard as V shot a lightning blade from her hand that sliced through the old warrior's neck.

V blinked, a halo from the bright light glowing behind her eyelids, and stumbled backwards. Panting, she scrutinised her hands. Front, back. Front, back.

She looked up. Everyone stared at her, friend and foe, the battle hung suspended, swords in mid-arc, attackers ready to pounce, fists raised and hovering, waiting to punch. Even those in the process of dying, seemed to stop what they were doing to gawp at the red-haired warrior.

V shook her head, as if the blistering sharp bolts hadn't just flown from her hands. *I am you, we are one.*

She pulled up Ashya's dismembered head and held it high, shouting, "Traitor warriors, look here! Ashya is dead, as you are all now dead to Peqkya."

She flung it across the courtyard. It bounced, rolled, rocked and came to a stop. The fighting resumed.

V crouched, and pushed her palms into her eyes, devastated to learn of Emmya's fate. All around her steel clanged and fists pummelled. She tried to collect herself, tried to block out the din that threatened to overwhelm her. *My Em.*

Lizya heaved V to her feet. "You have magic?"

V nodded.

Lizya laughed. "Well, there's plenty of cockfaces here

for you to practice on." A dagger flew past the warrior's ear, nicking the lobe. Lizya's face screwed up as she turned to seek out the fool who had thrown it and missed. "Let's finish this, V!"

V picked up her sword and snarled. She leapt into the fray yelling, "Take down Ashya's warriors!"

Fin arrived in the courtyard with the Jute fighters. Their little pink bodies were covered in markings, their blue hair shaped into monstrous spikes. They wore animal skin shorts, with leather strapping criss-crossed over their torsos to hold various weapons including small sharp knives, axes, and throwing blades. There were males and females, and they acted as one, Brinjinqa at the head.

The mass of pink and blue swarmed cammers, warriors, peons, washing over them like a huge foamy wave and fighting in a frenzy before plunging on, leaving only novice warriors loyal to the Melokai still standing. The novices looked startled for a moment, a sea of dead opponents at their feet, before turning to join another fight.

Fin fought her way to V, a grin on her face. "Evil, conniving little fighters, these Jutes," she shouted before the battle swept her away.

Poisoned warriors were starting to get up, as if rising from the dead, and re-joined the fight. The few remaining peons, alarmed at the withdrawing cammers and panicking as the blue and yellow marked warriors fell in droves to the Jute swarm, started to toss down their weapons and flee the courtyard, back into the bowels of the city. Novice warriors gave chase, hunting them down.

A mob of Riat women wrangled with soldiers outside the gates. The cammers were grabbing ponies and trying to trot away, clinging on to the rain soaked, bare backed ponies only to be snatched off by a furious Peqkian. Each fallen cammer was then set upon by a horde of clevercats who pinned the thrashing male to the floor. The cats clawed and scraped through cloth, skin, flesh and organs until they struck bone and then yowled in triumph before moving on to the next soldier.

Two of Ashya's traitor warriors were engaged in a dagger brawl with the senior warrior Gemya and V ran to assist. A dagger slashed Gemya's thigh and she fell, taking a second dagger in the throat.

The cockface who had wielded the dagger bellowed in celebration, only to feel the point of V's sword shoved through her skull. She looked down to see it come out her mouth. The remaining warrior welcomed V's dagger in her eyeball.

So much death, so many good women gone.

The noise of battle subsided and V sensed eyes on her back. She turned to take in their faces. Amongst the glut of dead, rows and rows of surviving warriors stood. In front of his fighters, who had formed up in tight lines, Brinjinqa bowed low. *Jutes in the Melokai's courtyard.*

They waited for V's orders.

She hesitated, *I am no leader of an army!* She wanted to chase after the fleeing armless male-child and torture him as he had tortured her friend. But she didn't. *There are more important things to consider… there are warriors willing me to lead them and the people of Riaow who need my protection. There will be time enough later to take revenge on that worm. Ammad will never escape my fury.*

"We are with you, V," Lizya said, banging her fist to her chest. Scores of Peqkian warriors repeated the same gesture. *They've chosen me...* She thumped her chest in gratitude for their belief in her. *And I choose them.*

V shouted, "Know this, our beloved Melokai Ramya is dead! Murdered by a cammer. A cammer assisted by treacherous warriors and treacherous peons."

The warriors bristled at the news of the Melokai's death.

An intense rustling of the leaves in the nearby trees reminded V of the noise of the vast, unknowable sea, and an all-encompassing sense of purpose surged through her limbs. Magic flowed out of every pore, exalted, free. She embraced it. Her skin shimmered, glowing red. *I can do this. Believe.* V extended her sword and pointed up to the menacing black clouds.

"Now we take back our city. Flush every cammer out of Peqkya. Cut them down. Make them suffer. For our Melokai, for Gogo, for Emmya. For every true Peqkian woman who has fallen tonight. We are the heart of these mountains! No one can stop us beating!"

V stormed into the streets, an army at her back.

AUTHOR'S NOTE

Enjoyed what you just read? I would be very grateful if you could take a couple of minutes to leave a review (even if only a few lines) on the book's online sales page at the store you purchased it from. Reviews help other readers to discover the trilogy and your help in spreading the word is hugely appreciated.

MELOKAI is the first instalment of the *In the Heart of the Mountains* trilogy. Book two, V, is coming in 2018.

Get a free ebook of THE FALL OF VAASAR here: www.rosalynkelly.co.uk/free-book This prequel novella is set 2,000 years before MELOKAI and tells of the event that sparked the bitter, bloody feud between the countries of Fertilian and Drome.

Subscribe to my email newsletter to be notified when V is released, and for giveaways, price promotions, free books, free short stories as well as exclusive extra content. You can sign up here: www.rosalynkelly.co.uk/subscribe

Thank you for taking the time to read MELOKAI.

Rosalyn Kelly
August 2017

ABOUT THE AUTHOR

Rosalyn Kelly grew up in the magical New Forest in the south of England and has lived around the country as well as in the Middle East, and travelled all over the world.

She studied English Literature and Language at Oxford Brookes University before embarking on a PR and marketing career.

After ten years telling the stories of international brands and businesses, she decided the time had come to tell her own and her debut novel MELOKAI was written in 2016 after quitting her job, going travelling for four months and then writing solidly for six.

The inspiration for her epic fantasy trilogy came when she was trekking in the mountains of Nepal's stunning Annapurna Sanctuary.

When she's not putting her heart and soul into book two of the *In the Heart of the Mountains* trilogy, she daydreams about where to travel to next, paints with acrylic, reads voraciously and writes book reviews on her blog.

Keep in touch:
Website www.rosalynkelly.co.uk
Blog www.rosalynkelly.co.uk/blog
Twitter www.twitter.com/rosalynkauthor
Instagram www.instagram.com/rosalynkauthor
Goodreads www.goodreads.com/rosalyn_kelly
Facebook www.facebook.com/rosalynkellyauthor
Pinterest www.pinterest.com/rozkelly

ACKNOWLEDGMENTS

Massive thanks to my parents Ann and Brian, and to my sister Kathy, for all their encouragement and help. My Mum has read every piece of creative work I have ever produced and her feedback has been invaluable in improving my writing. My Dad has a vivid imagination and he was the one who came up with the word 'peon' from some old Western movie he'd watched. And my sister turned out to be a back cover blurb maestro and helped me shape a compelling description.

I'd also like to say a huge thank you to my beta readers Becky, Jolly and Steph who gallantly read my early drafts and fed back with some brilliant and useful comments. Also, the early readers of my first chapters, Sian and Miriam. Thanks to blurb readers Robyn and Roo, to Esther who put me in touch with Steph, and to my editor Philip. Plus, big appreciation goes out to Naomi who encouraged me to start.

And thanks to all my friends and family who have supported me on this journey and have always been so enthusiastic about my decision to become an author. BIG LOVE xx

Rosalyn Kelly
August 2017

APPENDIX 1 – CHARACTERS

PEQKIANS:

Melokai Ramya – ruler of Peqkya, ruled for twelve years since age 20 (from Year 988 until present, Year 1000)
Sybilya – ancient prophetess, known as Stone Prophetess
Chaz – eunuch, Melokai's counsellor. Head Scholar
Ferraz – pleasure giver
Hanya (Hanny) – High Courtesan. Melokai's favoured female and counsellor
Gosya (Gogo) – Head Warrior and counsellor
Violya (V) – distinguished warrior
Lizya – distinguished warrior
Emmya – distinguished warrior
Monya – young warrior, looks like Emmya
Bevya – Melokai's clevercat messenger
Zekya (Zecky) – Head Speaker and counsellor
Rivya (Riv) – Head Trader and counsellor
Kafya – Mother of Mothers and counsellor
Omya – Head Teller and counsellor
Melokai Annya – ruled in Year 500 and brokered the truce with the Trogrs
Lomaz (Licky Licky Lo) – pleasure giver
Melokai Tatya – ruled in Year 700 and during her reign the last known sighting of a wolf was recorded during the Wolf Expulsion, 300 years previously
Jozya (Joz) – assistant trader
Robya – apprentice scholar
Irrya – courtesan
Ashya – high ranking warrior
Mikaz – pleasure giver
Stavaz (Slim / Stav) – pleasure giver
Toya – assistant trader
Naomya – new Mother of Mothers and counsellor
Marya – courtesan
Martaz – pleasure giver

Shit-pick – leader of the peon rebellion
Wevo – leader of the peon rebellion
Steely – leader of the peon rebellion
Laurya, Finya (Fin) – warriors with V in Majute
Parzya – warrior at Mlaw village
Wistorya – trader at Mlaw village
Urya – young scholar from Mlaw village
Denya – warrior captain leading 1,000 warriors in Fertilian
Kiya – warrior in wolf territory
Melokaz Ashrav and Melokaz Shavanaz – leaders of the warring Xayy armies turned to stone
Daya – warrior
Terya – Melokai Ramya and Gwrlain's baby
Sianya – warrior in Ashya's company
Gemya – distinguished warrior
Artaz/Artya/Artie – Ferraz's child with Melokai Ramya
Mother Samya – leads pen that Artaz is in
Melokai Rominya – the first Melokai of Peqkya 1,000 years before Ramya. Year Zero
Emmo – V's pet caterpillar

WOLVES:
Darrio – wolf, father of three, one of which is a standing female
Harro, Warrio – Darrio's sons, yearlings
Sarrya (Sarry) – Darrio's daughter, yearling, first standing female wolf
Arro – alpha breeding male wolf, head of the Wulhor-Aaen wolf pack
Lurra – alpha breeding female, head of the Wulhor-Aaen wolf pack
Ricarro, Berrio – children of Arro and Lurra, yearlings
Marro, Zirrio– male juvenile wolves (two years old), children of Arro and Lurra
Moirra, Herra – female juvenile wolves (two years old), children of Arro and Lurra
Sinarro and Norra – alpha pair of the Xulr-Aaen wolf

pack, Norra is a daughter of Arro and Lurra
Kurro and Jerra – alpha pair of the Maarr-Aaen wolf pack, they are Sinarro's parents
Temrro and Xocorra – alpha pair of the Vierz-Aaen wolf pack, Temrro is the brother of Jerra
Rrio and Varrya – alpha pair of the Dregil-Aaen wolf pack, they are Xocorra's parents
Zemrro – wolf from Dregil-Aaen, sent to pack-meet
Verra – wolf from Zegr-Aaen, sent to pack-meet
Alurro – wolf from Gurr-Aaen, sent to pack-meet
Benrro – old wolf from Karracht-Aaen who leads campaign onto the south bank of the Great River

DROMEDARS:
Ruler of Drome, Mastiq el Wakrime – has 23 known children with 1 official wife and 200 in harem
Crown Prince of Drome, Ammad – second eldest son of Mastiq and fifth child
Hallid – eldest son and first child of Mastiq, alcoholic. Mother is Mastiq's official wife
Jakira – mother of Ammad and Selmi, one of Ruler Mastiq's harem
Selmi (Sel) – second son of Ruler Mastiq and Jakira, brother of Ammad. Sixth son of the ruler, eleventh child
Ganni Deraasi – High Priest
Zeead Medra – new High Priest
Laetitia Medra – mother of High Priest Zeead
Whaled – Minister of War
Razanne – Whaled's daughter
Qabull – Ammad's most trusted guard with scar from ear to mouth and a brutal punch
Onhirid, Nuurad, Khasar, Haibal – Ammad's guards
Baghadd – Sel's childhood friend at mother's craterside villa, son of the cook
Samma – old chief in Urakbai village
Medi – Jakira's head slave
Laurie – Fertilian whore

Ruler Wahakbi – he lost Vaasar to Fertilians two thousand years previously (Vaasar now called Lian)

FERTS:

King Hugo Cleland – rightful King of Fertilian, he has ruled for 24 years. (Known by his family as Hugo Salmon, Cleland is the royal family name). Eldest son of Princess Olivia and Lord Ernest Salmon

Queen Jessima Cleland (nee Walter) – King Hugo's third wife, married for nine years since she was 20

King Edward and Queen Amy Cleland – deceased, murdered by false King Benjamin. Rulers before King Benjamin. Parents to Simon, Olivia and Timothy. Maternal grandparents of King Hugo, Ernest Jnr, Edward, Charles and Toby

Prince Simon and Prince Timothy Cleland – deceased, murdered by false King Benjamin. Sons of Edward and Amy and brothers to Olivia. Simon was King Edward's male heir to the throne. Uncles of King Hugo, Ernest Jnr, Edward, Charles, Toby

Princess Olivia Salmon (nee Cleland) – deceased, natural causes in old age. Daughter of King Edward and Queen Amy. Mother of five sons: King Hugo, Ernest Jnr, Edward, Charles, Toby. Married to Lord Ernest Salmon, ruler of Lian Harbour City

Lord Ernest Salmon – deceased, assassinated. Ruler of Lian Harbour City. Husband of Princess Olivia and father of King Hugo, Ernest Jnr, Edward, Charles, Toby. Son of Lord Hugo Salmon

Lord Hugo Salmon – deceased, natural causes in old age. Great friend of King Edward. Father of Ernest and paternal grandfather of King Hugo, Ernest Jnr, Edward, Charles, Toby

Prince Ernest Jnr (Ernie) – brother of King Hugo. Second son of Princess Olivia and Lord Ernest Salmon. Current Lord of Lian

Prince Edward – brother of King Hugo. Third son of

Princess Olivia and Lord Ernest Salmon. Presumed dead, lost at sea

Prince Charles – brother of King Hugo. Fourth son of Princess Olivia and Lord Ernest Salmon. Chief Cleric in Lian

Prince Toby – brother of King Hugo. Fifth son of Princess Olivia and Lord Ernest Salmon. Army General

Queen Gracie – deceased, in childbirth. First wife of King Hugo. Mother of Princess Matilda

Queen Jayne – deceased, in childbirth. Second wife of King Hugo. Mother of Princess Georgina

Princess Matilda – eldest daughter of King Hugo, mother is Queen Gracie. Married to Lord John Iddenkinge, and lives in the south of King Hugo's lands in Fertilian. Has two children, Johnny Jnr and Grace

Princess Georgina – second daughter of King Hugo, mother is Queen Jayne. Married to Lord Hadley Smyth

False King Benjamin Thorne – deceased, murdered by King Hugo. Ruled for 15 years until Hugo's rebellion. Took Kingdom by force from King Edward. Married to False Queen Charlotte. Father to twins Arthur and Mary

False Queen Charlotte Thorne – Wife to Benjamin and mother to twins Arthur and Mary

Mary Thorne (Miserable Mary) – eldest child of false King Benjamin and false Queen Charlotte, her twin is Arthur. She claims the throne and at war with her brother and Hugo. Married to Lord Clement Pullman. Has one child, James. Other three have died in infancy

Arthur Thorne (Awful Arthur) – Only son of false King Benjamin and false Queen Charlotte, his twin is Mary – claims the throne. At war with King Hugo and Mary. Not currently married and is a widower – has had four wives, all deceased. Has three children, eldest son is Jeremy

Lord Walter Berindonck – oversees farming for King Hugo, on war council

Lord Zachary– Army general, oversees North East watch on Arthur for King Hugo

Lord Alon Sumner – army general, oversees South East watch on Mary for King Hugo
Lord Simion, Lord Duggenham, Lord Littlehales – part of King Hugo's war council
Marcy, Tina – Jessima's handmaids in the castle
Lord Andrew Chattergoon – oversees the Lian tunnels for King Hugo
Elmgard – hapless soldier turned spy
Lord Gregory Doddy – oversees salt production in the vast salt flats in the south of Fertilian
King Edgar – ruled two thousand years previously, instrumental in the capture of Vaasar from Drome which he renamed Lian
Geraldina – Jessima's sister
Duke Ranulf Hawkins – first messenger sent to Riaow

TROGRS:
Gwrlain – Trogr from cave nation of Troglo
Gruack – Gwrlain's mother
Lulac – Gwrlain's sister
Bance – Gwrlain's friend and lover of Lulac

JUTES:
Amjin (front horn), **Oghril** (strange antler protrusion) and **Moqtoa** (two buns above the ears) – accompany V and traders
Utuli, Soogee, Yehep – three joint Potenqis (rulers) of Majute
Brinjinqa (Brin) – personal assistant and bodyguard of Utuli

APPENDIX 2 – PLACES AND PEOPLES

Peqkya – realm ruled by women, high elevation, surrounded by mountains. People are called Peqkians (referred to as cats, hisspits). Called Xayy before Peqkya. Speak Shella language

Riaow – capital city of Peqkya, residents referred to as Riats

Meliok mountains – circular mountain range that surrounds Peqkya to all sides (the north-east range is called the Small Mountains by the wolves)

Zyr Peq – highest mountain in the Melioks, north east boundary

Leqari Bridge – on the west road out of Riaow

Mount of Pines – hill where Sybilya resides

Inaly Lake – vast lake on outskirts of Riaow

Mlaw – village on border with Majute

Qipaz – village in central Peqkya

Strongcats – tigers who live in the wilds of Peqkya that worship Sybilya and do her bidding

Sarenky Sea – to the west of Peqkya

Jagged Canyon – to the north of Peqkya

Troglo – cave nation to the east of Peqkya. People are called Trogrs (referred to as cave creatures)

Zwullfr mountains and wilderness – wolf territory, vast, remote, mostly snow covered tundra and dense alpine forest that lies to the north east of Peqkya, north of the Meliok Mountains

Wulhor-Aaen wolf pack – one of the many packs in the wolf territory, led by Arro and Lurra

Aaowl Peak – highest and most iconic mountain peak in Zwullfr, shaped like the crescent moon

Wul-Onr valley – Great River runs through the valley that separates the Zwullfr mountains to the north and the Meliok/Small mountains to the south. (Called **Trequ valley** and **Trequ river** by the Peqkians)

Drome – desert kingdom to the south west of Peqkya, beyond the Meliok mountains. Shares a border with Fertilian. People known as Dromedars and speak Dromedari (referred to as desert rats, cammers)
Parchad – capital of Drome, situated within a giant crater
Orean – town near to Drome in a small oasis with water source (well)
Urakbai – village in northern Drome
Jhabia Ridge – ridge of rock outside Parchad
Wakrime (royal), **Qacirr** (holy), **Tamadeen** (high status), **Affarah** (majority peasants), **Yuurnan** (desert villagers), **Eqmadeh** (nomads), **Khumarah** (the assassins) – ancient Drome clans
The Cuttarrs (cutthroats) – Drome Ruler Mastiq's elite guard
Fertilian – lowland kingdom to the south east of Peqkya, beyond the Meliok mountains. People are called Ferts (referred to as southerners, thieves / occupiers). Speak Shella language
Lian – walled harbour city and major port on the Sarenky sea in the west, linked to Fertilian by tunnels (called Vaasar by Dromedars)
Cleland City – old capital of Fertilian, within King Hugo's lands
Rotchurch City – capital of Arthur Thorne's lands in Fertilian, north-east
Edester City – capital of Mary Thorne's lands in Fertilian, south-east
Yettle valley and Yettle Bottom plains – west of Rotchurch City
Majute – rainforest nation, people are called Jutes (referred to as pygmies, little people) and speak Juutayan
Ujen – capital of Majute
Qaziik, Janugah – ancient Jute tribes

Printed in Great Britain
by Amazon